OBSIDIAN HEART
BOOK THREE

ALSO AVAILABLE FROM MARK MORRIS
AND TITAN BOOKS

OBSIDIAN HEART

Book One: The Wolves of London
Book Two: The Society of Blood

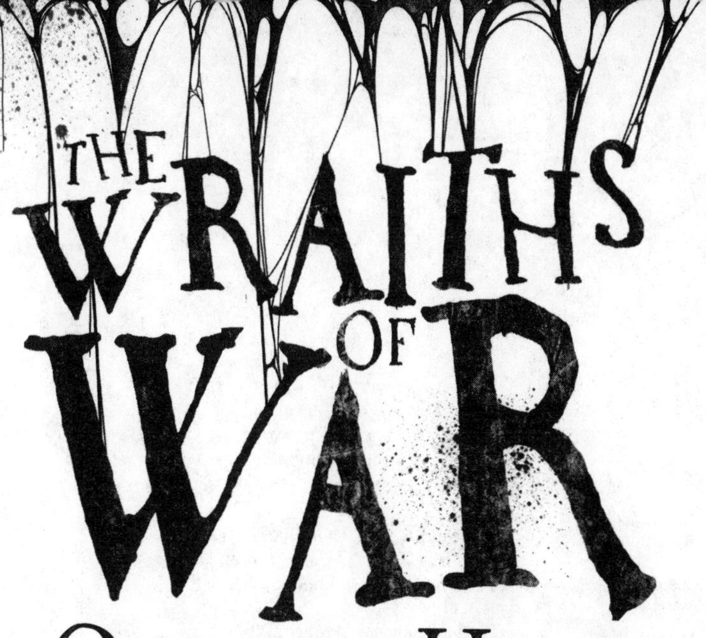

OBSIDIAN HEART

BOOK THREE

MARK MORRIS

TITAN BOOKS

Obsidian Heart Book Three: The Wraiths of War
Print edition ISBN: 9781781168745
E-book edition ISBN: 9781781168776

Published by Titan Books
A division of Titan Publishing Group Ltd
144 Southwark Street, London SE1 0UP

First edition: October 2016
1 3 5 7 9 10 8 6 4 2

Visit our website:
www.titanbooks.com

A CIP catalogue record for this title is available from the British Library.

Printed and bound in the United States.

To Gary and Emily McMahon, with love.
"I got some bad ideas in my head."

ONE

GOD

As soon as I opened my eyes, I thought: *I'm dead.*

Around me I could see only white. I could hear no sound. When I took a breath the air smelled of nothing at all.

Is this what death is? I thought. *A white nothingness? No pain? No sensation?*

Or maybe I was in limbo. Maybe I was awaiting sentencing, poised between one direction or the other.

I didn't know whether to panic or just lie there. I didn't know whether I was even *capable* of panicking – or of any emotion, for that matter.

I felt... empty. Did I even still *have* a physical body? I could *see*, and I could *breathe*, but was that only a memory? Were my senses the equivalent of phantom limbs? And if so, how did I feel about that – assuming I *could* still feel, of course?

Nothingness was better than pain, wasn't it? Well, wasn't it? My last memory was of excruciating agony, of vomiting blood as my body turned inside out.

Anything had to be better than that. I'd suffered enough in my life to know that when it came to a choice between suffering and death, death was preferable.

But that was when I'd thought of death as oblivion, not awareness. Maybe, though, this was what death truly was? Eternal awareness. But awareness of nothing.

The thought was terrifying. Or at least it would have been if I'd thought myself capable of terror.

I decided to close my eyes, and was thankful to find I could do so.

When I opened them again, God was sitting next to me.

He was smiling. He had white hair and a white beard. Blue eyes in a wrinkled face.

'Hi,' I said, only mildly surprised to find I could speak. 'Is it good news or bad?'

'Good,' God said. He was wearing a nice suit. It fitted him really well. It was a pale blue-grey colour that made me feel calm.

I sighed in relief – or at least in my head I did. 'Thank fuck,' I muttered, and then realised I'd sworn in front of God. I clenched my teeth in apology.

'Sorry. That just came out. It's just that I'm glad I'm not going... *down there*. I mean, I'll admit I've done some dodgy things in my time, but overall I think–'

'I'm not who you think I am, Alex,' he said. 'I'm not God.'

My mind felt like thick soup stirred slowly in a pot. I tried to think about what God had said. Was he trying to catch me out? I smiled – in my head, I smiled.

'You must be God,' I said, trying my hardest to remain respectful. 'If you're not him, how did you know that was who I thought–'

'You're still woozy from the procedure. Look again.'

Procedure? What procedure? I stared at him. His face looked familiar. But maybe that was because God looked like someone we all knew when we finally met him. Aren't we all supposed to be created in his image, after all? Aren't we–

Then the clouds parted and a shaft of light beamed straight down, and everything became clear.

'Fuck,' I said again.

God shrugged as if to say: *Sorry to disappoint you.*

'When do I grow that beard?' I asked.

The older me, who I'd mistaken for God, shrugged. 'A few decades down the line.'

'Bloody hell,' I said, 'you're old. You're the oldest I've ever seen you.'

'Why do you think I left it so many years before coming back to this moment?' said my future self. 'It was to delay these insults for as long as possible.'

But he was smiling. He wasn't really hurt by my comments, he'd been expecting them. After all, he must have spoken them himself years back, when he was me.

'So I'm not dead then?' I said, and realised that although I was pleased, I also felt wearied at the prospect of more life, more struggle.

'Not now,' my future self said. 'You were, though. Technically. For about thirty-two minutes.'

'Thirty-two minutes?'

'Give or take.'

Fuck. I'd been dead. Another thing to tick off the bucket list. The thought struck me as funny, and I sniggered.

'So where am I now?'

'A better question would be when.' He paused, as if giving me the opportunity to brace myself. 'You're in the future, Alex. 2097.'

Whoa. I wanted to say it, but the information hit me like a punch between the eyes, making my thoughts spin.

Maybe I shouldn't have been surprised. I'd known that with the heart I could travel through time. I'd used it to go back into the past, so it was only natural that it could also be used to go the other way, into the future.

Even so. The future. The great unknown. It seemed more impressive than the past, somehow, and more frightening. From the perspective of the present the future didn't exist, whereas the past did. You could read about the past; there were records, artefacts, photographs, graveyards full of people who had lived and died...

The future, though, had no bones to make it real.

'2097,' I said, as if testing whether, by speaking the date, I could make it *seem* more real. I couldn't.

My future self looked sympathetic. 'I know exactly how you feel. Give yourself a minute. Let it sink in.'

I looked up at the white ceiling. I was becoming more physically aware of myself now, but I still felt disconnected. I thought about raising my left arm, and then, with a slight mental effort that was normally so natural I didn't even *have* to think about it, I turned the thought into a command, at the same time tilting my head to look down the length of my body.

I was covered with a pristine white sheet, making me think of a body in a morgue. I watched as my arm rose into view. I looked at my hand and flexed my fingers, then curled them into a fist.

I felt okay. Despite my last memory before waking up here – the pain, the vomiting – I appeared to have suffered no lasting ill effects from my use of the heart.

Unless I was partially paralysed. Or under heavy sedation to allay the pain.

'What's the damage?' I asked.

My future self spread his hands, as if to say: *See for yourself.*

'It *was* extensive,' he said. 'But you're fine now.'

'Fine? How can I be fine? I thought I was dead?'

'You were. But future technology is a wonderful thing. Death is no longer fatal – or not always anyway.'

I tried to process what I was hearing.

'So what are you saying? That I'm... bionic? Like Steve Austin in *The Six Million Dollar Man*?'

'Nothing so crude. I seem to remember that when I was your age, I'd at least heard of nanotechnology; I knew the basic principles. Am I right?'

I nodded. 'Technology on a tiny scale, yeah?'

'Not just tiny,' he said. 'Atomic. Molecular. We're talking quantum-realm mechanics here.'

I shrugged, irritated at my future self's slightly patronising attitude. Had I always been like this? 'Whatever. I was never much good at science, as you know. But long story short, I'm guessing it was nanotechnology which saved my life?'

My future self confirmed it with a slight raising of his wiry white eyebrows. Then he lifted his hand, in which he was clutching something I recognised.

My notebook.

The one in which I jotted down all the dates and times a future version of myself had appeared, so that I'd know what I needed to do when the time came. It also contained other, less specific details of things I knew I needed to do, like set myself up in Victorian London so that everything would be in place when I arrived, and pay off my older daughter Candice's boyfriend's debt to the drug dealer who might otherwise endanger Candice's life.

'I've written it all down,' he said. 'Dates and times, both yours and mine; the details of this place; everything you'll need when you get to where I am. It's an important one, this, Alex. Forget it and we won't be here.'

'All right,' I said – snapped, in fact. 'I know. You don't have to spell it out.'

Unexpectedly he laughed. 'I know exactly what you're thinking. And you're right. I *am* a condescending twat. It comes with age. And experience.' He gave me a meaningful look, though whether it was laden with pity or envy I couldn't tell. 'You've got such times ahead of you, Alex. *Such* times. That's if you play your cards right, of course.'

'Any pointers?' I asked. 'Any advice?'

He drew in his lips so tightly I couldn't see them through his beard. His shoulders hunched in apology.

'Can't say a word. I mean, who knows where we'll be if I do, eh? Or rather, where *I'll* be.'

I rolled my eyes. 'No surprises there. All right, at least tell me about this nano stuff. Where are we, by the way?'

'Stuttgart.'

'In Germany?'

'Do you know of another one?'

His retort was more teasing than sarcastic. I said, 'But why here in particular?'

'Because it's the global centre of excellence for the application of medical nanotech.' He winked. 'Nothing but the best for us, old son.'

'So what is it, this nanotech? Does it mean I've now got millions of tiny robots running around inside me?'

'We,' he said, tapping his chest. 'They're still in here.'

The thought made me feel queasy. I raised my hand again and stared at the back of it, as if half-believing I might actually see the nanites jumping under the surface of my skin like fleas.

'So where are they?'

'Everywhere,' he said, as if enjoying my discomfort. His smile widened. 'Don't worry, you'll get used to them – or the idea of them, at any rate. And they do nothing but good. It's all thanks to them you're here talking to me.'

'So what *do* they do exactly? Apart from bring you back from the dead?'

'They repair you. Anything goes wrong with your body, they rush in and make it right again.'

'Anything?'

'Within reason. As long as your injuries aren't *too* severe. I mean, you get your head lopped off or you get smashed to bits by a tube train, that's your lot. But anything less drastic, they'll keep your system ticking over and undertake instant repairs. They're a preventative measure against cancer, heart attacks, strokes...' He wagged his finger at me. 'But that doesn't mean you're immortal. The nanites have their limits, plus they won't last forever. Even they're not immune to entropy.'

'What about when I use the heart?' I asked.

His smile reappeared. 'That's the beauty of it. You can use it more or less with impunity now. It will still make you feel ill, but the nanites will repair you, and quickly. This is the freedom I know you've been looking for. The magic formula. The big turning point.' His smile became a grin. 'Feels good, doesn't it?'

I stared at him in wonder. Yes, it did feel good. More than that, it felt wonderful. It opened up a whole new vista of possibilities.

'So what do I do now?'

He grabbed my hand, and at first I thought he was going to squeeze it, or clasp it between both of his, but then I felt something hard and cold and weighty being pressed into my palm.

I knew what it was immediately. The obsidian heart. It moulded itself to the cup of my hand as though that was its natural resting place.

'You go on,' he said. 'You pick up your journey where you left off, and you go on, and you get through it.'

He said nothing more, but I could see in his eyes just how tough this next stage of my life would be, and how it troubled him, and how he pitied me.

'Is it going to be really bad?' I asked.

His face seemed to sag, as though he'd been trying his best, but was no longer able to hold back the terrible weight of memory. At first I thought he wasn't going to answer me, and then finally he said, 'If you're careful, and if you're lucky, you'll get through it.'

There was a part of me that wished I *had* died. A part of me that wished I didn't have to do this. But I had no choice. If I wanted to keep my life on track, if I wanted to prevent a catastrophe that would affect not just me personally, but those I loved, I had to travel back in time, almost two centuries, to 1914.

I had to meet and befriend a man called Frank Martin.

I had to fight alongside him in the trenches of the First World War.

I had to watch him die, and then I had to use the heart that I now clutched in my hand to bring him back to life.

TWO
YOUR COUNTRY NEEDS YOU!

'Oi, you! Yes you, you little runt! How old are *you* then? Bloody Hun'll have you for breakfast, son, and still have room for seconds.'

The voice was raucous, the tone ugly, and the laughter that followed it uglier still. I stepped to my right, peering ahead of me, up the length of the long queue of men stretching all the way down the street and around the corner from the recruiting station.

It was August 14th 1914, and Britain had been at war with Germany for just over a week. Despite the season it was cold and drizzly, the men who were waiting in line with me hunched against the blustery, side-swiping wind, caps or trilbies on their heads, fags hanging out of their mouths, hands jammed into their pockets. We looked like an audition queue for an Andy Capp movie. The thought made me smile, though if I'd voiced it I'd have been met with blank faces, as it'd be another forty-odd years before the character would make his debut in *The Daily Mirror* cartoon strip. During the week or so I'd spent in this time period, acclimatising to the unfamiliar surroundings, I had come to the conclusion that the early twentieth century was a time of bad suits and bad haircuts. Most of the clothes the men wore (mine included) were grey and baggy, the trousers sagging at knee and crotch, the waistbands high and so loose that if they hadn't been held up by braces they'd have been puddling around our ankles. Beneath their shapeless, workaday jackets, a lot of the men wore home-knit jumpers over grubby white shirts, their Adam's apples bobbing above tightly knotted ties.

The men of Great Britain had greeted the declaration of war with a kind of gung-ho euphoria that was terrifying to behold. From my viewpoint their naivety seemed child-like, no doubt based on the fact that, in this day and age, information about the harsh realities of war was very much at a premium. There was no Internet, no TV, very few movies. There weren't even many photographs - not ones that were publicly available at any rate - and the newspapers I'd eagerly sought out were composed of little more than dry facts, densely and tediously presented.

People didn't seem to read books all that much either - not the general workforce, at any rate. The penny serials, or penny dreadfuls, which recounted lurid tales of pirates and highwaymen, had been popular during Victoria's reign, and were *still* popular, but even the works of, say, Charles Dickens were priced beyond the pockets of most working people. And though contemporary writers like James Joyce, Thomas Hardy and E.M. Forster were becoming more well known, books still tended on the whole to be heavy, daunting things, used by the rich to line the shelves of their libraries and read only by scholars and academics.

Basically, what I'm saying is that the male population of Britain had no fucking clue what they were letting themselves in for. It was horrible looking at the men queueing with me, many of whom were barely old enough to shave, and knowing that many - *most* - of them would be heading off to war and never coming back. No doubt they thought of war as a playground game, as a fun and exciting adventure. From the snippets of chatter I picked up, it was clear that the majority of them expected to send Jerry packing without too much trouble, and return home to a hero's welcome in time for Christmas, grinning and bedecked with medals.

From my modern perspective there was surprisingly little cynicism in these overheard conversations, surprisingly little doubt, and surprisingly little criticism - in fact, none whatsoever - of the powers-that-be. It seemed no matter what your status in life - whether you be king or politician, a member of the privileged classes or a humble working man - the general consensus was that you were all in this together, fighting side by side for freedom and justice, secure in the knowledge that evil would be conquered and good would prevail.

All of which made the belittling comments of the man ahead of me in the queue, and the sneery laughter that followed, strange to hear. It was a bum note in the general atmosphere of camaraderie. As I looked up the length of the queue I heard, but didn't see, someone (presumably the 'runt') respond to the bullish man's insult. The tone the 'runt' used was defiant, but his actual words were obscured by the bluster of the wind and by the fact that he was standing with his back to me, presumably facing his aggressor.

Whatever he said must have been cutting, though, because the laughter that followed *his* retort was a startled, even admiring, whoop of mirth. The tail end of the laughter was superseded by an animal-like snarl and the bullish man's voice again, angry with humiliation: 'Why, you little shit! I'll give you a hiding you'll never forget!'

As the queue ahead of me, about halfway between where I was standing and the door of the recruiting station, bulged and rippled, I was already moving, because suddenly I *knew* that this was it. I'd arrived in this time period wondering how I'd meet Frank, realising I had no idea which recruitment office to go to, and on which day, and at what time.

Then I'd realised it didn't matter. Frank had told me it would happen, which meant that therefore it would. It was a *fait accompli* – or maybe even a *Fate accompli*. All I had to do was act on what little information I had, and destiny would do the rest.

Thinking back to my conversation with Frank on the tube after he'd rescued me from the trap that Benny Magee had led me into in Queens Road Cemetery in Walthamstow, I recalled him telling me he'd been born in Lewisham and that he'd been training to be a draughtsman when war had broken out. I'd therefore headed to the Lewisham recruiting office, rather than the one closest to my house in Kensington, in the hope our paths would cross. Frank had also told me, during that same tube conversation, that he'd died (or *would* die) at Ypres in 1917 at the age of twenty. As 1917 was still three years away, that meant Frank would currently be seventeen. So like a lot of the men eager to head off to war he'd be little more than a kid. Younger even than my eldest daughter, Candice.

As I hurried towards what seemed to be a scuffle in the queue ahead, the knot of men surrounding it swelled even further, then broke apart. A few of them staggered back as two bodies hurtled sideways on to the pavement. One was a tall, burly guy in his twenties with red hair jutting from beneath the brim of a grey cap, and a complexion like lumpy, freckled cheese. The other, flailing and scrapping like a cornered cat, was Frank Martin. The burly man had him round the throat and had lifted him clean off the ground.

At seventeen Frank was even weedier than the version of him I'd known in my own time. His thin, slightly ferrety face was bright red through lack of air, and his dark hair was drooping over his forehead in oily strands.

To give him credit, though, he was making a good job of fighting his corner. The red-haired man was twice as broad as Frank and a good eight to ten inches taller, but Frank was lashing out at him as he hung in the air, landing punches wherever he could – which, to be honest, were mostly ineffectual thumps on his assailant's tree-trunk arms and bulging shoulders.

Almost casually the red-haired man drew back his free arm, as if to let loose an arrow from a bow, and curled his meaty fingers into a fist. From my perspective the fist looked about the size of Frank's head, and the arm about to propel it forward looked as if it would give the fist more than enough momentum to knock Frank's block clean off his shoulders.

By now I was running fast enough for the wind to catch hold of the brim of my hat and whip it from my head.

'Oi, Ginger!' I yelled. 'Try picking on someone your own size!'

Fist poised, the red-haired man was caught momentarily off-guard. He half-turned so suddenly that he stumbled, inadvertently both loosening his grip on Frank's throat and drawing him closer.

I'll say this for Frank – he had bloody good reflexes. Making the most of his opportunity, he kicked out at his assailant, his foot making a solid *thock* as it connected with the ginger man's shinbone.

His attacker's face contorted and he let loose a girlish howl of pain. His grip on Frank's throat slackened further, allowing Frank to wriggle free. Instead of making a break for it, though, Frank drew back his arm, jumped up and socked the ginger man in the eye. The man's head snapped back and his cap fell to the pavement. I was still running at him full-pelt, and before he could recover I thrust out both hands and shoved him as hard as I could.

The bloke was as compact as an ox, and if he hadn't already been tottering I might have done no more than jar my arms. But because he was off-balance over he went, a look of dumb incomprehension on his face, his arms windmilling behind him. He landed on his arse with a coccyx-crunching thump that made me wince. Sitting there, legs and arms akimbo, he resembled an over-sized baby. When I glanced at Frank, he looked at me and grinned. His face was flushed, his tie was askew and one side of his collar was sticking up in the air like a crumpled white bat's wing, but he looked utterly gleeful. I'd never seen him grin like that before, and it was an expression both joyous and heart-rendingly painful to see.

We were only able to enjoy the moment for a couple of seconds, though. As stunned as Ginger had been by the way the tables had been turned on him, he recovered quickly. With a roar he scrambled to his feet.

'You fucking sods! I'll have the fucking both of yer! Yer dead men!' he bellowed.

As he lumbered towards us, I tensed, poised between fight and flight. Although I was as tall as Ginger, he was a lot heftier than me, and despite coming from a rough neighbourhood and having the kind of face that sometimes made people uneasy (apparently my default expression, as I'd been variously told in the past, was moody and intense) I wasn't much of a scrapper.

I glanced at Frank again to gauge his intentions, wondering whether he was of a mind that we should join forces and put this bully down for good. Before it became a decision we'd be forced into making, though, fate intervened, in the form of several other blokes in the queue who started to pipe up on our behalf.

First to speak was a squat, dark-bearded, balding man with a Scottish accent. 'Ach, they beat ye fair and square, man. I'd accept that if I were ye.'

There were grunts of assent, nods of agreement. Like a cornered animal, Ginger rounded on the dark-bearded man and snarled, 'I'll lay you out too, Scotty, if you don't shut yer trap.'

Now another man jumped in, rangy like me, but pugnacious-looking. In an accent that was pure East End, he said, 'You have a go at him, mate, and you'll have to have a go at me too. Like the rest o' these gents, I'm here today to stand up to a pack of bullies across the sea. But before I give the Hun what for, I'd just as happily stand up to bullies on me own soil.'

The roars of assent were louder this time. Some of the men stepped forward, fists raised defiantly in Ginger's direction.

Ginger looked from one man to another, his anger turning to petulance and then to uncertainty. He looked to his knot of cronies, who had initially egged him on with their sneering laughter, but they'd lapsed into silence and were now looking at their shoes or huddling into their jackets, keen to disassociate themselves from their thuggish companion.

Ginger looked first at me and then at Frank. 'You haven't heard the last of this,' he said, and stabbed his finger in our direction, 'neither of you. I'll have you yet, you mark my words.'

'Yeah, you and the Kaiser's army,' retorted Frank, and everyone laughed.

Ginger's face went as red as his hair. He clenched his fists, gave us one more murderous look, then stalked away.

A few of the men catcalled after him, but the general mood was one of great good humour. The incident seemed to have stirred the collective blood, to have brought us all together, reminding us – on this unseasonably cold and wind-swept day – that we were here to unite against a common enemy. Conversation swelled and bubbled in the wake of the bully's departure; hands were shaken; strangers introduced themselves to strangers.

I stepped towards Frank, hand outstretched. 'Mate of yours, was he?' I asked, nodding towards Ginger's retreating back.

'Bosom pal,' Frank said. 'Wasn't that obvious?'

His hand met mine, and it was warm, his grip strong. He was so full of life I felt like weeping.

'I'm Alex,' I said. 'Alex Locke.'

'Frank Martin,' said Frank.

I nodded at a pub called The Crown, which was across the road, opposite the recruiting station. 'Fancy a pint once we've joined up?'

Frank's grin widened. 'Why not?'

THREE

COSMIC BALANCE

I mulled it over for a long time before deciding to go ahead. In the back of my mind, though, I always knew that now I had the means at my disposal – i.e. the ability to use the heart without it half-killing me – I'd have to give it a try. If I didn't, and everything went tits up at some later date, I knew I'd only end up wondering what might have happened if I had. And more to the point, whether, by avoiding what seemed like an obvious solution, I'd made things unnecessarily difficult for myself.

I reasoned too that if it wasn't meant to be then it wouldn't work out. And that if it *was* meant to be, then it would. In short, I'd be putting myself into the hands of Fate, just as I had when I'd gone along to the recruiting station in Lewisham. I'd left the timing of that up to destiny, and things had worked out just fine. I'd met Frank as I was supposed to, we'd joined up together, and now, despite the disparity in our ages, we were great pals.

In fact, it was Frank who I talked the whole thing over with, in a roundabout way, one night in The Globe over a few pints. The Globe was a poky little boozer in Lambeth, not far from the Bethlehem Royal Hospital – or Bedlam, as it was more popularly known.

It had been a couple of weeks since that blustery day when we'd first put paid to Ginger and joined up together. Since then we'd been kicking our heels, waiting for our call-up papers. Such was the enthusiasm among the men of Britain when war had been declared that many recruiting stations had had to temporarily close down in order to deal with the backlog of paperwork that needed processing before the thousands of eager volunteers could become bona fide members of the armed forces.

When Frank and I had reached the front of the recruitment office queue two weeks earlier, the flustered-looking officer on duty had simply taken our names and addresses and told us we'd be contacted 'in due course'. Frank had learned from a bloke at his work, whose cousin was in the Royal Fusiliers, that we could be waiting a couple of months before we heard anything further. According to Frank's work mate's cousin, it was a logistical nightmare trying to fix up quarters and find suitable training facilities for the huge influx of new recruits. Added to which there was a shortage of uniforms, weapons and food. The Great War might only be a few weeks old, but already it was taking a massive toll on the country's infrastructure and resources.

It was odd how a new century and a new monarch, or more especially the death of one who had epitomised the era that was named after her, could alter the mood and ethos of a country. Although the current year was only a couple of decades on from my three-month sabbatical in Victorian London, it felt like a different age entirely. The London of the 1890s had been a city of horse-drawn carriages, thick fog, gas-lit streets and elaborate, cumbersome clothing. More pertinently it had been a city of extremes – of astounding technological and commercial progress on the one hand and chronic poverty on the other.

Now, though, things seemed to have... the only phrase that sprang to mind was 'settled down'. Although ongoing social reform under the Liberal government, which had come to power in 1906, had to be a good thing, to me London seemed to have lost much of its colour and vitality, to have acquired a drabness, like a set of once fresh and fashionable clothes that had now faded and sagged out of shape.

Perhaps it was simply the dark cloud of war, which hung over everything; perhaps it was my own misconception of the world around me; or maybe it was even that I didn't have Clover here to keep me company, as I had in the 1890s. Whatever the reason, I couldn't help thinking that the London of 1914 needed a bloody good shot in the arm. The clothes that people wore were simpler, more sombre and less individual than they'd been twenty years earlier, and even the way people talked had changed. The mannered, formal, often colourful verbosity of the Victorians had, in a very short time, given way to a simpler, more homogenised way of speaking – one that seemed closer to how my parents and grandparents had spoken in the '60s and '70s, even though that era was still another half-century down the line.

The Globe, where I'd taken to meeting up with Frank most evenings (I had no idea whether, in this day and age, Frank was underage, and I didn't ask – if he wasn't, it would have seemed a bloody weird question), was poky and low-ceilinged, the furniture, floors and bar hewn of dark, dusty wood, the air grainy with pipe smoke. The local brew was strong – though it was also tepid and sometimes tasted a bit funky, on which evenings I favoured whisky to avoid the squits (not wine, though, which was my usual tipple at home; wine was for the 'toffs'). The clientele was one hundred per cent male, aside from the landlord's wife, who had a lazy eye and a permanent sneer. A fire roared in the grate to the right of the main bar, whatever the weather, and tarnished horse brasses adorned the walls.

By modern standards The Globe was a quiet pub, though sometimes, later in the evening, a sing-song would break out, occasionally accompanied by an enthusiastic plonk on the piano. For the most part, though, the only sounds to punctuate the smoky, somnolent atmosphere were the click of dominoes, the crackle of logs burning in the grate and the low rumble of conversation.

It hadn't been difficult cultivating a friendship with Frank, a fact that helped alleviate the guilt I felt at the sense that I was manipulating events, and therefore him, simply to keep Destiny, or Fate, or whatever, on the right path. He was a lively, bright lad, and he seemed mature for his age – though that might have been because the young people of this time were expected to shuck off the indulgences of childhood as soon as they left school and become adults almost overnight, usually marrying in their early twenties.

It was the last day of August, a Monday, which was significant to me only insofar as a couple of weeks earlier I'd promised myself I'd come to a decision by the end of the month as to whether I'd do what I'd been thinking of doing ever since (more or less) waking up in my new nanite-enhanced body. Halfway across the world the First Battle of Garua was taking place in Nigeria between British and German forces, a skirmish that would result in a German victory. But here in

Lambeth, even though talk in the country was of little else, the War still seemed not only impossibly distant, but not entirely real.

Frank and I were on our third pint of the evening, or maybe our fourth. He may have been only seventeen, and have weighed ten stone soaking wet, but I'll say this for him – he couldn't half put it away. In fact, sometimes I had a job keeping up – and so it was proving this evening. He still looked bright as a button, whereas I was feeling woozy and dull-headed, despite the nanites in my system. I'm not sure whether I'd been consciously planning to discuss my dilemma with Frank, or whether it was simply that I felt if I didn't share it with someone soon I'd burst. At any rate, all at once, my inhibitions loosened by alcohol, I heard myself asking, 'Listen, Frank, have you ever read *The Time Machine* by H.G. Wells?'

Frank looked momentarily surprised by the left-field nature of the question, then pushed out his bottom lip in lieu of a shrug. 'Can't say as I have. He's the coward, isn't he? Always going on about war being wrong and all that?'

'I don't think he's a coward,' I said. 'A pacifist maybe.'

'Same thing, ain't it?'

'Not really. But anyway – you know of it? *The Time Machine*? You know the story?'

Frank screwed his face up, as if trying to recall the name of a distant cousin. 'Is that the one about the bloke who can go into the future?' He snorted. 'A bit daft, if you ask me. Kids' stuff.'

Resisting the urge to discuss the merits and demerits of Wells's far-reaching vision, I said, 'Yes, but what if it was true? What if you *could* go into the future? Or the past for that matter?'

Frank looked at me as though I was simple. 'You can't, though, can you?'

'Just bear with me,' I said, trying not to become frustrated at his lack of imagination.

'Bear with what?' he said, a note of irritation in his voice. 'What's the point of this, Alex? Whatever I might look like to you, I'm not a bloody kid any more.'

'I know that,' I said, 'and I'm not making fun of you. Think of this as... a hypothesis?'

His eyes narrowed. 'You mean as something that's daft, but that we pretend is true? That we take seriously even though we *know* it's barmy?'

'Exactly!'

'Why?'

'Just because... well, because sometimes it's good to think outside the box.'

'What box?'

I waved a hand. 'I'm not talking about a real box. What I mean is... think of the world as having boundaries. Within those boundaries is everything we know about, everything we accept.'

'Everything that's true and real?'

'Everything we *accept* as being true and real. The sum of all human knowledge.'

'All right,' he said slowly.

'Now imagine there are things we *don't* know about. Things we haven't learned yet. And they exist outside these boundaries – not because they're not real, or because they're daft or childish, but simply because we don't know about them yet.'

'Like finding a way of travelling into the future?'

'Or the past, yes.'

He sighed indulgently. 'All right. But I still don't see what you're getting at.' Abruptly he laughed. 'Sometimes, I think you're half-cracked.'

I grinned, was about to agree with him, and then had a sudden thought. I put my hand in my jacket pocket, aware that my heart was beating hard. 'I want to show you something,' I said. 'To illustrate my point.'

He looked at me uncomprehendingly, but shrugged as if to say: *Go ahead.*

I glanced around me, ever wary, and withdrew the obsidian heart. Frank took a nonchalant sip of his pint, but to me it felt like a charged moment. Keeping the heart below the level of the edge of the table, out of sight of prying eyes, I extended my arm towards him and opened my palm.

'Here,' I said, 'take it.'

He glanced down, his expression dubious. In the gloom of the pub it must have looked as if I was offering him a lump of coal.

'What is it?'

'Take it,' I repeated. 'Have a look.'

He gave a little shake of his head, but then sighed and took the heart from my hand. I tensed as he lifted it in front of his face so he could peer at it more closely, and subtly tried to adjust my position so that I was shielding it from sight.

If I expected anything to happen, for the heart to respond to Frank in some significant way, or for him to respond to it, I was disappointed. He simply stared at it in bafflement, moving it from side to side. 'What is it?'

'What does it look like?'

He glanced at me, as if uncertain whether I was trying to catch him out. 'It's a heart, ain't it? Carved out of ebony or something.' He hefted it in his hand. 'It's a nice piece.'

My own heart was thumping harder now. I was half-surprised the vibrations weren't causing pint glasses to rattle on tables, curious eyes to turn in our direction. My mouth felt dry and I licked my lips. I said, 'Imagine that's *your* time machine, Frank. Imagine that with that you could go anywhere, backwards or forwards. That you just had to think yourself there and there you'd be. Where would you go?'

He looked at the heart and scowled. 'Well, I don't know, do I?'

'Isn't there anywhere you want to go? Anything you want to see?'

'I've never really thought about it.'

'Think about it now.'

'Why?'

I sat back, smiled, tried to take the intensity out of the situation, to make it into more of a game. 'Call it... an intellectual exercise.'

'The only exercise I want to do is lift me arm with a pint glass in it.'

I sighed, on the point of giving up. Then I had a brainwave. 'What about the War?'

'What about it?'

'Well, wouldn't you want to end it if you could? Stop it before it had even started?'

For a moment I thought he was going to say no. He looked almost sulky, like a schoolboy who'd been asked whether he wanted to cancel his birthday party. Then he said, 'Suppose so.'

'So what if, using the heart, you could travel back in time and... I don't know... stop Gavrilo Princip from shooting Franz Ferdinand? Would you do it?'

'Dunno,' he said, and then grudgingly, 'Maybe.'

'But what if, by stopping Princip, there was the possibility you'd be opening the door to something worse?'

Now he was looking confused. Hastily I said, 'Hang on, let me put it another way. What if someone said to you that if you didn't stop Princip there'd be a terrible war, the worst war this world had ever seen? What if they said that was a definite? What if they said the war would last for four years, and twenty million people would die, but then it would be over and the world would carry on? And what if they said that by stopping Princip you could stop that war? But that if you did that there was the possibility – not a definite thing this time, but a *possibility* – that something even worse would happen?'

Frank was now looking at me wide-eyed. It was as if I'd half-mesmerised him. 'What could be worse than twenty million people dying in a war?'

'I don't know. The whole world being wiped out maybe. What if, by stopping Princip, you might upset some... some cosmic balance–'

'God, do you mean?'

'Well... yes, if it makes it easier, think of it as God. What if, by stopping Princip, there was a *chance*, just a chance, that you could upset God enough to make him destroy the world?'

Frank was scowling, though not out of irritation this time; now he seemed to be genuinely contemplating the moral dilemma I'd set him.

'So I can leave things be,' he said, 'let Princip kill this Franz feller, knowing there'll be a war and twenty million people will die, but the world will be all right again afterwards. Or I can stop this Princip, and stop the war, and save those twenty million lives – but by doing that it *might* upset some... what was it you said?'

'Cosmic balance.'

'That's it. It *might* upset some cosmic balance, which would end us all.'

'That's the crux of it,' I said. 'Which would you choose? The terrible thing that was definite? Or the even worse thing that might or might not happen?'

Frank looked at me, then at the heart again. Then he placed the heart on the table, between our pint glasses.

'I'd stop the definite thing and take my chances,' he said.

I looked at him, surprised – but then realised I'd have been surprised whatever his answer.

'Would you? Why?'

'Because I can't cope with maybes. If you always think about what might happen, then you'd never do anything, would you? But if I can stop something that I know's going to be bad, I'll stop it. Every time.'

I put the heart back into my pocket, then picked up my pint and took a swig. I must have looked thoughtful, because Frank said, 'So? What about you?'

'The same,' I said automatically. 'I'd do the same.'

That night I used the heart.

FOUR
CHANGING HISTORY

The transition was smooth, the after-effects comprising of nothing but a slight tingling in my arms and legs, a few moments of light-headedness and mild nausea. I stood swaying in the darkened room, a room I was acutely familiar with, and for which I suddenly experienced an almost overwhelming ache of nostalgia.

It was this, combined with the now relatively mild effects of time travel, that caused me to grope my way to the squashy old settee and sit down. The springs creaked as the depression in the seat cushion welcomed back my familiar weight. It had been months since I'd sat here, although I guess as far as the flat (and the settee) were concerned, it had been only a matter of hours.

In front of me was the toy chest, which served as a coffee table, with Kate's *Toy Story* colouring book on top of it. At the sight of it the rush of nostalgia, which had made me feel jittery, was unceremoniously swept aside by a more powerful torrent of emotions – longing, loss, hope, excitement, fear. Last time I'd seen this room it had been trashed, the sofa I was sitting on shredded and overturned, the colouring book torn to pieces. But I'd now travelled back to a time before that had happened, to a time before the Wolves of London had been after me – or at least before I'd known that they were. If the heart had brought me to where I wanted to be, this was October 1st 2012. The reason the flat was empty was because my past self was currently on his way to meet Benny Magee at the Hair of the Dog, and Kate was across the hallway in the flat belonging to my neighbours – neighbours who my past self knew as Adam and Paula Sherwood, but whose real names were Linley and Maude Sherwood, and who had been brought here from Victorian London, presumably by the Dark Man, to abduct my daughter.

Although the sight of Kate's colouring book had set me off, it was the thought that she was probably, at this moment, no more than a couple of dozen metres away from me that caused me to literally *shake* with emotion. Ever since waking up in 2097 and discovering not only that I could use the heart to take me where and when I wanted to go (an ability I had only recently mastered), but also that the heart would now transport me to my chosen destination without also ripping me apart in the process, I'd been thinking about going back in time and preventing Kate's abduction. No, scratch that; I hadn't been thinking about it – I'd been *obsessing* over the idea.

The only thing that had prevented me from heading back here straight away was my fear that by changing history I would somehow make things even worse. I'd experienced the knock-on effects of altering events before, in the form of visions, which had been 'shown' to me possibly by the heart. In that instance I'd seen visions of what might happen if I failed to use the heart to meet Frank, or to pay off Candice's boyfriend's debt. In this case, though, it was different. Now my concern was what might happen if I used the heart to alter what to me was already established history.

Maybe nothing. Or maybe things would change not for the worse, but for the better. It could be that time was malleable, constantly in flux, and that altering history didn't necessarily always equal disaster.

Whatever the outcome, though, I knew deep down that I had to try it. I think I'd decided that even before my conversation with Frank in The Globe a few hours (and almost a century) earlier, but his words had served only to make up my already made-up mind. Before speaking to Frank I'd been teetering on the brink, bracing myself for the jump. His words had simply given me the extra push I needed.

I took several deep breaths in the hope it would stop my legs from shaking, and then I stood up. If the heart had brought me to the time of day I'd wanted to arrive – and judging by the darkening sky outside it had – it would now be just after 5 p.m. In truth, I had no idea what time Kate's abduction had taken place, but I knew it couldn't have happened during the school day, otherwise the school would have contacted me. It was possible that the Sherwoods, having cleared out their flat while I was at work, had picked up Kate and their own son, Hamish, at 3:30 p.m. and driven straight to wherever it was they'd disappeared to with my daughter. But if they *had* done that, then I'd just use the heart to try again; I'd use it to allow me to pick Kate up from school myself if needs be.

What, though, if that brought the Wolves down not just on me, but on the both of us? What if Kate was with me when they attacked?

No. I wouldn't allow myself to harbour doubts. I thought back to what Frank had said earlier: *I can't cope with maybes. If you always think about what might happen, then you'd never do anything, would you?*

'Who dares wins,' I muttered, and felt my lips twitch in a shaky smile at the dumb bravado of the phrase as I walked out of the room and across the short hallway of the flat. I fumbled at the catch of the main door with numb fingers, then tugged the door open and stepped on to the landing.

I half-expected to see the Sherwoods' door standing open, and them to be tiptoeing down the stairs, a suitcase in each hand. But the door of their flat was closed. I walked across to it and listened.

Muffled sounds, too vague to be called thumps or scrapes, suggested occupation, movement.

Gotcha, I thought, and raised a hand to thump on their door, imagining how shocked Paula's face would be when she opened it.

I couldn't believe it was really going to be this easy. Or was I being naive? Perhaps I should have come prepared for violence? I was about to thrust my raised fist forward when a hand grabbed my wrist from behind and tugged me off-balance. I stumbled backwards with a grunt of pain, then twisted to face my assailant, instinctively swinging my left arm round in a clumsy attempt at a punch. But my attacker anticipated the movement and stepped smartly aside, yanking my raised arm back even further. I cried out in pain, and my attacker's free hand immediately clamped over my mouth.

'For Christ's sake, shut up,' a familiar voice hissed in my ear. 'Do you want to ruin everything?'

My momentum spun me all the way round until I was facing my assailant. My eyes widened.

It was me.

An older version, of course, though I only knew that because I knew I hadn't yet done what he was now doing. He looked pretty much the same as me, which I guess meant he could have been anything from a few weeks to a few years older. I stopped struggling.

'For fuck's sake,' I said. 'What's the problem?'

He nodded back towards the door of my flat. 'We'll chat in here. Come on, quick, before it's too late.'

I glared at him, then sighed. 'Jesus Christ. Why are things never straightforward? What do you know that I don't?'

He let go of me and raised a hand towards the open door of my flat, like an estate agent inviting a prospective buyer to lead the way. I trudged ahead of him, rotating my right shoulder in its socket.

'That bloody hurt, you know,' I hissed. 'I wouldn't be surprised if it's still giving you gyp.'

My future self rolled his eyes. 'Jesus, I'd forgotten what a wimp I used to be.'

'Fuck off.'

I still found it odd talking to myself – arguing with myself especially. The oddest thing was that I knew exactly what my 'opponent's' limits were. To me, because he *was* me, he was entirely predictable. I knew he wasn't going to suddenly pull out a gun and shoot me – or hurt me in any way, come to that.

'So what's the problem?' I asked once we were back in the flat and he had closed the door behind us. 'Why can't I just stop them from taking Kate now and have done with it? Is it because you're scared of what'll happen to *you*?'

He went into the front room, turned the light on and looked around.

He picked up Kate's colouring book, then quickly put it down again. 'Good times, eh?' he said. 'Simpler times.'

'Are you still—' I started to ask, but he raised a hand.

'Don't waste time asking. But to answer your previous question – the one about what I know that you don't... what I know is that I remember being you, and I remember what *I* told myself when I *was* you. And I now know that it makes sense, which is why you shouldn't do what you're thinking of doing.'

I shook my head. 'What the fuck are you on about?'

He raised his hands, as if about to conduct an orchestra. 'Just go with me on this. It's like a time-loop thing, like a snake swallowing its own tail. It's best not to think about it too deeply, because it'll just end up tying your head in knots.'

I sighed. 'All right. Just say what you need to say.'

His hands were still raised, but now he pinched the thumb and forefinger of his right hand together, as if trying to squeeze what he wanted to say in between them, trying to make it as simple and as manageable as possible.

'The thing is,' he said, 'you've got a level of control over the heart now, right? You can use it to take you where you want to go, and the nanites inside you mean you won't end up in hospital or worse?'

'Yeah. So?'

'So there are better ways of doing things than just bludgeoning in like this and hoping for the best. *Safer* ways. With what you can do with the heart now – or maybe I should say, with what the heart can do *for you* – there's no need to use a hammer to crack a walnut.'

'I still don't get it.'

My future self sighed. 'You can change the past without *actually* changing it. Think about that. Think about it hard.' He tapped the side of his head with his forefinger. 'Use your noggin, Alex. But remember this: you don't have to be a victim any more.'

FIVE

BASIC TRAINING

Although my eyes were closed I was far from asleep. In fact, lying on my hard wooden bed beneath my thin, scratchy blanket I was beginning to think I might never sleep again. Not only was the hut so cold and draughty that I'd taken to wearing my long johns and woolly socks at night, but I was surrounded by such a cacophony of creaks, groans and snores that I felt as though my skull was vibrating with the din.

If the restless sleepers had formed an orchestra, then Howard Dankforth, who slept in the bed directly opposite mine, our feet separated by no more than the narrow aisle that ran down the centre of the hut, would have been its lead trombone. A big lad, six foot two and eighteen stone, he'd become known within the battalion as 'Bone Saw', because his snoring sounded like the electric teeth of that particular implement grinding its way through someone's leg.

It was February 5th 1915, and we'd been billeted in our hastily erected barracks – comprising a series of large wooden huts, each of which housed two dozen men – for just short of a week. Before this the three thousand or so of us who had travelled down from London to Dartmouth on a series of packed, rickety trains for basic training had been billeted with the local population, squeezed in wherever there was space. To reduce feelings of homesickness, disorientation and alienation, men from certain areas had been kept together in what were known as 'Pals Battalions'. If you were best mates with someone, the army had even gone out of their way to house you together where possible. Since receiving our call-up papers in mid-October, Frank and

I had been sharing digs in the home of Alfred and Edith White, a couple in their late fifties, who had a thirty-odd year old daughter called Elsie and two sons in their twenties, James and William. Alfred was the village undertaker, the latest in a proud family line stretching back to the mid 1700s. His boys had already gone off to war and were currently on manoeuvres in France. Alfred, a wiry, heavily moustached man, was of the opinion that the War would be over by the spring, whereupon his sons would come home and take up where they'd left off – helping with the family business with a view to eventually taking over when he retired. Such was his optimism I didn't want to disillusion him.

(Much later I discovered that both of Alf and Edith's boys were killed in the War – William, the younger son, in the summer of 1916, and twenty-seven-year-old James, who would be an officer in the Devon Light Infantry at the time of his death, in September 1918, just a couple of months before the cessation of hostilities.)

Alf and Edith had been kind to Frank and me – Edith, in particular, had treated us almost as surrogate sons – and it had been a wrench to leave them, particularly as it meant sharing a draughty hut with twenty-two other sweaty, smelly blokes. Even then, though, the camaraderie in barracks might have made up for it, if it hadn't been for one thing – or rather, one person.

He popped up like a bad penny the day we left London to begin basic training. Frank and I were sitting in the carriage of the train taking us from Paddington to Plymouth when the door flew open so violently that everyone jumped. Before then the mood had been raucous but friendly. In our carriage, aside from Frank and me, we had a barrister, a builder's labourer, a dentist, a butcher, a bank clerk and an engineer.

The bank clerk, Douglas Meadows, was a weedy lad with buck teeth and big ears. He was also a natural comedian, and had kept us in stitches with a string of jokes and funny stories. It was while he was in the middle of one of these that we were startled by the opening door. The bulky, scowling figure that appeared in the gap was like a thunder cloud. A thunder cloud with red hair.

'Well, well, look what we got here,' he barked. 'A couple o' nancy boys.'

It was Ginger, who Frank and I had humiliated the day we'd been standing in the queue at the recruiting station. We hadn't seen him since, and in fact I'd more or less forgotten all about him. I sighed and looked at Frank, who rolled his eyes. Although I was wary of Ginger, I wasn't scared of him – I'd faced far more frightening foes in the past few months – but I thought he might prove troublesome all the same.

Doug Meadows, cut off in mid-spiel, swallowed and blanched, and for a few seconds there was silence. Then the barrister, Bartlett Trent (a great name for a secret agent), said with a brightness which he clearly hoped would lighten the mood, 'Hello, old chap. Can we help you?'

Ginger's head swung round. 'No, "old chap", I don't believe you can. So why don't you shut your fucking mouth before I knock your teeth down your throat?'

Although the eight of us sharing the carriage barely knew one another, our common cause had created an instant bond. Jerking upright in his seat, Joe Lancing, the butcher, snapped, 'There's no need for that, old cock. We're all fighting on the same side here, if you hadn't noticed.'

'Yeah, you want to save that anger of yours for the Hun, mate,' Stan Little, the builder's labourer, chipped in.

There were nods all round. Ginger still wore a sneering expression, but now Frank sneered right back at him.

'You know what this is?' he said, circling his finger to indicate our eight-strong group. 'This is what's called making friends. You ought to try it, chum, otherwise you'll have a tough time of it once we get where we're going. It's not gonna be a picnic over there, you know. In fact, by all accounts, it's bleedin' Hell on Earth. So I reckon to get through it you're gonna need all the friends you can get.'

Doug Meadows looked alarmed, as if he hadn't contemplated what might actually happen once basic training was over. But everyone else was nodding.

'The lad's right, mate,' Stan Little said. He was a rugged, round-faced man with a scrubby moustache and a missing front tooth. He held out a hand that looked as if it had been moulded out of red clay. 'So why not drop whatever beef you got with these two and put it there?'

Ginger looked at the proffered hand, and for a second or two I thought he was going to accept Stan's offer. Then he glanced again at Frank, and I guess the memory of the day when the two of us had put him on his arse in a crowded street must have again risen to the forefront of his mind. The scowl crunched back on to his face and his lip curled.

'You'll get what's coming to you, sonny,' he barked, pointing at Frank. Then he shifted his attention to me. 'And so will your bum chum. You just see if you don't.'

I should have ignored him. But his stupidity irritated me. And so, before I could bite back on my words, I said, 'You want to be careful you don't get so angry that you spit your dummy out, mate.'

Admittedly it wasn't much of a riposte, but it was enough to rile Ginger. His eyes widened, his nostrils flared, his face went as red as his hair, and he lunged at me, his hand reaching for my throat.

What followed was ugly, stupid and embarrassing. In the confines of the railway carriage there was what I suppose you'd call a scuffle. It consisted mainly of a lot of flailing and shouting. Because I was sitting down I couldn't properly defend myself. I had to resort to hunching in my shoulders, fending Ginger off with my upraised arms while he loomed over me, swinging clumsy haymakers at my head and body. I used my legs too, pistoning out my right foot and catching him on the thigh with enough force to make him grunt and buckle slightly.

Before he could do any real damage, Frank, Stan and, perhaps surprisingly, Bartlett were up out of their seats and doing their best to pin Ginger's swinging arms to his sides and manhandle him out of the door. With a lot of pushing and shoving and tripping over one another's legs they eventually managed it, by which time half the train had been alerted to the commotion. Men started to pour out of the carriages flanking our own in such numbers that they were jamming the aisle, their necks craning to see what was going on. Some were egging on the combatants like spectators at a boxing match, while others laughed and clapped.

Not wanting to just sit there, I jumped to my feet, my left ear ringing and my right shoulder throbbing where Ginger had managed to get in a couple of half-decent clouts.

Doug Meadows stood up too and put a solicitous hand on my elbow. 'Are you all right, Alex?' he asked.

Looking into Doug's eyes it suddenly struck me how unprepared he was for what was ahead of him; how unprepared so many of these boys were. Because they *were* boys, a lot of them. Boys who might already have seen their homes for the last time. Boys who in a few months would leave the country of their birth and might never come back. I thought of photos I'd seen of twisted bodies lying in mud-churned battlefields; thought of the rows and rows of pristine white war graves in France and Belgium and Italy. Looking into Doug's eyes I suddenly felt like weeping.

Because I couldn't save them all. I wasn't sure, by resurrecting Frank, whether I'd even saved *him*.

He frowned, as if he sensed something of what I was thinking. '*Are* you all right?'

I laughed. It sounded hollow and ghastly in my ears. 'I'm fine, Doug,' I said, and clapped him on the shoulder. 'It was a bit of high jinks, that's all. Nothing to worry about.'

I almost added: *compared to what's to come*, but I didn't. As prepared as I felt Doug and Bartlett and all the other high-spirited young guys on this train needed to be, I couldn't do that to him. I couldn't whip away his optimism, illusory though that was, pre-empt the horror of the trenches. The War would do that soon enough.

We didn't see much of Ginger for the next three months. He was billeted in another village to us, and basic training consisted of so many men split into so many groups – an endless, drab round of drill, drill, drill, interspersed with trench digging, route marching, kit inspections, and instructions on how to skirmish, how to handle a rifle, and how to take cover from observation – that our paths barely crossed. When they did he would throw us filthy looks; he would even, on occasion, go out of his way to pass us by just so he could mutter some blood-curdling threat. Whenever that happened, Frank laughed in his face, and I ignored him.

After our tussle on the train, no doubt Ginger saw my silence as a sign I was running scared of him. The real reasons I wanted to avoid further trouble, though, were based more on calculation than emotion. Firstly, because of the heart and because I was a man out of time, I didn't want to draw undue attention to myself. Secondly, I didn't want to make army life even harder and more tedious than it already was by being up on a charge for indiscipline. And thirdly... well, to be honest, I had a certain reputation to uphold.

Purely because I was older than most of the other lads I was training with, I tended to be regarded as a bit of a father figure, as someone who was dependable, dignified, worldly-wise. I didn't do anything to encourage these views, or play up to them, but because a lot of the guys *did* think of me in these terms, I felt oddly reluctant to disillusion them. These young men, who were in the process of being hastily honed into soldiers, were about to be launched into a horror beyond imagining – and many of them would never see their loved ones again. In a way, therefore, I guess I saw it as my duty to be the rock that they thought I was. A reassuring presence they could depend on and take comfort from.

This Zen-like presence I'd acquired through no fault of my own was put to the test at the end of January. This was when we were moved into our newly erected barracks, and Frank and I discovered, either due to some nasty quirk of fate or because he'd wangled it to get at us, that Ginger would be one of the twenty-four blokes in our hut. In the week since we'd moved in it had been like living with a dangerous dog, one which snapped and snarled and constantly eyeballed us, but which hadn't yet had the opportunity to launch an attack. Not that either of us expected Ginger – whose real name was John Pyke – to confront us face-to-face. No, as stupid as he was, he'd be more likely to go for the stealth attack. He'd come at us when we were asleep, or sneak up on one or other of us when we were alone and unprepared.

We'd managed to be vigilant and tolerant up to now. We'd stuck together, deflected Pyke's sneered asides, laughed off his barbed comments as if they were nothing but banter. Frank had even treated it as a prank when he'd discovered a human turd under his pillow, and I'd done the same when I found that my shaving kit had been chucked in the cesspit. But it would surely be only a matter of time before things came to a head. Despite outward appearances I knew that Frank's blood was starting to boil.

The fact that Stan Little and Joe Lancing were in our hut too was both a blessing and a curse. A blessing because they provided a buffer between Pyke's hostility and our reaction to it, and a curse because they hated Pyke's guts almost as much as we did (or rather, almost as much as Frank did; I don't want to sound superior, but I genuinely regarded Pyke as little more than an irritant). I knew that if something *did* kick off, and Pyke ended up getting a pasting because of it, it would be all too easy for him to make out that he was the injured party; that he'd been singled out, victimised, his life made a misery, purely because he'd had the guts to stand up for himself.

As the aggressor, then, he'd win whatever happened – at least I'm guessing that was the way *he* saw it. The way *I* saw it was that Frank and I had to dig our heels in and not rise to Pyke's bait on the one hand, and watch our backs on the other. But how easy that would be over the next weeks and months I had no idea. I *had* contemplated taking Pyke aside, speaking to him as an adult, trying to make him see reason; in fact, I was *still* contemplating it. I was contemplating it as I lay in my bed in the hut, surrounded by the nightly chorus of creaks and snores. I was contemplating it when, unexpectedly, I fell asleep.

I didn't think I was asleep at first, though. I thought I'd simply... *moved*. One second I was lying in bed and the next I was somewhere else. I was no longer lying down, but sitting or standing up, and squinting into a bright light.

Was I about to be interrogated? Had I been drugged? Lost my memory? I braced myself for pain that didn't come. I felt warm, and instinctively took a step towards the warmth, as though my body was drawn to it.

'Hello?' I said, and from the quality of my voice I knew I was outside. I squatted down and touched the ground, felt a solid but shifting surface beneath my fingers. Sand. The grains so fine that when I lifted my hand they slipped beneath my fingers like silk. And now the light was receding as my eyes adjusted to it. The white, somehow pure sun was drawing back, spreading out its heat and its light, exposing my surroundings as if offering them to me.

I was in a desert. No, I was in *the* desert. I had been here before, and I knew what I had to do.

This is a recurring dream, I thought as I began walking. *I can wake up any time I want, but first I have to see this through.*

The sun beat down. The sand stretched around me in all directions, flat and featureless. My body was soaking up heat, but I felt good, I felt strong. All things moving in harmony, my mind clear, sharp.

Eventually I knelt down in the sand. I had arrived. There were no landmarks to tell me this place was different to any other, but I knew it was right just the same. I was the desert and the desert was me. The world was so new that I and everything in it was one and the same. We were unsullied by... what? Sin? Conflict? Progress? The march of evolution?

Primal sources. Primal sources and primal forces. They linked us. They linked everything.

I pushed my hands into the sand, the grains parting before my fingers like water. I linked my mind to the earth, and I found what I was looking for, and I pulled it out.

As before it was wet with the juices of its birth, and it squirmed and writhed, vibrant with energy, busy with life. I moulded it in my hands, using my core, the engine that drives me, as a template, shaping it in my own image. What I created was raw and ugly and vulnerable, but it was also *life*, beautiful and magical.

When it was complete I dropped it in the sand and walked away, leaving it behind, the first artefact. I knew it would find its way. I knew it would begin its journey here. I knew it would tumble through the centuries, until eventually it would end up where it was meant to be, whereupon we would be reunited, the creator and his creation.

I came awake.

There was no preamble, no drifting up from the depths of slumber. One moment I was in the desert, the next I was lying on my hard wooden bed, covered by a prickly blanket and encased in a cocoon of snores and restless creaks.

But something had changed. I could sense it as surely as a deer can sense a nearby predator. Since moving into the hut with the other men I'd taken to sleeping with the heart in my hand, with my hand under my pillow and my head resting on top of it. That way, if someone tried to take the heart from me I would know.

It wasn't this that had woken me, though. There was a dim night light by the door as a guide for those who woke in the dark and needed to stumble outside for a piss, and there was enough of an amber glow leaking from this to assure me there was no shadowy form looming over my bed.

So why were my nerves tingling like wires stretched between the outstretched arms of electricity pylons? Why was an internal alarm blaring in my head, warning me of danger? Was it something to do with the dream? Something I'd forgotten or overlooked?

I sensed stealthy movement in my peripheral vision, a worm-like creeping in the corner of my eye, that seemed to be coming from the narrow gap between the head of my bed and the wall behind. Thinking of the shape-shifter employed by my nemesis the Dark Man, I twisted on to my stomach, my head jerking up.

And that was when I saw it.

The heart.

Perhaps stimulated by my dream, it had become active, extending long, black, fibrous tendrils that had curled from under my pillow and were now climbing the wall behind my bed in sinuous, overlapping loops and spirals. The effect was that of a huge clinging vine growing at a remarkable speed, or of a multi-legged ink-black sea creature slithering out from its hiding place and tentatively exploring its surroundings.

The heart itself, the core from which the tendrils extended, was active too. I could feel it writhing in my palm, slick and hot like a newborn freshly expelled from its mother's womb. I had the notion that its 'flesh' was becoming one with mine, that we were one flesh, one mind.

And yet conversely the sensation was also a sensuous, almost sexual one. The tingling in my nerve endings became a swell of euphoria; my eyelids fluttered; I groaned.

Then, amid the snores and the sighs and the restless shifting around me I heard another sound, a purposeful and prolonged creak, as though someone had sat up in bed. And it was followed by a shocked gasp, almost a cry, sharp but brief, and just as quickly stifled.

Instantly I drew in my defences – that was what it felt like – and in a split second the heart was once again a cold, hard lump of obsidian in my hand. All evidence that it had ever been anything else was gone. With my hand still under the pillow, I half-turned my body, propped myself up on my elbow and surveyed the room.

No one was sitting up. No one was staring at me. As far as I could see everyone was asleep.

My gaze alighted on John Pyke's bed, four beds to the left (my right) of Howard 'Bone Saw' Dankforth's. I stared at his humped form without blinking. He was still – maybe *too* still? Was his the stillness of someone *pretending* to be asleep, eyes squeezed tightly shut, shoulders hunched, muscles tense?

I slipped out of bed as quietly as I could, padded down the central aisle until I was standing at the foot of his bed.

'Pyke,' I whispered. 'Pyke, I know you're awake. There's no use pretending.'

He didn't respond. Didn't move. His body remained motionless.

Had he seen? And what would it mean if he had?

I stood there for another minute or so, staring at the dark mound of his body.

Then I went back to bed.

SIX
THE WITCH

'Come on,' Frank coaxed. 'Come on, old son. That's it. You know you want it.'

Stan Little, rain dripping off the brim of his steel helmet, chuckled, and was immediately shushed by the rest of us. He put a hand over his mouth, looking both contrite and amused. Squatting in the trench, plastered in clinging mud, which oozed up over the ankles of his boots, he reminded me of the Speak No Evil monkey.

The rat crept closer, its fur so slick with mud and rain it looked metallic. It was wary, but hungry too, and the gobbet of bread on the point of Frank's bayonet was proving impossible to resist. Out in No Man's Land, amid the mud and the corpses, the barbed wire and the shattered remnants of ordnance, it would be able to see nothing of us, hunched below ground level in our water-filled trench. Neither would it be able to smell us; the stink of death on the battlefield would mask our scent. But if we made too much noise it would hear us, whereupon it would be gone in a flash.

Like all the rats here – and there were so many of them they often scampered across our bodies at night – this particular specimen was a big bastard, but mangy and diseased-looking. Frank remained motionless as it moved to within a few feet of his bayonet, the tip of which was poking at an angle above the sandbags stacked on the lip of the trench. I glanced at the men. Stan had removed his hand from his face, leaving brown streaks, and was now grinning, his eyes almost feverish with excitement. The others, shivering in the cold, their uniforms soaked through and plastered with mud, their faces drawn with the effects of dysentery and exhaustion, were staring avidly at the lump of white bread, as if they wouldn't mind snaffling it themselves.

After prevaricating for a moment the rat suddenly darted forward. As it clamped its teeth around the bread, Frank almost casually pulled the trigger. As ever his timing was perfect. As the rat turned away with its prize, the bullet from Frank's gun transformed it from a living creature into a red explosion of unrecognisable meat. We watched it, or rather the bits of it, scatter across No Man's Land. Geoffrey Ableman, a new recruit, barely eighteen, was so entranced by the spectacle that he forgot himself for a moment and raised his head above the lip of the trench to watch its progress.

Instantly there was the crack of a rifle from the German trenches and a bullet whined over our trench and smacked into the mud somewhere behind us. It might have drilled through Ableman's skull if Reg Coxon hadn't grabbed him and yanked him back down a split second before the bullet's arrival.

'That were yer one and only chance, lad,' Reg told him in his broad Barnsley accent. He stabbed a finger at the sky. 'Him up theer'll not grant thee another one.'

As a grinning Frank descended the wooden ladder propped against the inside wall of the trench, the men surged forward to clap him on the back. His skill at 'rat bagging', one of the few things that kept us amused during the grinding hell of trench life, had earned him the nickname 'Dead Eye'. The only member of our squad who didn't come forward to congratulate Frank was John Pyke. As ever he sat a little removed from the rest of us, beneath the sheet of rusty corrugated iron that was laid over the top of the trench and served as our only shelter. Eyeing us balefully, Pyke was hunched like a gorilla over the brazier we used to keep warm and to boil water for tea. When I glanced his way he dipped his head, as if he was afraid I might hypnotise him.

It was early December 1915, and we'd been on the front line for five weeks. From when I'd first signed up to becoming a battle-ready soldier had taken around fifteen months. On 5th November we'd set sail for France, the men joking that although we'd miss Bonfire Night at home we'd be seeing plenty of fireworks once we crossed the channel. From Boulogne the eight hundred plus men and thirty or so officers who made up our battalion had boarded yet another rickety train, which had transported us to a railhead south-east of Abbeville in the valley of the River Somme. Although we'd camped there for the night with the intention of getting some rest before the next stage of our journey, it had been so cold that none of us had been able to sleep. Instead we'd walked around for hours, fully clothed and wrapped in our blankets, in an effort to keep warm. Another long train journey the next day, followed by a ten-mile trudge, during which each of us had been loaded down with equipment (rifle and ammo, blanket, ground sheet, eating utensils and other kit), had brought us to the village of Bellancourt. By the time we arrived in what turned out to be a filthy little place, the streets strewn with refuse, we were so exhausted and hungry that we'd been fit for nothing more than collapsing into our billets. Mine was a draughty barn, full of dirty straw, on the edge of the village, but I made myself a makeshift bed and fell into an immediate deep sleep. I woke several hours later to find my body covered in flea bites and the place swarming with rats, some of which had nibbled at my boots and clothes.

We spent the next few days marching from one village to another through thick mud and driving snow. It was so hard going, and the equipment we carried so heavy, that we were almost looking forward to reaching the front line just so we could have a break from putting one foot in front of the other. Although we'd only been a few days out of England, we were already having to endure appalling conditions. We spent most of our time hungry, wet, filthy and exhausted. We'd been wearing the same set of clothes since arriving in France, which was mainly because we didn't have a fresh set and wouldn't be issued with one until we reached our destination. In truth, though, even if we *had* had fresh clothes I doubt any of us would have bothered changing into them. For one thing, it was too bloody cold to get undressed (the sheep pens and barns, in which we were billeted, did nothing to protect us from the sub zero temperatures), and for another it would have meant having to carry our wet, mud-plastered, and therefore heavy, clothes in our knapsacks.

There were times, I admit, when I wondered if it was all worth it, times when I (probably selfishly) told myself this wasn't *my* War, and when I asked myself whether I *really* had to go through all this. These moments usually came at the end of a long, long day, when I was more exhausted than I'd ever been, but couldn't sleep because of the cold and the continual grinding apprehension in my belly. If it hadn't been for my sense of duty, combined with the fear of what might happen if I *did* jack it in, I might well have given in to temptation and called it a day. And even then I might have given up if it wasn't for the other blokes.

Because despite the hardships, and despite signs that the War was getting ever closer – or rather, that *we* were getting closer to *it* – the men managed to remain pretty cheerful, which both moved me and gave me a boost when I needed one. Granted, there were one or two moaners, and one or two who were clearly scared and trying not to show it (I admit to being one of them, but then *I* knew what we were in for), but I'd been lucky enough to have Frank, Stan Little, Joe Lancing and Doug Meadows as my constant companions. The five of us had formed a tight-knit group, within which Frank and Doug, in particular, could always be relied on to keep our spirits up. On our second day's march out of Bellancourt, the peace of the French countryside (which was admittedly pretty dismal, given the horrible weather and the churned-up roads) had been suddenly shattered by a dull but persistent barrage of heavy guns in the distance. With perfect comic timing, Frank had wafted a hand behind the seat of his pants and exclaimed, 'Would you pardon me, chaps? I think that bully beef stew has come back to haunt me.'

It probably doesn't seem as funny written down, but we were in such a state of heightened emotion – almost delirious with exhaustion and jittery with the pent-up fear of what was to come – that we all collapsed with laughter, as did the men around us, the effect expanding outwards like a Mexican wave. Soon those who hadn't heard the quip were laughing too, even if it was simply at the sight of the five of us, clinging to each other in an effort to stay upright, with tears rolling down our faces. Eventually the officers in charge managed to pull us back into line, but even they were grinning. There may not have been much to laugh about in our immediate futures, but I'll say this for the British Tommy: whatever the circumstances (and often, there was carnage and terror so overwhelming that in hindsight I'm astonished the survivors managed to remain even part-way functional) his spirit and sense of humour couldn't be dampened for long.

As I said, it had been just over a month since we'd arrived in France, during which time we'd mostly been living in mud, sleeping in mud, even eating mud, because with no cutlery among our kit apart from our jack-knifes, we had to use our muddy fingers to hold our rations. In the five weeks we'd been in the trenches we'd already lost little Doug Meadows to a sniper's bullet, and both Joe Lancing and Barty Trent to a shell, which had landed right next to them and exploded while they were on guard duty.

Losing our friends, and more particularly witnessing their deaths, was gut-wrenching, and something that even now I don't particularly want to dwell on. Yet already – though it sounds awful to say it – we were starting to get used to the idea of life as an expendable commodity. Because there was something hideously unreal, even other-worldly about the trenches, I (and I know a lot of the other guys felt the same) found myself retreating into a kind of invisible bubble, viewing what was happening around me almost as if it was a hideously vivid dream.

Part of this was no doubt due to the fact we were all in a state of perpetual trauma. The daily shell bombardments, often augmented by rifle grenades and trench mortars, could sometimes last for three hours, and even putting aside the sustained terror of knowing that a direct hit could end your life (or worse, leave you hideously mutilated and in unimaginable agony – and my fear of this happening was no different to anybody else's; I had no idea whether my glimpses into my own future made me immune or not), it's no exaggeration to say that the sheer *noise* of the bombardments was almost enough to literally drive you mad. Unless you've directly experienced it, it's impossible to put into words how *awful*, how *overwhelming*, that hellish din is. It makes you feel not only as if your thoughts are being shaken loose from your head, but as if your very soul is in danger of being ripped from your body. There were times, under bombardment, when I felt sure the noise alone would be enough to make my teeth splinter, my ear drums burst, my skull split in two.

It wasn't just my hearing, though, that was temporarily obliterated during these nightly attacks; *all* my senses were as badly affected. The constant explosions would cause the ground to shake, my jittering vision to fill with nothing but the sight of flying mud and shrapnel, and the blinding flash of exploding shells. Often I couldn't even see *that* much, because my eyes and nose would be streaming from the stinging effects of gas and sulphur. The drifting smoke would catch in my throat, making me cough until I could taste blood, and filling my mouth with a nasty chemical taste. At such times even my sense of touch was unreliable. There'd be nothing but shifting, shaking, sliding mud beneath my hands and feet, making it impossible to orientate myself.

With more mud buffeting my body from all sides, I'd sometimes feel as though I was drowning, unable to tell up from down. On these occasions, when it became impossible to stand upright, impossible to see what my friends were doing or hear what they were saying – impossible to function in any useful way at all – I would simply give up and sink into the filth and curl my body around the heart, which I always kept in the button-down hip pocket of my uniform jacket. Sometimes I'd clutch it in my hand and think about leaving, think about using the heart to project myself somewhere else, *anywhere* but here...

But I never succumbed to temptation. I was too afraid that if I did I wouldn't have the nerve to come back. And even if I did come back I was afraid the temptation to take a break might come upon me again and again, with increasing regularity, and that the War for me would therefore become horribly protracted, the nightmare stretching on and on, to a point where even my 'breaks' from the conflict would become blighted by the terrible knowledge that at some point I'd have to return to it.

Although the War is long behind me now, the memories of those terrible times are still fresh in my mind. I'm still haunted by them; they still give me nightmares – so many, in fact, and of such intensity, that often I find myself wishing only for peace, for an end to it all.

But the simple fact is, I endured the trenches. All of us who were there endured them.

Well, that's not true. Not all.

Some died, of course.

Others went mad.

And yet others were mad, or at least half-mad, before they even set foot on foreign soil.

Which brings us back to John Pyke.

After that night during our training when the heart became active, Pyke avoided me. He still slid me sidelong looks at regular intervals, but from that point on they were full not of aggression and intent, but of mistrust, wariness – even fear.

So I sometimes believed anyway. Because for all the times when I was convinced he had seen the heart in full flow, and was running scared because of it, there were just as many other occasions when I told myself I was being paranoid, and that his wariness was down to the fact that he was alone and outnumbered, and therefore worried that our little band of brothers might at some point gang up on him.

I don't know for certain, because I never got to know him that well, but I'm guessing that back home, on the streets of Lewisham, Pyke had been a big cheese, a cock o' the walk, the kind of bloke it was easier to back up than to oppose. Under normal circumstances, young blokes like Pyke who lived in tough areas would abide by the law of their particular jungle, every man for himself, with the strongest, usually bolstered by an entourage of weaker hangers-on, rising to the top.

The War, though, changed all that, and the prevailing mood from 1914 became one of all lads together, of local rivalries being forgotten in the face of a common enemy. The previously diffuse population of Britain's young men had discovered there was strength to be had in numbers – which was bad news for men like Pyke, who'd become used to being top of the pile, having achieved their status through bullying and intimidation, and who now found themselves suddenly weakened by dint of becoming one of the herd. Now, when Pyke and his ilk tried to throw their weight about, they'd find themselves confronted by a single body of men prepared to stand together and defend the weakest. Some of these tough guys – the smarter ones – adapted; they bought into the group mentality and became better men because of it. Others, though, those who were too stupid, or too crazy, to conform, all at once found themselves ostracised and friendless.

Pyke was not only one of the stupid ones, he was also one of the crazy ones – and I'm afraid it was me who'd made him so.

All right, so maybe that's exaggerating it a bit. Maybe it wasn't me that had made him crazy, but the heart. And maybe the heart didn't actually *make* him crazy. Maybe Pyke was already three-quarters of the way there, and the heart, combined with the effects of the War, had just nudged him over the edge.

All the same I felt guilty about it. And the likelihood that Pyke, if he had survived the War, would have remained a nasty piece of work, didn't make me feel any *less* guilty.

'Time for a spot o' tiffin, I think,' Frank announced once the back-slapping had died down. 'Stick the kettle on, Pykey.'

Despite Pyke's surly manner, Frank often addressed him in a breezy way, as if they were old mates. I knew Frank was doing it to wind him up, and sure enough Pyke flashed him a venomous look.

'Do it yourself,' he muttered.

Frank snorted a laugh. Aside from one or two barbed comments, he and Pyke had pretty much managed to steer clear of each other this past year or so. Today, though, for some reason – maybe because Frank was buoyed by his 'rat bagging' triumph; maybe because he'd simply lost patience with Pyke's constant hostility – he was in a provocative mood.

'You really take the biscuit, you know, Pykey,' he said, still in that same cheery manner. 'When it comes to priorities you really are arse about tit.'

The men were piling into the shelter now, huddling round the brazier to get warm, rain dripping from their helmets and clothes. Some, like Reg Coxon and Geoff Ableman, who'd been drafted in from other battalions and knew nothing of Frank and John Pyke's past history, watched the exchange curiously.

'Just leave it, Frank,' I said. 'It's not worth it.'

As soon as Frank flashed a glance at me, I knew he wasn't going to listen. After months of simmering silences, dark looks and the occasional muttered insult, clearly things, for him, had come to a head.

'Why should I leave it?' he retorted, and gestured disdainfully at Pyke. The big man was still sitting by the brazier, glaring up at us, a filthy, rat-nibbled blanket around his shoulders, his elbows resting on his thighs and his hands dangling between his knees.

'Look at him,' Frank continued. 'He's a fucking wet weekend. Like a fucking big kid he is. Harbouring his stupid grudge, as if it really fucking matters. As if it really fucking matters *after all this*.'

There were tears in Frank's eyes, and suddenly I understood. He and Doug had been the battalion's chirpy chaps, the ones who kept spirits up when things were tough, the ones who could always be relied on for a quick quip or a funny story. But now Doug was dead, and Frank, though he'd been trying to hide it, had been feeling the strain. And all at once he was at the end of his tether. He needed to vent. And

Pyke, the dark, energy-sapping hole at the centre of our group, was the obvious target.

Jock McDaid, a thick-set Scottish engineer, who after the War would go on to become a Labour MP and serve in Ramsay MacDonald's 1924 government, said, 'What grudge is this then?'

'Has tha' 'ad a lover's tiff?' asked Reg Coxon, raising a ripple of laughter.

'It's something and nothing,' I said quickly. 'It doesn't matter.'

'It *does* matter,' said Frank, struggling to speak. 'People have died, and it *does* matter…' His voice choked off.

I would have half-expected Pyke to have jumped up by now, stung into action, but he was still sitting there, his body not relaxed but utterly motionless, as if he had a poisonous spider on his shoulder and was waiting for someone to knock it off. He was still staring at Frank, but oddly he wasn't *glaring* any more. Then his eyes shifted to me, and I almost took a step back, shocked at how depthless, how empty, they looked.

Barely moving his lips he said, 'Yeah, well, that's hardly my fault, is it?'

Reg Coxon leaned over him, water dripping from the rim of his helmet and sizzling on the hot rusty metal of the brazier. Above us rain clattered on the corrugated metal roof.

'Eh, lad? What's tha' say? Speak up.'

'He said it wasn't his fault,' someone piped up.

'What wasn't?'

'I haven't a clue, old cock.'

Stan Little, standing on the other side of the brazier, scowled and said, 'Like Locke says, it's something or nothing. He's half-cracked, this one.'

Pyke's head turned, the movement strangely lizard-like, his eyes sliding darkly to regard Stan. 'You would say that, wouldn't you? You're another one under his spell.'

Stan's scowl deepened. 'Whose spell? You're addled, old lad.'

'You know who.'

'I don't, you know. You're going to have to tell me.'

I knew it was coming. And sure enough Pyke's head turned slowly again and his empty eyes drilled into mine. When he raised a hand and pointed at me, I realised how much he was trembling, how scared he was.

'Him,' he whispered.

Then, as if the effort of pointing had been too much for him, his whole body seemed to droop. He lowered his head and wrapped his arms around it as if to defend himself from blows. All eyes turned to me. McDaid said, 'What's the lad talking about, Locke?'

I shrugged, trying to look as bemused as everyone else, though the heart in my chest was thumping hard, and the one in my pocket seemed to be getting heavier and heavier.

'Search me.'

In a muffled voice, from behind the barrier of his entwined arms, Pyke said, 'That's a good idea.'

'What is?' asked McDaid, more confused than ever.

'Searching him. He'll have it on him somewhere. Then you'll see. Then you'll see what's causing all this.'

All the men were looking at me now, and for once I was glad of the mud on my face. It meant they couldn't see me turning red. I grinned and raised my arms.

'Be my guest. I have no idea what Pykey's on about, but if anyone wants to find what he thinks I've got, they're welcome to try.'

Still the men hung back, many of them eyeing Pyke warily, some raising their eyebrows at each other, one or two tapping the sides of their heads.

'This is daft,' Stan Little said. 'I told you the lad's lost it. Now let's forget all this rubbish and have a cup of tea. I'm parched.'

There was a general murmur of agreement. Someone said, 'Maybe you ought to have a lie down, Pykey. Get a bit of kip.'

Pyke unpeeled his arms from around himself. He looked like a turtle emerging from its shell. He fixed his gaze on me again, and now his face was drawn, stricken, as if he believed he had come too far to turn back.

'It's in his pocket,' he croaked. 'His left hip pocket. I've seen it.'

Attention swung back towards me. I still had my arms half-raised. Under the scrutiny of the men I did my best not to look nervous, guilty.

Jock McDaid said, '*Have* ye got something in your pocket, Locke?'

I laughed. 'Only this.'

I had to concentrate to stop my hand from shaking as I unbuttoned my pocket and took out the heart. The moment I produced it, Pyke whimpered and put his hands over his face. The rest of the men leaned forward.

'What is it?' Geoff Ableman asked.

'What's it look like?' someone said. 'It's a little heart.'

'But what's it for?'

'It's not *for* anything,' I said with a shrug. 'It's a family heirloom. A good-luck charm. My old mum gave it to me, said it'd keep me safe. Daft, really.'

The lie came easily. I saw several of the men relaxing, glancing at Pyke with renewed pity.

'Why is the lad so afraid of it?' McDaid asked.

'Beats me.'

'Can I have a look at it?'

As ever when someone asked me this question, I felt a pang of reluctance, had to fight a knee-jerk reaction to snatch it back, hide it away. But I forced myself to grin. 'Sure.'

I held out the heart and McDaid took it.

Pyke jumped up so suddenly that all the men jerked back. The heel of his boot caught the wooden box he'd been sitting on with such force that it flew backwards, clattering against the wall of mud behind him.

'*Don't touch it!*' His voice was high and thin, almost a screech. '*It's evil!*'

'Fuck's sake, Pykey!' someone exclaimed.

'Sit dahn, lad,' said Reg Coxon.

McDaid held up his free hand, as if appealing for calm, then extended it slowly towards Pyke as though soothing a nervous animal. Pyke had scooted backwards and was pressed against the wall, his face stark with fear.

'Take it easy, lad,' McDaid said. 'There's nothing to be scared of. Look for yersel.'

He raised his other arm, the heart sitting on the flat of his hand. I tensed. I wanted to take it back off him. I imagined it erupting into life, entwining its black tendrils around all the men packed into the shelter.

Pyke cowered, quailed. He half-turned, pressing himself against the wall, digging his fingernails into the oozing mud as if he wanted to claw his way through it.

'It's tricking you,' he wheezed. '*He's* tricking you. I've seen what it can do.'

McDaid's voice was still soothing, but there was a hint of impatience in it now.

'Come on, lad, settle yersel. It's a rock, that's all. It can't hurt ye. Ye need to pull yersel together.'

Pyke was still clawing at the wall, almost sobbing. 'You don't understand. Only *I* understand.'

'*What* don't we understand?' said McDaid.

'*It's alive!*' Pyke hissed, making me think immediately of Colin Clive in the old black-and-white *Frankenstein* movie. 'It's why we're here. It's what made all this happen. *It'll kill us all!*'

Not surprisingly Pyke's wild claims were met with bewilderment, amusement and scorn.

'Come off it, lad!'

'What does he think it is, a bloody shell?'

'You need a holiday in the funny farm, mate.'

But Pyke, as if drawing on every last ounce of strength and courage he possessed, suddenly rose to his full height and pointed his finger at me again. His arm was rigid this time, no sign of a tremor there at all.

'*He's a witch!*' he exclaimed. 'That's what he is! A witch!'

The amused sniggers turned into howls of laughter, the scorn into outright ridicule.

'Oh, aye! Where's his broomstick then?' Reg Coxon said.

'Hubble, bubble, toil and trouble!' cried Geoff Ableman.

But as the men around me dissolved into laughter, I continued to look at Pyke. His face was twisting, turning bestial. And then suddenly he leaped forward. Before I could shout out a warning, he snatched the heart from McDaid's hand and barged into him, knocking him backwards into the brazier. The men jumped back with cries of alarm as the hot brazier rocked, puffing up a great cloud of orange sparks. As a couple of the guys lunged forward to steady McDaid and stop him falling headlong on to the hot coals, Pyke bolted past them, heading for the shelter's entrance. One of the men made a half-hearted grab for him, but Pyke shoved him out of the way. He loped into the trench, hunched and long-limbed, like an orang-utan that had broken out of its cage.

'Hey!' I shouted, panic surging in me as I ran after him. But it was like running in a dream. The rain was battering down, and the deep mud at the bottom of the trench was clinging, slippery. As my right foot went from under me and I fell to my knees, I saw Pyke ahead, apparently having no such difficulties, clambering up the ladder that Frank had been standing on a few minutes before.

'Pykey, no!' I shouted, fear sluicing through me. '*Please!*'

But desperate though my plea was, I knew he was too far gone to listen to reason. As I clambered to my feet, my thoughts were racing, flicking through possibilities at breakneck speed.

There was nothing *I* could do to stop him, short of putting a bullet in his back, which was never an option. My only hope, therefore, was that, if Pyke didn't slip off the ladder and knock himself unconscious, the heart itself would intervene, perhaps transform in some subtle way that wouldn't freak the men out. I clung to this hope even as Pyke scaled the ladder; even as – to my horror – he reached the top and kept going, scrambling up over the lip of sandbags and loping out into No Man's Land.

Most of the other guys had followed me out of the shelter, just as horrified as I was to see what Pyke was doing. From behind me came a chorus of raised voices:

'Fuck's sake, Pykey!'

'Pykey, come back!'

'No, mate, no!'

But Pyke kept going, disappearing from sight, though we could still hear his footsteps over the rain, splashing through the mud towards the German lines as if he hoped to find salvation there. Plastered in mud, I regained my feet and plunged towards the ladder. I began to climb it with only one thought in my head – to get the heart back. Though *how* I was going to do that I had no idea.

I was halfway up the ladder when I felt the bottom of my uniform jacket snag on something. I glanced down, to see that Frank had grabbed my jacket and was tugging me back.

'Not you too, mate,' he said, his face streaming with rain. 'Not for a family heirloom. It ain't worth it.'

I glanced at the men, all of whom seemed to be staring at me with wide, shocked eyes, then turned my attention back to Frank.

'I wasn't going after him,' I said. 'I just wanted to see–'

Then I heard the crack of a rifle above me, and Pyke started screaming.

He wasn't screaming in pain, though. His voice was a high screech of anger.

'*This is for you, Jerry!*' he was yelling. '*This is for you!*'

Distracted by the rifle shot and by Pyke's voice, Frank allowed his grip to slacken on my jacket. I took advantage of the moment to wrench myself free and scramble up the ladder until I was high enough to poke my helmeted head over the top.

In other circumstances, the Germans holed up in their trench several hundred yards away might have taken a pot shot at me, but just now they had a much bigger target to aim at. A man-shaped target that was charging at them like an enraged bull, one arm raised and what looked like a grenade in his hand.

I clapped eyes on him just in time to see him hurl the heart with all his strength towards the German trench. Even as it arced through the air, a dwindling black speck, and was lost in the slashing murk of the rain, there was a barrage of gunfire that made me flinch and dip my head, though not before seeing Pyke's body twitch and twist and crumple, as if boneless, to the ground.

'*No!*' I screamed. '*No!*'

But – although I'm ashamed to admit it – my sudden outpouring of distress and desolation was more for the loss of the heart than for the death of John Pyke.

I felt a tugging on my jacket again. I looked down. Frank's wet face was pallid with shock. Suddenly he looked very young.

'He's gone, mate,' he said. 'He's gone, and it was his own doing. There ain't no helping him now.'

SEVEN

NO MAN'S LAND

'I've got to get it back.'

It was 1:15 a.m. and Frank and I had been on sentry duty for fifteen minutes. Everyone else was asleep, or at least resting, either huddled round the brazier in the shelter or curled up in their groundsheets in one of the many cubbyholes that had been hacked out of the muddy inner walls of the trench. Although the cubbyholes were colder and (marginally) dirtier than the shelter, at least they were off the ground, which meant you were not so bothered by rats. The little bastards were bolder and more plentiful at night; they'd run not only past your feet but right over them. We always did sentry duty in pairs, each shift lasting two hours. Whoever was on duty in the early hours, when it was quiet, would often pass the time with a game of 'rat football', where a 'goal' was scored every time you managed to kill a rat with a single kick.

Frank was sipping tea from a tin mug, each mouthful making him grimace. The tea here was foul, but we kept drinking it, partly because it was hot and partly because it was a reminder of our far-distant homeland. The water was transported to us through the winding maze of communication trenches in old petrol cans and was then boiled over a wood fire in pots that we also used to make stew, and that we had no way of washing properly. As a result the tea tasted mainly of wood smoke, petrol and old bully beef – an irresistible concoction.

Frank's eyes narrowed over the rim of his mug. 'Get what?'

'The heart. The thing that Pyke threw into No Man's Land. I've got to get it back.'

Frank sniggered, thinking I was joking, then he saw my face and his expression changed in an instant. 'You ain't serious?'

'It's important to me, Frank. That heart... well, it's been in my family for years.'

It was the feeblest of reasons for putting myself in peril. Frank's boggle-eyed response was almost cartoon-like.

'Maybe so, but it ain't worth getting your head blown off for.'

'I won't get my head blown off. I'll be careful. I'll just go for a quick recce.'

'A *quick recce!*' His response was too loud and too shrill, and I gritted my teeth and glanced towards the shelter, knowing that if the others came to see what the commotion was about my chance would be gone.

To his credit, Frank responded to my grimace, his voice dropping to a murmur, though his tone was still urgent and anxious – like that of someone trying to persuade a potential suicide not to jump off a bridge.

'It's pitch black out there, Alex. It'd be like looking for a needle in a bleedin' haystack.'

'Exactly,' I said. 'It's pitch black. Which means that if I'm careful the Germans won't see me.'

'But you'll *never* find what you're looking for!' His face was flushed, his voice tight with frustration. 'Can't you see that? Can't you get that into your thick head?'

'I have to try,' I said stubbornly. 'I owe it to my family.'

'You owe it to them to stay alive, more like.'

'Don't worry, I'll be fine,' I promised him. 'I'll be back before you know it.'

Frank shook his head. 'This is madness, old chum. You're as tapped as Pykey was. You know I can't let you do this, don't you?'

'Oh? And how will you stop me? Knock me out and tie me up?'

'Yeah, if I have to.'

I gave him a look.

'All right, maybe not. But you've got to see how crazy this is! In fact, it's more than crazy, it's...' He wafted a hand in the air, unable to think of an appropriate word.

'I'll be fine,' I told him again. 'I'll take it nice and slow. Jerry won't even know I'm out there. And I'm pretty sure I know where the heart landed. I saw Pykey throw it.'

'But it's different in the dark,' Frank said. 'You can get turned around till you completely lose your bearings.'

'I won't get lost,' I said. 'Straight there and straight back. I promise.'

I could see I was wearing him down. His shoulders were slumping. He looked defeated.

'You'll die, Alex.'

'I won't, I promise. I'll be back.'

His head had drooped. He wouldn't look at me now. 'Well... it's been nice knowing you, mate.'

'I'll be back,' I told him again, unable to stop myself saying it like Arnold Schwarzenegger in *The Terminator*.

If my using what sounded like a German accent puzzled him he didn't say so. In fact, he didn't say another word, just turned his back on me and dragged his ground sheet tighter around his shoulders. It wasn't a show of pique; he simply couldn't bear to watch me scale the ladder and disappear into No Man's Land, as Pyke had done a few hours before me.

I thought about reaching out, patting him on the shoulder, but in the end I turned away too and began climbing the ladder. Outwardly I might have seemed calm, but my insides were in turmoil, my guts roiling with anxiety and fear.

Frank was right, of course. This *was* madness. And the chances of finding the heart *were* infinitesimal. But I had to try. I had to trust that things would work out okay, and that this wasn't simply one of a multitude of potential alternative timelines. I had to believe that in this reality I wasn't destined to be shot and killed by a German sniper.

At the top of the ladder I paused a moment, and then slithered up and over the sandbags lining the lip of the trench. In many ways this was the most dangerous part of the exercise. If a Jerry soldier had his gun trained on our trench at this moment I'd make a pretty bulky target. But I had to hope that the Germans were like us – concerned, in the early hours of the morning, only with keeping warm and getting a bit of much-needed kip. By the time I'd negotiated the sandbags without hearing the familiar crack of an enemy rifle (though, to be fair, a killing bullet would almost certainly have reached its mark before I heard a thing) and had slid on my belly into the muddy depression in front of the trench, my heart was hammering so hard it felt as if something was trying to burrow out of the ground beneath me.

I lay there a few moments, panting, my face so close to the ground that I could have stuck out my tongue and lapped at the freezing mud. And it *was* freezing, a thin crust of ice having formed over the deeper puddles that speckled the quagmire dividing the zigzagging lines of the Allied trenches from the German ones. At least the earlier rain had stopped, though the cold, smoky fog that drifted constantly across No Man's Land left not only a greasy film of moisture on your skin and clothes, but also a lingering odour of sulphurous decay.

After a minute or so had passed with no apparent activity from the German trenches I cautiously raised my head. Much of what I could see was black, though here and there certain shapes that bulged from the surface of the mud were given sketchy definition by the background glow of the distant German searchlights that constantly scoured the night sky for the approach of enemy aircraft. It helped too that I'd seen No Man's Land in daylight, through the crude periscope we used to save us having to stick our heads up above the lip of the trench. That, at least, enabled me to get my bearings, to identify not only certain landmarks, but also potentially troublesome – even lethal – obstacles.

Although what stretched before me was basically an expanse of severely churned mud, I knew that it was scattered with often partially submerged debris. There were the blackened remnants of trees that had been smashed to burning splinters by shell fire; there were twisted jags of metal ordnance that could slash a man's body open if he crawled over them without realising; there were broken weapons and dented metal helmets; there were coiled stretches of barbed wire...

And, of course, there were bodies. Lots of bodies. Some whole, or mostly whole. Some mangled, or in pieces.

One of those bodies, and not so very far away, belonged to John Pyke. I couldn't see it, but I knew that he had managed to progress – what? – thirty or forty yards before being cut down in a hail of gunfire? Which meant he would be lying somewhere in front of me now, dead and probably still bleeding, his limbs twisted, his face slack, his eyes greyed over and full of mud. Rats would probably be scampering over his body; he'd be a feast for them.

I felt sick. I'd never liked Pyke, but it was still awful to think that less than eighteen months ago he'd joined up to fight for his country, dreaming no doubt of glory, of returning home a conquering hero, and now there he was, lying out in the mud like so much rubbish, the life smashed out of him.

Did he have family? It was likely. It was likely that someone at home – parents, brothers or sisters, a girlfriend – loved him and was anxiously hoping and praying he'd get through, that he'd be all right. How long before they heard the devastating news? A few days? A week? A month? And what would they hear? That he'd died bravely? That he was missing in action?

My breathing had slowed now, and my heart was beating less rapidly. In the near distance, jutting above the foreshortened horizon of No Man's Land, I could see the sagging and splintered remains of a tree trunk sticking out of the churned mud like a vast taloned claw clutching at the air. I knew the trunk lay about a hundred yards in front of the German lines, because the lads manning the Howitzers and sixty-pounders often used it, among other landmarks, as a distance mark during bombardments. I knew too that Pyke had lobbed the heart in that general direction. And so, like a turtle, I began to crawl through the mud towards it.

I tried not to think about how exposed I was, how long it would take to crawl even these several hundred yards across No Man's Land, and how unlikely were the chances of finding what I was looking for when I reached my destination. All I could do was cling to the hope that the heart and I were connected, that we had a mission to fulfil (whatever that might ultimately turn out to be) and that we were therefore *destined* to be together.

Woolly thinking, but it was all I had. All I could do was build a barrier in my mind to keep out the doubts and the uncertainties, and try to stay concentrated on the task in hand.

The mud was like glue, which made the sheer physical toil of crawling through it on my belly utterly exhausting. I tried to stay as quiet as I could, but sometimes I couldn't prevent myself grunting with effort as I propelled myself forward using only my elbows and knees. Although my extremities were cold – my hands in particular were completely numb – I was pouring with sweat inside my uniform. I probably stank (I hadn't changed my clothes since our last rest period away from the line almost a week ago), but the odour of sulphur and decay that hung over the battlefield – 'the stink of Hell', Frank called it – was far worse than any amount of BO generated by the unclean bodies of the living.

How badly I smelled, though, was the least of my concerns. What really worried me was the fact that if I wasn't careful the sweat pouring from my body would eventually cool, even freeze, leaving me in real danger of dying from hypothermia. It was important, therefore, not to give in to exhaustion, but to keep moving. I tried to picture myself, having completed my mission and made it back unscathed, warming myself by the brazier, my freezing-cold, mud-plastered hands wrapped around a mug of army tea. I imagined myself sipping the tea, imagined it trickling down my throat, warming my insides. I knew it would taste disgusting, but that didn't matter, because if I managed to make it back with the heart in my pocket, I also knew that the tea, foul though it was, would be the best I'd ever tasted.

The longer I crawled, the pain in my limbs and back steadily increasing, my skin continuing to ooze sweat, my breath becoming a series of ragged gasps, the more I felt my mind trying to break away, to drift. At one point I found myself wondering what Clover and Hope were doing now, whether they'd discovered I'd gone and how they'd reacted – and then I snapped to, like a sentry on duty trying desperately to stay awake during the graveyard shift, and I remembered that time didn't work like that, that Clover and Hope didn't exist in this world, in this time; that my life now, in 1915, wasn't on some track that was running parallel to theirs in the future.

Time was an elusive beast, an ever-coiling snake, difficult to grasp and hold on to. And like a snake it had fangs that were full of poison, and the poison was loneliness. Or worse than loneliness, it was an all-encompassing desolation, one that forced you to realise we were all cast adrift on a vast, dark, endless sea, each of us friendless and forever lost and endlessly, endlessly...

It was the stench that snapped me out of the meaningless, sleepy ramble that my thoughts had become. My head jerked up as if someone had thrust a bottle of smelling salts under my nose. For a moment I couldn't remember where I was. And then my eyes focused and I recoiled. On the ground in front of me, wrapped in muddy rags that must once have been part of a uniform (though whether it was one of ours or one of theirs was impossible to tell) was an entire but badly mangled leg.

It was bloated with green and purple-black rot, and the stench coming off it was unbelievable. Hideous too was the fact that the decaying foot was still encased in an army boot, the laces neatly tied.

I turned my head and vomited, hunching in my shoulders to avoid the spatter. Then I paddled frantically with my right elbow, trying to steer away from the sight and stench of the hideous obstacle in my path. I'd seen worse things, both in the trenches and earlier – I'd witnessed Hawkins, my butler and friend during my time in Victorian London, have his arm severed in front of me and die from the resulting blood loss, for example – but at that moment I was feeling at a particularly low ebb, my body and mind more vulnerable than usual. As soon as I was out of range of the leg, or at least of the worst of its smell, I paused to gather my strength, at which point a sudden wave of despair washed over me.

What was I doing? What could I possibly hope to achieve here? This was hopeless. Utterly hopeless.

Luckily the feeling lasted for no more than a few seconds. No sooner had I been gripped by it than I rallied, shrugging it off angrily.

No, I *wouldn't* give in. I'd come too far to simply stop. If I was going to die here – whether that be my ultimate destiny, or whether I was simply unlucky enough to be in one of many alternate timelines that would simply peter out with my pointless and premature death – then I wouldn't allow it to happen without first expending every last ounce of energy available to me. I would struggle and fight to the end. Either that, or be stopped by outside forces.

As if Fate were mocking me, the Germans chose that very moment to start firing.

I made myself as flat as possible, closing my eyes as my cheek smacked into the mud. At first I assumed the shots were nothing but routine – now and again in the dead of night, those on sentry duty, whether on our side or theirs, let off a volley just to prove they were doing their duty, and to let the enemy know they were still around and alert – but when bullets started splatting into the mud somewhere to my left, I realised I must have been spotted. Perilous though it was to move, I knew it was more perilous still to just lie there, because sooner or later I would be hit.

Trying to still the frantic terror of my thoughts, I lifted my head a fraction and looked around, searching for a place to hide or something I could use as cover. Perhaps ten yards ahead of me I spotted what looked like a shell crater – a black depression in the ground rimmed by a ridge of earth where the mud had been forced upwards by the impact. I waited for the initial burst of gunfire to subside, knowing there would be a slight pause between one volley and the next, and then, my ears throbbing, I scrambled up into a semi-crouch, ran forward and dived into the shell crater.

Although I didn't have much choice, I was all too aware that throwing myself into an unknown hole in No Man's Land was a move born of utter desperation. Full of future technology I might have been, but I knew if I landed on the jagged remains of a shell and slashed my belly open, then no amount of nanites could repair me. I knew too that if the hole was more than, say, six feet deep and full of thick, muddy water then the likelihood was I would be sucked under and drown.

Luckily, though, the hole turned out to be only four or five feet deep, added to which I had a soft landing. Not so luckily, the soft landing was a dead and rotting German soldier. How long he had been there I had no idea, but he stank to high Heaven and was crawling with maggots. He was lying on his back, his head – what was left of it – partially submerged in a pool of black water.

I landed across his midriff, part of which promptly broke with a gristly snap. Worse than that, though, was the feel of his flesh through his uniform. Decomposition had caused slippage, which meant that the violent pressure of my body resulted in the flesh, which had become soft like old bananas, sliding away from the bone beneath. In my revulsion, I unthinkingly put my left hand on his chest to lever myself up and away from him – whereupon his rib cage cracked like a lattice of dry sticks and my hand plunged into a cold, stinking pulp of rotting internal organs.

I clapped my free hand, which was caked in mud but not guts, over the bottom half of my face to stop myself from screaming. Not that it was likely the enemy would have heard me. Above my head, loud enough to make the bones of my skull ache, the Germans were still blazing away. Ordinarily I would have covered my ringing ears and kept my head down until it was over, but in the circumstances the gunfire seemed oddly divorced from me. Gagging, I withdrew my hand from the dead German's innards with a slurping plop, then plunged it into the pool of muddy water between his booted feet.

The next few minutes were spent heaving and shuddering with reaction. I couldn't tell whether the appalling stench that seemed to have wrapped itself around my head like a warm, damp towel, was coming from the dead German or my own hand. Certainly the thought of using that gut-smeared hand to eat, or even scratch myself, in the immediate future made me gag anew. As did the sight of the fat white maggots wriggling with frantic glee over the dead man's body, some of which I had to brush off my own clothes, such was their eagerness to make friends.

Eventually I managed to calm myself, to stop the shakes that kept wanting to ripple through my body. At around the same time the gunfire from the German trenches, which had already become intermittent, stopped altogether. I knew that if Frank and I had been on sentry duty, and we'd looked out over No Man's Land and spotted movement, we'd have blazed away too. I also knew that if, after several minutes, we'd seen no further signs of movement, we'd have assumed that either we'd been mistaken, that the enemy had been hit or that they'd retreated back to where they'd come from. We'd then have been vigilant for a while, our senses heightened. But at last the draining conditions, our jittery tiredness and the sheer constant boredom of waiting for something to happen would have taken their toll, and we'd have sunk back into our usual state of edgy torpor, secure in the knowledge that no human being could cross that blasted heath between us and them without being spotted.

Despite my anxiety about the onset of hypothermia, not to mention my instinctive desire to put distance between me and my gruesome companion, I forced myself to sit tight for a while. I wondered, with all the racket from the German guns, whether my absence had been discovered back in the home trench, and what Frank would say to cover me if it had.

But that was something to worry about later. If I found the heart I might even be able to use it to backtrack an hour or two, to return to my post only ten minutes or so after setting out on my mission. I could tell Frank I'd changed my mind – or better still, that he'd changed it for me, had made me realise that what I intended to do was hopeless and stupid. Of course, I'd have to keep the heart hidden from then on, but with Pyke no longer around to cause trouble, that shouldn't be a problem.

After what felt like half an hour or so, the cold really started to bite, to embed itself into my bones and guts. I began to shiver, and then to shudder, and no amount of willpower could stop it from getting worse. Even more alarming, my mind started to drift again; I felt sleep stealing over me in ever-increasing waves. The fourth time I snapped awake, I thought I'd lost the ability to move. For a moment my mind battled between caring and not caring – there was a big part of me that just wanted to give up, to let it all go. If it hadn't been for Kate, for my overriding desire to find her, to see this through, to make everything all right again, I might have given in to that temptation.

Instead I forced myself to move, groaning and wincing as I rose from the huddled sitting position into which I'd sunk. My feet were wet and frozen. My uniform clung to me like cold cardboard. With a grimace I flicked another maggot off my sleeve. Looking down at the dead German, his ravaged face half-turned away from me, his teeth clenched in a ghastly grin through shrivelled lips, I could just about make out that over his uniform he was wearing what appeared to be an officer's overcoat made of some thick woolly material. Fingers trembling from the cold, I extracted my box of army-issue matches from my breast pocket and struck one. I half-expected it to be too damp to light, but it flared into life immediately. I glanced up at the lip of the shell hole, hoping that the bloom of flame couldn't be seen over the top. If it could, it would be only a matter of seconds before the Germans started blazing away again.

When all remained silent, I extended my arm, the flame shaking as its glow spilled over the dead soldier, illuminating some of the grislier details of his condition. I tried not to look too closely at the hideous cavity in his chest, at his twisted limbs and caved-in head, at the black patches of slimy rot on his uniform. Instead I focused on his coat, which was open and spread out in the mud beneath him like a cape, and tried to think only of how much warmer I would be with it wrapped around me. Yes, it had been lying in muddy water, and would therefore be wet and filthy, and yes, its dead owner had been decomposing into it for God knew how long, which meant that the stench would be unspeakable, but if I wanted to avoid freezing to death I'd have to get over my revulsion. Beggars couldn't be choosers.

I shook out my match and tossed it aside. With one foot planted either side of the man's sprawled legs, I shuffled forward, moving slowly to prevent myself slipping over in the mud and landing on top of his maggot-riddled corpse for a second time. As I moved up past his knees, and then his thighs, the stench of rotting flesh intensified, rising so thickly to envelop me that I couldn't help but imagine it as green, sinuous vapour coiling serpent-like around my body. I gagged, but managed to prevent myself from vomiting again.

Once my feet were either side of his hips, I steeled myself, then bent forward. I kept my breathing shallow, blocking off my nose and taking in small sips of air through my mouth. Even that, though, was bad enough. To me the air tasted sour, almost brackish, like polluted water. Although it was dark, I could still see the basic shape of the German beneath me, the white wriggling commas that were maggots, the greyish flesh of his dead face and hands.

My aim was to peel his coat from him without touching him, to roll him gently out of it. I took hold of a sleeve with the intention of tugging it down over the arm inside, hoping that the body wasn't so far gone that attempting to move it would cause it to come apart. Bracing myself against further gouts of stench I gripped the sleeve tighter and started to pull at it.

And felt the body squirm beneath me.

Letting go of the sleeve, I jerked upright, a shock of primal fear making my nerves tighten, the hairs on my body prickle. What had I just felt? *Thought* I'd felt?

Hands moving quickly, I snatched the matchbox from my pocket, opened it, picked out a match, lit up, held it up.

Shadows slid away from the light, like cockroaches seeking shelter in the darkness.

I looked down at the gnarled and discoloured hand of the dead German.

It was moving.

At first I thought the activity must be caused by things beneath the skin – maggots, or beetles, or worms, which had burrowed into the dead man's flesh and become agitated when I'd disturbed the body. But then I saw there was a purpose to the writhing of the corpse's fingers. They were bending and straightening like the hands of someone who'd been outside in freezing conditions, and was now coaxing their joints back to life in front of a warm fire.

Horrified, I staggered back from the body, almost slipping in the mud. As my arms windmilled in an effort to stay upright, I dropped the match, which hit the ground and fizzled out. For a few seconds, while my eyes tried to adjust to the sudden absence of light, the darkness seemed absolute and full of terrors. With my vision compromised, my hearing all at once seemed intensely acute, picking up every tiny sound within the immediate vicinity.

I could hear movement. Lots of movement. And not just the busy rustling of maggots feasting on the dead man's flesh, or the scampering of nearby rats. No, I could hear other sounds too – most notably, from right in front of me, a prolonged, somehow stealthy succession of glutinous plops that might have been made by a body shifting in a bed of thick mud. But perhaps even more disturbing were the sounds coming from all around me. Out there, in the blackness of No Man's Land, something, or what sounded like a *lot* of somethings, were stirring.

Having regained my balance, I lit another match. Immediately I saw that the body of the German soldier was indeed twitching and jerking. He looked as though his dead limbs were being animated by an electrical charge, as though his body had become a series of involuntary reflexes.

It was a horrible sight.

Then, with a wet ripping sound, he pulled his shattered head from the mud and turned to look at me.

I say 'look', but perhaps it might be more accurate to say that he seemed to use his head like a kind of radar, and had turned his face in my direction in an attempt to home in on me. His eyes had shrunk to little more than raisins in black sockets, and his skull, to which mud and clumps of hair clung, resembled a deflated football, the right side of which had caved in and crumpled. His mouth hung open, and as he sat up in a series of jerking, uncoordinated movements, a drool of maggots and black gunge spilled from it, and also from the hole in his splintered skull.

He was lifting an arm, his hand clawing towards the muddy wall beside him as if to haul himself upright, when my match burned out once more. If I hadn't witnessed many worse horrors since the heart had come into my possession, I might well have been hauling myself out of the shell hole by now, running in mindless terror across the churned-up death trap of No Man's Land, an easy target for German snipers. I'm not saying I wasn't shit-scared, because I was – but I wasn't gripped by blind panic. Instead my thoughts were racing, trying to make sense of what the hell was going on.

Was this the Dark Man's doing? Was he somewhere nearby? Could he be in possession of the heart, and had used its power to reanimate the dead, in order to prevent or delay me from pursuing him and retrieving it? Or was the heart itself, lying out in No Man's Land, somehow responsible? Perhaps it was animating the dead for some reason of its own? Or maybe it had been damaged and its power was leaking out like radiation from a faulty nuclear reactor?

I lit another match. The dead German was clambering shakily to his feet, like a frail old man rising from a bath. Maggots trickled from his body, spattering on the ground like solidified water droplets. As he rose to his full height, I did too, but only for a moment – only briefly enough to peer over the rim of the shell crater and take a quick recce at what was going on beyond the confines of my little home from home.

As I'd suspected, the dead were rising up around me. Out there in No Man's Land, silhouetted against the burnt umber of the night sky, I could see at least a dozen ragged black shapes, some still recognisable as men, pulling themselves from the mud, creaking to life like animated scarecrows, shuffling or lurching or squirming their way across the rutted mud of the battlefield.

It was an awful sight, but looking quickly to my left and right, I saw, with a thrill of horror, something that made it even worse: every single one of the reanimated dead was heading in my direction!

I'd seen my share of zombie movies; I knew the lore. Zombies ate people, didn't they? They feasted on human flesh. So was that why they were heading for me? Because they could smell me? Because I was the closest available meal?

I barely had time to contemplate this before the guns started firing.

The shots came from the German side, a blistering barrage of machine-gun fire, which lit up the night sky with white flashes of jerky light. I dipped my head quickly beneath the rim of the shell hole, but the bullets weren't aimed at me. This time the Germans had taller, more obvious targets to go at. Scooting backwards until I was as far away as I could get from the reanimated corpse that was sharing the space with me, I pressed myself against the curved 'wall' of the crater and lit another match.

The dead German was swaying backwards and forwards as if acclimatising to the fragile body into which he (or whatever animated him) had woken. His overcoat had slid off his bony shoulders and was now lying in a crumpled heap behind him. I looked at his ravaged face and wondered if there was anything still left of him in there. Could he still see me, although he had no eyes? And if so, did he still recognise me as the enemy? As he took a lurching step in my direction, I transferred the still-burning match from my right hand to my left and drew my revolver. If he *was* a zombie, and if zombie lore held sway here, then I ought to be able to stop him with a bullet to the brain.

Even as I raised the gun, though, I realised how ridiculous that was. Zombies weren't real. And the method recommended to dispatch them wasn't a medical fact; it had been invented by a screenwriter or a movie director or someone who wrote comic books. What good would it do to put a bullet in the dead German's head? His brain had already turned to black mush that was leaking out of his crushed skull. A more sensible option, surely, would be to disable him as much as I could. He wouldn't be able to walk if his legs were shattered, would he? Wouldn't be able to crawl towards me if his arms had been smashed to bits.

Shifting my aim from his head to his thigh, I pulled the trigger. The bullet spun him round with such force that when he splatted into the mud on his back he was facing away from me. His arms paddled for a moment, then he started to push himself back to his feet. I shot him again, this time in the elbow, which shattered in a spray of stinking black goo.

Down he went again, and this time his body rocked from side to side, as he tried to use his good leg and remaining arm to rise. It was a ghastly thing to watch, but it was pitiful too. He reminded me of a stranded sea bird, its wings coated with oil, trying desperately to take to the air and unable to work out why it couldn't.

With the dead soldier all but out of action, I moved forward in a semi-crouch to finish him off. Above me the German guns were still blazing, and now I was pretty sure they'd been joined by shooting from our side too. Which presumably meant, unless Frank was blasting away by himself and the other guys were sleeping through it, my absence had been discovered. But again I pushed that thought to the back of my mind. At that moment a potential court martial for desertion was the least of my worries.

The German soldier was still rocking from side to side, still stoically trying to rise. He gave no indication of being aware of my presence as I stood over him. He didn't claw at me, or turn his head to try to bite my ankle. He just kept rocking backwards and forwards, his face little more than a yawning black skull, no pain or anger or animosity in it.

'Sorry, mate,' I muttered, and I shot him in the centre of his face. It burst like a papier-mâché mask full of sludge, some of which spattered over my boots and up my trouser legs.

In *The Walking Dead*, whatever malign force animated the zombies was instantly extinguished when the creatures' brains were destroyed. But, as I had suspected, the rules that applied to zombies in movies and TV shows didn't apply here. Although my German friend no longer had much of a head above his lower jaw, it didn't stop him from trying to rise to his feet, or even slow him down all that much. He continued to scrabble in the mud, and got as far as levering himself up on one elbow before the failure of his shattered leg to hold him caused him to flop to the ground again. Even when I put further bullets into his 'good' leg and 'good' arm, grimacing as I pulled the trigger, his body continued to spasm and jerk, and would carry on doing so, I suspected, until it was completely destroyed.

Trying to ignore the twitching corpse at my feet, I wondered what to do next. It was hard to think with the din going on above me, and as yet showing no signs of abating. Lighting another match, I checked the rim of the crater, shuffling in a slow circle to ensure that nothing undead was about to imminently drop or roll or lurch down the slope in my direction. It was horrible to think that bodies, or bits of bodies, were more than likely dragging themselves towards me at this moment.

As I pivoted, my feet sliding in mud, I wondered whether I had ever been in a more wretched situation, and vowed to myself that if I ever got out of this, and became one of the older versions of me, I would make bloody sure that I came back to this moment to save my younger self.

Then I suddenly thought: *Why wait? I mean, why the fuck should I when I had the means to make it happen?* I might not have the heart, but I had *something* that could potentially influence future events. But would it work? Was my logic watertight? There was only one way to find out.

My hands shaking not only with cold now, but with excitement, I cast aside my latest match and unbuttoned the left breast pocket of my uniform jacket. I took out the notebook I always carried with me, the one in which I kept a record of where and when I needed to be at certain points along my timeline, and what I needed to do to keep events consistent with my experience. Strictly speaking, we weren't allowed to keep diaries or notebooks in the army, for fear they would fall into enemy hands and give away vital information, but this was one rule that was flouted by a large number of men. Committing thoughts and experiences to paper, rather than keeping them bottled up, was an outlet which prevented many of them – many of *us* – from going insane with the grief, horror and anxiety we were forced to live with on a daily basis.

Along with my notebook was a stub of pencil, which I sharpened with my jack knife whenever I needed to. In truth, I hadn't made many entries in the book during the course of the War, as so far it had simply been a case of ploughing through the days, one after the other, with no deviations into the past or future, and no interference from my future self (selves?).

Holding the book up to my face so I could see the white glimmer of its pages in the dark, I opened it and riffled through it until I came to what seemed to be a blank page. Then, with the stub of pencil, and working mostly blind, I wrote down the date, the approximate time, and the words 'Shell Crater'.

No sooner had I finished than a laconic voice, close enough and loud enough to be heard above the gunfire, said, 'You rang m'lord?'

It was my voice, although gruffer, more weathered, and it was coming from behind me. I turned to see an older version of myself – even older than the last version of me I'd seen in the hospital in 2097, his (my) hair and beard whiter and thinner than it had been back then, his face even more deeply lined. He was perhaps a bit skinnier too, and more stooped, though admittedly the heavy-duty cagoule that swamped him, and the green rubber waders that came up to his thighs made it difficult to tell.

I was trying to get over the weird existential shock of seeing myself looking so *old* when the future me cocked an eyebrow, as if he knew exactly what I was thinking (which he obviously did), and barked, 'As you can see, I came prepared.' He flicked the beam of the torch he was holding up into my face, making me flinch and cover my eyes.

'Christ,' I said, 'did you *have* to do that?'

He neither apologised nor answered my question. Instead he countered with a question of his own. 'Bloody hell, did I *really* look that bad when I was your age?'

Only then did he lower the torch so that its beam was no longer blinding me. As I tried to blink the green after-image from my eyes, he said briskly, 'Let's get this over with then,. When you get to my age you'll realise how anxious you are not to be reminded of all this.'

He jerked his head up to indicate the flashes of gunfire above us, and as he did I noticed he was deliberately avoiding shining his torch in the direction of the German soldier's still-twitching corpse, or even glancing that way.

'Fair enough,' I said. 'How much can you help me?'

'As much as I remember me helping you when I was you.'

'And how much is that?'

You'd think, wouldn't you, that if you ever met yourself, the two of you would get on like a house on fire? But the truth was, I found him pretty irritating. In some ways I even found it hard to believe this old geezer was me, not because I had any real doubts, but simply because there was such a distance between us that he seemed like an entirely different person to my present self. It was as if he was a grumpy uncle, or maybe an older brother who I'd lost contact with years ago, and with whom I now had nothing in common. He looked at me askance.

'I know what you're thinking.' Then all at once his voice became quieter, less confrontational – so much so that I had to lean in to hear him. 'But when you reach where I am, kid, when you see this from my point of view, believe me, you'll feel exactly the same way I do.'

Throughout our exchange he'd been holding the torch up, pointing it vaguely at the muddy wall beside us, but now his arm drooped as if the thing had suddenly become too heavy for him, the beam shrinking to a tight, bright circle on the ground between the toes of our boots. I noticed the circle was vibrating, and when I looked at him I was surprised to see not only that his hand was shaking, but that his bottom lip was too.

'Are you all right?' I asked, suddenly feeling as awkward and embarrassed as if he were a stranger.

He sniffed and nodded, but even in the dim light I could see his eyes were gleaming with wetness.

Oh God, he was crying. Had I made him cry? Had I made myself *cry?*

I hovered, not sure what to say, not sure whether to reach out and give him a hug.

But knowing exactly what I was thinking, he raised a hand, and blurted a choking sob of a laugh.

'Fuck me, I'm making a right scene, aren't I? I promised myself, having seen it once, that I wouldn't do this, that I'd be stronger when it came to my turn. No doubt you're now thinking the same as I did. Yet when it comes to it, you'll probably blub like a baby too.'

'Probably,' I said, though only to make him feel better. I put the notebook back in my pocket, then placed a filthy hand on his shoulder. 'Sorry,' I said hesitantly. 'For bringing you back, I mean. I never thought how bad it would be for you. The things we do to ourselves, eh?'

He nodded ruefully and wiped his eyes with a wrinkled, trembling hand. Even though I knew it was me I was looking at, it was heart-wrenching to see how badly affected he was by returning here. How vulnerable he suddenly seemed.

'I can't stay long,' he said, and he cleared his throat in an attempt to strengthen his voice, stop it from cracking. 'It's not that I'm not allowed to, it's just... I *can't*.'

'I understand.' I spread my hands, knowing he wouldn't take offence if I got down to business – knowing, in fact, that he'd welcome it. 'So what can you give me? Can you take me to the heart?'

He shook his head, though simultaneously grimaced in apology. He knew from first-hand experience how desperate I was, and how disappointed his reply would make me feel.

'Sorry. I can help you solve your immediate problem, but that's all.'

'Because it's all you remember from when you were me?'

'That, and the fact that if I stay much longer the strain of it'll give me a bloody heart attack. And I'm damned if I'm going to die in this shit hole at my age. What an irony that would be, eh?'

'You won't have a heart attack,' I said, and I tapped my own chest. 'We've got nanites, remember. At least, I assume you've still got them?'

'I have. And they're good, but they're not miracle workers.' Then unexpectedly he grinned. 'Mind you, you don't know the half of it. From what I remember, when I was you, you think I'm about eighty, don't you?'

I was about to reply, but before I could, something loomed up behind his right shoulder – a black figure, silhouetted against the dying glow of a Very light, standing on the rim of the pit.

Not sure whether it was an enemy soldier or a zombie, I yelled a warning and reached out to grab him, my instinct being to... I don't know, drag him to the ground, or at least out of harm's way.

Before I *could* grab him, though, his arm came up and deflected my hand. I was surprised by the swiftness of his reflexes, but then realised that what was happening now was just an action replay for him, and that he'd known what I was about to do.

In a voice that was still shaky, but strong enough to be heard above the now intermittent gunfire, he said, 'It's all right, kid. No need to panic.'

The black figure behind him took a lurching step forward, and then, with a complete lack of coordination, tipped forward into the pit. I winced as it face-planted into the mud at the bottom. My wince became a cry of horror as, with a wet crack that could be heard in a moment of silence between one burst of gunfire and the next, I saw the falling body flip up and over despite the fact that its head remained in the same position, face down in the mud. Only when the figure finally came to rest, the head on its broken neck now stretched so impossibly backwards that it was trapped between the ground and the figure's shoulder blades, did I see that it was little more than a near-skeletal frame draped in the tattered rags of a mud-caked uniform. The figure's emaciated limbs were moving slowly and jerkily, like the legs of a beetle on its back. Then, motivated by some primal instinct to regain both mobility and momentum, it began to rock from side to side, presumably with the intention of first flipping over on to its front, then clambering to its feet.

My older self still had his back to the figure. Looking at the blankly determined expression on his face, I saw this was a deliberate choice, that by refusing to obey his natural instinct to turn around he was showing he had no desire to re-live this particular moment, to see for the second time what was admittedly a sickening sight.

'Time to end this,' he said, and switching the torch from his right hand to his left, he reached into the pocket of his cagoule and withdrew the heart. He held it up in a way that made me think of a wizard in a fantasy story, striking fear into his enemies by displaying the source of his power. He closed his eyes and his face settled into an expression of grim concentration. And then there was a... I'm not sure what to call it. A pulse? A beat? It felt like a deep, throbbing convulsion in the pit of my belly that seemed to temporarily empty me of all sensation, all thought.

When I blinked what felt like a split second later I was amazed to see that the torch had reappeared in my older self's right hand, and that the heart was nowhere to be seen.

'What did I just miss?' I said, and then I noticed that not only had the skeletal figure that had tumbled into the pit disappeared, but also that the dead German officer I'd been sharing the trench with was now back where he'd been before, and was no longer moving. He had reverted back to his previous and proper state – that of an inert mound of decaying flesh, bone and cloth.

'Did you do that?'

He shrugged, patted his pocket. 'Not just me. I had some help.'

'But you controlled the heart? I mean, you... directed its energy or whatever?'

'I wouldn't say control. I'd never say control. But... I guess so, yeah.'

I felt a thrill go through me. 'So... when did you learn to do that? When will *I* learn to do it? And what else can you make it do? Can you–' Then, seeing the stubborn look on his face, I raised a hand, forced myself to stop. 'All right, I know. I'm asking too much. You're not allowed to say anything in case it fucks up the future. But... what *can* you tell me? What can you give me to make my life a bit easier – *our* life a bit easier?'

He seemed to relent. He smiled, shrugged. But he said, 'Not much. The thing is, when you get to my age, you only dare do what you know you've already done. You *want* to do more, but you can't risk it. Every time you go back in time you're scared you'll fuck up. You're scared you'll say too much or do too much, and everything will unravel.'

'Which must mean things are okay with you,' I said. 'If you don't want to change things, I mean. It must mean things have turned out okay.'

He smiled – a little bitterly? I wasn't sure.

'Or maybe it just means I'm scared of things turning out *even worse* than they have.' Before I could respond he made a zip motion across his mouth with his fingers. 'My lips are sealed. For both our sakes. There's a line in the sand, and there's too much at stake to risk stepping over it.'

I sighed. I was freezing cold, and miserable, and desperate to get the heart back – but he was *here*, in front of me. I couldn't pass up the opportunity to get what I could out of him.

'But what if you *are* stepping over it? I mean, what if you're stepping over it without knowing, and your memories are constantly changing to accommodate that without you realising it? Have you thought about that possibility?'

'Of course I have. I've thought about everything. At your age, you're still relatively new to all this, but me – I'm old. It's become both an obsession and a way of life.'

'And a trap?' I said, maybe a little spitefully. 'One that you can't escape from?'

He acknowledged this with a shrug. 'Maybe that too.'

I sighed – and then realised that something else had happened since he had used the heart to kill (or should that be *re*-kill?) the dead: the guns had stopped. Once again there was silence in No Man's Land – aside, of course, from the constant scuttling of rats.

'Did you undo what just happened?' I asked. 'Did you stop the dead or just take us back to before they came back to life?'

'Both,' he said. 'As far as the Germans are concerned, they've just taken a couple of pops at you, but they're not on full alert. You wouldn't stand a chance of getting through their lines if they were.'

I narrowed my eyes. 'So is that what I do? Get through their lines?'

His smile was both enigmatic and smug, and I thought to myself:

I'm never *going to smile like that. It's so fucking irritating!*

'It is, isn't it?' I said. 'You've got the heart, so it must be. So am I untouchable now? I mean, if you're me, and you're helping me out, then that must mean I'm going to get through this, right? I'm going to be okay?'

I was testing him, playing Devil's Advocate. This was old ground, and I pretty much knew what he was going to say before he said it.

'Don't try and be smart, kid. You know that *I* know that *you* know it's never that simple. Even at my age, there are still no hard and fast answers – that much I can tell you. You should never assume, you should never be blasé. In fact, yes, you *should* assume. You should assume that time is constantly in flux, which means that it can change in an instant. Yes, I got to where I am now, but I didn't do it by being reckless. And I didn't do it just by listening to me when I was you – don't make the mistake of thinking it's that simple. I did it by being careful, and by being lucky, but who's to say that you'll be as lucky as I was? Maybe you'll fuck up and we'll both blink out of existence. Maybe you'll make decisions that change what I've got, where I am – or maybe you already have. How would I know? I mean, it's not as if you *feel* your memories changing, is it?' He reached out a hand and grabbed my arm. He looked fierce now, even angry. 'There were times, kid, when I needed help and for whatever reason it didn't come. Times when I got hurt, badly hurt – when I could have died, in fact. But you've had a few of those already, haven't you, so you know all about that? What I'm saying is, just because I'm here now isn't any kind of insurance that you will be. So be careful. Be *fucking* careful. And be lucky.'

And with that, he was gone.

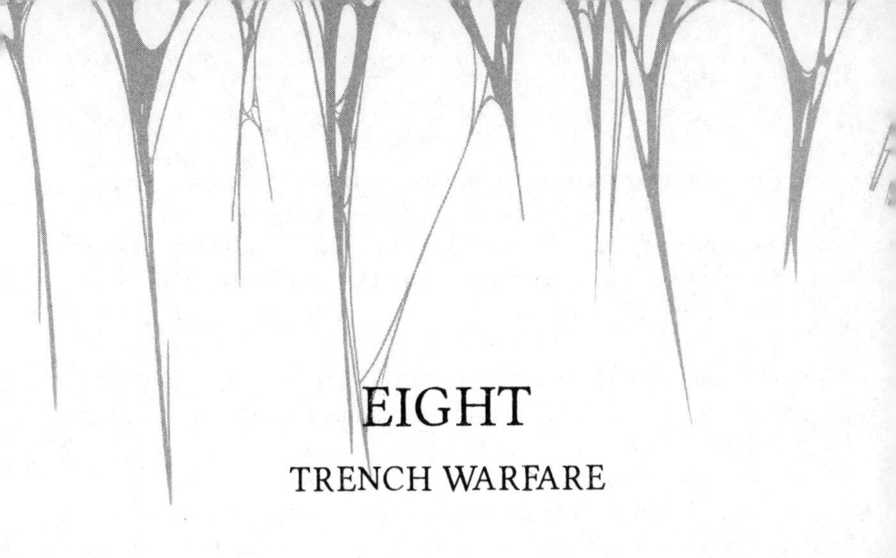

EIGHT

TRENCH WARFARE

So what now? I thought.

I was cold, wet, exhausted, and the way I saw it I had two choices: either I could go on or go back. But in truth, those two choices were only one choice. If I went back, I might lose the heart forever, because who knew when I'd get chance to look for it again, and where it might end up in the meantime?

Added to which, although the older me hadn't actually *led* me to the heart, he'd not only removed a couple of obstacles in my path to it, but had given me more than a hint that continuing with my self-imposed mission was the right course of action. What was it he'd said? He'd rolled back time so the Germans wouldn't be on full alert, which would make it easier for me to get through their lines – something like that.

A one-man mission to penetrate the enemy's defences and retrieve a valuable artefact. It sounded like the plot of a *Boy's Own* adventure story. But it was what I was going to have to do if I wanted the heart back. And I was going to have to do it on the double, while it was still dark. Leave it any longer and I'd be out in No Man's Land when dawn broke, and hiding would be impossible.

Shivering with cold, I looked over at the dead German soldier, who was once again lying in the position he'd been in before he'd started to stir. Did that mean the bullets I'd shot into him were now back in my gun? I checked and saw that they were. I puzzled briefly over how I could have a memory of an event that effectively had not now taken place – and then I put the thought from my head. I'd need my full wits and strength to concentrate on the here and now, on what was directly ahead of me. There was no point pondering on imponderables.

Remembering what I'd been about to do when the dead German had first stirred to life, I moved forward and, bracing myself against the stench, began once again to peel his coat from his decomposing body. This time I managed it without incident, and a couple of minutes later was standing with the stained and stinking coat in my hand, shaking and concentrating as hard as I could on not throwing up. I had nothing left inside me except bile, and I knew that if I succumbed to the urge to puke it would do nothing but twist my guts into knots and drain me of more energy than I could afford to expend. I moved as far from the German as I could, though some of the stink of him, contained within the coat, came with me. Grimacing, I held the coat in both hands and shook it out as if it was a bed sheet I was trying to flap free of creases. It helped – but only a little.

Although every instinct urged me to fling the coat as far away as possible, then wash my hands in one of the muddy pools dotted around the base of the shell hole, I gritted my teeth and shrugged it on. Not only would the coat keep me warm, but it would also effectively hide my British uniform if and when I managed to cross the German lines. If I was lucky, it might even wrong-foot any German soldiers I might come across long enough for me to take advantage of the situation.

Luckily the coat was a decent fit. Not perfect – I'm tall but fairly lean, whereas the German had been shorter and stockier, which meant that the sleeves came up over my bony wrists – but good enough. When, bent over double with one hand on my belly, I had once again conquered the urge to puke, I straightened up and spat on the ground.

Okay, I thought. *Time to go.*

Digging my fingers into the muddy walls of the shell crater, I heaved myself up and out. As I ascended I moved as slowly as I could and kept my head down. It was an awkward manoeuvre, and tough on the biceps, which had to take the majority of my weight, but having been on guard duty many times over the past few weeks, I knew that what tended to catch a sentry's sleepy eye at night were sudden, jerky movements – a fact that had caused many a scurrying rat to be blown to Kingdom Come.

It took me a long time to slide up and out of the shell hole, and by the time I managed it I was knackered, and at first could do no more than lie spread-eagled on the ground, breathing hard and trying to recover. I'd like to have lain there for at least twice as long as I did, but after about five minutes the cold oozing up from the muddy ground once again started to seep into my limbs through my layers of clothing, and so I slowly and reluctantly raised my head and tried to get my bearings. Ahead of me I saw the shattered tree trunk I'd been heading towards earlier. I estimated it was now something like thirty metres away.

How long had I been out in No Man's Land? It seemed like forever, but it was probably no more than about ninety minutes. Possibly less, as far as Frank back in the home trench was concerned, when you took into account how the older me had helped by winding time back a little. No need to panic just yet then – I still had several hours of darkness ahead of me. Trying to stay calm, I moved forward on my belly, inch by painstaking inch, negotiating a route through the mangled bodies and darting rats and often lethal chunks of shrapnel.

At last, having traversed a distance that would have taken me no more than a minute to cross on foot, I reached the tree stump. I paused here a few moments to catch my breath, my curled-up body pressed behind the stump for shelter as my lungs laboured and my ribs heaved. Once again, although my hands and feet and face were numb with cold, I was pouring with sweat inside my uniform. The muscles in my arms, legs and stomach were aching as if I'd been pumping iron for the last hour, and my head was swimming both with exhaustion and with the stink of decomposition from the coat, which was rising with the heat from my body and enclosing me in a reeking fug.

Again, I waited until the cold started to creep through me, and then pressed on, though more cautiously than ever now that I was nearing the German lines. Just ahead of me, like thin, dark, looping scratches on the marginally lighter horizon, I saw coils of barbed wire rising from the rutted mud. Many a soldier, both from the German side and ours, had come a cropper on this stuff. If you ran into it in blind panic, as many did, you became ensnared, and therefore an easy target for enemy snipers. The trick, when approaching it horizontally as I was, was to take your time, to flatten it down bit by bit, keeping your movements slow and, most importantly, your mouth shut whenever you felt the hot, sharp sting of barbs scraping across your flesh. Eventually, if you were both patient and lucky, you would succeed in flattening a section of it down enough to be able to roll over it – though even at this point you had to be careful. If a stray upstanding barb snagged on your coat, you might end up pulling the wire taut and setting off a rattling chain reaction down the length of the coils, which would alert the enemy just as effectively as if you were to leap to your feet and wave your arms.

It took me a good twenty minutes – my fingers as cold and numb as icicles even as the sweat trickled down my face and stung my eyes – to deal with the barbed wire strung across my path. The process involved delicately isolating each loop between the fingers of my two hands and then very carefully flattening and twisting each of those loops into corkscrew-like lengths, like the twist of wire at the top of a metal coat hanger, until I could squash them down into the mud. I had to repeat this process maybe a dozen times in all, taking care not to tug too hard on each loop of wire and make the whole coiling length of it jerk like a fisherman's line. It was back-breaking work, not least because I had to do it flat on my belly with my chin resting in a pool of mud and my outstretched arms raised no higher than an inch above the ground, but eventually I managed to create an area wide enough to crawl over.

Five minutes later, having successfully negotiated the German defences without raising the alarm, I came upon an upward-sloping ridge of mud, stretching to the right and left of me as far as I could see (which admittedly wasn't far in the darkness) and topped with a layer of sandbags. I'd known the German trench must be close, but now that I could actually see it, no more than half a dozen yards in front of me, my heart quickened and my body started to shake with nerves. Once again, doubts assailed me. What the fuck was I doing here? Who was to say that the heart wasn't lying out there in No Man's Land somewhere, half-buried in the mud, and I had simply crawled past it in the darkness?

Then I again remembered my older self's words. He might not have said it outright, but hadn't he strongly hinted that in order to get the heart back I would have to penetrate the German lines? But what the fuck could I do? I was one man against the entire German army! All right, so maybe that was exaggerating. Instead of panicking I needed to stay calm, think this through, break it down. What exactly was I likely to be faced with here? What obstacles would I have to overcome?

If the Germans operated a similar system to ours, and I had to assume they did, they'd have somewhere between a dozen and two dozen men occupying each traverse – by which I mean a single section of trench, the trenches themselves being dug in a zigzag pattern to confine the blast of any explosives that might find their mark, and thus reduce the number of casualties. At this time of night most of those men would be asleep, with maybe only a couple of sentries on duty. So initially, if I were lucky, I'd have only two men to overcome. Which still made the odds two against one. But at least I had the element of surprise. Plus I was wearing a German officer's overcoat.

I crawled a little closer, moving so slowly now that a snail could have overtaken me. After reducing the distance between myself and the trench to only a couple of yards, I froze again.

I could hear voices.

There were two of them, and they were conversing quietly in German. I had no idea what they were saying. I'd never done German at school, and the only words I knew I'd picked up mainly (and ironically) from old war movies – '*Achtung*!' '*Schnell*!' '*Auf Wiedersehen*,' '*Heil*, Hitler!' Lying flat on my belly and listening to the voices for a minute or two – one light, almost boyish, the other deeper, more jovial, the words often accompanied by a rumbling chuckle – I was relieved to hear that they sounded both relaxed (which meant they must have decided the movement they'd seen and shot at in No Man's Land earlier was nothing to get alarmed about) and that they were endeavouring to keep their voices low (which meant the other men must be asleep, as I'd hoped). It was odd to think I was only a few yards away from them, and that if I'd been so inclined I could have ended both their lives with a grenade or a couple of bullets. Odd and creepy too, because on numerous occasions Frank and I had been in the same situation as the two German sentries, and my presence here was a reminder of how easy it was to become complacent, how close you could be to death without realising it.

After a couple of minutes I retreated from the edge of the bunker, inching myself backwards and wincing at every tiny slurp and squelch of mud caused by the movement of my body. Once I was out of earshot of the German sentries (or at least, I *hoped* I was) I swivelled round and headed to my right, my intention being to drop into the trench some distance from the two men. I was now utterly plastered in mud from head to toe, but aside from the fact that it clung like glue, which meant that crawling through it was an enervating business, it didn't worry me unduly, because most of the other men in the trenches were in a similar condition. After five minutes or so I reckoned I was far enough along the trench that I wouldn't alert the sentries, whereupon I crawled up to the line of sandbags and after a quick peek to make sure there was no one about, I slithered up and over them.

My heart was hammering now, the adrenaline rushing through me. I slid to the bottom of the trench, then clambered to my feet, my boots and the dead German's stinking coat now so caked in mud they felt as heavy as lead. I did what I could to scrape off some of the filth, but it was a pretty hopeless task. I had nothing to scrape with except my hands, and they too were gloved in mud. In the end, hoping I wouldn't have to move quickly any time soon – whether that be to fight or flee – I took a couple of deep breaths, then drew my revolver. Holding it by my side, concealed behind a fold of the mud-caked overcoat, I moved along the trench towards the two sentries.

Be brash. Be confident. Act as if you own the place. I had no idea whether anyone had ever specifically given me that advice, or whether it was just one of those general life tips that you hear repeated every so often (the kind of approach interviewees and new employees and insurance salesmen are encouraged to adopt), but it was a mantra I was fully committed to right now. My best chance of success was to catch the enemy off-guard, and I knew I couldn't do that by sneaking about like a thief.

That said, my limbs were so stiff with cold and tension, and I was shaking so much inside, that as I moved in the direction of the murmuring voices I couldn't help but think I must look like some ghastly, grinning marionette. With each step the voices, though still conversing quietly, grew louder and clearer, a fact which I tried (and failed) not to find increasingly unnerving. Ahead of me was a natural curve in the muddy wall, from a few metres beyond which both the voices and a faint bloom of lamplight were drifting. Bracing myself, I strode, with as much confidence as I could muster, around the corner.

As soon as I appeared the heads of the two sentries snapped up and they fell immediately silent. The bulkier, older, dark-haired one who had been sitting on a box, leaped to his feet, though whether to confront me or as a mark of respect, having seen my officer's overcoat, I wasn't sure. The younger one, his hair a flaxen yellow, the cheekbones of his thin face so sharp that he looked cadaverous in the dim candlelight, raised his rifle uncertainly. Ignoring it, I gave both of them what I hoped was an easy smile and spoke one of the few German phrases I *did* know: '*Guten abend.*'

At first the men just gaped at me, which made me wonder whether I'd misremembered what I'd thought was the German for 'Good evening'. Then the older man nodded, albeit warily, repeated my greeting, and said something else in German, which by the inflection of his voice was clearly a question.

Taking a gamble, I smiled again, nodded and said, '*Ja.*' But this only made the two men frown. I was no more than four or five steps away from them now, and still strolling unhurriedly forward. Perhaps deciding that I had misheard his question, the older man began to repeat it.

Instead of answering him I brought up the gun, which I'd been holding by the barrel, and smashed it down on the bridge of his nose. Almost before the blood had started to gush I hit him twice more, once on the forehead and once, as his legs gave way beneath him, on the top left side of his skull.

I didn't want to kill him, but neither did I hold back. I couldn't afford to. If I was going to get through this, I had to do everything full-bloodedly; there could be no half measures. Having chosen the bigger and tougher-looking of the two men, I knew that my first blow had to incapacitate him, and my second and third had to render him unconscious. I knew too that it had to happen quickly, while the younger man was still in shock and before he had time to work out what was happening. I'd gambled on the fact that because I was wearing a German officer's overcoat, the young soldier's instinctive assumption would be not that I was an enemy soldier launching a one-man attack, but that I was a superior officer inflicting a punishment for some unknown but serious misdemeanour on his unfortunate comrade.

And so it proved. As the dark-haired man slid to the ground, his face a bloody, ruined mess, the younger soldier continued to gape at me, his mouth open but silent, his rifle drooping, momentarily forgotten, in his hands.

So incapacitated by surprise was he, in fact, that I had ample time to flip my revolver round, so that I was holding it by the now blood-stained butt instead of the barrel, and press its muzzle against the centre of his forehead, directly between his bulging, terrified eyes. With my other hand I yanked the rifle from his nerveless fingers and threw it into the mud behind me. Then, raising that hand, I extended my forefinger and placed it to my lips.

'Shh.'

The young soldier's face crumpled in shame, but I only realised he had pissed himself when a stink of urine wafted up between us. I could hardly blame him. He was no older than eighteen and more than likely a raw recruit, who having been dumped into the sheer hell of trench warfare, had just seen his friend battered unconscious by a mud-spattered mad man who was now pressing a revolver to his forehead. As if the full implication of this had only just entered his stunned brain he abruptly began to cry. To his credit he did it quietly, his blubbering lips emitting almost silent gasps of breath as tears poured down his face.

There was a part of me that felt desperately sorry for him, and ashamed of my actions. I was immediately transported back almost a couple of decades, to when I was barely older than this young soldier was now, and I had been part of a gang that had held up a van carrying around £100,000 in cash. There'd been a kid in the van that day, a boy of about ten riding shotgun with his uncle, and the stark, blubbering fear on his face when we forced the van to the side of the road and appeared with our stocking masks and baseball bats was exactly the same as the expression on the German soldier's face right now. Weird to think that that incident had taken place almost twenty years ago for me, and yet in linear terms was still eighty years in the future.

'Do you speak English?' I whispered, but the German soldier's eyes were now screwed up tight as he continued to weep, and he seemed not to hear me.

I gripped his chin tightly in my muddy hand and forced his head up.

'Open your eyes,' I hissed, and then groped for the same words in

German. 'Offnen... offnen...' What the fuck was the German for eyes?

But I didn't need it. He got the message. His eyes, shimmering with tears, opened and he stared at me in stark terror.

'Do you speak English?' I repeated, and bared my teeth at him when he didn't reply. 'Answer! *Schnell!*'

He wasn't being stubborn. He was simply too scared to speak. His lips moved, but nothing came out. I could see his face tightening with desperation as he struggled to make a sound, the flesh turning white and waxy as if the blood was draining out of him.

For fuck's sake, don't faint, I thought. I smiled to try to put him at his ease, and spoke words that if I'd have been in his situation I wouldn't have believed for a second.

'I don't want to hurt you. All I want are answers. Now, tell me – do you speak English?'

He nodded so vigorously that the muzzle of the gun scraped his forehead hard enough to break the skin and draw blood. He winced, and as if the sudden pain had awakened his voice, managed to whisper, '*Ein bisschen*... a little.'

'A little may be enough. You understand what I'm saying?'

'*Ja*.'

'Okay. I'm looking for something.' I released my grip on his face, my fingers leaving muddy streaks, and held my thumb and index finger a few inches apart. 'A small black heart. Made of stone. About this big. You understand?'

He looked almost childishly eager to please. '*Ja, ja*.'

'Have you seen it?'

'*Ja*.'

'Where?'

In heavily accented German the young soldier said, 'British soldier... he throw it. It... er...' Carefully, evidently wishing not to antagonise me by making any sudden moves, he mimed the arc of a projectile with his right hand, which he then clapped softly into the cupped palm of his left.

'Fell? Landed?'

'Landed! *Ja*. Outside. Not far. This man...' he indicated his unconscious companion with a grimace '...he go. Get it.'

My heart leaped. Could it really be this easy? Could the heart be in the possession of the unconscious man?

'Does he still have it?'

The young soldier's face fell. He was clearly sorry, albeit no doubt for his own sake, to give me disappointing news.

'*Nein.*' He wafted a hand. 'Taken.'

'Who by?'

He shrugged nervously, as if to let me know it wasn't his fault.

'*Kapitan*... how you say?'

'Captain. An officer?'

'*Ja, ja.* Officer.'

'What was his name? This *Kapitan*?'

'Heidrich.'

'Heidrich?' I tried out the pronunciation. 'Kapitan Heidrich?'

The young soldier started to nod, then remembered the muzzle of my revolver was still pressed to his forehead. '*Ja.*'

'And where is Kapitan Heidrich now? Where is the heart? Is it still here?'

'*Nein*...' Again he wafted a hand. 'Away.'

'He took it away?'

'*Ja.*'

'Shit. Where?'

The soldier turned the corners of his mouth downwards – an apologetic facial shrug. 'Camp perhaps. This is most... like?'

'Likely?'

'Likely. *Ja.*'

My mind was racing. I had the sense that the heart was receding from me, that soon it would be unreachable – if it wasn't already.

'How far away is this camp?' I asked.

Again that facial shrug. 'Perhaps... ten kilometres?'

'Ten kilometres. About six or seven miles?'

'*Ja*,' he said, though I suspected he had no idea what the equivalent was in miles and was agreeing simply to please me.

'The camp is that way?' I pointed back behind the German lines, in the opposite direction from where the British trenches lay.

'*Ja.*'

'There are communication lines from here to there?'

He looked puzzled at this, so I tried to indicate what I meant by drawing lines with my finger running back from the trench. 'More trenches? Like this one? You travel through them to get to the camp?'

His face brightened with understanding. 'Oh. *Ja*.'

'How many men?' I asked. 'Between here and the camp?'

He did that facial shrug again. 'Some. Er... not much.'

I frowned. 'Is that the truth?'

Alarmed he said, '*Ja, ja*, is truth.'

It was going to be a tremendous risk, a ludicrous and foolhardy mission, but what choice did I have? I looked at the young soldier contemplatively. 'I'd better go there then. Question is, what am I going to do with you?'

He seemed to understand that all right. His features seemed to sag, as if he had suddenly aged twenty years. He began to shake, and his eyes flickered upwards, towards the gun pressed against his forehead.

'You say not hurt.' His voice was a quavery whisper. 'Please, please... I... I help.'

'Relax,' I said, but either he didn't understand, or was too scared to register what I was saying. I raised a hand, palm out, the universal sign for *calm down*. 'I won't hurt you, I promise. I'm a man of my word. You understand?'

He looked at me like a frightened puppy. In the mud at our feet the dark-haired man groaned, shifted a little, then settled again. I was going to have to go, and soon, but I couldn't leave the young soldier here to raise the alarm. Within minutes I'd have armed soldiers after me. I'd have no chance.

'I won't hurt you,' I repeated, 'but I'll have to tie you up. Okay?'

Still he looked scared, but he gave a jerk of a nod, the muzzle scraping his skin again. I knew exactly what he was thinking. He didn't trust me not to kill him, but his only choice was to follow my instructions and hope for the best, hope that this untrustworthy enemy would somehow, miraculously, spare his life.

'Good lad,' I said, and I took a step back from him, giving him room, while still levelling my revolver at his head. 'Take off your uniform. Your jacket. And your trousers.' I pointed at the items as I named them.

He frowned at me, troubled, unwilling. It was obvious he had understood my instructions, but was uncertain as to where this was going. There was a raw bindi-like spot on his forehead, rimmed in smeared, partly dried blood, where I had pressed the revolver against his skull.

'I have no rope,' I said. 'So I must use your uniform. You understand?'

He nodded slowly, and then, even more slowly, began to unbutton his jacket.

'*Schnell!*' I hissed, my reassuring expression scrunching instantly into a scowl. 'Quickly! Don't take the piss.'

He got the message, popping open the buttons of his jacket and tugging it off in double-quick time, and then stripping off his trousers with such clumsy urgency that he almost slipped and fell in the mud. When he was standing, shivering in his long johns, I ordered him to lie on his stomach in the muddy water at the bottom of the trench, and then used his trousers to tie his legs together, his jacket to secure his arms behind his back. I also stripped off one of his stinking socks (seeing that the Germans were living in the same squalid and miserable conditions as we were was oddly heartening) and stuffed it into his mouth, securing it in place with the belt from his trousers. Then I did the same to his unconscious companion.

Before leaving I put the young soldier's right boot back on his sockless foot, as it was bad enough leaving him lying in freezing water wearing just his underwear without having the added guilt that he might get frostbite so bad he'd lose his foot, or get his toes chewed off by rats. Then I rose to my feet and looked down on him for a moment. He looked pathetic, scared, and he was shivering with cold and fear. Even now he probably thought I was going to put a bullet in his brain. For a moment I thought about getting out my notebook and writing down his name, with the obscure intention of somehow compensating him at some point in the future. But it would have meant removing his gag in order to ask him, and I had wasted enough time already; I couldn't afford to push my luck any further.

So in the end I simply said, 'I'm sorry. *Auf Wiedersehen.*'

And then I left.

NINE

HEIDRICH AND THE HEART

Notebook in one hand and revolver in the other (albeit concealed within the pocket of the German officer's overcoat), I hurried through the communication trenches that led back from the front line to the German camp. The labyrinthine network of ditches was familiar to me because we employed a similar system on the other side of No Man's Land. During the day and early evening the British communication trenches saw plenty of foot traffic, but at quiet times, like now, they were generally little used and therefore virtually unmanned – and I was relieved to discover, as I ploughed my way doggedly onwards, that the German trenches were no different. All the same, I knew I couldn't take it for granted that I wouldn't meet *anyone* on my journey. Walking miles along narrow, mud-filled ditches with heavy rounds of ammunition or pots of stew was such back-breaking, time-consuming work that there were frequent dug-outs along the way, which the 'couriers' could use for rest and recuperation. It wasn't unusual for anyone tramping through the trenches, whatever the hour, to come across an individual, or perhaps a group, taking a lengthy breather – or sometimes, if the prospect of trudging all the way back to camp was too much for them, even bedding down for a night's kip.

Even when there was nothing, or virtually nothing, to weigh you down, the trenches were a nightmare to negotiate. Each trudging step, through a quagmire of clinging mud, which often oozed up to your shins or higher, was a thigh-straining effort. When there had been a lot of rain it could sometimes take an hour or more to walk a mile. And unluckily for me, there *had* been a lot of rain recently, but no matter how bad it was I knew I couldn't afford the 'luxury' of a six-hour plod. At best I had three or four hours of darkness left, and if I was going to get to the German camp before Reveille at sunrise (or whatever the German equivalent was), then I was going to have to get a shift on. Therefore, despite the fact that I was already knackered both from the crawl across No Man's Land and the stress of the last few adrenaline-pumping hours, I forced myself not just to walk but to jog – or at least to try to maintain a half-decent pace given the fact that the mud caking my boots and sticking to their soles made my feet feel as if they were encased in cement.

As it turned out, I met only one pair of men on my journey. They were sitting hunched in a dug-out with what looked like chunks of cooked meat – possibly sausages – in one hand and tin mugs in the other. They both looked filthy and exhausted, and their eyes were half-closed as the steam from their mugs coiled around their whiskery faces. At my sudden appearance they both sat up, startled. Then one of them said something in German, albeit in a respectful rather than confrontational tone, presumably having clocked my coat. I muttered, '*Guten abend*,' and hurried by without slowing, flapping my notebook in the hope they would assume I had an urgent message to deliver and couldn't stop to chat. I had no idea what customs or protocols I might be breaking, both with my greeting and my notebook waving, but the men neither challenged nor pursued me.

I think if I'd have been in their position I wouldn't have given my actions much notice either. Certainly from the British perspective, there was such a changeover of staff at the front line that a stranger in an officer's coat would simply be assumed to be another new officer come to join the fun. Besides which, if the Germans were like us, they would be dull-eyed and dull-witted through boredom, lack of sleep, the dreadful conditions and the sheer exhaustion that followed periods of extreme stress. Such a combination tended to lead you to lower your guard, accept things at face value. It would never have occurred to me to think that a British officer could in reality be a German soldier who had crawled across No Man's Land to undertake a private mission which involved him journeying deep into enemy territory. Such a thing just didn't and wouldn't happen. No soldier would be crazy enough to do something like that – not even the crazy ones.

Maybe because I was so strung out, I started to giggle at that thought. And I kept on giggling intermittently, until, after what felt like a good two hours since I had left the young soldier and his companion trussed-up in the mud, the muddy walls flanking me gradually began to get lower – or, perhaps more accurately, the ground beneath my feet started to rise like a slope or ramp. I was so shattered by this point that I had to bend forward at the waist and clutch my thighs to keep going. As I slowly ascended, the muscles in my legs not just protesting but screaming hotly at the extra effort, I felt like a miner emerging into the light after spending days underground.

Not that it *was* light, mind you. If it had been I'd have been screwed. Reaching the top of the 'ramp' I found myself in an open field looking down from the top of a gradual slope at a sweep of countryside below. The vast night sky that seemed to fill eighty per cent of my vision was so awash with stars that tilting back my head to look up at them made me feel dizzy. The effulgence above only made the earth below seem blacker, so much so that it was hard to pick out details. There appeared to be a clump of woodland about half a mile directly ahead of me, to the right of which was a cluster of what looked like buildings, tents and vehicles that I guessed was the German camp. A few lights were glowing from somewhere within it, but they were by necessity sparse and dim. If the German camp was like ours I knew it would be makeshift, its perimeter fencing perfunctory at best. With all those miles of trenches between the camp and the Allied forces, there was no need for high security. The danger came not from enemy raids, but from bombs dropped by enemy aircraft.

I was lathered in sweat, plastered in mud, and every muscle in my body seemed to have been pummelled and stretched beyond endurance. I wanted nothing more than to sink to the soft ground and sleep for twenty hours. I might even have done that, and damn the consequences, if I hadn't forced myself to bring Kate's face to mind. The memory of her chestnut hair, her big blue eyes behind her pink-framed spectacles, and her cheeky, half-crooked smile instantly brought a lump to my throat and tears to my eyes. I swayed for a moment, vision blurring, my defences so low that simply allowing the memory of my five-year-old daughter to emerge from the shadows, where for reasons of self-preservation I usually kept it, was almost enough to reduce me to a quivering mess.

Paradoxically, though, it also gave me the impetus I needed to carry on. After the weakness came the strength – a surge of energy and determination, like a shot of pure adrenaline.

My plan was sketchy, to say the least. I'd approach via the woods, in case there was a sentry on the gate, seek out an officers' billet, and take it from there. God knew how long I had left before daybreak, before the camp started to rise. I'd got this far through guts, luck and endurance, but my luck now felt like the thinnest of threads, and as frayed as my nerves. All I could do was hope it held out for a little while longer.

Trudging down the hill I felt exposed, though there was no way anyone from the camp could have seen or heard me, not without shining a great big spotlight up the slope. All the same I was glad to reach the clump of woodland which flanked the left side of the camp, by which time a shower of soft winter rain had started to fall, the droplets hissing in the highest branches of the skeletal trees, as if a thousand people were whispering up there. I welcomed the rain. Later its cold might seep through to my bones and make me shiver, but right now the light, cool touch of it against my skin felt soothing and oddly protective, the sound of it masking my squelching progress through the woods. I felt as though the rain was cleansing me too, spiritually as well as physically, ridding me not only of a layer of mud, but also the stench of death. A fanciful notion, but that was where my head was at that moment. I was focused on my task, but at the same time my thoughts felt as if they were floating free.

When I felt I'd gone deep enough into the woods I turned sharp right. Five minutes later the trees thinned out and I found myself on the fringes of the German camp. I was relieved to discover I'd been right about the lack of security. The only thing blocking my way was a waist-high wooden fence, which was so dilapidated I guessed it must have been erected by the camp's former owner, who, I decided, must have been a farmer, because the billets were wooden outbuildings – a couple of big barns and a selection of smaller, rickety-looking sheds which I guessed must have housed livestock or stored things like tools, machinery and animal feed. The wooden buildings were clustered around what had clearly been the farmhouse – a grim stone construction with a low roof and small windows through which a little light bled.

Parked in the yard, a large open area composed of muddy cobbles with puddles of black water filling the ruts and dips, were a dozen or so armoured cars that looked as if they had seen plenty of service. Beyond these, off to my right, was the camp entrance, separated from the outside world by a wooden gate topped rather pointlessly with coils of barbed wire. Just inside the gate was a lone sentry with a rifle over his shoulder. Thanks to the lantern perched on the gatepost beside him, I could see he had his back to me. He was smoking a cigarette and gazing off into the darkness.

There was no one else about, though I could hear soft sounds, which I associated with horses – snuffles and the occasional hoof-clack – coming from an outbuilding to my left. Beyond that, perhaps drifting from the farmhouse, I could faintly hear a buzz of conversation and the odd burst of laughter.

Was that where the officers were billeted? It seemed likely. But if that was the case, how was I going to get in undetected? How the hell was I going to find this Kapitan Heidrich and retrieve the heart?

Even if all the officers had been asleep it would have been a daunting task. But they clearly weren't asleep. At least some of them (I guessed there were at least three and possibly as many as half a dozen) were awake and having a few drinks, maybe even a party.

What time was it? Four, five in the morning? It might even be six, in which case I had only an hour or so of darkness left. I was starting to feel desperate, but I tried to stay calm, to think through my options. I could create a diversion, draw the men out of the cottage – but how? By freeing the horses? That, though, would only cause a commotion, and my best chance of success was to rouse as few people from sleep as possible.

Maybe I was over-thinking it. Maybe my best and simplest choice was to sneak round to the back of the farmhouse, try to find a way in, then sneak upstairs while the officers were still occupied in the room at the front of the house. Maybe I'd strike lucky. Maybe I'd find the heart in one of the unoccupied bedrooms. But what if Kapitan Heidrich was one of the men I could hear carousing, and what if he had the heart on him? In that case I guess I'd have to wait, try to conceal myself, take my chance if and when it arose.

It was all ifs and buts, and I told myself irritably that there was no point just standing there pondering on them. What would be would be. The important thing now was to actually do *something*.

Keeping an eye on the sentry at the gate, I climbed over the fence and scurried across the farmyard, aiming for the nearest armoured car. With every step I expected the sentry to whirl round, bring up his rifle, order me to halt, but I reached the vehicle undetected. I slipped into the shadow between that and the next one, and paused for a moment, breathing hard. Sweat was pouring off me even though I was shivering inside. In getting this far I felt I'd used up not only every ounce of strength I had, but all my reserves as well. If I'd been a car I'd have been running on nothing but fumes by now. But I had to keep going. Had to take the next step, then the one after it, then the one after that. I tried not to think about what I'd do if Kapitan Heidrich wasn't here, or if the young soldier had given me false information. As long as I had a target I'd carry on. Beyond that... who knew?

I decided not to run. Once I broke free of the shadowy cover of the cars, I decided that I would stroll casually and unhurriedly across the open stretch of maybe fifty metres to the corner of the farmhouse; I would walk as if I owned the place. It went against all my instincts, but I told myself that not only would running exhaust me, but I'd be more likely to attract attention. And yes, walking would take longer, which meant there was more chance the sentry at the gate would turn and spot me, but even if he did, what would he see? An officer walking towards the officers' billet. Granted, I had no knowledge of German army etiquette, but what I did know was that if I'd been that sentry in the British army and I'd turned to see what looked like a British officer walking towards the officers' billet, I wouldn't have challenged him. I probably wouldn't even have wished him a good evening unless he wished me one first.

I slipped from the cover of one car to another until I was standing behind the rear bumper of the last vehicle in the row. I hovered a moment, looking at the open ground in front of me, my stomach doing slow cartwheels.

'He who dares,' I murmured, and then I stepped out into the open and began to walk towards the farmhouse.

It felt like a fuckload more than fifty metres, but eventually I reached the corner of the building. I slipped behind it, into a black wedge of shadow, and then sagged against the wet stone wall, panting as if I'd not walked fifty metres but sprinted two hundred. I waited until the shakes subsided, then made my way along a narrow path dividing the side of the house from a long wooden outbuilding next to it. At the end of the path was another cobbled yard, this one smaller and strewn with filthy straw and broken farming equipment.

It was dark at the back of the house and the rain was coming down harder now. It ran down the roof of the farmhouse and dripped freely from the eaves and guttering, which gave the impression that the building was melting or slowly decaying.

However, even though I was getting soaked, I was thankful for it. At least the rain's hissing clatter would mask the sounds I might make breaking in. The building had a back door, set into a recessed stone porch, but to my despair it looked stout enough to withstand a battering ram.

There was a window to the right of the door, but like the rest of the building's windows it was small – perhaps even too small to crawl through. I approached it to examine it, and was actually in the process of leaning forward to peer into the house, when all at once the window flared with orange light, as if a fiery eye had opened.

I leaped back, startled and alarmed. My first thought was that this was a trap, that the Germans had known of my presence all along and had lured me into an enclosed space from which there was no escape. Then my scrambled thoughts settled. Staring at the light even as I backed away from it, I saw that it came from a lantern held by a figure who had entered the kitchen – a figure who, I could tell at a glance, had no inkling of my presence; was not even looking in my direction.

All the same I had to hide, in case the figure looked out of the window and spotted me in the yard. I scuttled across to a broken-down cart and crouched behind it. Peering around the edge of one of the remaining wheels, I saw that the light in the window had grown more diffuse, though only because the lantern was no longer visible. From the way the light swayed and shifted and gradually brightened, I could tell its bearer was heading in the direction of the back door.

Was he coming out? Why? Perhaps I *had* been spotted. Perhaps the young soldier had somehow managed to get a message to the German camp ahead of me? I had no idea how, but exhaustion was making me paranoid, and paranoia doesn't care about logic. Perhaps the Germans had *ways*. Ways we didn't understand. Could it even be that the heart was involved? Surely it hadn't betrayed me?

I found that thought more alarming than the prospect that I might be discovered. And my fears seemed borne out even further a moment later when I heard the grinding judder of the back door being pulled open.

Here it comes, I thought, squeezing my eyes shut and drawing myself into as tight a ball as I could. I wished I could somehow melt into the shadows in which I was crouched, become one with them. What would the Germans do to me if they found me? Torture me for information? Shoot me? My hand slipped into my pocket and closed around my gun. But even now I wasn't sure whether, if it came down to it, I'd be able to kill anyone in cold blood. Zombies and monsters, yes, but another living, breathing human being? Maybe if my own life was threatened, maybe if it came down to a cold choice between him and me... but even then I wasn't sure. There was no doubt I'd become more ruthless and resourceful these past few years, but taking someone's life changed you. It broke something inside, something intrinsic. Even killing someone accidentally, as I had done, took something away from you that you could never get back. And not even finding out that the victim had orchestrated their own death at your hand made a difference to the sense of desolation you were left with.

Crouched behind the cart, I heard the lantern-bearer moving about in the yard. Was he looking for me? A moment later I heard a metallic clunk as he placed the lantern on the cobbled ground, and then I heard him stop, settle.

What was he doing? Perhaps if I opened my eyes I'd see him grinning down at me, pointing a gun at my head? Then I heard a spattering of liquid more concentrated than the rain, and a sigh. I sagged with relief. He was taking a piss! Whoever the lantern-bearer was, he'd come out of the house to relieve himself.

I felt another hysterical giggle bubbling up and raised a hand to stifle it. But the hand stopped halfway to my mouth. It had suddenly occurred to me how I might take advantage of this situation. I had to act fast, though; almost before thinking about it, in fact. And even as the half-formed idea was taking shape in my head, I was rising from my hiding place, moving swiftly across the yard, drawing my revolver from my pocket.

The German soldier was standing with his back to me, his left hand raised above his head, palm flat against the wall of the house, his right hand holding his cock. He was finishing off, oblivious to my presence, as I moved across the yard towards him, was shaking out the last droplets when I pressed the barrel of the gun to his head, just behind his ear.

He jumped, flinched away, started to turn. Acting instinctively I pushed him from behind, slamming him into the wall, and pressed my gun hard against the side of his cheekbone, maybe even hard enough to bruise.

'Don't move!' I hissed. 'Move and you're dead! You understand me?'

He went rigid, and even though I could see only part of the right side of his face I could tell he was scared.

'Yes, yes,' he said, eager to please.

'You speak English?'

'Yes.'

'Good. I'm looking for Kapitan Heidrich. You know him?'

Silence.

I pushed the gun harder into his cheek, making him grunt in pain.

'Are *you* Kapitan Heidrich?'

'*Nein!*' He blurted out the word, his voice shrill, then immediately tried to compose himself. 'No. It is not I.'

'Where is he?'

'He is inside. Sleeping.'

'You're sure about that?'

'Yes. Yes, he is up the stairs.'

My mind was racing. My captive was young, maybe mid to late twenties, and, though I may have been wrong, he struck me as the German equivalent of an upper-class English officer – well bred, private school, privileged background. He certainly spoke English well, with only a slight German accent. He seemed genuinely scared – and who wouldn't be with an enemy soldier holding you at gunpoint? – but was he scared enough to co-operate fully with me, to betray a fellow officer?

'Put your cock away,' I said.

'My...?'

'Your cock. Your knob. Your penis.'

He understood that all right. Without another word he did the necessary, then buttoned himself up.

'Now I want you to take me to Kapitan Heidrich. He's got something of mine and I want it back. But if you raise the alarm, I'll kill you. You understand?'

'Yes, I understand.'

'Good. Come on then.' I grabbed the scruff of his collar.

'Wait,' he said.

Wait? This was unexpected. I was thrown for a moment. Then my sense of self-preservation kicked back in. I was deep in enemy territory. I had to keep the upper hand here, had to keep my captive compliant, in fear for his life.

Still maintaining a tight grip on the back of the soldier's collar, I yanked him backwards, then slammed him into the wall again. He gave a gasping cry of pain.

'Fuck your "wait",' I said. 'I'm in charge here. I give the orders. You understand?'

'Yes.' A breathless croak.

'Good. Come on then.'

Leaving the lantern on the ground, I manhandled him towards the open back door and the darkness beyond.

I wondered why he'd asked me to wait. Perhaps because he wanted an assurance from me that after he had led me to Heidrich, I wouldn't kill the both of them. So maybe, in order to *keep* him compliant, I ought to give him that assurance. Stepping into the sparse and functional kitchen, I said, 'Stop.'

The soldier tensed, but complied. Leaning in close, I said, 'Before we proceed, let me tell you how this is going to go. You're going to take me to Kapitan Heidrich and I'm going to take back what's mine. If you do as I say, no one will get hurt. When I have what I want I'll tie you both up, and then I'll leave, and you'll never see me again. You understand?'

He gave two quick, jerking nods.

'Not good enough. Say if you understand.'

'Yes, yes, I understand.'

'Good. So there's no need to do anything stupid. You're not going to try to be a hero, are you?'

'No,' he whispered.

'Good lad. As long as we understand each other. Now take me to Heidrich. And remember – stay quiet.'

He led me through a door on the opposite side of the kitchen into a narrow corridor with rough stone walls and a stone-flagged floor. My hair and clothes wet from the rain outside, I tried not to shiver. Despite the warm glow of a candle, which was set into a recess in the wall halfway along the corridor, the interior of the house was like an ice-box. In fact, it was arguably colder in here than it had been in the yard.

At the end of the corridor, on the right, was another stout wooden door, from behind which came the sounds of men talking in German, interspersed with gouts of laughter. They sounded drunk, their speech – though I couldn't understand what they were saying – sloppy and slurred, their laughter over-raucous. That was good. If they were drunk it meant their reflexes would be slow.

On the left, curving round and up, was a wooden staircase. It looked uneven, worn, roughly hewn. The handrail atop the twisted and haphazardly spaced support posts of the banister looked like it would give you splinters if you ran your palm across it.

'He is up here,' the young soldier whispered, indicating the staircase.

'Up you go then.'

With my left hand still holding his collar and my right hand holding the gun which I was still pressing to his head, he preceded me up the stairs. Inevitably the steps creaked as we ascended, some so loudly that I clenched my teeth and glanced behind me, certain that the conversation below would dwindle and stop, that the door would suddenly fly open and half a dozen armed and drunken German officers would tumble into the corridor.

But nothing happened. Either the stone walls were thick enough to block the sounds of our ascent or the officers were too drunk or too blasé to investigate. Or maybe they just thought my captive had decided to hit the sack after taking his piss. Maybe they were even now joking about his lack of staying power.

Even so, I was glad when the stairs curved round far enough that we were out of sight of anyone who might emerge from the room below. Even happier when we reached the upper landing.

'Where now?' I asked, looking at the corridor ahead of us, at the four wooden doors – three on our right and one facing us at the end – which were so warped and irregularly-shaped that they looked as though they had been hacked to fit gaps in the bulging stone rather than being part of the farmhouse's original design.

'The second door,' the soldier replied, pointing.

'You're sure about that?'

'Yes, that is Kapitan Heidrich's room. I swear it.'

'Open it.'

I tensed as the young soldier reached out and curled his hand around the doorknob. He had said that Heidrich was asleep, but what if he wasn't? What if he was even now sitting up in bed, reaching for his gun, alerted by the sound of the opening door? Or worse, crouching in ambush, the heart in his hand, ready to unleash its power against me?

I had come to regard the heart as an ally. Up to now it had protected me. But would it continue to do so in the hands of someone else, or would it transfer its loyalty to its new owner? Even now I didn't know.

The young soldier twisted the knob and pushed at the door. It was as badly fitting as it looked, scraping grittily across the floor as it opened.

I shoved the young soldier ahead of me, pretty much using him as a shield. The room was small and square, and at first his body blocked my view of the bed, which was against the wall on our left. When he jerked and cried out, my initial thought was that he'd been shot, even though I'd heard no sound. I half-expected him to fall, but instead he took a quick step backwards, which was so unexpected we almost clashed heads. Thinking he was making an attempt to overpower me, I lunged forward and, still gripping his collar, pushed my left hand downwards against the back of his neck with all my strength in an effort to force him to his knees. Unable to resist the pressure he stumbled and fell, and I staggered forward too, almost sprawling on top of him. I just about managed to regain my balance, and glanced up at the bed, to check what Heidrich was doing.

But Heidrich wasn't doing anything.

Because Heidrich was dead.

He wasn't *just* dead, though. He had been gutted. There was a candle flickering in one of the stone recesses in the wall, and it was illuminating a lot of red and a lot of wetness. Head back and arms out in a cruciform shape, the dead man had been killed with just two cuts. One had slashed so deeply and savagely across his throat that he had been virtually decapitated. The other had opened him up from his Adam's apple to his pubis, releasing not only a hell of a lot of blood, which I realised now was running down the walls and dripping from the ceiling, but also a slippery snake's nest of fat purple intestines. Heidrich, assuming this was him, was naked, and I could see his ribs sticking out through the rent in his chest. I could also see that nestled in the palm of his limp right hand was the obsidian heart.

The shock of finding Heidrich dead, of seeing the violence that had been done to him, and also of realising he was holding the heart, momentarily diverted my attention from the young German officer sprawled at my feet. Unbeknownst to me, my grip had slackened on his collar and my gun arm was now hanging limply by my side. Taking advantage of my lapse of concentration he suddenly rolled on to his back and kicked out, sweeping my legs from under me. I flew sideways as if hit by a car, sheer exhaustion making me feel as if I was light and hollow, my flesh thin as paper, my bones dry old sticks.

I hit the floor so hard my brain jarred in my skull, causing black pixels to swarm across my vision. My overwhelming thought was to keep hold of the gun, but I felt so weak, both physically and mentally, that the revolver flew from my numb fingers and went skidding and clattering across the bare wooden floor.

Fuck, I thought, still struggling to see, still struggling to get my body to do what I wanted it to, *I'm dead.*

I expected the young German to leap over my body, scoop up my gun and turn the tables on me, if not put a bullet in my brain. But instead he was out of the room in an instant, thumping along the corridor, clattering down the stairs.

In my dazed state I heard him yelling for help, his voice shrill, boyish. Although I was still dizzy, I knew I had no more than ten or fifteen seconds before the young German's fellow officers, drunk though they were, would be pounding up the stairs and bursting into the room. Gritting my teeth, I pushed myself up onto all fours, and then I brought my knees up, planted my feet flat on the floor, and rose shakily but as swiftly as I could to a standing position, fingers gripping on to the cold rough wall for support.

The room dipped and swayed. It felt like the cabin of a ship in a terrible storm. I heard a roaring in my ears. The rain outside? The enraged men downstairs? My own blood rushing through my head? I forced myself to turn towards the bed, to focus on the black, blurred shape in the outstretched hands of the corpse. As I stumbled towards it, I heard feet pounding on the stairs.

I slipped in blood, went down on one knee, got up again. The heart was a black pulse, going in and out of focus. I reached out, grasped for it, but my hand swiped through empty air.

I heard a shout behind me, half-turned.

A man was in the doorway. Red complexion, moustache. Shock and outrage on his face. He had a pistol in his hand. He pointed it at me.

I turned away from him, took another step towards the heart, grasped for it again.

As I did, I heard a bang.

TEN

HOME IS WHERE...

The heart was in my hand. The bang was the sound of me hitting a hard floor as if I'd dropped from a height of maybe three or four feet. I was curled up in an almost foetal position, and my knees took the brunt of the impact. Spikes of pain shot up through both kneecaps and seemed to meet and shatter somewhere around my midriff.

Panting for breath, I curled around the pain, trying to contain it. At any moment I expected to be hauled upright, screamed at by a jostling crowd of drunken German officers.

If it wasn't for the nanites in my body, constantly repairing me, I doubt I would have made it this far. But in spite of their ministrations, I was now completely spent. Plastered in mud, spattered with blood, my clothes reeking of death, I must have looked like one of the zombies that had attacked me in No Man's Land. It was almost certainly thanks to the nanites that I hadn't got dysentery like most of the other lads, but even so I knew I'd lost weight these past few weeks. I'm a naturally tall bloke, with a long, lean, slightly knobbly face, so whenever I shed a few pounds I end up looking not healthy but cadaverous.

I don't know how long it took me to realise I'd shifted. When I'd grabbed the heart my instinctive desire had been to return to the trenches, but that wasn't where I was now. As the throbbing pain ebbed – nanites again, doing their stuff – I realised my cheek was resting on some kind of rough material – a carpet! I pushed myself up on shaky arms, and immediately felt nauseous. I leaned over and tried to vomit, expelling only bile, which burned the back of my throat. My eyes watered, my stomach felt as if it was twisting in on itself, my muscles felt on the verge of going into cramp or worse... and then (Praise be to the nanites!) all these sensations smoothed out, and within thirty seconds had melted away.

The first thing I saw when my blurred vision came back into focus was the bed beside which I was kneeling. At the same time, mostly subconsciously, I realised it must be evening, because the room I was in was lit by electric light rather than daylight. As I tentatively sat up, rising above the level of the bed, my attention was grabbed by something which was sitting on the middle of the mostly red duvet. It was a sheet of white A4 paper.

My eyes widened. *No! It couldn't be!* I reached out a filth-caked hand and grabbed the sheet, smearing it with mud. I held it in front of my face and peered at it, my mind racing so quickly that at first the words seemed to jitter and jump on the page. I blinked and concentrated harder and the words settled. I read:

Dear Clover
I'm really sorry, but I've had to go. I know you'll think I'm stupid and reckless, but I don't think I've got a choice...

My hand started to shake so much that I couldn't read any more. But I didn't have to. I knew what the rest of the note said. Because I'd written it myself, about eighteen months ago, just before using the heart to travel back to August 1914. And yet such were the convolutions of time travel that here the note was, as fresh as if I'd finished it only moments ago – which as far as this timeline was concerned I probably had. How long had it sat here undiscovered? How long had I missed myself by? Seconds? Minutes?

My own thoughts were so busy, so *noisy*, that I didn't grasp someone was close by until I heard a floorboard creak outside the room. Frantically, still on my knees, I looked around for the heart, which I only now realised wasn't in my hand. I wondered whether the heart and I had somehow become separated, or even whether it had moved on without me. Then I spotted it, on the floor a foot or so to my right. I groped for it – but too late.

After a perfunctory knock the door opened and Clover stepped into the room, her eyes screwed into a half-squint as if she was afraid of catching me naked or doing something embarrassing. As she entered she was saying, 'Are you all right, Alex? Only I called up three times to let you know the pizza was here and you didn't...'

Then she turned and saw me, and her voice abruptly cut off. The weight of her mouth dropping open seemed to yank her eyes wide. She stared at me in horror.

I stared back.

It was the first time I'd seen her for over a year and I was immediately overcome by a flood of emotions. Maybe if I hadn't been in such a raw and traumatised state I would have been able to stay in control – who knows? Although Clover and I had become friends almost by default, having been brought together by a common enemy, I can only describe the love and affection I felt for her at that moment as both deep and familial. To my shame (I'm not generally given to blubbering like a goon) it was also powerful enough to break through my defences and make me crumble into tears.

'Oh God, Alex,' she said, her shock wrong-footing her, causing her to half-stumble into the room. 'What the fuck's happened to you? Who's done this?'

I couldn't answer. Now that the floodgates had opened, there was no way they could be forced shut. The nanites inside me might have been able to repair me physically, but they were useless against naked emotions.

Raising a hand, I waved it feebly, as if to say: *give me a minute*. I couldn't see her through my tears, but I heard her drop to her knees in front of me, felt her grab the hand I was waving and squeeze it hard.

'You're filthy,' she said. 'And you stink. And you're covered in blood. Christ, what have they done to you?' She paused, as if drawing breath. Then I sensed her going still, stiffening, and I knew that she was putting two and two together; that having regarded me properly for the first time, having perhaps registered what I was wearing, the penny was beginning to drop. She was silent for ten, maybe fifteen seconds, and when she next spoke her voice was different. Hurt. Accusatory.

'You've been travelling, haven't you? You used the heart without telling me?'

Try as I might to stop them, the tears were still gushing out of me.

But now I was keeping my head down and my gaze averted not because of that – or not entirely anyway – but because I felt guilty, ashamed, of lying to her, letting her down. The note I'd written, now mud-smeared and partly crumpled, was on the floor by my left knee. I pushed it towards her, felt it slither beneath my fingertips as she snatched it up.

It's amazing how the crackle of paper can convey tension and disapproval. As she read the note I made an attempt to pull myself together. I pushed the heels of my hands into my eye sockets, tried to contain my snivelling by alternately swallowing and taking deep breaths. Once I'd managed to force the floodgates shut again, I raised my head and looked at her blearily. I was embarrassed by my outburst, even though I knew it was nothing to be embarrassed about. I'd seen men break down in the trenches who'd been subjected to far less stress than I had in the past few hours.

'The plan was that I wouldn't be here when you read that,' I said, my voice clogged. 'That went a bit wrong, didn't it?'

She sighed, looked at me. It was impossible to read her expression. In a softer voice than she'd used moments before, she asked, 'How long have you been away?'

'Eighteen months,' I said.

She flinched as if someone had touched her neck with a cold hand. 'Eighteen months! Are you serious?'

'Afraid so.'

She reached out, and at first I thought she was going to slap me. But instead she touched my chest gently, as if checking whether my uniform was genuine.

'You've been in the War? The trenches?'

I nodded.

Something flickered across her face. The threat of tears? But whatever it was, she brought it under control. Her voice, though, was husky.

'Why didn't you tell me?'

'I did tell you. In the note.'

This time it was anger that flashed in her eyes. 'Don't be smart, Alex. I deserve more than that.'

'Sorry. I didn't mean to be smart. It was just...'

'Just what?'

I squirmed, struggling to express myself. 'Well, I could hardly have taken you with me, could I? War is men's work.' I pulled a face to show I was joking. 'At least, it was back then. And I just thought... if I went and did what I was supposed to do – what I *had* to do – then maybe I could be back before you knew I'd even gone.' I nodded at the note she was still holding in her hand. 'That was just meant to be insurance. In case anything went wrong.'

'But what about the heart?' she said. 'What about the danger of that? Of using it? Last time you tried, it nearly killed you.'

I forced a smile. A weak attempt to make light of the situation. 'It nearly killed me this time too. But it was something I had to go through. A gamble I had to take. To keep things on the right path.' Stumblingly I told her what had happened – about my future self rescuing me, about the nanites in my system.

She reached out and touched my chest again. 'And they're inside you now? Those tiny robots?'

'Yep. Like a swarm of microscopic doctors, ticking things off on their little charts.'

She shuddered. 'Creepy.'

'It's just science, that's all. Science that's not available to us yet.'

'It's the origin story of a villain in a bloody superhero movie, is what it is. This is how it always starts. Some normal bloke tries some snazzy new scientific doo-dah on himself, which then goes wrong and turns him into a...'

'Mutant?' I suggested.

'I was going to say "monster".'

'Oh, thanks. So that's what you think I'll become? A monster?'

She groaned and clapped her hands to her cheeks.

'I don't know. This is such a lot to take in. Twenty minutes ago you were FaceTiming Hope before popping upstairs for a lie-down while I ordered pizza. And now...' She wafted a hand almost exasperatedly at me. '...all this. I mean... you really haven't seen me for *eighteen months?*'

I shook my head. 'And I can't tell you how good it is.'

'Not seeing me?'

My laughter sounded like a weary cough. 'The opposite. It's *so* good to see you. So good to be back here.'

'And you're done now, are you? You're back for good?'

'I wish I was.'

'What do you mean?' Her eyes narrowed. 'Don't tell me you're going back?'

'I *have* to, Clover. I've got no choice. You know as well as I do what'll happen if I don't.'

She sighed. I could see she was struggling. Not to understand – she knew what was at stake – but simply to allow me to go through it without her help. By default we had become a team, but in this instance there was nothing she could do, no way she could watch my back.

Struggling to make it easier for her, I said, 'Look, don't worry. I've got the heart, remember. I can be there and back before you know it.'

'If you survive.'

'I will. I promise.'

She glared at me. 'Don't make promises you can't keep. I'm not a child. I know how this works.'

I held up my hands in apology – and was struck by the fact that ten minutes earlier, if I hadn't got to the heart in time, I might have been doing the same thing under different circumstances.

Her expression softened. 'You look done in. *Really* done in. You don't have to go back straight away, do you?'

I hesitated. Weirdly I couldn't help thinking that if I *didn't* go back straight away I'd be cheating somehow. The other guys going through the War with me, sharing the hell of trench life, didn't get any respite, so why should I? On the other hand, this was not my war. I was born in 1977, for fuck's sake! I was a man out of time.

'You look as though you need a good meal and a sleep,' Clover said. 'And you *definitely* need a bath. Much as I love you, Alex, you stink like road kill.'

'It's this coat. I had to nick it from a dead German to disguise myself. He wasn't too fresh. In fact, he was oozing a bit.'

She bulged out her cheeks, as though trying to keep in a mouthful of puke. 'That may be the grossest thing I've ever heard. That may even put me off my pizza.'

Pizza. I briefly closed my eyes and actually shivered with pleasure at the thought.

'Well, it doesn't put me off. I'll have yours as well as mine if you don't want it.'

She smiled a crooked smile. 'I'll run a bath for you. Do you want me to wash those clothes?'

'Better not. It'd be weird if I arrived back in the trenches looking spotless.' With an effort, my limbs so tired I could hardly manipulate them, I struggled out of the overcoat. 'You can chuck this, though. Or preferably burn it. I won't be needing it again.'

She pulled a face, picking the coat up by pinching the edge of its collar between her thumb and forefinger, holding it at arm's length. She carried it across the room to the open door. At the threshold she paused.

'Why *did* you come back? Why here and now, I mean? I can understand you needing a break, but if you didn't want me to find out what you'd been up to, why didn't you come back to a time when you knew the house would be empty?' She nodded at the heart, which was still lying on the carpet a foot or so away from me. 'I thought you had better control over that thing. I mean, I knew it made you ill, but in terms of where and when, I thought you just had to think of the date and place and there you'd be.'

'Me too,' I said, and rubbed a filthy hand over my filthy forehead. 'But I was stressed and exhausted. Maybe I wasn't thinking straight. I didn't even mean to have a break at all, to be honest. I meant to go back to the trenches. Maybe the heart... I dunno... picked up on my subconscious or something. Maybe it brought me where I needed to be rather than where I wanted to be.'

Still standing by the open door, Clover was peering at the heart, a frown on her face. 'Is it okay, the heart? It looks... different somehow.'

'Yes, it's fine,' I said automatically. But when I looked down at the heart, when I looked at it properly for the first time since I'd got here, I realised she was right: it *did* look different.

'It's just got mud on it,' I said. 'From my hands.' Though even as I spoke the words I knew it was an attempt to convince myself rather than because I truly believed them. Then, when I picked up the heart and felt how light it was, my worst fears were confirmed: there *was* something wrong with it. Something seriously wrong.

Cupping the heart in my palm as if it were a sick hamster or an injured bird, I held it up to my face and examined it. As well as feeling light, as if all the life had been drained from it, it looked dull and misshapen, its fine detail scoured away, like the face of a stone gargoyle on the outside wall of a church that has been eroded by the elements.

I touched it with my fingertip, and realised it was brittle and flaky, shreds of it coming away and leaving a residue on my skin. I felt a spasm of alarm, which manifested as a stab of actual pain somewhere between my breastbone and my belly.

'It's sick,' I said, as if the heart *were* a pet. 'There's something wrong with it.'

'It looks old,' Clover said. 'Ancient, in fact.'

Her words transported me back to my time in Victorian London, to a night just after the Christmas of 1895 when Hawkins and I had been lured to a riverside dock called Blyth's Wharf in Limehouse. The Dark Man and his cronies had been waiting for us there, and in his possession that night the Dark Man had had a heart which looked, if anything, even more ravaged than the one I held now.

Could it be possible...? My mind raced as I thought again of the dead rising from the mud of No Man's Land; of Heidrich's savagely mutilated body; of the way the heart had been nestled snugly – and conveniently – in his outstretched hand.

'It was him,' I breathed.

'Who?' When I didn't immediately answer, Clover's voice hardened. 'Alex, who do you mean? What are you talking about?'

I looked up at her, my mind still whirling. 'The Dark Man. He was there. He must have been. He knew what would happen, so he took advantage of the situation. He stole my heart and left his old one in its place. That's why it didn't take me where I wanted to go. Because it's... malfunctioning. It's clapped out. Unreliable.'

'But the Dark Man's dead,' said Clover, and then she checked herself. 'Hang on. I get it. Time travel, yeah? The Dark Man you mean is an earlier version, before he died.' She checked herself again, rolled her eyes. In a goofy voice she said, 'Duh. Obviously.'

'Shit,' I muttered, looking at the brittle, gnarled lump of stone in my hand and trying to work through the implications. 'Shit, fuck and bollocks.'

'Sounds like a pretty accurate summing up of the situation,' she said, though her expression told me she was thinking hard too.

Sure enough, a few seconds later she said, 'We saw the Dark Man die in Victorian London, yeah? He was so fucked-up that the power of the heart – your heart, I mean – was too much for him and it killed him.'

'So?'

'So,' she said, 'judging by *that* heart,' (she nodded at the one in my hand) 'which is old, but I'm guessing not as old as the one the Dark Man showed you back in 1895, the Dark Man who took your heart and left you *that* one must be pretty old too – but he must be young enough to be able to handle the power, or at least he thinks he is. I guess it depends on whether he knows what happened to the older version of himself or not.'

I scowled. 'None of this is helping. Whether he knows or not, the fact is, he's got my... *Ferrari* of a heart, whereas I've been left with his old, clapped-out Hillman Imp.'

A wave of despair washed through me, and seemed to take with it what little energy I had left. I slumped forward until my forehead was resting on the carpet.

'So how the fuck am I going to find him and get my own heart back now?' I said.

ELEVEN

IN LIMBO

I had no idea what to do next.

So for the next few days I did nothing.

Well, no, that's not strictly true. I spent a lot of time shut away with the heart, trying to 'commune' with it as I'd done on several occasions before. This involved holding the heart in my hand and staring at it until my perception changed and I slipped into a meditative, almost trance-like state, whereupon the heart would seem to blur, to shimmer, to both shift out of phase and become intrinsically linked to my mind.

Although I'd had visions before, I didn't know – particularly on this occasion – how much of what I'd seen had been conjured from my own subconscious and how much had been a consequence of the heart gifting me the ability to view the world through *its* eyes. I *do* know that whereas before I'd let my mind roam free, had let it go wherever the heart, or my own subconscious, had wanted to take me, this time I was more tentative. Because of the state of this particular heart, I didn't know how reliable it was, or how dangerous. I didn't want to risk using it to travel, not yet anyway, because who knew what might happen or where I might end up? If it had brought me here when I had intended to go back to the trenches, who was to say that next time it wouldn't simply return me to my starting point – the farmhouse in the German camp, where I'd have to face down a horde of drunken German soldiers who thought I'd murdered one of their comrades? Or maybe it would plunge me into the midst of the Dark Man and his cohorts? Or what if it simply shattered through overuse and I shattered along with it, my pieces scattered through time?

My aim, during these 'communing' sessions, was to see whether I could somehow get the 'old' heart to link with its younger self, or at least give me some clue as to where or when the Dark Man might have gone with it – though to what end I don't know.

'Maybe this is what's *supposed* to happen,' Clover said, trying to reassure me.

'Well, if it is, why the fuck doesn't someone enlighten me? Why doesn't a future version of me pop back to explain what I'm supposed to do next?'

The simple fact was, I was in limbo, and I'm afraid that didn't make me easy to live with. I stomped about the place, being grumpy and snappy, feeling like a caged animal.

'Maybe you should just look at this as a chance to recuperate for a while,' Clover suggested one evening as I sat slumped miserably in front of the fire.

I scowled at her. 'I don't want to fucking recuperate.'

'Because you're enjoying the War so much you're eager to get back to it?'

I glared at her. 'Do you know how fucking insensitive that question is? If you had any inkling of what it's like in those fucking trenches—'

'Stop!' she barked, raising a hand. 'Just stop right there!'

Now we were both glaring at each other. In a steely voice she said, 'I'm sick of you mooching around, whining like a spoiled brat. *That's* why I said what I said – because you're driving me up the wall. Now, I'm going to get a bottle of good red wine and we're going to sit by the fire and talk this through. Okay?'

Frustration that manifested itself as anger was still boiling inside me, but I could see how earnest she was, how much she wanted to help. It caused my anger to evaporate a little, leaving a residue of melancholy tiredness behind.

I rubbed a hand over my face. 'Okay,' I said. 'Sounds good.'

And it *was* good. Good just to sit by the fire and drink fine wine and talk things through.

Admittedly we didn't get very far. We didn't come up with any answers. But it untangled the angry knots inside my head, helped me see that when it boiled down to it I had two choices.

Either I could do nothing and hope that at some point Fate would intervene, as it had in the past.

Or I could be both proactive and reckless. I could try using the heart, whether to take me back to the trenches or in pursuit of the Dark Man, and see what happened – which I guess was merely another way of giving myself up to Fate, albeit in this case having first given Fate a boot up the backside to stir it into action.

'Is that all we are, though?' I said, swirling the wine round in my glass, enjoying the way the firelight turned it into a glowing, blood-red whirlpool. 'Puppets? Creatures of Fate? No will of our own?'

'Guess we'll never really know, will we?' We were well into the second bottle and Clover's words were slightly slurred by now, her eyes sleepy with heat and alcohol. 'Do we do what we do because we choose to or because we're meant to? It's an enigma. An enigma wrapped in a conum... com... comundrum.' She pushed herself to her feet and gave a cat-like stretch. 'And with that tongue-twister I'm off to bed. G'night.'

After she'd gone I took the heart from my pocket and sat staring at it again, my eyes smarting, my thoughts fuzzy. I'd seen the Dark Man die in this very room, had seen the heart consume him. But what did that mean? That the future was secure? That I was destined to get *my* heart back, leaving him with his? Or was the Dark Man a rogue element, a trickster who rode roughshod over the timelines, twisting and breaking them without compunction? Maybe, by stealing my heart, he had already caused things to start unravelling? I couldn't help but see time as a complex plait, composed of many threads, all of which were now not only fraying, but actually coming apart, each strand separating from the others and spinning off into God knew where.

Or maybe that was bollocks. Who knew whether our actions were already pre-ordained, part of some great cosmic scheme or structure from which there was no possibility of deviation, or whether we had been given free will, in which case every little thing we did, every decision we made, subtly – or maybe not so subtly – altered all our pasts and presents and futures, creating a multiverse, a realm of endless alternate realities?

The questions swirling in my head felt like a multiverse in themselves, a cascade forever tumbling and intertwining, never coming to rest. *Was* there an answer, or answers, to these questions somewhere? And more to the point, would I ever find those answers?

'Do I want to?' I murmured to myself. 'Do I want to know everything?'

Still holding the heart, my mind broke up, my consciousness washed away in the torrent of thoughts and questions that were rushing through it. And in front of the fireplace from which, over a century before, I had seen a shape-shifter emerge in the form of a black crow and kill my butler and friend Hawkins, I fell asleep.

And dreamed.

I have an impression of noise, people, dim lighting. I'm with someone, but I don't know who it is. My attention is drawn to a figure across the room. It's as if we're linked in some way, but at the same time I feel repelled by the figure; it exudes an aura of horror or dread. Although I'm staring directly at it I can't seem to properly focus on it. Is it standing in shadow, or is its face partly concealed, perhaps by a hood or a mask? I know the figure is aware of me, and when it sees me looking at it, it turns and flees. Although I'm afraid, I immediately give chase.

It was a simple dream, and yet it seemed forbidding, overwhelming, as if it possessed a peculiar and terrible darkness all its own. And although I thought I had remembered all of it, in my memory it still seemed somehow more protracted than my telling of it, as if each individual second had been saturated, engorged, with its own dreadful significance.

Despite feeling sure I'd recollected the dream in its entirety, I nevertheless had the sense that something had happened within it that had shocked me out of it, though when I snapped awake, shivering and disorientated in front of the grey embers of the fire, weak daylight leaking through the gaps in the curtains, I couldn't for the life of me remember what it was.

I was still gripping the heart. Gripping it so hard that my white-knuckled fingers ached when I uncurled them. Slipping it into the pocket of the hoodie I was wearing, I looked at my palm and saw a black imprint had been left there, like a charred stigmata. I staggered upstairs, and into the bathroom. After turning on the tap, however, I paused, my hand hovering inches from the column of running water.

Was it wise to wash part of the heart down the sink?

'Fuck it,' I muttered, and put my hand under the running tap. Because when it came down to it, what else could I do? Even if I cleaned my hand with a Wet Wipe, and then burned the Wet Wipe, the particles would still end up in the air, where they'd be breathed in, absorbed.

Besides, it wasn't as if the heart was something alien. It was of the earth, part of the planet. I had seen myself as its creator, forging it from the clay and sand with my bare hands. It was ancient and elemental; it was a repository for primal forces.

My head was pounding. I leaned forward over the sink until my forehead was resting against the cool glass of the mirror.

'You look how I feel.'

My skin squeaked against the glass when I turned my head. Clover was standing in the bathroom doorway in a white vest top and blue-and-yellow checked pyjama bottoms. She looked pasty, though her eyes were dark-ringed, partly due to smudged mascara, which she'd evidently been too tipsy to remove before going to bed.

'What time is it?' I asked.

She held up her mobile. 'Nine twenty-two. I had a text from Jackie, Hope's nurse at the hospital. She wants to see us.'

'Which one?'

'What?'

I closed my eyes. My thoughts still felt jumbled and jittery. 'Who wants us to see us? Jackie or Hope?'

'Oh. Jackie.'

'Why?'

'I don't know. She doesn't say.'

'Is Hope all right?'

'As far as I know. She was yesterday when I spoke to her. So do you think you can find a window in your busy schedule?'

The question was delivered as nothing more than a gentle quip, but I was in the mood for neither banter nor sarcasm.

'What time?'

'Jackie asked if we could be at the hospital by midday. That's when she has her lunch break.'

'Sure. I'll need a shower first, though.'

'And I need coffee,' said Clover. 'Lots and lots of it.'

We arrived at the hospital at ten to twelve. The plan was to speak to Jackie first, who I'd met a couple of times, and then go see Hope afterwards.

When we entered the swish foyer of Oak Hill, Jackie, a slim, attractive, dark-haired woman of about thirty, rose from one of the plush armchairs in the waiting area and came hurrying towards us, hand outstretched.

'Hi,' she said. 'Thanks for agreeing to see me.'

Her velvety voice had the barest hint of a Welsh accent. Her large chestnut-coloured eyes regarded us earnestly beneath a fringe that seemed to be balanced on her long upper lashes.

'No problem,' Clover said, shaking her proffered hand.

It was only when I shook it too that it struck me for the first time how small and fine-boned she was. My own hand swamped hers.

'Shall we grab a coffee?' Jackie said, gesturing towards an open door on the left-hand side of the wood-panelled corridor behind her, beyond which I knew was The Library Café, whose walls were lined with shelves of leather-bound books. 'My shout.'

'Sounds good,' said Clover.

When I nodded Jackie gave me a quick, hesitant smile, then turned and led the way.

Once we were installed around a corner table with our various beverages – a cappuccino for Jackie, a mocha for Clover and a double espresso for me (I needed the caffeine kick) – Jackie said, 'As I'm sure you've guessed, I wanted to talk to you about Hope.'

She was clearly nervous, and that made me nervous too. Anyone who spent any time with Hope, as Jackie had, would realise pretty quickly that she was anything but a normal girl. I braced myself for a barrage of questions – and hoped not only that I'd remember the fictional back-story that Clover and I had hastily worked out in the car on the way over, but also that I'd be able to make it sound convincing as I lied through my teeth.

'Okay,' Clover said easily, and sipped her mocha, leaving the floor open for Jackie to continue.

Jackie glanced briefly at each of us and then down at her drink, her finger prodding at the handle of her china mug as if she didn't quite trust it. A little falteringly she said, 'She's a lovely girl. A real sweetie. My son Ed thinks so too. This last week or two they've become great friends.'

'We heard,' said Clover. 'Hope talks about him all the time. And also about you. Thank you for being so kind to her.'

Jackie smiled, and this time it was less hesitant, more genuine. It turned her from an attractive woman into a beautiful one.

'It's no effort at all. Hope makes it easy for me. She's a model patient.'

'But?' I said.

Her smile slipped. 'Pardon?'

'There must be a but. I'm sure you haven't asked to see us just to tell us how lovely she is.'

Clover flashed me the briefest of frowns, as if to let me know I was being too aggressive, too confrontational.

'No,' Jackie said, 'I haven't.' She picked up her mug, then put it down again. 'It's just... well, do you mind... can I ask... what's the situation with Hope?'

'The situation?' Clover said.

Jackie's cheeks were reddening. 'I don't want to cause offence. And I don't want you to think I'm being nosy. But... well, Hope tells me you're not her parents. She says you're not even married... though you pretend to people that you are.'

'Is that a problem?' I said, making an effort *not* to sound confrontational.

'Of course not,' said Jackie, a little too shrilly, then she glanced around to check she wasn't attracting attention. Unless they were being terribly polite, the customers sitting at the only other two occupied tables seemed embroiled in their own conversations. In a quieter voice she said, 'If what Hope says is true, then of course your reasons are entirely your own affair–'

'But you're concerned for her welfare?' said Clover.

'Well, yes. But not because I think you've been mistreating her, or anything. It's obvious that Hope loves and trusts both of you, and that you've treated her well...'

'But her "situation", as you called it, still makes you uncomfortable?'

'Well... not uncomfortable as such...'

'Curious then?'

Despite what she had said, Jackie *did* look uncomfortable. 'I'm sorry, it's just... there seem to be so many loose threads. And Hope herself is... well, it's as if she's been kept in isolation all her life. The gaps in her knowledge are... startling. As I say, I know it's none of my business, but the thing is, I do *care* about Hope. I've grown to care about her *a lot*. And I thought...'

'You thought you owed it to her to find out if she's safe?' said Clover gently.

'Well, partly that.'

'She is,' I said. 'You don't have to worry about that. We care about her as much as you do. All we want is for her to be happy and healthy, to have a good life.'

'Oh, I don't doubt it,' said Jackie. 'And I really do mean that. You can call me naive if you want, but... well, you get a feel for people, don't you? And often you can tell, by how children behave, whether they're being mistreated, and I know that Hope isn't. Despite all she's been through, with her arm, I mean, she's a happy little girl. Happy and bright and... *loved*.'

Clover was nodding. 'She is,' she said. 'She is loved.' Then she paused and looked at me. 'Should we tell her?'

I frowned, playing my part. 'They'd have our guts for garters if we did.'

'Only if they find out,' said Clover, 'and I'm not going to tell them. Are you?'

I snorted. 'Course not.'

Jackie was staring at us, wide-eyed, her fingers gripping the edge of the table, as if she was anticipating a bumpy ride. Her lips were pursed as if she dare not speak, or even breathe.

'Jackie, can we trust you?' Clover asked earnestly.

Jackie nodded, and hesitantly said, 'Y-yes, of course.'

Clover looked at me. 'What do you think, Alex?'

I stared at Jackie until her eyes flickered away from me, as if I was evaluating both her and the situation. I shrugged. 'On your head be it.'

Clover leaned in, as though to take Jackie into her confidence, and almost unconsciously Jackie leaned in too.

'What I'm going to tell you must not be repeated,' Clover said. 'This is a delicate situation, and we're only taking you into our confidence in order to impress upon you the importance of discretion in this matter. Do you understand?'

'Yes,' Jackie whispered.

'Good. We're very grateful to you for lavishing so much care and attention on Hope – aren't we, Alex?'

I nodded.

'That little girl has been through a lot,' Clover said. 'And it's our job to protect her.'

'Job?'

Clover nodded. 'Alex and I are undercover police officers. We rescued Hope after a raid on a people-trafficking ring in East London four months ago.'

Jackie's hand flew to her mouth. 'Oh my God.'

'We don't know anything about Hope's background. We don't know where she came from, who her parents are or were, or how and when she lost her arm. When we found her she was filthy, malnourished and all but feral. Her captors had been keeping her in a cage so small she couldn't even stand up.'

'Oh God,' Jackie breathed again, her eyes now glittering with tears. 'That's... *horrific*.'

'What we *do* know, and thank God for it,' Clover continued, 'is that she hadn't been sexually abused. And aside from the obvious neglect and the injury to her arm, there were no signs she had been physically abused either. For the past few months she's been living in a safe house with Alex and I, and together with a number of household staff we've been carefully rehabilitating her. The state of her arm has been a major worry, particularly with regard to infection, but the medical team who've been monitoring her round-the-clock initially made the decision to delay the added trauma of an operation until it was thought she'd be psychologically able to cope with it.

'Happily, though, as you can see for yourself, she's come on in leaps and bounds in a very short time – in fact, her progress has been remarkable. And now that her arm has been repaired there's no reason why she can't go on to live a happy and healthy life.'

Tears had spilled from Jackie's eyes and formed glittering lines down her cheeks. Looking shell-shocked, she wiped them delicately away with the tips of her fingers.

'So... what'll happen now?' she asked, her voice throaty with tears. 'Will Hope be taken into care?'

I shook my head. 'She'll live with me.'

'With you?' It was clear from Jackie's tone that she had already decided I was a forbidding and unapproachable presence. 'With your family, you mean?'

I hesitated. 'I don't... I have a daughter, but my wife doesn't live with us. I have two daughters, in fact.'

I realised straight away that that sounded neither convincing nor reassuring, and sure enough Jackie looked troubled.

'You don't sound very sure.'

I cleared my throat. 'I *am* sure. It's just... it's a complicated situation.'

Clover reached across the table and rested a hand on Jackie's forearm. 'Believe me, Jackie, Hope's future welfare is our main priority. That little girl will get the best of everything.'

I nodded in agreement, but even I was wondering how Hope would fit into my present lifestyle and how I – or we, if Clover continued to be part of my somewhat uncertain household – would be able to provide her with security and protection, given our current circumstances.

Jackie took a deep breath, and then, speaking quickly as though to get it out before either we could stop her or she could change her mind, she said, 'Why don't *I* take her?'

I blinked. 'You?'

'Yes.' She sat up straighter in her chair and drew back her shoulders, as if gathering her courage. 'Why not? It's not such a crazy idea, is it?'

Clover glanced at me, then said slowly, 'When you say take her...'

'I mean adopt her. Legally. She and Ed get on so well it would be lovely if they could be together all the time. And I always wanted more children, but after Ed, well... I couldn't. And Steve, my husband, and I, we've got plenty of room – we live in a big old farmhouse in a lovely village about five miles from here. There's a lovely village school, which Ed and Hope could go to together. And Ed would look after her – not that he'd need to, of course. Hope is such a lovely girl that she would soon make friends. It would be...'

'Lovely?' said Clover with a smile.

Jackie had become flushed with the enthusiasm of her idea, but now she smiled wryly.

'Well, yes, but I was going to say "ideal".' She looked at us eagerly. 'It would be, though, wouldn't it? She'd have a settled family environment – not that I'm saying yours isn't settled. And you could both visit her any time you wanted to.'

She brought a hand up to her mouth in an almost child-like gesture, which I found oddly charming.

'Sorry. I'm getting ahead of myself. It's probably an impossible idea, isn't it? A pipe dream?'

'Actually...' Clover looked at me. 'Maybe it isn't. What do you think, Alex?'

I looked at Clover, and then at Jackie. Aside from the emotional wrench of letting Hope go, of effectively giving away the little girl I'd rescued from certain death in Tallarian's laboratory, I was actually thinking it was a wonderful idea. With Jackie and her family, Hope would have love and stability, and she would be far from the danger and uncertainty that Clover and I were likely to have to contend with in the foreseeable future. Plus it would solve any potential problems that might have arisen if – *when* – I eventually managed to get Kate back.

I nodded slowly. 'It might work,' I said. 'In fact, it might be the ideal solution for Hope – if she's agreeable to it, of course.'

As we were to find out a short time later, she *was* agreeable. In fact, she was more than agreeable; she was ecstatic.

'Yay!' she yelled, bouncing up and down on her bed, her eyes blazing with joy. 'Yay!'

'Are you really so desperate to see the back of us?' I asked, but I was grinning.

Hope scrambled down off her bed and gave me a clumsy clout with her artificial arm. 'Course not, silly! You'll come and see me every week. You *will* come and see me, won't you?'

'You just try and stop us,' I said.

'And we'll FaceTime too,' said Clover. 'You'll be sick of the sight of us.'

'No I won't,' Hope protested.

It was wonderful to see Hope looking so happy and lively. Although in this timeline it was only a few days since our last meeting, in the eighteen months that had passed for me between then and now she seemed to have become an entirely different girl to the one who, a few weeks earlier, had left Victorian London and accompanied Clover and me to the twenty-first century.

Jackie had left it to the two of us to propose her adoption idea to Hope, saying it would be unfair on Hope if Jackie were there to see her reaction and hear her verdict. Instead of accompanying us, Jackie elected to wait in the café, and it was there I found her fifteen minutes after leaving her, looking like a patient anxiously awaiting crucial test results. The fearful anticipation in her eyes when she looked at me as I walked in convinced me that Hope would be going to the best home Clover and I could have wished for.

'She loves the idea,' I said. 'It's a yes.'

'Oh!' said Jackie, as if shocked, and then, with genuine delight, '*Oh!*'

Then she burst into tears. I crossed the room and enfolded her in a hug, which might have surprised her, but which she seemed grateful for.

'I'm so happy,' she said, her shoulders shaking and her voice muffled against my chest. She was so tiny that hugging her wasn't all that different from hugging Hope. 'I'll look after her, I promise.'

'I know you will,' I said.

The four of us celebrated with chocolate cake bought from the café (Jackie getting teary-eyed again, but laughing, when Hope asked, 'When I come to live with you, am I to call you Jackie or Mum, like Ed does?') and then Clover and I gave the two of them hugs and left, promising we'd be back soon.

Crunching across the gravel forecourt towards the car, Clover asked, 'How do you feel? About the prospect of Hope going to live with Jackie, I mean?'

'Grateful that at least one of our stories will have a happy ending,' I said. 'Hope'll have a wonderful life with Jackie and her family.'

Clover nodded. 'I think so too.'

As I was folding my long legs into the passenger seat of the car, my mobile rang. I twisted myself awkwardly to prise it from my jeans and prodded the 'Answer' button. 'Hello?'

'Alex,' a voice said bluntly, 'it's Benny Magee.'

'Benny,' I said, earning a raised-eyebrow look from Clover in the driver's seat. 'How are things?'

Ignoring the question, Benny said, 'I'm not promising anything, but it looks as if one of my contacts might have come up trumps.'

It was so long since I'd seen him that I was momentarily thrown.

'What do you mean?'

'What do you think I mean? I've got a lead on your missing daughter. My bloke reckons he knows where she is.'

TWELVE

BIG MOMENT

'I don't like this,' I said.

Clover, who was driving, shot a scowl in my direction. 'Oh, for God's sake, Alex, we've already been through this a million times. Read my lips: *It's not a trap.*'

I slumped further into my seat, arms crossed tightly over my churning stomach.

'Yeah, but how do you know? He's done the dirty on me before. Who's to say he won't again?'

We were following Benny's grey Jag through increasingly wild countryside. For the past half-hour the roads had been getting narrower and hillier, the hedges flanking us higher and more unkempt, and the sight of buildings and people increasingly scarce. As if to compound my mood of foreboding the skies had been growing darker too, the previously wispy white clouds now multiplying into a gloomy mass above us, squeezing out the light and throwing the surrounding fields and hills into shadow.

As Clover sighed, the first drops of rain began to fall, splatting on the windscreen like transparent bugs. She switched on the wipers and said with exaggerated patience, 'Let's break this down, shall we? Let's look at the facts. *Again.* Number one, Benny's motivated by money, and you've already said you'll pay more than whoever else might approach him to do the dirty on you. Number two, he's shit-scared of the Wolves of London. Facing them took him *way* out of his comfort zone, and I personally don't think he'd go near them again even if they offered him ten times what you could pay – which, before you say anything, I know contradicts my first point, but fuck it. Number three, despite the fact that he's a cold-hearted bastard, I genuinely believe he has proper father-daughter-type feelings for me, and would never knowingly put me in danger. And number four, you've seen the photographic evidence.'

I was silent for a few moments. I looked out of the window so I didn't have to meet her exasperated gaze. The way the tree trunks and the crumbling stone walls had turned black and gleaming in the rain reminded me of the obsidian heart – my heart, that was, not the dull and brittle version I was currently carrying around in my pocket.

Wearily I said, 'Photographs can be faked. And how do we know Benny himself isn't being taken for a ride? How do we know that wasn't the shape-shifter on that picture we saw? How do we know we're not *all* being lured into a trap?'

'Because... what would be the point?' Clover said. 'The Dark Man has the heart – *your* heart. So why would he need to do that?'

I shrugged. 'To kill us. To stop us hunting him down.'

'But why expend the time and energy to drag us all the way out here? Presumably, with your heart he can go anywhere, do anything. If he wanted to kill us, he could do it any time, any place. He wouldn't have to go to the trouble of luring us into an elaborate trap.'

'Maybe he's as tied to circumstances and situations as we are? Maybe he doesn't want to upset the apple cart in case it fucks everything up for him too.'

'Maybe, maybe, maybe,' Clover muttered. 'Why can't you just be optimistic for once? Don't you *want* to believe?'

I could have responded angrily to that – of *course* I wanted to believe that my missing daughter was waiting for me at the end of this journey; there was nothing I wanted to believe *more* – but I knew Clover was only asking the question out of frustration at my cynicism. Or was it pessimism? Maybe both.

'Who are you? Fox Mulder?' I said, aiming for jokey and ending up closer to snide.

She glanced at me again, I guess because she was unable to gauge my mood from my voice, and her expression softened a little. 'If I am, that makes you Dana Scully.'

I snorted a laugh. 'I just... don't want to get my hopes up, that's all. After everything we've been through, it's hard to believe my search might end at a little Welsh farmhouse in the back of beyond. It all seems too abrupt, too...'

'Anti-climactic?'

'I suppose. Does that sound stupid?'

'No, not stupid. But I think you expect this whole thing, this quest of yours, to culminate in some great showdown, some final battle. But things don't always work out that way. Real life is far less dramatic and more predictable.'

'Maybe.'

'There's no maybe about it. It's true.'

'Okay, okay,' I said, raising my hands as if to ward off an attack.

'So let's just go with the flow for now, shall we? Let's keep an open mind and see how things work out.'

'Yes, boss,' I said.

The rain abruptly increased, dashing against the car with a light, clattering hiss that made me think of spilled paperclips, and instantly transforming the windscreen into a writhing mass of colourless jelly. The brake lights of Benny's car were twin smears of glowing red ahead of us. Clover coolly flicked a lever and with a rapid and repeated creaking the wipers doubled their speed, sweeping away arcs of rainwater before they could properly form on the glass.

As she hunched over the wheel to concentrate more fully on the road ahead, we lapsed into a silence that was filled only with the sound of rain and the constant sigh of the heater as it buffeted us with soft waves of delicious warmth. Despite – or perhaps partly because of – the nervous tension that thrummed through my body like the onset of fever, I started to feel drowsy. I closed my eyes and thought about Benny's phone call earlier that afternoon, about how my brain had seemed to freeze and my body lock at his words.

'My... daughter?' I finally managed to say after he'd told me about the lead one of his contacts had given him. 'You mean Kate?'

Laconically he'd said, 'How many other missing daughters have you got?'

'No, I mean... who is this contact? What has he heard? And who from?'

'That's all irrelevant, Alex. It's just people I know asking people they know asking people they know. Their names aren't important. What *is* important is that we've got a location. It's a cottage in Wales, middle of nowhere. It's being rented by a young couple who've got two kids with them, a boy and a girl, both about five years old. All the descriptions match. And I've got a photo.'

'Of Kate?' I sounded like someone trying to speak whilst being strangled.

'No, of the geezer. The dad. Give me two ticks and I'll send it to you.'

About fifteen seconds later the image arrived in my inbox. I clicked on it, expanded it with trembling fingers, and my heart gave a lurch. Fuck, it *was* him! Linley Sherwood – or Adam as he was known in the twenty-first century. He was standing side on to the photographer, who from the fuzzy nature of the photograph had clearly been some distance away from his subject and had had to zoom in rapidly to catch the image before Linley disappeared – which presumably would have been only a moment or two later, as Linley's hand was already reaching towards the doorknob of a house or cottage with white, ivy-covered walls. He was wearing what looked like a Barbour jacket and a tweedy cap, and his expression was bland – he was neither smiling nor scowling. He looked, in fact, like a man who had not the slightest inkling he was under observation.

I showed the picture to Clover, who nodded confidently. 'That's definitely him,' she said.

Despite her conviction, however, the more I stared at the photograph the more I began to doubt my initial reaction. *Was* it really him? Or was it someone who just looked like him, and it was our – or rather, my – own need to believe that had done the rest? Maybe this was a wild goose chase. Maybe I was getting worked up for nothing.

I opened my eyes, took out my phone and clicked on the picture again. And again, that first, instinctive response – *It's him!* – before the doubts started to creep in.

'Maybe you're right,' Clover said.

I glanced at her, surprised at how alarmed I was to hear her express doubt. 'What?'

'To be wary. Dubious. Whatever. There's no point continually building your hopes up, only to have them come crashing down.'

'Do you think they *will* come crashing down?'

'Honestly? I've no idea.' She glanced at the sat nav, which she'd set in case we got separated from Benny en route. 'But we'll find out in about twenty minutes.'

By the time we arrived at our destination, it felt as if my guts had petrified into a hard, painful lump in my belly. The cottage was on our right, nestled into a fold of land on a rise. Despite the white-painted walls, the building's low roof of dark-grey slate and the ivy rambling across its façade made it appear furtive, as if it was trying to conceal itself. Bordering the property was a black stone wall, and behind it fields climbed towards the bleak horizon like a succession of undulating green and brown waves.

Benny eased his Jag into a lay-by about ten metres beyond the cottage and Clover just about managed to squeeze our hired Ford Focus in behind it. As she edged up to Benny's rear bumper he climbed out of his car and watched her do it, his face like granite. Just as it seemed inevitable she'd clip his car, she cut the engine, then leaned forward, grinned and gave him the thumbs-up through the windscreen. He shook his head, his expression unreadable. Although it was pissing down the rain seemed not to touch his dapper grey suit.

'Do you think he's armed?' I asked.

'Course he is,' said Clover. 'He's hardly likely to change the habit of a lifetime, is he?'

As soon as I opened the passenger door of the car and climbed out, I started shivering. Although it was unpleasantly wet and chilly after the warmth of the car's interior, the reaction was precipitated more by my apprehension than because of the cold.

'How do you want to do this, Alex?' Clover asked – mostly, I suspected, to make it clear to Benny that I was in charge here.

'I'll just walk up and knock on the door,' I said, 'see what happens.'

Clover nodded and indicated I should lead the way. Benny said nothing. I walked around the back of the car and crossed the road on hollow legs, my guts juddering, my thoughts like balloons that felt as if they wanted to break free of my skull. I tried to move naturally, though I felt as if I was a novice trying to get to grips with the controls of an unwieldy machine. My skin prickled with raindrops; my scalp felt as if cold spots were trying to hatch from it. I slipped my hand into my pocket and closed it around the heart. I was hoping it would flood me with strength, or at least provide me with succour, but it felt flaky and insubstantial in my grasp, as if it would take nothing but a good squeeze to crush it to powder.

Pushing open a wooden gate in the stone wall, I ascended half a dozen uneven steps. At the top a gravel path, bisecting a patchy lawn, ended at a blue front door. It wasn't a strenuous route, but as I trudged up the path towards the door I was panting hard with stress and expectation. I wondered who would answer my knock and what kind of reception I'd get. I wondered whether the heart in my pocket would protect me if this *was* a trap.

I was still wondering when the door opened and Paula Sherwood stepped out.

I froze. For a moment, caught halfway between the top of the steps and the house, I felt completely exposed. I wondered whether Benny was pulling out his gun behind me, and what it would take to provoke him to start shooting. I felt an urge to throw up my hands, to tell Paula we'd come in peace. It was she who spoke first, though.

'Hello, Alex,' she said. 'Come in out of the rain. We've been waiting for you.'

I glanced over my shoulder, wondering whether Benny had set me up after all. He was standing about five metres behind me. He didn't have his gun out, though he had his right hand in his jacket pocket and an expression of surly mistrust on his face. A couple of metres behind him Clover caught my eye and pulled an exaggeratedly baffled expression.

I turned back to Paula – or Maude, as she had been christened – and asked, 'Who told you we were coming?'

She smiled. 'Believe it or not, you did – although you were older. You told me to say, "Tell him I'm sixty-five. Tell him to write it down in his book."' She half-raised her hands as if to say: *Don't shoot the messenger.* 'I hope that makes sense?'

'It does.'

'Good. So are you coming in? I've put the kettle on.'

For a moment I couldn't answer. Of all the scenarios I'd envisaged this hadn't been one of them. 'Is—' I started to ask, and then found my throat had closed up. I took a deep breath, swallowed with difficulty, and tried again. 'Is Kate in there with you?'

'She is.' Paula's voice had grown soft, as if she was fully aware what

I'd been going through. 'She's upstairs playing with Hamish.'

A breathy groan escaped me, as if I'd been punched in the stomach, and my knees turned to water. I might even have started to sag, because all at once Clover was beside me, sliding a supportive arm around my waist. She said something, but my pulse was pounding in my ears and I couldn't hear.

The next question seemed to tear out of me, harsh and uncontrolled. 'Why did you take her?'

Paula looked contrite, even distressed. She half-raised her hands again. 'Because you told us to.'

'Me?' I boggled at her. 'What... how... *what are you talking about?*'

Paula glanced at the sky. It was getting dark and the rain was coming down harder. I felt it trickling down my face, mingling with the hot sweat. 'Just come inside,' she said. 'Come and get warm and dry. I'll explain everything over a cup of tea.'

She retreated into the house, leaving us no choice but to follow. Clover kept her arm tight around my waist as if I was an invalid. Staggering up the path towards the open front door whilst trying to come to terms with what I'd just been told felt almost like having an out-of-body experience. I was only vaguely aware of Benny bringing up the rear, and despite the fact that I still didn't entirely trust him, I was glad to have him with us. Although he was a slight man, easy, almost balletic, on his feet, he was nonetheless a solid and steadying presence. He was the best kind of guy to have on your side in a crisis.

Clover and I paused on the threshold of the front door, peering suspiciously into the room beyond. The door opened directly into a large kitchen, the unevenly plastered walls painted a soothing eggshell blue. To our immediate left, beneath a small window with a deep wooden sill, was a sink and dishwasher. To our right was an enclosed wooden staircase, with a door, currently shut, at the bottom. Jutting from the centre of the left-hand wall was a tiled hearth, logs crackling merrily in the old cast-iron fireplace, filling the room with smoky warmth. Beyond that was a dining area, and to the right of that was the main kitchen area – cooker, fridge, cupboards and shelves, a breakfast bar on which stood a chopping board, a knife block, and a cluster of large glass storage jars full of pasta, rice, muesli, teabags.

It was all very normal, very homely. The pictures on the walls were hunting scenes, still lifes, old framed railway posters advertising the seaside. The curtains at the windows were floral, chintzy, edged with lace. There was a bowl of fruit on the dining table; a biscuit barrel in the shape of a cat licking its paw on top of the fridge; a collection of unusual rocks and shells on the window sill above the sink, next to a half-empty bottle of Ecover washing-up liquid.

'Where's your husband?' I asked, not sure whether to call him Adam or Linley.

Paula had moved back as far as the dining table, as though anxious not to antagonise us by getting too close. She indicated a door between the breakfast bar and the boxed-in staircase.

'He's in the living room. He thought it best to keep out of the way at first, so you didn't feel...'

'Threatened?' said Clover.

Paula expelled a nervous chuff of laughter. 'I was going to say crowded.'

'Tell him to come in here,' I said.

'And tell him to keep his hands where we can see them,' added Benny, who had sidled into the room behind us, his own right hand still nestled in his jacket pocket.

'Adam,' Paula called – evidently the Sherwoods were sticking to their adopted names whilst in this time period, presumably to avoid slip-ups. 'You can come in now. But keep your hands where they can be seen.'

We all stared at the door, which, after about five seconds, slowly opened. Adam Sherwood stood there, smiling sheepishly at us. He raised his hands, showing us his empty palms.

'Hi,' he said.

No one returned his greeting.

After a moment Paula stepped away from the dining table, drawing our attention. Half-turning back towards it, she flapped a hand. 'Please won't you sit down? I'll make us all some tea.'

She hadn't been lying when she said she'd put the kettle on. Steam was drifting from the spout of an electric Russell Hobbs model beside the cooker. Cautiously Clover and I sidled across to the dining table and lowered ourselves onto the cushioned pew inset into the left-hand wall, beyond the fireplace. From here we had a clear view of the kitchen, and everything that was happening in it.

Adam was still hovering by the open door through which he'd entered the room. When we were seated he turned to Benny, who had only ventured a few steps into the cottage, and was now standing to the left of the front door like a bouncer, his backside pressed against the edge of the white porcelain sink.

'Won't you sit down too?' Adam said.

Benny shook his head. 'No, I don't think so.'

Adam opened his mouth to reply, then clearly thought better of it. Flashing Benny a nervous smile, which wasn't reciprocated, he crossed the kitchen and sat in a chair opposite Clover and me.

Paula, who was making tea and looked more edgy than I'd ever seen her, possibly because of Benny's reptilian scrutiny, had said that the children were playing upstairs. Glancing up at the ceiling, I wondered if that was true; if it was, I couldn't hear them. Of course, they could have been engrossed in a DVD or a board game. 'Playing' didn't *always* mean pounding up and down the floorboards, shrieking at the tops of their lungs, not even for five-year-olds. Nevertheless I had to resist an urge to jump to my feet, run across the room, tear open the door at the bottom of the stairs and call Kate's name.

'Can I see my daughter?' I asked.

As I spoke I was looking at Adam, who was sitting in a slightly hunched position with his hands meshed together on the table top, and an almost ingratiating half-smile on his face. Unlike his wife he still closely resembled the young clerk whose house Clover and I had visited in Victorian London – a bright but unworldly man who couldn't help but be overawed by his elders and 'betters'. Even now he didn't answer my question, but glanced over his shoulder, deferring to his wife. She was putting the tea things on a tray and looked as if she'd been expecting my question – which, as it turned out, she had.

'Your older self said you'd ask that. And the answer is, yes you can, if you like. But he also said to tell you that it would be in your best interests to prepare yourself first. He said you'd be desperate to see her, but that your head would be all over the place, and that it would be better in the long run if you sat tight for ten minutes or so, and calmed down, and let me tell you about how she came to be here with us. He also said to remember what he told you that night you tried to prevent

Kate's abduction, and he stopped you. He said...' She narrowed her eyes as if visualising the exact words in her mind. 'He said you could change the past without changing it, and that you didn't need to be a victim any more.'

I stared at her. After all that had happened in the past ten minutes, my mind was such a whirlwind of thoughts and emotions that much of her little speech was swept up and tossed around like dead leaves in a November storm. I was so intent on trying to pluck her words from the maelstrom, to make sense of them, that when Clover laid her hand over mine I jumped, having forgotten for a moment she was sitting beside me.

'Are you okay?' she asked.

Her eyes, fixed on mine, were soft, concerned.

'Yes, I... I'm fine... I...' I put my free hand on my hot forehead. It was blessedly cool, and seemed to momentarily calm my thoughts, if not clear my mind. 'Tell me again,' I said to Paula. 'That last part. What was it my older self said?'

She carried the tray to the table and set it down, then slid into the seat next to her husband. There was a pot of tea and five china cups on the tray, along with a sugar bowl, a jug of milk, five plates and a Victoria sponge cake on a glass stand.

As Clover poured the tea and Adam cut the cake, Paula said, 'He said you could change the past without changing it, and that you didn't need to be a victim any more.'

'Change the past without changing it,' I repeated. 'What does that mean? It doesn't make sense.'

Clover was still pouring the tea, but all at once she put the teapot down heavily enough to draw everyone's attention. There was an expression of dawning realisation on her face.

'Yes it does,' she said.

'How?'

Instead of answering me, she glanced at Benny, who was still leaning against the sink on the far side of the room. 'What is it you're always saying to me about luck, Benny?'

He frowned. 'Fucked if I know.'

'Don't you always say there's no such thing as being lucky or unlucky?'

Now he nodded. 'That's right. The concept of luck is a load of bollocks. A man makes his own luck in this world.'

She turned triumphantly back to me. 'You see?'

From her expression I felt as though I *should* see, but I was still baffled.

'Sorry. I think you're going to have to spell it–'

And then, all at once, it came to me – and it was a real light bulb moment. *Ping!* I think I may actually have jerked back in my seat as though I'd been slapped. Then I started to laugh, and had to clap a hand over my mouth to make myself stop.

Paula was smiling indulgently, and Adam was nodding in relief – which I guess meant they were already ahead of me, having been briefed by my older self. The only one of us who still looked puzzled (and pissed off about it) was Benny.

'You going to let me in on the joke?' he growled.

Looking at him, I realised I must resemble a kid who'd just been shown the best magic trick ever.

'All this time,' I said, 'I've been looking for Kate, frantic with worry because I thought the Wolves of London had taken her; because I thought she was a prisoner of the Dark Man.'

Benny's face was like stone. 'And?'

'And she wasn't!' As it unfolded in my head, like the petals of a lily that had been tightly budded for what seemed an age and had now suddenly and gloriously come into blossom, the words started to tumble out of me. 'Don't you see? It was *me* all along! Me who arranged to have her taken away! To keep her safe! To keep her out of the Dark Man's clutches!'

'You've lost me,' Benny said. 'So you're telling me you arranged to have your own daughter abducted and then... what? You forgot?' He scowled at Clover. 'Am I being taken for a ride, Monroe?'

'No.' Clover shook her head. 'Not at all, Benny. It's... complicated, that's all. There's a lot of it you won't believe – that you won't *want* to believe.'

He snorted. 'Try me. I've already been forced to believe a lot of fucked-up shit these last few weeks, and it's all been because of him.' He pointed at me. 'Those fucking freaks in the crypt. That... *thing* that attacked my house.' He rubbed his temple above his right eye as if he had a knot of pain there. 'There were times I thought I was losing it.

Going seriously doolally. Times I thought...' He shook his head, as if deliberately derailing that train of thought. 'But I'm an adaptable man. I've had to be. And seeing is believing. However fucking crazy it might look.'

Clover nodded almost affectionately. 'Yeah. Sorry, Benny. For dragging you into all this.'

'It's not you I blame, Monroe. It's him.' He jabbed a finger at me again.

'All the same,' said Clover. She finished pouring the tea, then stood up and carried one of the cups over to him. 'Drink this. I think you're going to need it. And promise me two things.'

He narrowed his eyes. 'What?'

'When Alex tells you what he's going to tell you, try not to have a meltdown. And try not to shoot anybody.'

'It's that bad, is it?'

She nodded sympathetically. 'It's a bit... out there.'

He sighed, but to my relief he slipped his right hand out of his jacket pocket to take the cup she was offering him. As Clover walked back to the table to sit down, he took a swig of tea and fixed me with his ice-blue eyes.

'Go on then,' he said almost wearily. 'Let's hear it.'

I looked at Paula and Adam Sherwood, who looked back at me expectantly, and then I looked at Clover, who gave me a single encouraging nod, as if to say: *It's time.*

And so I began. When I'd entered this cottage I thought I'd be the one listening to a story – or rather, an explanation of how and why Kate happened to have ended up here with the Sherwoods – but as it turned out, I was the one telling it, the one with all the answers, even though I hadn't *realised* I had them until today.

As my story unfolded – Candice's boyfriend's debt; contacting Benny; meeting Clover; Kate's abduction; stealing the heart and finding out what it could do – something fundamental occurred to me. Something which had resulted in too many convolutions, had been too bound up in cause and effect, to occur to me until now.

I realised that the reason I had been drawn into this whole tangled mess in the first place was not because of outside forces, but because I had been *caught in my own trap*. The Dark Man aside, I had stolen the heart to try to get Kate back – but because it was me (or would be me) who had had Kate abducted in the first place, that meant I had been forced back into a life of crime purely as a result of my own actions!

But, of course, I had only arranged for Kate to be abducted (or *would* only, because it hadn't happened yet) in order to prevent the Dark Man from taking her. Because what my future self had been trying to tell me was that with the heart I could *create* my past, rather than being a victim of it; in other words, I could be the manipulator rather than the manipulated.

The problem, of course, was that by creating my past, I was also wrapping heavier and more numerous chains around myself. Because now, to maintain the timeline that would lead to this moment, I presumably would have to set up the rest of it, starting with the message I'd have to send to Clover, claiming to be Kate's kidnapper and giving myself instructions as to what to do next. Which in effect meant I would have to move my past self around as though he (I) was nothing but a piece on a chess board; a pawn in an elaborate, inescapable game.

All of this was whizzing round my head as I told my story, and had the paradoxical effect not only of freeing my mind, of furnishing me with possibilities, but also of making me realise how irrevocably tied into the web of my own past I was, and of how my actions might unwittingly have had a devastating effect on those around me.

Was it because of my future involvement in my own past, for instance, that Lyn had endured five debilitating, draining years of mental illness? Because if I hadn't become enmeshed in this web I'd created, if I'd somehow found a way to avoid becoming the owner and guardian of the heart, wouldn't the Dark Man have left us alone – or rather, left Lyn alone? Hadn't it been entirely *because* of my involvement that he'd used the heart to go back in time and plant the seeds of madness in her mind? But *why* had he done that? Out of spite? Or were there still questions to which I didn't yet know the answers? Or perhaps answers to which I didn't yet know the questions?

'Time travel?' Benny said. 'Do you honestly expect me to swallow this shit?'

Even as my story had been spilling out of me I'd become so preoccupied with my inner voice that I'd almost forgotten I had an audience. Benny's contemptuous interruption snapped me back to the here and now. Before I could gather my wits enough to answer him, Clover jumped in.

'I told you it was a bit out there.'

'There's out there and there's fucking taking the piss,' Benny retorted. He put his cup and saucer down with a clatter on the draining board behind him and swiped a hand through the air as though crossing all our names off some invisible list. 'I don't know what you're on – and that includes you, Monroe – but I don't have to listen to any more of this bollocks. I've done my bit, and I expect to be paid accordingly.' His eyes, fixed on mine, were like daggers of ice.

'You will be,' I said.

'Oh, I know I will. I have no doubt about it. And now I'll leave you to your fairy stories.'

Abruptly he turned from the sink, stomped across to the door and yanked it open. He stepped out into a squall of rain, then reached back and pulled the door shut behind him. After he'd gone the four of us looked at each other, a little taken aback by the suddenness of his departure. It was Clover who broke the silence.

'Well,' she said chirpily, 'at least he didn't shoot us.'

I could hardly blame Benny for his reaction. He had only responded with such venom because, underneath it all, he was scared. There was a time when I'd thought nothing could scare someone like him, but the fact is he was an inflexible man who'd believed that what he took to be reality was as inflexible as he was. Finding out that he was wrong had pulled the rug from under him. And although it had pulled the rug from under me too, unlike Benny I'd been able, after a period of adjustment, to alter my thinking, to adapt.

I realised that with Benny's departure there was no more reason to delay.

'I'd like to see my daughter now, please,' I said.

Paula nodded and stood up. Clover's left hand snaked across to my right one, grabbed it and squeezed.

'Big moment,' she murmured. 'You ready?'

Now that the time had finally arrived the knot in my belly had untied itself and was now thrashing about inside me like an angry octopus.

'I don't know,' I said. 'I might throw up.'

'Have some tea and cake. It'll settle your stomach.'

I grimaced. 'I think it'd make me want to throw up more.'

I watched Paula move across the room, pausing only to switch on a couple of lamps. It was late afternoon now – early evening, in fact – and getting dark. Rain was still throwing itself against the cottage outside, though the walls were so thick, designed to withstand fierce winters, that we could only hear it against the windows. As Paula opened the door at the bottom of the stairs and started up, the wooden steps creaking beneath her, I shuddered and muttered, 'Please don't let this be another trick.'

'It's not a trick,' said Adam. 'You know it's not.'

I heard a creak above me. Then another. Then footsteps descending, softly at first.

My mouth was suddenly very dry. My eyes burned. It was stuffy in the kitchen, the fire giving out plenty of heat, but I was shivering. I tried to swallow, but couldn't. I stared at the wooden door at the bottom of the stairs. It had swung to behind Paula, leaving only the thinnest of black lines around the frame. The stairs were creaking under the weight of... how many bodies? The door started to open. Paula stepped through it, smiling.

'There's someone here who wants to say hello,' she said.

The little girl was holding Paula's hand and concentrating on negotiating the last few steep wooden steps, the tip of her tongue poking out between her teeth. Her curly brown hair had grown since the last time I'd seen her, and had she got taller too?

I felt waves of heat, or perhaps euphoria, rushing through me; felt my arms and legs tingling; felt my head swimming, as though I was about to faint. As if she knew exactly how I was feeling, Clover squeezed my hand, anchoring me. She slid out of the wooden pew, tugging me behind her.

Stepping off the bottom step, the little girl looked up, wrinkling her nose as though that might help adjust the pink-framed spectacles perched there. Her blue eyes fastened on me and widened. Her cute little bud of a mouth became an 'O' of surprise, then stretched into a huge smile.

'*Dadeee!*' she squealed. She yanked herself free of Paula's grip. At the same moment Clover let go of my hand, allowing me to drop to my knees as my daughter raced across the kitchen towards me. Kate threw herself into my arms and I hugged her tight, feeling the wonderful, wriggling warmth of her, breathing in her familiar smell - fresh, uncategorisable, unique.

If I had any doubts that this was really Kate, they were dispelled in that instant. Even so, after all I'd been through, all the heartache, it was hard to believe we were back together, and that she was safe, and all was well. It was the moment I had yearned for, the moment I'd feared might never come.

'Daddy!' she cried. 'Daddy! Daddy!'

She was an eel in my grip. She wriggled free and looked into my face, as if to check it was definitely me.

'Kate,' I said, laughing even as my vision blurred with tears. 'It's so lovely to see you, scamp.'

She frowned and touched my face, then examined her wet palm.

'Why are you crying?' she said. 'You should be happy, not sad.' She shook her head, tutting in weary exasperation. 'You really are a very, very silly man, Daddy.'

THIRTEEN

NIGHTCAP

'Still awake?'

I jerked upright from my seat by the fire, which provided the only light in the room. I hadn't been asleep, but I'd been far away, my thoughts roaming. Blue-green images of the flames I'd been staring into were still dancing in my vision as I turned to look at Clover, framed in the darkness of the staircase doorway. She was wearing clothes that Paula had lent her to sleep in – a white T-shirt with a Hollister logo on it and pink shorts, under a white towelling dressing gown that was hanging open as if she'd thrown it on in sleepy haste.

'Too much adrenaline,' I said. 'My head's buzzing – and not because of this.'

With my foot I nudged the half-empty bottle of Southern Comfort perched by the leg of my chair like a faithful pet. After the girls had gone to bed, Adam and I had shared a nightcap and chatted a while. Then Adam had gone to bed too, leaving me by the kitchen fire with the bottle.

How long ago had that been? An hour? Two?

'What time is it?' I asked.

Clover squinted at the digital display on the cooker across the room. 'If that clock's right, three eleven. You're going to be knackered in the morning.'

'I don't think I'll ever sleep again.' Then it came over me once more – that warm rush of euphoria; happiness in its purest, most complete form. 'We've done it, Clover,' I said, grinning. 'We've got Kate back.'

She matched her grin to mine. 'I know.' She tiptoed across the stone floor on bare feet, wincing at the cold even though the fire was breathing out heat, and squeezed my forearm. Then she dragged a chair out from under the dining table in the corner and set it down opposite mine. She perched on it, bringing up her legs until her heels were resting on the edge of the seat, feet curled together like puppies seeking warmth from one another's bodies, bony knees sticking up in the air. She reached out, stretching her hands into star shapes, holding them up to the fire. Orange warmth lapped at her long shin bones and her face perched above her knees; fire flickered in her wide-set eyes.

'Join you?' she said, abruptly uncurling herself so she could bend down and grab the bottle of Southern Comfort.

'Be my guest.'

She unscrewed the cap, held out the bottle and jiggled it. 'Top up?'

I looked down at the glass I'd all but forgotten I was holding. There was no more than a sip of liquor left in the bottom. I tilted it to my mouth, savouring the sweetness of it on my tongue, then held out my glass so that Clover could pour me another. The liquid looked beautiful in the firelight; it was the deep, smooth brown of freshly shelled chestnuts, shot through with flashes of red and gold. I was struck by the beauty of it. But then this was a night for beauty. For perfection even. I couldn't remember ever being more content than I was at that moment. I wanted it to stretch on for ever and ever. I wanted it never to end.

As Clover tilted the bottle to her lips and took a slug that made her eyes water, I laughed. 'Peasant.'

She exhaled a sharp breath from the O of her mouth as if trying to create a smoke ring out of alcohol fumes. 'Well, I don't have a glass, and the floor's too cold to go get one.'

'Allow me.' Smiling, I rose from my chair and went into the kitchen area and opened cupboards until I found one that was full of glasses. Selecting a whisky tumbler I returned to my seat by the fire. 'Here you go.'

'Gee, thanks,' she said in a sparky American accent. She poured herself a generous measure, then put the bottle down on the hearth with a soft clunk. She held up her glass; firelight trapped in amber. 'Cheers.'

'Cheers.'

'To happy families.'

'Happy families.'

We chinked glasses and drank.

For perhaps thirty seconds we sat in companionable silence, sipping our drinks and gazing at the sinuous, ever-changing patterns in the fire. Clover stretched out her legs and wriggled her toes, warming them. Eventually, as though she'd been building up to it, she said, 'So... where do we go from here?'

I glanced at her, not sure how to interpret the question. She wasn't coming on to me, was she? Not after all this time?

'What do you mean?' I asked.

She looked at me – then arched an eyebrow and laughed. 'Not what you think I mean. Let's not even *begin* to go there. Let's keep that can of worms firmly closed.'

Ordinarily, no matter whether I felt the same way as the woman or not, my male ego might have been a little bruised at such a firm rebuff. With Clover, though, it was different. She was a mate. And mates don't... well, they just don't, do they?

'Fine by me,' I said – then immediately felt the need to qualify my statement. 'Not that you aren't... I mean...'

She held up her glass and mimed screwing a lid on it. 'This is the can of worms. Well... jar, cause you don't screw a lid on to a can. But the point is, it's firmly closed. See? Can't open it.'

'Good.' I took a sip of my drink. 'So... what did you mean?'

'I meant – where do we go from here? Literally. Now that you've got Kate back...' She spread both hands, slopping Southern Comfort up the inside of her glass '...what's the next move?'

I expelled a long breath. 'To be honest, it's something I haven't wanted to think about. Something I've been deliberately *avoiding* thinking about. Because...'

I paused, wondering how to say it and how it would sound. But Clover got there ahead of me.

'Because now that you've got Kate, now that your quest, as it were, is at an end, you're wondering why you *need* to carry on, why you shouldn't just let everything else slide.'

I shrugged. 'That's about the size of it.'

'And are you *really* thinking that? Seriously, I mean?'

'I'm seriously wondering what would happen if I did nothing. If I took Kate home and… just started living my life again.'

'Do you want me to play Devil's Advocate?' Clover said softly.

'Not really. But I've a feeling you're going to.'

She held up her glass and peered into it as if staring into a crystal ball. 'Remember the visions you had a while ago? Remember how awful they were?'

I nodded, grimacing.

'Wasn't that the heart's way of showing you how, if you don't play your part in the past, it'll impact on the present?'

I sighed. 'But this *is* the present.' Though even as I said the words I knew I was being obstinate.

'Is it?' She took another sip and gazed into the fire. Her tone was lazy, casual, as if we were discussing something insignificant, something which had minimal impact on our lives – the performance of a favourite football team, or the latest season of a TV show.

'Maybe this is only the present because of what you've still got to do to make it so,' she said. 'Maybe if you ignore what you've got to do…' She left the comment hanging.

I frowned. She was only verbalising what had been lurking in the back of my mind, but I still felt cross with her for puncturing my balloon. Knowing it would be unfair of me to blame her for that, though, I stayed silent for a few seconds, gathering my thoughts.

At last I said, 'It's all changed, hasn't it?'

'What has?'

'My… quest. My purpose. From today it's no longer a search for Kate. Now it's a mission to manipulate the past and the future, to shore it up, keep it from falling down around our ears.' An image came to my mind of a vast edifice, a huge tumbledown mansion with cracked walls, encased in an exoskeleton of scaffolding and surrounded by signs warning of falling masonry. I gave a small, bitter laugh. 'It's a restoration project, that's what it is. The past and the future are in danger of collapsing, and I'm the one who has to stop it. I'm a fucking… temporal builder.'

'Or an architect,' she said.

'Or maybe just some bloke trying to do a jigsaw puzzle. A massive jigsaw puzzle through time, of a picture that keeps changing, along with the pieces.' I scowled at my own analogy. 'Trouble is, how will I know when it's finished?'

'Maybe it never will be,' said Clover.

'Oh, thanks for that. That's *very* reassuring.'

She gave a sheepish, clench-teethed grin. 'Sorry.'

Churning with frustration at the hand I'd been dealt, I turned my attention once more to the flames. For a few seconds the scowl stayed on my face, and then I thought again of the moment I'd seen Kate – the *real* Kate – for the first time in what for me had been over two years, and how it had felt when she'd gleefully shouted my name, and run across the room to greet me, and I'd wrapped my arms around her.

As long as she's safe, I thought, *as long as she's safe and well and happy, nothing else matters.*

When I looked up, Clover was staring at me as if she'd been scrutinising every little change of mood on my face. 'Sorry,' she said again.

'What for?'

'For opening my big mouth. For not giving you more time to enjoy the moment.'

I waved away her apology. 'It's okay. It's not your fault. And it's not as if I wasn't aware I'd have to go back to the trenches and finish the job at some point. Not to mention... well, all the rest of it.'

'You do have a lot to do, don't you?' Clover said sympathetically. 'I hope you've been taking notes.'

I patted my pocket. 'I have. I've jotted it all down in my little black book. I just wish...'

'What?'

'Well, that I could do everything right now, get it all out of the way. Or better still, just press a button and make everything right.'

'If only life were that simple.'

'If only.' I took another sip of my drink, then sighed and glanced up at the ceiling. 'I can't tell you how torn I feel about this whole situation. I mean, on the one hand I'm so happy to have Kate back, and it's lovely to know she's up there right now, cosy and safe and fast asleep in bed. But on the other hand it's agonising to think that no sooner have I got her back than I'm going to have to bugger off and leave her again.'

'We'll look after her while you're away,' Clover assured me. 'I'm a brilliant babysitter. She'll be in the safest of hands.'

'I know she will. And thank you. Though if it all works out, hopefully you won't have to do much babysitting. Once the War's over I'm planning to come straight back here. If I'm lucky, no one will even notice I've left.' I saw her wince and held up a hand. 'And before you say anything, I haven't forgotten that I've got the Dark Man's old, knackered, unreliable heart, and he's got mine. Which means my first priority has to be to get my heart back.'

'Any ideas how you're going to do that?' Clover asked.

'No. But I am. I *have* to. And I will.'

'I admire your determination.'

'I'll get Benny on the case,' I said. 'I might not be his favourite person in the world, but I don't think he'll turn my money down. I'll look for the Dark Man everywhere. I'll leave no stone unturned.'

'And what if he's not here? In this time, I mean?'

'Then I'll use the heart, and fuck the consequences. If I'm meant to find him, then somehow or other I will.'

Clover looked thoughtful – either because she was debating whether to tell me not to be an idiot, or because she had an idea brewing. Eventually she said, 'Maybe you're not the right person to track down the Dark Man.'

I frowned. 'What do you mean?'

'Maybe, to find him, you need someone with a stronger connection to him.'

'Like who?' I said. 'Tallarian?'

Clover shook her head. 'I was thinking of someone closer to home. Someone whose every waking thought for the past five years has been dominated by the Dark Man and what he did to her. Someone who finds comfort and solace in the heart, and feels an affinity with it.'

The penny dropped. 'Lyn?' I said, surprised.

'Lyn,' she confirmed. She took a slow sip of her drink, allowing the suggestion time to take root in both our minds. Finally she said, 'I know it's a long shot, and I know it might come to nothing, but he was in her mind, Alex – *right* inside. I mean, surely, on that basis, it's at least worth a try?'

FOURTEEN

FIND HIM

It was tough saying goodbye to Kate, but being an eminently adaptable five-year-old she took our latest parting far more easily than I did. She was thoroughly enjoying her 'holiday' with Adam and Paula – and most especially with her best friend, Hamish – and, of course, had no inkling of the two years or so of torture I'd endured searching for her. When, after an uproarious full English breakfast, I gave her a farewell hug, I found it hard to let her go. So hard, in fact, that in the end she started to wriggle like an eel.

'Daddy, you're squishing me.'

'Sorry, peanut.' When I opened my arms her cheeks were flushed and the static electricity from my jumper had made her hair stand up in wavering spikes.

'Do you know what your problem is?' I said solemnly.

She pushed out her bottom lip. 'What?'

'It's that you're just so incredibly huggable.'

Her frown dissolved into giggles. 'And your problem is you're a great big silly sausage. Will you be coming back soon?'

'Very soon,' I promised.

'And when you come back, will we be going home and will I be going to school?'

I thought of the flat we'd lived in, torn apart by the Dark Man's mob (unless, of course, I'd done it to maintain the timeline, in which case I'm sure I'd find out in due course), and of the house in Kensington I owned now.

'Probably,' I said, thinking it would be easier to explain all that when the time came.

'Yay!' cried Kate. 'We like school, don't we, Hamish?'

Hamish was chewing a slice of toast. He had egg yolk, ketchup and jam around his mouth. 'I like drawing aeroplanes,' he announced. 'Mrs Mason said I drawed the best aeroplanes in the class.'

Kate wrinkled her nose. 'Aeroplanes are boring. Tigers are better.'

'Are not!'

'Are!'

'Are not!'

'Talk to the hand,' Kate said haughtily, showing him her palm, which made us all guffaw.

By 10:30 a.m. Clover and I were on the road. As we ate up the miles and put Kate and the Sherwoods further behind us, I felt hollow, shrunken, as if I'd left a major part of myself back in that little cottage, and what was left was like an unravelling ball of twine that was shrinking ever smaller.

After dozing in the chair by the fire for a while, Clover and I had finally crawled up to our separate beds at around 5 a.m., where, with rain dashing against the window like handfuls of pebbles, I'd managed to get three or four hours fitful sleep. When I'd woken up – to the glorious sound of Kate and Hamish whooping as if imitating police sirens – bright morning sunshine had turned the field outside my tiny bedroom window into a carpet of emeralds. Now, though, the clouds were closing in again, as if imitating my mood. I closed my eyes, which felt gritty and hot, and within seconds I was asleep.

Clover woke me at lunchtime, prior to pulling off the motorway so we could grab a bite to eat in a service station Costa, and then I spent most of the afternoon alternately staring unseeingly out of the window as the M4 unrolled before us, and drifting back off to sleep. In one of my wakeful periods I also called DI Jensen and told him Kate had been found safe and well, and that he could call off the police search for her. It was an awkward conversation, but he'd seen my future self on the beach, and eventually swallowed my rather sketchy explanation. After calling Jensen I called Candice, which was an altogether more pleasurable experience. When I told her the good news, she screamed in delight, then abruptly burst into tears. In a rushed, blubbery, emotion-filled voice she asked me a ton of questions, but I managed to deflect them, telling her things were still hectic and that I had to go, but would give her the full story in due course (which I didn't say would be when I could come up with an explanation she'd be likely to believe).

We hit pre-rush hour traffic on the M23 at around 3:30 p.m. and eventually drove in through Darby Hall's imposing iron gates just before five. Clover cut the engine in the tree-lined car park behind the main building, and groaned and stretched before squinting at me.

'How you doing?'

'Okay.'

'You haven't exactly been scintillating company these past few hours.'

'Sorry. Had a lot to process. Needed the head space.'

She told me she'd have a walk round the grounds to stretch her legs while I went up to see Lyn. Five minutes later one of the orderlies, a gangly black guy called Richard, was leading me up the wooden staircase towards Lyn's room on the first floor.

'Where's Dr Bruce today?' I asked, more to make conversation than anything.

Richard briefly wrinkled his nose as if at a bad smell. 'She's around somewhere.' He gave me what I thought was a reluctant sideways glance. 'I can find her if you wanna see her.'

'No, that's okay.'

Lyn was sitting by the window, reading a book by lamplight when I entered. Outside the sun was creeping towards the horizon, filling the room with pre-dusk shadows.

'Alex,' she said, closing the book and smiling up at me.

'Hi,' I said, and put out a hand to the light switch.

'Don't,' she said. 'I like this time of day. I like to see the colours in the sky.'

The only colours I could see were grey and black, with maybe a hint of murky green at the horizon, but I let it slide.

'How are you?'

'Good,' she said. 'Getting better all the time.' She stood up, dropped the book on the chair and gave me a twirl. 'What do you think?'

She *did* look better. Less scrawny, less hesitant in her movements.

There was even a flush of pink in her cheeks, a suggestion of vitality in her previously lank hair.

'You look great,' I said. 'Every time I see you, you look better.'

'I feel great,' she replied. 'Well, maybe not great, but better than I was. Dr Bruce said she might even reduce my medication soon if I keep improving.'

'That's brilliant,' I said, crossing the room towards her. I felt uneasy, though, because despite coming all this way I suddenly began to wonder whether asking her to help might not be the right thing to do. In the early hours of the morning, by the cosy glow of a cottage fire, and with several Southern Comforts inside me, Clover's suggestion had seemed reasonable, even inspired. But now that Lyn and I were in the same room, facing each other, I was starting to have doubts.

Although her condition had improved dramatically in recent weeks – since I'd acquired the heart, in fact – that shouldn't lull me into thinking she wasn't still fragile and vulnerable. The main reason she was *getting* better, it seemed to me, was due to her interactions with the heart, to whatever succour it gave her when she held it, and to her belief that I had trapped the Dark Man within it, which meant not simply that he could no longer harm her, but that we now had power over him.

How would it affect her, therefore, if I showed her the now-crumbling heart? And if she discovered the Dark Man was not trapped, as she had thought, but still at large, and that I had come to seek her help in tracking him down? Would she have a relapse, retreat back into herself?

Convincing her that we were in a position of strength, and that the Dark Man would be running scared of both of us, was, it seemed to me, the way to go. Perching on the edge of the bed, I said as earnestly as I could, 'Look, the reason I've come to see you today is because you're the only person strong enough to help me. There's something I need to do, and I won't pretend it'll be easy, but if we work together I know we can do it.'

I'd certainly grabbed her attention. She was all eyes. Nodding solemnly, she said, 'If I can help you, Alex, I will. What is it you want me to do?'

I took a deep breath. 'I want you to help me find the Dark Man.' Before she could respond – almost before she had chance to assimilate what I'd told her – I said quickly, 'He's running and he's weak and he's scared of us. All I need is for you to help me find him and then I can do the rest. Can you do that? *Will* you do that?'

I looked at her steadily, calmly, but inside I was bracing myself, more than half-expecting her to freak out.

Her eyes, though, remained as calm as I hoped mine were. She regarded me for a moment, as though coolly assessing what I'd told her, and then she held out a hand.

'Give me the heart.'

Just like that? I wanted to ask. *Don't you even want to know what happened, how he escaped?* I didn't know whether to feel alarmed or heartened by how well she seemed to have taken what could – and maybe should – have been a devastating piece of news.

Looking at her outstretched hand, though, I realised there may yet be a further hurdle to negotiate.

'One thing I should tell you before I do,' I said, 'is that the heart is... not as you remember it. What I mean is, it's damaged. But that doesn't mean it can't still be effective. And it doesn't mean it can't be renewed.'

She gave me an indulgent smile. 'You don't have to mollycoddle me, Alex. I know you're trying to protect me, because you think I'm still liable to fall apart at any moment, but I'm much stronger now than I've been for ages. I'm genuinely getting better.'

'I *know* you are,' I said, with so much conviction that I only ended up sounding – to my ears at least – entirely *in*sincere.

If Lyn picked up on that, though, she decided to ignore it. Still smiling she held out her hand again. 'So will you give me the heart?'

I slipped my hand into my jacket pocket, wondering whether she had already come to the same conclusion I had – that her link with the heart might be the best way to track down the Dark Man – or whether she simply wanted to glean some comfort from holding it. Feeling I ought to clarify this, I said, 'I will, but be careful in case–'

'Just give it to me!' she snapped.

I froze, startled. Okay, so maybe she *wasn't* quite so sanguine and stable as I'd thought. But before I could decide how to respond to her flare-up, she was raising her hands, a sweet smile of apology replacing the momentary anger on her face.

'Sorry,' she said, 'that was uncalled for. It's just that–'

Something moved under the bed.

Instinctively I jumped up from where I was sitting, half-turning to look behind me.

'What was that?'

'What?'

'Didn't you hear it?'

'I didn't hear anything.' That indulgent smile again. 'I've never seen you so jumpy, Alex. Look, why don't you just give me the heart and we can–'

Another sound from under the bed. Another scuffle-creak of movement. But it was accompanied by a groan this time. A decidedly human groan.

I took a couple of steps back from the bed, half-expecting someone – or something – to lunge out at me. I kept my eyes on the shadowy space between bed and floor, diverting my attention only for an instant to flick a glance at Lyn. The groan had been unmistakeable, and I expected her now to look as startled and alarmed as I felt. If anything, though, her face had become hard and blank.

'Lyn, what's going on?' I said. 'Who's under there?'

Instead of waiting for an answer I dropped to my hands and knees and lowered my face to the floor. I felt horribly vulnerable, but I had to see.

Due to the gathering dusk, there was very little I *could* see at first. Only a vague, elongated shape smothered in shadow with a pale patch at one end. Almost immediately my eyes began to adjust, and I realised the pale patch was a face. As I stared at it, the features formed through the murk, like the image on a developing photograph. Recognition suddenly hit me like a cold electric shock and I cried out.

It was Lyn.

Her eyes were closed and her mouth was open, but she was stirring, as if from a long sleep. As she drifted back to consciousness another low groan drifted up and out of her. By then my head was already snapping round to regard the woman sitting in the chair by the window.

'You're not–' I began.

At which point the imposter's body erupted upwards and outwards into a nightmarish mass of thrashing, tar-black tentacles.

The transformation happened so suddenly, so abruptly, that I registered it purely on a subconscious level. Recalling it later, I could only liken the sight to footage I'd seen of oil strikes, whereupon a huge geyser of viscous black liquid would burst under enormous pressure from the newly ruptured ground.

In this case, though, the 'oil' was *alive*, and it shot not just up into the air but outwards in all directions. Tendrils of it crawled across the ceilings and walls and smothered the window, blocking out what little daylight remained. It reminded me of a fungus, or a virulent climbing plant, which had somehow managed to condense many years' growth into an explosive split second.

The 'oil' was the shape-shifter, of course, one of the Dark Man's cohorts.

Before I could even think about how to react, several of the tentacle-like strands swooped down and smashed into me with tremendous force, pinning me face-first to the floor. The thickest of the strands was no more than the circumference of a broom handle, but each of them was nevertheless so incredibly strong that, try as I might, I couldn't move a muscle. The strands had me pinned by my wrists and ankles, and there were also several pressing into my back – one of them exerting such effortless pressure on the base of my spine that I had no doubt it could crush my bones to powder if it wanted to.

Why the shape-shifter didn't simply kill me I had no idea – though that wasn't a question that occurred to me until later. Feeling movement around my hip area, I turned my head (the only part of me I could still move) and saw another of the black, rope-like strands delving into my jacket pocket, where I kept the heart. The Dark Man already had the 'new' heart, so why he should now want the old, crumbling one, which he had left me in return, I could only guess. Maybe it was to prevent us from tracking him down?

As the shape-shifter's rope-like appendage rose almost gracefully from my pocket, its tip curled around the 'old' heart like a long black finger, I tried to project my will into the heart, tried to impel it to react, to burst into life and fight back.

But nothing happened. Either the heart was too weak and decrepit to respond or it needed a physical link between us to do so – needed, effectively, to match its energy to mine to complete a circuit and create a charge.

When the door to Lyn's room smashed open, I assumed at first that the shape-shifter had ripped it from its hinges, perhaps prior to making its escape. Turning my head towards the sound, however, my chin scraping the carpet, I saw the door had been shoved open from the outside and that Dr Bruce was now standing on the threshold, her arms outspread, her eyes wide and fixed, as if her mind, presented with the impossible sight in front of her, had checked out, shut down.

I opened my mouth, intending to shout a warning to her to get out, but then an extraordinary thing happened: Dr Bruce's body began to *glow*. It flared into life like an energy-saving light bulb, and within seconds was glowing so brightly that I could no longer make out the doctor's features; could only, in fact, vaguely discern the shape of her body within the nimbus of radiance that engulfed her.

Just as extraordinary as the light emanating from her was the fact that the shape-shifter was reacting to it, shrinking back. The tendrils of its tarry flesh that were closest to her body were flinching and drawing themselves in like a slug poked with a stick.

And then, like the shape-shifter before her, Dr Bruce's body *exploded.* Light erupted up and out of it, though it was a light that seemed sinuous, thick, *purposeful.* It was as if lava, bursting from a volcano, had become sentient; as if molten rock was creating a semi-fluid, multi-limbed form for itself. I saw it fly at the shape-shifter, gained a fleeting impression of two vast leviathans clashing together in combat. Then the radiance became overwhelming; my eyes began to smart, and I was forced to shut them.

I lay prone and unmoving as the battle raged above me. At least, I *assumed* it was raging; the combatants were silent. Indeed, I felt *encased* in silence – a silence that was profound, that blocked my senses; a silence that was like being underwater, or sinking in mud. I only knew the battle was over when the silence was broken by the discordant clamour of breaking glass, and I suddenly realised that I could move, that the tendrils that had been pinning me to the floor had released their grip on me. Groggy and bruised, I sat up and tentatively opened my eyes.

I was facing the row of windows overlooking the hospital grounds, one of which – the one the shape-shifter had been sitting beside when I'd entered the room – had burst outwards in a cascade of shattered glass. Not only that, but the anti-suicide bars across the window had been snapped and twisted back as if they were sticks of liquorice. Through the window I could see a long, undulating ribbon of black birds – crows perhaps – staining the dusky sky. Perhaps it was my imagination, but I got the impression they were ragged, panicked, in retreat. Within seconds the flock had become a speck in the distance, and then it was gone.

Shifting my attention back to the room, I saw Dr Bruce lying on the carpet at the foot of the bed. She was on her back, arms outspread, her white coat open like wings beneath her. Her eyes were closed and her thin, freckled face looked even paler than usual, but she was breathing slowly and steadily. Nestled in her right palm was the heart.

Dropping onto my hands and knees, I shuffled towards her. 'Dr Bruce,' I said, and touched her shoulder. 'Dr Bruce, can you hear me?'

'Alex?'

The voice came not from the doctor, but from behind me. I half-twisted to see Lyn emerging from beneath the bed. She looked confused, groggy, though I could see no blood or bruises on her face, no obvious injuries.

'Hey,' I said gently. 'Are you okay?'

'What happened?'

'Can't you remember?'

She half-shuffled, half-rolled all the way out from beneath the bed and levered herself into a sitting position. But then, as if the effort had been too much, she slumped back against the bed frame, blinking, and put a hand to her forehead.

'Whoa,' she said, her voice thick and slightly slurred. 'I feel dizzy. And a bit sick.'

'Deep breaths,' I said, as I clambered to my feet. For a few seconds I felt dizzy too, but then it passed. I crossed the room and went out of the open door to the small bathroom on the opposite side of the corridor. At the side of the sink Lyn's yellow toothbrush was standing upright in a transparent plastic cup. I removed the toothbrush, rinsed out the cup and filled it with water. Then I crossed back into her room, walked across to the bed and crouched beside her slumped body.

'Here you go,' I said, handing her the cup. 'Drink this. Sip it slowly.'

She took the cup with a trembling hand. 'Thanks.' After several long sips of water, some of which trickled down her chin, she lowered her arm until the cup was resting on her thigh, and tilted her head back.

'Better?' I watched her closely, hoping that whatever had happened to her wouldn't set back the progress she'd been making in recent weeks.

'Yes,' she said, though she sounded drowsy. 'Much, thanks.'

I wondered again whether to ask her what had happened, then decided against it. I didn't want to push her. If she wanted to tell me she'd do so in her own time. Leaving her to recover, I moved across to Dr Bruce, took the heart gently from her limp palm and dropped it into my jacket pocket. I touched her shoulder and said her name again, but she didn't respond. I hesitated a moment, then slid one arm beneath her neck and the other beneath her knees, and lifted her up. She was heavier than expected – or perhaps I was weaker than I'd thought – and at first, as I straightened up, I staggered forward, thinking I was going to drop her. Then I recovered, and carried her over to the bed. I laid her gently on top of the duvet.

'What's happened to Dr Bruce?' Lyn asked.

'She's going to be fine,' I said. 'She saved us.'

'From what?'

I hesitated, then decided to risk it. 'The Dark Man.'

Lyn was silent for a moment, then she asked, 'How did he escape?'

I crouched in front of her, took her hand in mine, and said gently, 'He tricked me. I was careless. But he won't get far. He's weak and we're strong. He's scared of us.'

'I saw a light,' said Lyn, and she lowered her voice to a whisper. 'Was it Dr Bruce?'

'Yes.'

It was hard to read her expression, to judge how all of this was affecting her. I consoled myself with the thought that at least she wasn't catatonic, or panicking, or obviously scared. Levelly she asked, 'What is she?'

'She's... a guardian,' I replied, saying the first thing that came into my head. 'She's here to protect you.'

I glanced at Dr Bruce, who was still sleeping peacefully. Lyn's question was a good one. Who or what *was* Dr Bruce? Could she be *my* equivalent to the Dark Man's shape-shifter? Had a future version of me, using the heart, either created my own shape-shifter to protect

Lyn, or imbued the doctor with shape-shifting powers? She had clearly been stronger than the Dark Man's shape-shifter – but why? Because she had been created with the 'young' heart, whereas the Dark Man had created his Wolves using a heart that was older, weaker? Could this also explain why Frank had been able to repel the shape-shifter's assault in the basement of Commer House? It all seemed to add up – and it made me think again of what my future self had told me when he'd stopped me from preventing Kate's abduction: that I didn't have to be a victim, that I could create my own destiny.

Perhaps, then, the Dark Man had created his Wolves of London only when he had realised the power of *his* obsidian heart was waning, and that to hold on to it he might need guardians to protect him, or warriors to fight for him. And so in retaliation I had created – or *would* create – my own 'Wolves' using the heart when it was younger, stronger, more powerful.

If this was true, then it was a delicate balance of power – and one which at this moment was tilted in the Dark Man's favour. Was the fact that he was currently in possession of the younger, more powerful heart, whereas I was lumbered with the older, weaker version simply part of the existing timeline or a dangerous variation on previously established events that might, for me, have far-reaching and disastrous consequences?

Whatever the answer, Dr Bruce's timely intervention had taught me one thing – that I couldn't be complacent; that as long as I knew there was still work to be done, I couldn't simply sit back, accept my lot and hope for the best.

No, I had to be proactive. In order to set events back on the 'right' path (as I saw it anyway) I had to pursue the Dark Man; I had to do all I could to retrieve 'my' heart.

'Where did she come from?' Lyn was asking. 'How did she know about the Dark Man?'

'The heart gave her some of its powers,' I said, wondering whether, by speaking the words, I was making them true. 'Dr Bruce doesn't *know* about the Dark Man, not consciously anyway, but the part of the heart that was sleeping inside her knew that she would be here to protect you if ever you needed it.'

Lyn's wide-eyed expression made me think of a child whose

imagination had been captured by a fairy story. 'And she *did* protect me, didn't she?'

I nodded. 'She did.'

Lyn twisted her head to look at Dr Bruce's serenely sleeping face. 'Will she be all right?'

'She'll be fine. She won't remember anything about what happened. When she wakes up she'll carry on as normal. She won't even wonder why she's been asleep on your bed.'

Lyn turned back to look at me. 'So what do we do now, Alex?'

I felt a flash of déjà vu, only this time it was the real Lyn I was talking to. 'We go after the Dark Man. We hunt him down. Because we're stronger than he is. Together we're stronger, and we can beat him. Do you believe that?'

Her eyes gazed into mine, and for a moment I saw, quite clearly, the beautiful young woman I had fallen in love with. Then she nodded, breaking the spell. 'Yes,' she said, 'I believe you.'

I slipped my hand into my jacket pocket, withdrew the heart and pressed it into her hand. She put down her cup of water and wrapped both hands around it, as if it was a small animal she had been instructed to protect.

In turn I wrapped my own, larger hands around hers.

'Find him, Lyn,' I told her, and leaned in to kiss her forehead. 'Find the Dark Man.'

FIFTEEN
PUNCH AND JUDY

It was only the second time I'd travelled using the Dark Man's old heart, and as before, it was a rough ride. It was like being administered with a drug that scrambled both my senses and all notion of linear time, whilst simultaneously being hurled around on a particularly violent fairground Waltzer.

After a pummelling, bruising journey that seemed, conversely, both instantaneous and interminable, I found myself deposited... where? With my senses mostly out of action, all I had to cling to at first was the vague notion that I had a solid surface beneath me, and another one at my back. As self-awareness slowly returned, I realised two things: one, that the surface behind me was cold and hard and smooth – a wall? – and two, that I was sliding down it, as if my unresponsive legs were crumpling under the weight of my upper body.

Was Lyn with me? I had no idea. I blinked my eyes, but my vision stubbornly refused to clear. I wasn't blind; I could see moving shapes, shifting light, colours that bled into one another. But I couldn't make sense of anything. And neither could I pick out individual sounds from the clamour that filled my head. I tried to call out, but didn't know whether I'd managed to make the sound that I'd intended, or even whether I'd moved my lips. I felt detached from too much of my body.

And then a black, crippling wave of nausea surged up through me, overwhelmed me, and even my limited sense of my surroundings dissolved for... how long? Seconds? Minutes? I stayed conscious, though, which I told myself was a good thing – even if the notion of oblivion *did* at that moment seem preferable to how I was feeling.

Eventually – though in truth it may only have been seconds – the wretchedness in which I felt I was drowning began to ebb. *Thank God for nanites*, I thought, spluttering to the surface, certain that without their protection, and with the heart in the condition it was, I'd probably be dead of acute organ failure by now, the journey having damaged my system beyond repair. This time when I blinked my vision began to clear, the blurred shapes in front of my eyes becoming more sharply defined. At the same time the clamour in my ears began to separate into individual sounds, a weave of words spoken in a mixture of human voices. It was chatter, conversation. I was in the midst of a crowd. I could hear laughter, the chink of glasses. A party? Then I became aware that one voice was louder than the rest, and its tone was different – not jovial, but shot through with a shrill edge of distress. It was repeating one word over and over. A short syllable followed by a letter. *Al. X. Al. X.*

At once my fuzzy thoughts tuned in, as if I'd broken through the membrane of sleep and snapped back into the waking world.

Alex. That was what the speaker was saying. My name!

I suddenly became aware that my arm was hurting, that it was being squeezed as though in a vice.

'Ow,' I said.

A pale oval loomed in front of me. Something black blossomed in it.

'Alex.' I realised that the black thing was a mouth. 'Alex, can you hear me?'

'Lyn,' I said, and as if I'd uttered the magic word the pale oval became her face. She looked scared, confused, her eyes flickering with panic. The vice crushing my arm was her hand, wrapped around my wrist and clinging on as if she feared I might disappear like smoke if she let go.

'Alex,' she said. 'We've moved. We're not where we were. I don't know what's happening.'

Her voice was thin and shrill. I cursed myself for not preparing her better, though in fairness there hadn't been time.

'I know,' I said, 'but it's all right. The heart's looking after us. It brought us here to find the Dark Man.' Then a thought struck me. 'Where *is* the heart, by the way?'

Irritably, as if I was worrying about trivialities, she patted my jacket with her free hand. 'It's in your pocket. I put it back there when we... arrived.'

My faculties were returning quickly now. I thought I'd come round to find myself sitting on the floor, but in fact I was slumped in a chair beside a small round table, Lyn across from me, so close our knees were touching. Had I found the chair myself, perhaps guided by some instinct of self-preservation, or had Lyn helped me into it? Certainly she seemed less affected by the rigours of the journey than I was, physically at least. Once again then, it seemed that even though I had handed the initiative to find the Dark Man over to her, I was the one who had suffered the brunt of the heart's effects – presumably because, as its guardian, it was my mind, my energy, my resources it had linked with and utilised to bring us here.

But where was 'here'? I looked blearily around, absorbing what information I could.

There were lots of people and noise. The people were drinking and smoking, and mostly paying us not the slightest attention. There was a bar to our left, a crowd gathered around it, waiting to get served. There were plenty of other small tables, like the one beside us, with laughing, chattering groups seated around them.

A pub. We were in a pub. But the air was thick with smoke; it hung over us like a blue-grey net. And only a few people were talking or texting on mobile phones. But they were not the sleek smartphones that most people carried about nowadays. These were chunky little grey Nokias, like the first phone I'd owned back in... when was it? The early 2000s?

I was trying to remember when the smoking ban had come in – 2005? 2006? – when Lyn said, 'But the Dark Man's not here. He *can't* be. But *we're* here.'

She looked stricken. Not just scared now, but terrified. Her statement was odd. It didn't quite seem to make sense. Was she losing it?

I took her hand in mine as if to anchor her, the one that wasn't still squeezing my arm hard enough to leave bruises. Gently I said, 'Yes, we *are* here, Lyn. But the Dark Man must be close by too. Otherwise the heart wouldn't have brought us.'

She shook her head rapidly from side to side. 'No, no, I don't mean *we're* here. Me and you. I mean...' But her voice petered out, as if she couldn't find a way to express herself. She scowled in frustration, then half-rose from her seat, tugging at my arm to get me to stand with her. 'Look. *Look.*'

'Look at what?' I said, allowing myself to be pulled upright in order to humour her, to stop her becoming more manic than she already was.

'I have to show you something.'

'Can't you tell me?'

'No, I have to *show* you.'

'Okay,' I said gently, 'but try to be calm. Take a couple of deep breaths.'

For a moment she looked at me uncomprehendingly. Then her taut features relaxed a little.

'I'm fine, Alex. Really. It's just... well, I'm freaked out by this.' She wafted an arm to indicate our surroundings. 'But no more than anyone else would be in my situation.'

I smiled and said, 'I'm sorry. This is my fault. I should have prepared you for this. I meant to, but everything was a bit... frantic.'

She nodded distractedly and tugged at my arm again. 'Just look at this and tell me I'm not delusional.'

'What?'

'There, look. Over on that table near the door to the Ladies. Tell me what you see.'

She was deliberately keeping her face averted from whatever she wanted me to look at, as though afraid the sight might send her over the edge. I swept my gaze across the chattering throng of people. Using the door to the Ladies as a marker, I glanced down...

A tingle went through me.

I'd seen older versions of myself several times now, and although I couldn't exactly say I'd got used to it – or ever would – it was an experience I was at least half-familiar with. But this was different. This gave the notion of time travel a whole other perspective. Not because it was the past, but because it was *this* particular night in *this* particular place. I knew exactly where we were now – and when.

It was Thursday 19th June 2003, and we were in the Punch and Judy pub in Covent Garden. Sitting on the other side of the crowded room, completely wrapped up in one another even though they'd only just met, were younger versions of Lyn and me. I was twenty-six and she was four weeks away from her twenty-third birthday. I was two months out of prison and feeling giddily happy. Lyn was… well, she was beautiful. So radiant, so full of life, that I felt emotion welling in me, tears prickling in my eyes.

I became aware that Lyn – the Lyn of today – was staring into my face, and that there were tears in her eyes too.

'I'm right, aren't I?' she murmured. 'It is…'

Her voice tailed off. I nodded. 'Yes,' I said, 'you *are* right.'

She leaned into me, and I put my arm around her. Her voice dropped to a whisper. 'I'd forgotten how… I'd forgotten what I was like.'

Her voice at that moment was the saddest thing I'd ever heard. There was so much regret, so much longing, in her words. I hugged her tight, enfolded her in my arms. Around us people chatted and drank and laughed, oblivious.

'Everything will be okay,' I told her. 'I'll make it right.'

Maybe it was wrong of me to make such a promise, but I couldn't not respond to her anguish. Looking at the young couple across the room who had eyes only for each other, I wondered why the heart had brought us here. I'd told Lyn to find the Dark Man, but had the heart simply latched on to her happiest memory and made a beeline for that instead? Was the heart now too damaged to take me where I wanted to go? In which case, would I have trouble getting back to *my* present day? To Kate? And what about all the other things I needed to do?

I tried to stay calm for Lyn's sake, but I felt my anxiety escalating. Perhaps we ought to get out of here now, give the heart another chance to find the Dark Man.

But then, diverting my eyes from my and Lyn's younger selves for a moment and sweeping my gaze once more around the pub, I realised I wasn't the only one watching the couple. Leaning on the far side of the bar, only visible now and again because of the ebb and flow of the crowd, was a figure whose attention seemed also to be fixed on the two lovebirds. It was hard to tell for certain because he was wearing dark glasses – though, in fact, it was these and the rest of his clothes that had caused me to notice him in the first place. As befitting a warm June day, most of the pub's customers were wearing light summer clothes, but this man was dressed in a black baseball cap, shades, and a black leather jacket, whose upturned collar concealed all but his nose and mouth. Although it was difficult to tell, I also got the impression there was something wrong with his face. Had he been scarred or burned?

Lyn must have felt me tense, because she asked, 'What's the matter?'

'Look over there,' I said. 'No, not at us. Over to the left. At the figure in black at the far end of the bar.'

She had broken our embrace and twisted around to see where I was looking, but now she stepped back so smartly that she almost cracked the back of her skull on my chin. I put my hands on her arms to steady her, and felt her body trembling.

'Oh my God!' she said. 'That's him!'

'Who?' I asked, then realised. 'The Dark Man?'

She shrank back against me, head nodding rapidly, jerkily.

I don't know what it was – sixth sense? Foreknowledge of our presence? Or perhaps he had simply been peripherally alerted by Lyn's evident fear of him? – but all at once the black-clad man's head snapped round. I couldn't see his eyes through his shades, but I felt certain he was scrutinising us coldly, intently.

I stared back, wondering what he would do, whether he was about to launch an attack in a crowded pub – but if he did wouldn't the younger me have remembered it? Then he turned and began to make his way towards one of the pub's several exits, his shiny black form slipping through the crowd like an eel through water.

'Stay here,' I said to Lyn.

Before she could respond, I set off in pursuit.

SIXTEEN

A SCREECH OF RAGE

It was tough pushing my way through the crowd around the bar, but despite my urgency I tried to do it without spilling a drink or nudging anyone aside. I was paranoid about making a scene and drawing the attention of my younger self. What if he clocked me and realised who I was. Would history change? Would the timeline as I knew it fall apart? It really wasn't something I wanted to find out.

It seemed an age before I managed to wriggle my way through to the spot where the Dark Man had been standing, though in truth it was probably no more than thirty seconds or so. The exit he'd used led into an equally crowded sunken courtyard that was five or six metres below ground level, from where a set of stone steps over to my left ascended to the complex of swanky retail outlets that occupied the elegant, neo-classical structure that had once housed London's main fruit and veg market.

I knew that if I lost track of the Dark Man here I'd have little chance of finding him again. There were so many exits out of the vast building of which the Punch and Judy was only a small part, and indeed out of the central square itself in which the building stood, that it would be the easiest thing in the world for him to perform a vanishing act in the surrounding maze of streets. It helped him too that the June sky was now darkening rapidly, which put the time at somewhere between 9 and 10 p.m.

A few streets away was the building which in the late 1800s had been occupied by Mr Hayles, the ill-fated proprietor of the junk shop

Tempting Treats, in which the heart had fetched up before it had found its way into my hands. The area was far more salubrious now, but the layout of the streets was no less dense and convoluted than it had been just over a century ago. Plus there were many escape options available to the Dark Man these days. To evade my clutches, he could jump on a bus or dive into a cab or lose himself in the labyrinth of the Underground. As I manoeuvred my way slowly through the milling crowd of drinkers in the courtyard, I wondered if my task was already a hopeless one.

But no. As I came to the top of the steps, leaping up them two at a time, I saw his black-clad form ahead of me. He was at the far end of the walkway that stretched up the left-hand side of the piazza, rows of now mostly closed shops on his left and Ponti's bustling, open-air restaurant on his right.

I was heartened not only by the fact that the Dark Man was still in sight, but also that, despite moving fairly rapidly, he was hobbling. I guessed this meant that although he was a younger version of the creature I'd encountered in Victorian London, he was already afflicted with whatever illness or disability would reduce him to the twisted, emaciated wreck he'd ultimately become – which could only be good news for me.

As I broke into a run, I attracted the attention of various onlookers, and a pair of Japanese tourists even scuttled out of my way in alarm, as if they thought I was going to attack them. Aside from the crowded pub, though, and the various eating places in the vicinity, the rest of Covent Garden was sparsely populated, for which I was thankful. I couldn't let him escape.

I had gained on him by maybe ten or fifteen metres when he glanced over his shoulder, and saw me.

He put on a spurt of speed, limping out through the wide, colonnaded exit at the far end of the building and into the square itself. Although I was already going full pelt, I tried to speed up too. Who knew which way he'd turn now that he was temporarily out of my sight? He might even use the heart to transport himself elsewhere.

Even as this thought occurred to me I felt a tingling, like a warm electrical current, on the right side of my stomach, just above my hip. Still running, I slipped my hand into my jacket pocket. Sure enough, the heart had come alive; I could feel energy rippling through it. But why? What had activated it? Could it be in its death throes? Might it be expending whatever energy remained in it before it died altogether?

Alarm spiking inside me, I burst out from under the roof of the main building and looked wildly around the square. A few couples were strolling about, but there was only one person on his own – a dark-clad figure, about twenty metres to my right, who was hunched over as if in pain. He was holding something in his hand – I couldn't see it, but I knew it must be the heart – and he appeared to be blurring and jittering, as if he was shifting in and out of phase. It hurt my eyes to look at him.

My right hand was still stuffed in my jacket pocket, still wrapped around the tingling heart. Not entirely sure what I was doing I drew the heart from my pocket and held it up, as if it was a grenade I was about to throw.

'No!' I shouted, and was peripherally aware of a few passers-by casting startled glances in my direction. I shouted again and began to run towards the jittering, flickering shape of the Dark Man.

As I drew closer to him, so the heart in my hand began to tingle more strongly. Electrical ripples coursed down my arm and through my body. My vision blurred, my surroundings not only moving in and out of focus, but altering too, the buildings around the square constantly brightening and going dull, as if hundreds, perhaps even thousands of days were passing in the blink of an eye.

The buildings themselves were also changing – new details appearing and then disappearing just as quickly, the frontispieces altering shape and structure and colour, as if a vast series of photographs taken through time from exactly the same angle were being laid rapidly over one another, like the images in a flicker book. Here was the row of buildings blackened by soot; here were the same buildings with bomb damage; here they were encased in scaffolding; here they were with repositioned windows.

There were more peripheral things too that appeared and disappeared: greenery, people in various styles of historical dress, carts pulled by horses, street lamps, market stalls.

I felt dizzy and sick as the array of images flashed before me – more than that, I felt buffeted, hurled about, as if I was desperately trying to hold a tiger by its tail.

And so I was in a way. Perhaps it was because the two hearts were linked – or rather, because the older heart was linked to its younger self – but I knew without a shadow of a doubt that the Dark Man was using *my* heart, the younger heart he had stolen from me, to flit haphazardly through time, to jump from one day, one year, one century to another in an effort to escape.

But clearly he was finding it impossible. Though whether that was because the hearts, when active and in such close proximity to one another, were inseparable or because the heart in my possession was latching on to my desire, my need, my desperation even, to stick with him, I had no idea. All I knew for certain was that, try as he might, he couldn't shake me off. If there *was* a way of detaching me, of breaking the link, then he was not strong enough, or perhaps simply not canny enough, to make it happen.

As though not only the hearts but our thoughts were linked, I sensed him deciding to abandon that tack, to try something different. I knew what he was going to do before he did it. I knew that rather than jumping from one *time* to another, he was instead going to try to escape by jumping from one *place* to another.

What happened first, though, was that we returned to the present day – or rather, to the point at which we'd started our tussle: 19th June 2003. Our surroundings settled, became sharper and more *fixed*; the sense of being buffeted about slowed and then ceased altogether.

The Dark Man's body stopped jittering and phasing for a moment. It became solid, entrenched wholly in the here and now. I knew, though, that this was only a temporary thing; knew that he was, in effect, briefly taking stock, getting his bearings, before launching himself elsewhere. I knew too that if I wanted to stop him, trap him, then this might be my only chance. But I was also reeling. I, too, needed a moment to orientate myself, get my breath back. Even so, I tried to imagine using the heart to throw a lasso of energy around him, ensnare him.

Just then, however, someone shouted my name, breaking my concentration. The voice was harsh, urgent, and very close. I heard running footsteps.

And then the Dark Man *leaped*.

That was what it felt like. I know because I leaped with him. There was a sense of propulsion, of hurtling through space, of my surroundings flashing by in a smear. I had the notion both that I'd been dragged after him and also that I was giving chase, determined not to lose him. For a long moment I had no inkling where or when I was. I was rushing through darkness, the heart's energy rippling through me. I was screaming – or someone was.

And then I arrived.

I hit hard ground. I stumbled and fell, gasping at the flash of bone-jarring pain as my knee impacted with something sharp. I heard the clattering of stones or bricks; more distantly I heard traffic. I felt a brief but warm summer breeze on my skin. As my vision cleared I became aware of shapes around me, some blurred by darkness, others sketchily defined by a grainy, yellowish light that leaked in from... somewhere.

There were walls surrounding me, either crumbling or unfinished. There was a roof high above, or at least the skeleton of one, through which patches of night sky could be seen. Beneath me the ground was uneven, scattered with rubble and other debris. I was on a building site, or perhaps in an old, abandoned factory or warehouse.

Still lying on the ground, I glimpsed rapid, whitish movement out of the corner of my eye. Alarmed, I twisted to my left, and saw pale, flapping shapes ascending towards the roof. Birds. Pigeons perhaps. Disturbed by my – *our?* – arrival.

Where was the Dark Man? Twisting my body again, I looked around. At first I couldn't see him. Had he given me the slip, after all? And then, twenty metres or so away, I saw a hint of murky movement, black on black. As my vision adjusted and my perspective shifted, I realised that the black silhouette in the foreground was the Dark Man. He was struggling gingerly to his feet, clearly feeling as battered and bruised as I was. I took a breath, then scrambled upright, wincing at the pain in my knee.

As small stones tumbled from my clothes and pattered to the ground, the Dark Man turned towards me. All I could see was a hunched silhouette, but I got the distinct feeling that he was glaring at me.

I took a step towards him, rubble crunching beneath my feet. Immediately he held up his right arm, as if ordering me not to come any closer. I snorted. Fuck that. Then I realised he was holding up the heart, brandishing it like a weapon.

Feeling like a duellist compelled to defend himself, I held up my heart too. I barely had time to wonder which would be the more powerful combination – a physically fit man with an older, weaker heart or an infirm man with a younger, stronger heart – when the Dark Man unleashed a flailing bolt of energy at me.

It came like a multi-tipped whip, sizzling through the air between us. Instantly I retaliated – or the heart in my hand did. I felt a great pulse rush up through my body, gathering every shred of bile and anger and outrage en route. The heart then seemed to convulse, to both suck up the venomous distillation of energy inside me and spit it out in one instantaneous movement. It was like a screech of rage hurtling towards the Dark Man, like a heat-seeking missile. Our two expulsions of energy clashed in mid-air. Clashed and grappled, each seeming to extrude black tendrils, which wound over and around one another like opposing, or perhaps complementary, cultures blending together into one enormous mass.

My whole body started to tremble, and then shudder, my muscles aching in the way they would if I was trying to lift a boulder as big as myself, or push a truck uphill. Wondering how long I could hold back the Dark Man's energy, I clenched my teeth, blinked away sweat that was trickling down my forehead and into my eyes, and looked across at him.

It gave me a savage satisfaction to see that he too was suffering. His twisted body was bent almost double, like a man trying to forge ahead through a hurricane. Somehow the sight of him struggling to maintain his attack reminded me again of everything he'd done, and caused my fury to boil up anew. Unclenching my teeth I yelled at him.

'Who are you? Why the fuck are you doing this? Why are you trying to ruin my life?'

I knew the answer – or thought I did. It was because he wanted the heart. He wanted power. And I was the one standing in his way.

His head creaked up. I saw the movement, but it was still too dark to make out his features. His voice when he answered was cracked and rough, a sign that his body was already beginning to fall apart.

'All I wanted,' he croaked, 'was acceptance. But all I got… was rejection… and disgust… and hatred.'

It was a surprising answer, but it didn't make me feel any less vitriolic towards him.

'Why was that *my* fault?' I sneered. 'Why was it *Lyn's* fault, for fuck's sake? What gave you the right to steal the heart from me, and then use it to go back and destroy the mind of the woman I loved? What kind of sick, twisted *cunt* are you? Lyn was pregnant! All she wanted was to love me and to love our child… to be a mother…'

The anger choked me up. It wadded in my throat and gut like a lump of dough infested with fire ants. It bit and burned, preventing me from ranting at him further. Instead I tried to channel my fury through the heart. At that moment all I wanted to do was crush him, tear him apart.

Then I heard the tumble and clatter of stones behind me, and the next second something flew past me, shrieking and whirling. At first I thought it was something conjured by the heart – an independent source of energy, perhaps even my rage made manifest. The notion persisted even when a slim dark figure darted in front of me, its arm raised as it faced the Dark Man. Only when its shrieks became words – 'You bastard! You bastard!' – did I realise it was Lyn.

At once I remembered the voice that had called my name in the square, the patter of running footsteps behind me. Lyn's presence here could only mean she'd been close enough to me when the Dark Man and I had 'leaped' to hitch a lift with us. Until now she must have been lying in the rubble somewhere behind me, dazed, perhaps even unconscious. But now she'd woken up.

And she was every bit as fucking furious as I was.

In *her* upraised hand she held not another version of the heart, but a half-brick. I discovered this when she hurled it at the Dark Man, still spitting vitriol. It flew straight and true, glancing off the side of his forehead and spinning away into the shadows. The Dark Man dropped without a sound, like a boxer felled by a knockout blow. Instantly the heart energy that he'd attacked me with evaporated like smoke in a strong wind. As the Dark Man's body hit the ground, his fist opened and the heart rolled free. I saw Lyn scoop up a chunk of rock and run towards him as if she intended to smash his brains to pulp.

For me, the sudden dissolution of the Dark Man's heart energy was like the unexpected snapping of a rope in a tug of war. I staggered back, exhausted and momentarily disorientated, almost tripping over a pile of rubble. In fact, if Lyn hadn't been there I might well have succumbed to my weariness and fallen flat on my arse. But seeing her standing over the Dark Man's prone body, raising the rock above her head, somehow gave me the impetus to shoot a leg out behind me and allow me to regain my balance, to stay upright.

'Lyn,' I shouted, putting as much urgency into my voice as I could, 'don't.'

She paused, but she didn't lower the arm that was holding the rock. She turned her head towards me, and although I couldn't see her features clearly, the harsh stripes of light and shadow on her face and the rubble-dust in her now wild and tangled hair made her look haggard, feral.

'Why not?' She spat out the words. 'He deserves it.'

'He does,' I said, 'but this isn't the way. I've seen him die and this isn't how it happens.'

'You've seen...' Her arm sagged. This was clearly all getting too much for her. When she next spoke her voice sounded almost plaintive. 'What do you mean? What's happening, Alex? I don't understand any of this.'

Still holding the old heart in my right hand, I held up my left in a calming gesture and approached her cautiously. 'I know,' I said. 'I know it's hard. But you've seen what the heart can do. You know it can give us the ability to travel in time.'

She stared at me. She didn't respond, but I thought – or hoped – she was listening.

'I've seen him die,' I said softly. 'I've seen the heart destroy him. But if you kill him now, everything will change – and maybe not for the better. Do you understand?'

I was close enough now to make out her features. Despite the years of suffering she'd endured that had prematurely aged her, she looked almost child-like in her confusion. Looking down at the Dark Man she said, 'He deserves to die. For what he did to me, to *us*, he deserves it.'

'I know,' I said (and part of me wondered what would happen if Lyn *did* kill him now; wondered whether, in fact, things might turn out *better*), 'and he *will* die. Just not here. Not now. It isn't worth it, Lyn. *He* isn't worth it. Kill him and you'll be a murderer forever. You don't want that, do you? A taint like that... it never leaves you.'

Still looking down at the Dark Man's crumpled body, she said,

'How could it be murder? He's not even human.'

'We don't know that,' I said. 'Throw away the rock, Lyn. Throw it away and pick up the heart. That's what will *really* hurt him.'

I watched her hesitate, wondering what I would do if she rejected my advice, what would happen.

But then she sighed once more and reluctantly dropped the rock. Stepping forward, she bent to pick up the younger heart. I half-expected it to react to her touch, but it remained inert. She straightened and stepped away from the prone figure, turning towards me.

The Dark Man groaned, stirred – and then, in a sudden burst of movement, lunged and grabbed at Lyn, his hand encircling her ankle. Her forward momentum was abruptly curtailed, his grip so strong, despite his infirmity, that she was almost yanked off her feet. As she stumbled forward, trying to maintain her balance, her head came up and she looked at me, and then, like a rugby player passing the ball while being tackled by an opponent, she lobbed the heart in my direction.

It wasn't the first time the heart had been thrown to me. Mayla, an African prostitute who'd been one of my 'watchers' in Victorian London, had once flung the heart to me up a flight of stairs, eager to be rid of it. Even though on this occasion it was dark and the heart was black, I knew, as I'd known then, that I'd catch it – and I did. I shot out my arm, opened my hand, and the next second the heart was smacking snugly into my palm. I closed my fingers around it with a sense of elation. The heart – *my* heart – was at last back in my possession.

My satisfaction lasted for only a second, though. Because as soon as I closed my hand around the 'younger' heart, both it and its older twin erupted into life. I'm not sure entirely why it happened. I can only guess that because my body was providing a physical link between two versions of the heart it created some sort of temporal short circuit. All I know for sure is that my body was suddenly engulfed in a blistering discharge of energy. It was as if the two versions of the heart were resuming hostilities using me as their battleground. My spine snapped into an arch and my head was thrown back. All at once I couldn't see, couldn't scream; my every nerve ending was on fire. I felt as if I was being torn apart – or as if each version of the heart wanted to return to its own particular time stream, taking me with it. I might have been the heart's guardian, but what the heart didn't seem to understand was that I couldn't be in two places at once. Dimly, through the roaring in my head, I heard Lyn screaming at me to let go of the heart.

But I couldn't. Each version of it was fused to my hands. The next thing I was aware of was that she was with me – she must have kicked herself free of the Dark Man's grip – and was clawing at my right hand, the one that was holding the old heart, trying to prise my fingers apart. I wanted to help her, but I couldn't; I was paralysed. I heard a crack, and then another, and although I felt no pain I knew she was breaking my fingers to get at the heart.

Then I felt what I can only describe as a sideways *whoosh*, and suddenly the energy was draining out of me – or rather, *shooting* out of me, as if I was a water pipe that had sprung a leak. As the power flowed from me, my senses came back – and to my horror the first thing I saw was Lyn flying backwards through the air, like someone caught in a bomb blast.

It was so dark that I didn't see her land – but I heard her. She came down with a horrible dead-weight thud and a clattering of bricks and rubble that made me flinch and cry out. I knew in that moment that if she'd saved my life by sacrificing her own I'd never forgive myself. I'd use the heart to go back and change things, and fuck the consequences.

The heart. I looked down at my left hand and saw that the younger heart – *my* heart – was still tightly clutched in it. My right hand, though, two fingers now swelling and going blue and (now that I came to think of it) hurting like *fuckery*, was empty, with the old heart nowhere in sight.

That wasn't my concern right now, though. All I cared about was Lyn. Goading my wobbly legs into life, and trying to ignore the sickening waves of pain that were throbbing up from my broken fingers and through my arm, I lurched and stumbled over the uneven ground towards the place where I'd heard her land. All the way I was muttering, 'Please be all right, please be all right.' It was unbearable to think that only a short distance away, while all this was happening, our younger selves were meeting for the first time.

When I finally found her, she was so still that I thought at first she was just part of a pile of weeds and rubble. I almost walked straight past her until I noticed the paleness of her outstretched hand. She looked crumpled, one leg twisted beneath her, one arm outflung, her chin tucked into her chest.

'Lyn,' I said, dropping to my knees beside her, even though the right one was still aching from when I'd whacked it earlier. She was covered in dust and there was an ominous-looking dark patch on the right side of her clothing that stretched from beneath her ribs to her hip. Unable to use my right hand (I was holding it against my body like an injured pet), I slipped the heart into my jacket pocket and reached out with my left hand, tentatively touching the dark patch with my fingers. The patch was wet and sticky. *Oil*, I told myself stubbornly, *or mud.* I raised my wet fingers to my face and smelled the unmistakeable coppery tang of blood. *Fuck.* There was such a lot of it. And the dark patch on the right side of her body wasn't all of it, by any means. There were more dark smears on her face, and yet more clotting her hair and on the rocks beneath her head.

Touching her cheek, I spoke her name again. 'Lyn. Can you hear me?'

Leaning forward, I put my ear to her chest, but before I could tell whether or not her heart was beating I heard a gritty shifting of rubble behind me.

Still on my knees, I twisted around, my hand reaching for my jacket pocket with the same speed and instinct that a gunslinger might reach for his gun.

The sound was the Dark Man. But he wasn't sneaking up on me. He was down on his hands and knees, scrabbling for something on the ground.

I realised it must have been the 'old' heart only when his hunched silhouette smeared and disappeared. Clearly he'd decided that with the younger heart back in my possession he was no longer a match for me, and so had gone away to lick his wounds. I had no doubt I'd see him again, though right at that moment such a prospect seemed less than inconsequential.

My head starting to swim from the pain in my right hand, I drew the heart from my pocket with my left, then hunched forward and slid that same arm carefully beneath Lyn's shoulders. I had to push through the blood-sticky rubble beneath her, but eventually I had her in an awkward but fairly secure grip. Holding her as close to me as I dared, I rested my forehead against hers and instructed the heart to take us home. As our surroundings bled away and the world went momentarily black, I prayed it wasn't already too late.

SEVENTEEN

THE CROSSROADS

'Penny for them?'

I was so deep in my own thoughts that I didn't hear Clover come in. I looked up from my chair, feeling dazed.

'Just the usual boring stuff that any time-travelling killer thinks about,' I said.

She frowned and crossed the room to sit in the seat beside me.

'You're not a killer.' She put a hand on my arm. 'Well, not a *bad* one anyway.'

I snorted a laugh.

'How are the fingers?'

I held up my right hand. It had been five days now since, thanks to Lyn, I had got the younger heart back. My forefinger and the one next to it were still buddy-taped together, but there was virtually no pain from them now.

'Fine,' I said. 'Good old nanites doing their work. The doctors are baffled by my amazing powers of recovery.'

She smiled, waited a couple of beats, and then said, 'So? Do you want to share?'

'My fingers?'

'Your thoughts, dumbo.'

I sighed. 'I'm just... taking stock. Trying to work out what my next move should be. Trying to apply logic to the situation.' I tapped the side of my head. 'It's hard to be logical, though, when you're on the inside looking out, when you can't see the bigger picture.'

She nodded. 'Go on.'

'It's just... time travel creates so many ripples... so many consequences and conundrums and inconsistencies. By doing what I'm doing... going through the War with Frank, making notes in my little book to remind myself of things I need to do in the future... it just feels like my life's become a constant process of patching up, of making sure everything continues as it should... or as I *think* it should... of, I don't know, retro-fitting the past so it correlates with the present, and hopefully the future.'

'It's a big responsibility,' she said.

'It's not *just* that, though, is it?'

'Isn't it?'

I'd looked away from her to stare down at my hands, but now I slid another glance in her direction.

'What if we're wrong, Clover? What if *I'm* wrong? What if time travel isn't an exact science? What if none of this is set in stone? What if time is constantly in flux, and whenever I use the heart, thinking I'm keeping things on the straight and narrow, or putting them back to where *I've* been led to believe they should be, I change things? Maybe not big things, but... what if, by establishing or restoring the timeline, I'm making things happen slightly differently each time, creating ripples?'

'That's a lot of what ifs,' she said.

'My life's become a whole series of what ifs. And here's another: what if I just decide not to do it any more?'

She was looking at me steadily, and although her expression was thoughtful rather than disapproving I couldn't help feeling a bit like a child that has stamped a petulant foot.

'You've said this before,' she said.

I threw up my hands in exasperation. 'Yeah, I know. It's just that now I've got Kate back my whole mindset's changed. Before, I had a purpose. I was searching for my daughter, and I wasn't prepared to stop until I'd found her. Now, though...'

'You've still got a purpose,' Clover said. 'You've got to keep things on the right track for Kate's sake. Who knows what might happen if you don't?'

'But that's my point, don't you see? *Who knows?* Maybe things will be better without my interference. Maybe, if I hadn't got involved in the first place, Lyn wouldn't have ended up the way she did.'

Clover was silent for a moment. Then she glanced across at the recumbent figure in the hospital bed.

'Lyn's fine,' she said firmly. 'She's going to be fine.'

I looked across at Lyn too. We were back at Oak Hill, the private hospital in which I'd recuperated after returning from the Victorian era with Clover and Hope. Lyn, who was now a patient here, was in an induced coma, having fractured her skull. With the top half of her shaven head swathed in bandages she looked incredibly vulnerable, child-like. She had also broken three ribs and her right arm, and she had a nasty gash on her right hip. But aside from that her injuries were superficial – cuts and bruises, most of which were already healing.

'I'm not talking about her physical injuries,' I said. 'I'm talking about the five years she spent raving and terrified out of her wits because of that... that bastard.'

'The heart seems to be helping her with that.'

I had placed the heart in Lyn's limp hand, and despite being unconscious she was now cupping it gently between her palms.

'It calms her,' I said. 'Whenever she's held it before, she's said she can feel it healing her.'

There was silence between us for a moment. Then Clover said, 'Do you really think you can keep Kate safe by doing nothing?'

'By protecting her, you mean?'

'Don't split hairs, Alex.' Clover's voice was mild, though, not irritable. 'You know what I'm talking about.'

I felt weary. Weary of the way my thoughts constantly batted to and fro. Weary of everything I might prospectively still have to do to maintain the status quo. Weary of the uncertainty of it all. I slumped back in my seat.

'Truthfully?' I said. 'I don't know. I just don't know. I mean, how do you keep someone safe? How do you *guarantee* their safety?'

Clover considered the question. 'You eliminate all threats to them, I suppose.'

'And what's the biggest threat to Kate?'

Clover shrugged. 'The Dark Man?'

'The Dark Man,' I confirmed. 'So you'd think, wouldn't you, that what I *really* need to do is find out, once and for all, who the Dark Man is and nullify him in some way? But is that possible? Is it even *wise*? Because we've already seen the Dark Man die. We know how it ends for him. We know that he becomes an ancient, crippled creature who's eventually destroyed by the power of the thing he most covets. So the question is, can I change that version of our past by dispatching the Dark Man sooner? More to the point, *should* I change it? *Dare* I? And what'll happen to us, to our past, to our memories, if I do?'

'It's a tricky one,' Clover admitted.

'That's putting it mildly.' I hesitated, then said, 'Thing is, I have been thinking pretty seriously about going to a point in time where I *know* the Dark Man's going to be and... well, stopping him from doing what I know he's going to do.'

'What point in time is that?'

'The moment when Lyn first met the Dark Man. The moment when he first... poisoned her mind.'

'Do you know when that is?'

I nodded. 'With Lyn's help I've worked it out. This could be the pivotal point for both of us – the point when both our lives began to go off the rails...'

'I sense a "but".'

I grimaced. 'But what if I'm wrong? What if I do manage to stop the Dark Man? The change to both of our lives would be... monumental. Lyn and I would live happily together with Kate, as a family, and maybe none of this' – I waved my hand around vaguely – 'would ever happen. Or maybe it would happen so differently that I'd never get to this point, and so would never be in the position to go back and change things. Classic time anomaly.'

'Or maybe only *some* things would change,' Clover suggested. 'I mean, maybe your older daughter's boyfriend would still get in trouble with that drug dealer, and maybe you'd still contact Benny, who'd still put you on to me, and I'd still tell you about the heart...'

'But Kate would be with Lyn, and so Adam and Paula would never need to look after her, which means they'd never abduct her, which means I wouldn't have to steal the heart, which means I'd never kill McCallum...' I put a hand to my head, as though to contain my thoughts. 'Unless...'

'Unless?'

'Unless something worse happened. What if, in this new scenario, it's the Dark Man who abducts Kate, after all? What if he hurts Lyn, or worse, and abducts Kate?'

'Why would he do that?' asked Clover.

'I don't know. But that's the point, don't you see? I don't know anything! And that's what's tearing me up. If I nip things in the bud, and stop the Dark Man from doing what he did to Lyn, I might make things so much better. On the other hand, I might make things so much worse. I mean, what about Hope for one thing? If I change things, I might never go back to Victorian times, might never rescue her. She'd die a horrible, lingering death in one of Tallarian's cages...'

'Nothing is without consequences,' said Clover softly. 'And at the end of the day all you can do is what you think is right.'

I looked across at Lyn on the bed. She looked nothing like the bright and bubbly girl I'd fallen in love with. Her skin was waxen, her face sunken and care-worn.

'But I don't know what that is,' I said. My guts felt clenched; my head ached. 'That's the problem, Clover. I don't know what that is.'

EIGHTEEN

A HOUSE OF NIGHTMARES

My hands are buried deep in the sand, but I push them deeper still. I feel the sun scorching my back, the hot sand burning my knees, but it doesn't matter. I am connected to the earth; I am connected to creation. I reach and I reach, and eventually I grasp the soul of the planet.

It is an unknowable force, but in that moment I know it, and it knows me. It is the stuff of all things; I am its Creation, but also its Creator. I am both Frankenstein and his monster. We are indivisible, a loop that continually circles, and never meets its beginning, nor its end.

I close my eyes and reach out, both with my hands and my mind. I draw the soul of the planet towards me, even as it lures me in. Then the essence I am searching for implodes, compacting and compacting until it becomes both compliant and pliable, a substance to be manipulated.

When I draw it from the sand it is black and dripping, and squirming with energy, with life – the *first* life. Then it gathers the sun and the air to it, or rather the knowledge of what and where it is, of what its limits are within this environment. And it adapts accordingly, becoming clay and stone and root matter. And I use my hands, and the energy we share, to shape it, knowing it will find its way...

When I opened my eyes I was immediately overwhelmed by the sense that I had returned from a monumental journey, and that in the split second it had taken me to slip from sleep into consciousness I had crossed impossibly vast distances of time and space. As I lay in my warm bed, staring into a swirl of shadows and pre-dawn light, I fancied I could hear the unending hum of the universe, which had accompanied me forward through time. More than that, I fancied I was a part of it; that not only my flesh and bones but also my thoughts, my ideas, my perceptions, my *soul* were composed of stardust, which still crackled with the faint white static of the beginning of everything.

Mad thoughts. *Cosmic* thoughts. Old Dennis Jasper, wherever he was, would have been proud of me.

I smiled, but couldn't shake the notion that when I breathed it was the universe breathing, and that when I shifted in bed I could hear that white static underlying every tiny rustle of movement.

Movement. I saw it out of the corner of my eye, flickering and dark. Slowly I turned my head on the pillow. The universe crackled.

'Oh, my...'

The heart was blooming with life. Perched on the bedside table between my phone and a John le Carré paperback I'd started last night in the hope it would dilute my racing thoughts, it was extruding a mass of long black tendrils, which were writhing and waving gently, as though tasting the air. Still partly swaddled in the freewheeling and seemingly limitless nature of my dream-thoughts, I wondered if this was an omen, or perhaps even an answer of sorts to the many questions constantly orbiting inside my head. Trying to clear my mind of clutter to facilitate the link between the heart and my own subconscious, I reached out a hand and pushed my fingers deep into the tendrils, caressing them, as if they were the silky strands of a lover's hair. The tendrils responded, wrapping themselves around my fingers and wrist. Immediately I felt the heart-energy swirling through me, becoming part of me, like ink injected into water. I gave myself up to it, trusting it would take me where I *needed* to go...

Maybe it was because I hadn't imposed my will on the heart – or not consciously anyway – but this time the transition was both effortless and instantaneous. This time I didn't even get a sense that my surroundings were shifting around me. All at once I was simply no longer lying in bed, but standing in a room that I recognised instantly. The walls were a soft butter-yellow, and there was a mobile of little felt clouds and a smiling sun hanging over a wooden cot containing a padded mattress. Stood against the opposite wall was a chest of drawers with a changing mat on top of it, and in the corner, next to a window which was still waiting for curtains, was a well-padded armchair, still wrapped in plastic, which Lyn and I had bought under the assumption that Lyn would need somewhere comfortable to sit when she got up to feed our new baby in the middle of the night.

This room was the nursery in our little flat in Shepherd's Bush, and the smell of fresh paint and fresh fabric, coupled with the lack of curtains, placed the timeframe at mid 2007. In fact, I could be even more accurate than that, because I knew without a shadow of a doubt that the heart had brought me to the date I'd had bobbing in my head for the past week or so.

Thursday May 10th 2007. As closely as Lyn and I had been able to ascertain between us, this was the day when she had first encountered the Dark Man.

He had come in the evening, she'd told me, when I was out teaching. Aside from that she had little recollection of the incident. She said she could remember it now only as an awful dream – or as less than that; as the *flavour* of an awful dream. It was a memory which even now her mind veered away from, or erected barriers against, whenever she tried to focus upon it.

All she remembered with any certainty was waking up at around 9 p.m. that night, and thereafter of having a little wriggling *something* in her mind. Something which made her think of a worm burrowing into an apple, and which, little by little, blackened and poisoned her thoughts.

'It's like... like he'd made my mind into a dark and terrifying place. Like a house of nightmares that I couldn't escape from. At first, sometimes I'd be there, trapped in this horrible place, and sometimes I wouldn't. But when I was there I couldn't make myself understood, and when I wasn't there I'd forget about it – or almost forget, enough at least that I couldn't explain what I was going through. And then, more and more, I'd find myself trapped in the nightmare house until finally I couldn't get out at all. And all the time I was looking for you, Alex, but I couldn't find you. And I was so scared that I lost the ability to function on my own. I couldn't speak... couldn't think...'

Even telling me this much had made her tremble. And although I'd wanted to know everything about her first encounter with the Dark Man I hadn't pushed it. Looking around now, at the half-finished nursery, at the chair that Lyn would never sit in, I felt sad and angry.

We'd been so happy together, and so looking forward to the birth of our first child. And it wasn't as if we'd been asking for much. We'd just wanted a simple, straightforward life. Thinking of how the Dark Man had casually and spitefully destroyed all of that made the anger boil up into something vicious and murderous inside me. The Dark Man was nothing but a cancer, and if I got the opportunity I would eradicate him, cut him out.

I could tell by the sky through the curtainless window that it was already evening. But what time in the evening? It was May and edging towards dusk, so I guess that would make it... 7:30? 8 p.m.? Lyn couldn't remember exactly what time the Dark Man had showed up, but what she *did* remember was waking up on our bed, fully clothed, at around 9 p.m. I used to leave the flat for my class at 6:30, and be back around 9:45, so was it possible the Dark Man's visit had already happened? That I was already too late? No, surely not. The heart wouldn't be so cruel – would it? Feeling a little panicky, I crossed the room to the door, opened it a crack and listened.

Faintly I could hear music. One of the female vocalists that Lyn used to like: Norah Jones, Tori Amos, someone like that. Along with the clatter-clink-bump of pots and pans and crockery, and cupboards opening and closing, which I knew was the sound of Lyn clearing up after dinner, the music was coming from the kitchen, which was the last door on the left at the end of the corridor. And now that I had the door open I could hear Lyn half-singing, half-humming along with the music. It was a distracted and fairly tuneless sound, to be honest, and yet the sweetness of her voice, the innocence of it, was like a knife to my heart.

But there was no time for sentiment. I was here for a reason – but what reason? How *exactly* was I going to stop the Dark Man? By making myself known to Lyn, announcing my presence, acting (unbeknownst to her) as her protector? But wouldn't that lead to some awkward questions? Like why had I come back? Why wasn't I teaching? Why was I wearing a T-shirt and boxers, and looking all rumpled and tousle-haired, as if I'd been asleep? And, perhaps most pertinently, why did I look the best part of a decade older than I had an hour or so earlier?

Suddenly I had a horrible thought. What if *I* was the Dark Man? Or rather, what if it had been *my* presence here now – an older, more care-worn version of the man she knew and loved – that had sent her over the edge? Was that possible? But she had identified the Dark Man in the Punch and Judy, hadn't she? And I had had run-ins with him; he wasn't a figment of our imagination.

Even so, I dithered, wondering how best to do what I had presumably been brought here to do.

I was still dithering when Lyn screamed. But I was running barefoot along the corridor as the scream became words, as her voice, shrill and raw with fear, demanded, '*Who are you? Get out! Get out of my flat!*'

I was a metre or two from the kitchen door when I heard *his* voice – the Dark Man's. It was a clotted rasp, and it sounded not malicious, as I'd expected, but wheedling, even regretful.

'Don't be scared. I've been looking for you. It's taken me so long to get here. I just... just want you to remember me.'

I hit the partly open door with my shoulder and burst into the kitchen. I saw Lyn pressed back against the kitchen sink, her hands soapy, terror on her face. The Dark Man, looking similar to how I'd seen him in Covent Garden, was looming over her as she leaned back, his gnarled hand reaching out. Before I could do anything to stop him, I saw him touch her cheek lightly with the tips of his fingers, saw (or thought I saw; it happened in a split second) a black spark, like a shot of poison, spasm from the withered obsidian heart in the Dark Man's other hand, pass in an instant through his body and into the fingers of the hand that was touching Lyn. Then the blackness passed through his fingers and into Lyn's skin, forming a bruise-like blemish on her cheek. I saw Lyn's eyes widen in utter horror – and then her body dropped as if her bones had been removed, her legs folding beneath her.

'*No!*' I screamed as I ran at the Dark Man.

But he was no longer there. Suddenly I was alone with Lyn, who was lying in a crumpled heap at my feet. I dropped to my knees beside her, saw that the dark blemish on her cheek was already fading, being absorbed through her pores and into her body. Frantically I pressed the heart against her now-pale cheek, hoping I wasn't already too late, that I could use it to draw the poison out of her before it became embedded, wormed its way into her mind.

It didn't work. The heart remained inert in my hand, nothing but a cold black stone.

'Come on,' I muttered. 'Come on, you fucker. Why did you bring me here, if not for this?'

I kept the heart pressed against her cheek for several minutes, willing it to come to life, *ordering* it to undo what the Dark Man had done – but to no avail. The heart refused to play ball. In the end, snarling, I drew back my arm to hurl it across the room. But I arrested the action before I could carry it through, forced myself to calm down.

'Useless bastard,' I spat, holding the heart in front of my face, before, due to my lack of pockets, tucking it under my arm. With both hands free I picked Lyn up, carried her through the flat and into our bedroom. I laid her on top of the bed, and after putting the heart down on the bedside table, placed a hand gently on her swollen stomach. I felt nothing at first, and then there was a squirm of movement, followed by a little thump, which, despite the situation, made me smile.

'Hang in there, Kate,' I whispered. 'I'll see you soon. I love you.'

I sat on the edge of the bed and stroked Lyn's hair, and then her cheek where the Dark Man had touched her, wondering what else I could do. Remembering how Lyn had gained comfort from simply holding the heart, how she had said that she could feel it healing her, I grabbed it from the bedside table and pressed it between her hands. Then I simply held it there, my hands over hers, for a long time, looking at her face.

She looked peaceful, but then she had looked peaceful from the moment she'd passed out. I thought again of how the Dark Man had said that he had been looking for her, that he wanted her to remember him.

The words themselves could have constituted a threat, but the way he had said them hadn't seemed threatening. Was it possible that what he had done to her, therefore, had been an accident? In which case, could he be *persuaded* not to touch her? Maybe if I'd just been a bit quicker off the mark, if I hadn't stood dithering in the nursery...

Perhaps it wasn't too late. I had the heart, after all; I could try again. Gently I extricated the heart from Lyn's hands, then leaned forward and kissed her on the forehead.

'See you earlier,' I whispered and closed my eyes. I willed the heart to take me back to the nursery, to the exact moment I'd arrived this evening.

I opened my eyes, and felt a moment of disorientation. I wasn't where I'd expected to be. I was so thrown that it took me a moment to recognise my surroundings – and then it struck me.

I was in my bedroom, in my house in Kensington. My bed sheets were rumpled, as if I'd just crawled out of them, and there on my bedside table was my phone and the John le Carré book I'd been reading the previous evening.

So the heart had transported me not to the nursery, but back to where I'd started from this morning. And from the quality of the light pressing against the closed curtains it looked as though I hadn't been gone long either – possibly only minutes.

I paused just long enough for the post time-travel nausea to peak and then ebb as the nanites kicked in, and then I tried again. I wondered whether the misunderstanding had been mine or the heart's. Or was the heart sulking because I'd got cross with it? The thought would have been funny if it hadn't made me uneasy.

There was a slight sense of shifting, and then my bedroom simply solidified around me again. What was going on? Was I losing my touch? I waited for the sickness to come and go, then tried again.

And again I didn't move.

I tried three more times, thinking that nothing was happening at all, until I realised that, subconsciously, I had heard the same faint bird call outside my window more than once. I tried again – and yes, there it was again. The exact same cawing screech of a distant crow.

So I *was* moving each time I used the heart, but only in time, and only backwards by the same few minutes. Was I stuck in a loop? Had the heart become defective in some way?

In truth, I think I knew the answer. I just didn't want to face up to it.

I'd had my chance, and I'd blown it. Or perhaps this was the heart's way of letting me know there were some things I *couldn't* change, no matter how much I wanted to. Perhaps when it came to events in my past, events that I *knew* had been established in my own timeline, then – even taking into account interference from my future selves, which was *also* part of my established timeline – there was no changing them further.

In some ways this was reassuring (it was as if the heart had a built-in safety cut-out switch that came into effect whenever I tried to do something with potentially cataclysmic consequences), but shittily it also meant there was seemingly no leeway to rectify the wrongs and regrets of the past.

Or was there? Perhaps I was accepting defeat too easily. Perhaps there was another way round it.

I pondered on the problem for a while. Wondered whether the solution might be not to try and overlap an event I'd already lived through, and failed to influence, but to go even further back in time – or even forward.

Yes, maybe that was it. Maybe the easiest and best thing to do was simply to go forward, into my own future, and seek advice from my older self. Would my older self be prepared to help me when I got there? I had no way of knowing. But what I *did* know was that if my older self was simply a future version of me, then when he was my age he would have had this thought too.

In which case, he would be expecting me.

NINETEEN
INTO THE FUTURE

Moving forward was easy.

I'd decided to go forward five years – *exactly* five years – from the day I left, which was Friday November 2nd 2012. It was mind-boggling to think that in what I considered *my* timeline, the one I'd lived in before acquiring the heart, and the one I felt most anchored to, only a few weeks had passed since I'd first got in touch with Benny and met Clover at Incognito. I'd lived for considerably more than a few weeks during that time, of course, having spent three months in Victorian London and another eighteen or so from the late summer of 1914 to early 1916. Soon I'd have to head back there again and live out the rest of the War. Which meant that by the time Candice, my eldest daughter, next saw me I'd have lived through something like five years in what for her would be roughly the same number of weeks.

I'd been thinking a lot about that since finding Kate. About what it really meant. It was something of a headfuck living on a different timescale to everybody else. I hadn't got used to it, nor probably ever would. A few weeks ago the prospect of going months, even years, without seeing my daughters would have seemed inconceivable. I wondered whether Candice would be shocked at my appearance when she saw me again. Or would she, in that oblivious way all teenagers seemed to have, not even notice how much I'd aged? Or maybe the nanites inside me would slow the effects of ageing right down, and I actually *wouldn't* look all that different to how I'd looked before I'd gone off to war?

This, of course, was assuming that everything went as intended, and I returned from the Front unscathed.

Once the usual time-travel nausea had subsided, the first thing I did when my bedroom, after shimmering slightly, reappeared around me, albeit subtly altered (the bed stripped, a few things replaced or moved around), was head for the office, which as I think I've said before was white, spotless and full of snazzy gadgets. I logged on to the main computer, a flash, flat-screen model, and checked the date, smiling as it showed me I'd arrived when I'd intended: November 2nd 2017.

Turning from the computer screen, I shouted, 'Hello?' but received no reply. I prowled the house in the hope of finding either my future self or someone who could tell me where he (I) was.

But the house was empty. Moreover, it didn't look as if it had been lived in for a while. The beds were stripped, the place inordinately clean and tidy, and there were no perishable foods in the fridge or cupboards.

In fact, the place seemed to me to be sending out a clear message: *Don't bother hanging about. You'll be wasting your time.* Despite the fact that the message was most likely from my future self, I found it teeth-grindingly infuriating. My future self had known I'd be here at this time, so why was he being evasive? Then again, it was presumably because he remembered being me, and therefore remembered arriving to find the house like this, and so didn't want to risk disrupting the timeline by doing anything different. Would I be the same five years down the line? I liked to think not. In fact, I was so annoyed that I told myself I'd definitely make sure I was around to greet the younger me. But when it came down to it... well, who knew?

I jumped another year into the future – November 2nd 2018 – and once again found the house both clean and tidy, and empty and closed up.

'I can do this over and over again, you know,' I shouted, my voice echoing in the empty house, 'and I bloody will. You can't avoid me for ever.'

I made myself a cup of black tea (there was no milk) and sat in the armchair by the unlit fire, wondering if there was any way to out-manoeuvre my future self. I wondered whether perhaps I could just leap around through time, so randomly and rapidly, without recording my journeys, that the future me would simply forget where and when I might appear.

But even if I managed to catch myself that way, what would stop the future me from escaping by immediately activating the heart and using it to send himself, say, a few hours or a day or two into the future? And as soon as I considered that possibility I cursed myself for thinking of it, because now that it was in my head my future self could, and probably would, make it a reality.

I tried to put myself in my future self's shoes by wondering how I'd feel if my past self popped forward to ask my advice. First of all, I guess I'd be alarmed, because I didn't do that and it would therefore mean that my past had changed. But looking at the situation purely hypothetically, I guess, depending on what the past me wanted to know, I'd be... wary.

Let's say, for instance, that my past self popped forward after receiving the text sent apparently by Kate's kidnapper, telling me to meet him at McCallum's house. And let's say he wanted to know whether he should go, or whether it was a trap. What would I tell him? Because, yes, it *had* been a trap, and it had led to my arrest – but it was as a indirect result of being incarcerated in the police station that I had ended up as a prisoner of Tallarian's in Victorian London, and it was because of that that I'd first encountered Hope, and had ultimately been able to give her a life she would otherwise never have lived.

So... there were always consequences. Each separate event was a link in a chain, and if one of those links were to break... well, who knew what might happen.

But all of this was old ground. And on the other hand, there would surely be a way of giving my past self advice that would at least ease his passage without breaking the chain. Besides which, I was pig-headed and impatient. And I could just as easily believe that I was *meant* to be persistent, was *meant*, at this point, to receive some advice from my future self. Because whereas I could understand not wanting to upset the apple cart as regards my past, surely (if you'll forgive my mixing of food-related metaphors) this was an entirely different kettle of fish? Because wasn't I now, by my actions, *creating* my future? Whatever I chose to do at this moment would surely be my future self's *memory* of what I did?

With this in mind, I decided to try one more thing. I told myself that if it worked, it was because it was *destined* to work; it was because my future self *remembered* it working. Using the phone in the hall, I rang my daughter Candice's mobile number, hoping she hadn't changed it in the six years that had passed since 2012. After a couple of rings a voice said, 'Hello?'

'Candice,' I said, trying not to sound too unsure.

'Dad. How come you're home? What's happened?'

I paused, then said, 'What do you mean?'

'I thought you were in South Africa for the next month. How come you're not?'

My mind raced. South Africa? Why would I be in South Africa? Then it struck me that my 2018 self may possibly be in another time zone, and had simply told Candice that he had a job which took him abroad for long periods.

'Yeah, I... er... there was a change of plan. Bit too complicated to explain.' Before she could respond I said quickly, 'Anyway, the thing is, my mobile's on the blink, and I can't get access to my address book and diary, and I... I was trying to remember the date of a business meeting, because I need to get in touch with this guy. And... anyway, it's a long story, but I'm pretty sure this meeting was the day after I saw you last, but I can't remember exactly when that was. So I thought–'

'Calm down, Dad,' Candice said. 'You sound really stressed.'

'Yeah, I am,' I admitted. *Don't overdo it. Play it cool.* 'I'm just having one of those days.'

'Sounds like it.'

I laughed. 'Sorry for being so manic. But if you *can* remember...'

'Hang on a sec, I'm on it. Just crossing to the calendar on the wall. You came for Sunday lunch, didn't you? About three weeks ago? Yeah... here we are. It was the fourteenth. So I guess your meeting must have been Monday the fifteenth.'

'Sounds about right,' I said. 'Thanks, Candice.'

'No probs.'

'Oh, hang on. There is one other thing. You're going to think I'm a complete idiot, but like I say, my address book's gone up the swanny, so I'm jotting down everyone's addresses as I speak to them. So... sorry, but could you remind me what *your* address is again?'

'Dad!' She sounded shocked, and I thought: *Oh God, what if I've made a massive faux pas? What if she lives next door or something?* Then she tutted and said, 'I can't believe you can't remember your own daughter's address!'

'I know,' I said, putting on my what-a-prat-I-am voice, 'but you know what I'm like. I've got a terrible memory for these things. Sign of age.'

She tutted, but reeled off an address, which I jotted onto the pad beside the phone. I'm glad I asked. I'd thought it likely she'd have left the house she'd been living in with her mum and Glenn by now, and moved into a place of her own, and sure enough she had. The address she gave me, in the genteel environs of Tufnell Park, was not one I recognised.

I was dying to ask her how she was, what she was doing now, whether she was with anyone – but from her point of view my questions would have been too weird. So instead I said, 'Right, well, thanks, honey. Speak to you soon.'

'Yeah, bye, Dad.'

Five minutes later, having paused just long enough to put on some of my future self's clothes so that I didn't a) look odd, and b) freeze to death whilst hanging around on my daughter's street, I used the heart to take me back to Sunday October 14th 2018, timing it to arrive at 11:30 a.m. Trying to appear as unobtrusive as possible, I half-hid behind a tree a few houses down on the opposite side of the road and staked out Candice's place.

It was a nice house. Semi-detached, but tall and set back from the road behind a thick hedge and a front lawn maybe four metres square. A wrought-iron gate led up a garden path to a set of stone steps, a tiled porch and a blue front door flanked by stained-glass panels. If the place had a cellar, then the house was at least four stories high – maybe five if a couple of cramped attic rooms had been squeezed under the neatly tiled roof.

I was dying to know more about Candice's present circumstances, would have loved to have knocked on that blue door and asked my daughter to fill me in on the last six years of her life. But of course I couldn't. All I could do was speculate – so speculate I did.

The way I saw it there were four options. One, she had graduated, landed herself a plum job with a megabucks wage and bought herself a prime piece of London real estate. Two, the place belonged to her current (and obviously rich) boyfriend/fiancé/husband. Three, the house, despite appearances, had been divided into flats or bedsits, one of which she was renting. Or four, she was a live-in nanny/housekeeper with a well-to-do family.'

I was still wondering when a metallic red Vauxhall Vectra appeared at the end of the road and headed towards me. Because I didn't want it to look as though I was loitering, and because I had no mobile on me with which I could have pretended I was having a conversation, I dropped to one knee, dipped my head and picked at the laces of the black Timberland boots I'd borrowed from my future self's house.

Instead of driving past, though, the car slowed and stopped beside me. Hoping the driver might simply be after directions, I raised my head as the passenger window slid down – to see my own face staring back at me.

'I think you're wearing my clothes,' my future self said.

I looked down at myself and sighed. 'These are *my* clothes. I just haven't bought them yet.'

My future self smiled. 'Get in,' he said, 'quick before she sees us.'

I took one more look at Candice's house, half-expecting to see my eldest daughter staring at me from an upstairs window, eyes boggling and mouth open wide in astonishment, and then I opened the passenger door and slid into the seat. The car pulled away from the kerb as soon as I shut the door.

'Nice flowers,' I said, eyeing the large bouquet in fancy pink paper on the back shelf.

'They're exactly like the ones you'll buy in six years' time,' my future self said drily. 'The wine too. That's in a cooler in the boot.'

'Should I make a note of it?' I said, and then realised I'd left my little black book in my jacket pocket, which was draped over the back of the chair in my bedroom in 2012.

'No need. These kinds of things take care of themselves.'

At the end of the road we turned left.

'Where are we going?' I asked.

'Why? Are you nervous?'

'Oh yeah. Because taking me to a remote location and putting a bullet through my head would be a great idea from your point of view.'

What we did, in fact, was park at the south end of Hampstead Heath and go for a walk up and down the hills and through the woods. Because it was a chilly Sunday morning, and because we kept off the beaten track, we didn't see many people about. The occasional jogger or dog walker who *did* walk or run past us paid us little or no attention. I guess that anyone who happened to glance our way would just assume we were twin brothers out for a morning stroll. Apart from having slightly longer hair than me, I was pleased to see my future self looked pretty much identical to how I looked now.

Tramping through a mushy carpet of autumn leaves, I said, 'Unless I'm stricken with amnesia in the next few years, I don't suppose you need me to tell you why I'm here?'

'No, I don't,' said my future self. He shot me a sidelong look and said, 'As you'll appreciate in a few years' time, this is fucking weird for me.'

'Because you're having to remember to say exactly what you said when you were me?'

He screwed up his face. 'Not exactly. Because you don't remember conversations you had years ago word for word, do you? But at the same time... yeah, whatever I say there's a kind of... weird echo. It's sort of like déjà vu, except not.' He shrugged. 'It's hard to explain.'

'I'll try to remember that,' I said.

He grimaced. 'You won't. Not properly anyway.'

We grew quiet when a woman in a headscarf approached and then scuttled past, swinging a lead. As I idly watched her dog, a white Fox Terrier with a saddle-like patch of black fur and brown ears, snuffle its way through every pile of damp leaves as it trailed in her wake, my future self said, 'There's not much I can tell you, you know.'

'I guessed you'd say that.'

'I know you did. Sorry.'

The dog gave us a wary glance and bustled past. I said, 'When you were me, did you ever think you'd go against the grain? Do things differently when it came to your turn? Just for the hell of it? Or maybe not exactly that–'

'Because I was frustrated and pissed off with what people *weren't* telling me?'

I nodded.

'Course I did.'

'So?'

'So now that I'm here I'm thinking it's not worth the risk. I'm thinking there's probably too much at stake.'

'Probably?'

He shrugged. 'Believe it or not, I'm not some sort of oracle. There's still loads I don't know.'

'But there must be loads you *do* know that I don't?'

'I know there's big changes coming.' He halted for a moment, eyes widening. 'Wow, what I just said was *exactly* how I remembered me saying it when I was you. *That* was weird.'

'What kinds of changes?' I asked. 'Can't you give me a hint?'

He looked momentarily thoughtful. 'Hang in there. That's all I can really say. You'll find out soon enough.'

We lapsed into silence again, though only because my head was buzzing. In front of us the sinuous grey blur of a squirrel darted up a tree. Breath pluming as my frustration made me snappish, I said, 'Can't you give me *anything* concrete?'

'I'm sorry.' And to his (my) credit he truly *did* look sorry. 'If I thought it would help, I'd tell you. I really would. You know that.'

'Do I?'

'Well... you will do. Look, why don't you try asking me some specific questions and I'll see what I can do.'

'What should I do about the Dark Man?' I said immediately.

'Next.'

'Oh, come *on*!'

This time he didn't even say anything; just gave me a look.

Scowling I said, 'All right then. Where are Kate and Lyn? *How are they*?'

His smile was both crooked and inscrutable. 'Ask me something else.'

'Oh, for fuck's sake! Is that going to be your answer whatever I ask? Because let me tell you, when I get to be you, I'm going to do it all differently. I'm going to spill every fucking bean imaginable.'

Even as I was saying it, though, I knew I probably wouldn't. And what was worse was that my future self knew how frustrated I was, and therefore knew exactly what I was thinking and feeling. All of which made me feel like a petulant child, stamping its foot to no effect.

Instead of making fun of me, though, my future self was sympathetic.

'I wish I could tell you everything, I really do. But all this – who you are, who I am, where we both are right now – is so fragile that one slip could fuck up everything. I'm not saying it *would*, because I don't know

– I genuinely don't. What I'm saying is, it *could*, and that's enough for me to keep schtum.'

'Which means you must be in a good place right now, yeah?' I said. 'I mean, if you're scared I'll change everything by knowing too much, then you *must* be in a good place, otherwise you'd *want* it changed, wouldn't you?'

My older self just shrugged and pulled an imaginary zip across his lips.

'I can see it in your eyes,' I said – though I couldn't, not really; I was simply trying to draw him out. 'You're contented. Which must mean everything's okay. Which must mean Kate and Lyn are okay. And what about Clover and Hope? How are they?'

To his credit, his face didn't flicker; he gave nothing away.

'You're good,' I said. 'Which means *I'm* good. Maybe we ought to take up poker.'

He gave a throaty laugh and produced a pack of Marlboro Lights. He offered me one and we strolled along, smoking in companionable silence for a moment. I'd always been a social smoker, though the War had made me into more of a habitual one; it was one of the few pleasures you could get in the trenches. This was the first cig I'd had since returning, though, and it tasted good.

As if reading my mind, my older self said, 'If you really want my advice, it's this: go back to the War. Sooner rather than later. It'll be a grind – in fact, it'll be a fucking nightmare – but just live through what you have to. Get it over with before taking things any further.' He shot me a narrow-eyed look as though assessing my mettle. 'But keep your head down. Be careful, and be alert. Don't take things for granted. Just because you're talking to me now doesn't mean you're invincible. I don't want to wake up one morning to find I'm a paraplegic. Or maybe not wake up at all.'

'It's not as if you'll know much about it if I get blown up, though, will it?'

He shuddered. 'Suppose not. But... just don't, all right?'

'I'll do my best.'

I watched the leaves drifting down from the trees. The sky was a grimy, unyielding white. I hadn't learned much coming here, but even so I now felt calmer, more focused on the way ahead. Looking at my future self, I allowed myself to at least begin to believe that things might turn out okay. Misplaced optimism, maybe, but it was optimism all the same.

I said, 'Just let me know one thing about the future.'

Before I could go on, my older self said, 'No. No way will I tell you how *Breaking Bad* ends. Do you think I want to spoil it for myself?'

I laughed, and he laughed along with me. We finished our cigarettes, then turned and headed back to the car.

TWENTY

THE MISSING

Later that day I went back to the War.

When I say 'that day' I am, of course, using the term in its loosest sense. Because since waking up, my day had already encompassed five dates – May 10th 2007, three November 2nds (2012, 2017 and 2018) and October 14th 2018. So to put it more accurately, the day I left to head back to the War was the day I'd woken up on that morning – November 2nd 2012.

Before heading back after speaking to my future self, though, I first jumped ahead to November 2nd 2018 and (to avoid creating a possible anomaly, the ripples of which might do who-knew-what damage) left the clothes I'd borrowed back where I'd found them. Then, wearing only the T-shirt and boxers I'd woken up in that morning, I went back to the morning of November 2nd 2012. Once there, back in what I thought of as my own time, I felt more than tempted to hang around for another day – to have a last long soak in the bath, eat good food, and sleep in my comfortable bed for one more night. However, I knew if I stayed even a day longer, it would become that extra bit harder to leave, and therefore that extra bit easier to convince myself to stay a few *more* days, or maybe a week... perhaps even a month...

Only a couple of minutes after arriving back, therefore, I steeled myself, then changed once more into my mud-caked army uniform. The mud had dried now, but it still whiffed a bit, plus it flaked off in chunks as I walked, leaving a dirty trail on the floor behind me. Once I was ready, I walked with heavy steps and a heavy heart along the corridor to Clover's room and knocked on the door.

'Yeah?' she said, conveying in that one word the fact that she'd been plucked from sleep, but was instantly alert – or at least trying to be.

I opened the door and stuck my head round. 'I'm off,' I said.

She sat bolt upright, her sleepy eyes widening, her maroon hair sticking up in tousled tufts. 'What do you mean – "off"?'

'I mean I'm going back to the War. There's no time like the present.' I grimaced at my own joke.

'When will you be back?'

'From your point of view, hopefully in about five minutes. But just in case I'm not, I came to let you know where I was going. And to say goodbye.' Another lump of dried mud detached itself from my trousers, powdery particles of dirt puffing up as it hit the carpet just inside Clover's room. 'And also to tell you, you might need to get the hoover out.'

Clover swung her legs out of bed, graceful as a ballet dancer, and crossed the room towards me. She was wearing a white T-shirt with a picture of Daffy Duck on it, and blue-and-green tartan pyjama bottoms, and as she got to within a couple of metres of me she held out her arms.

'I wouldn't,' I said. 'I'm pretty rank.'

'Bugger that.'

She wrapped her arms around me and hugged me tightly, tucking her head under my bony chin. As I hugged her back, I said, 'Not only is your hair the colour of plums, it smells like them too.'

She tutted. 'That's raspberry, not plum, you plum.'

'Well, I knew it was *something* fruity.'

She laughed, and then fiercely said, 'You look after yourself, okay? Don't do anything stupid.'

'You'll see me again in five minutes.' *Hopefully*.

'Yeah, but you won't see me. Or Kate. You've got a tough couple of years ahead of you. So keep yourself safe.'

'I will.'

'You'd better.'

I didn't want her to see me leave, so I went back to my room, shedding more dried mud en route, and took the heart from my pocket. I pictured myself back in No Man's Land close to the Allied trenches, my intention being to arrive about fifteen minutes after I'd assured Frank I'd be back.

It worked like a dream. One second I was standing in my warm bedroom in 23 Ranskill Gardens, and the next I was in pitch darkness, lying on my belly in freezing-cold mud. Although it was what I'd been hoping for, I gasped both at the stink and at the icy shock of it. Immediately I felt the familiar time-travel nausea rising in me. I lay still, riding it out, waiting until the nanites had kicked in and done their work. Then I slowly raised my head.

Directly ahead of me, like a thick line between the black mud and the black sky, was a kind of dun-coloured bank or ridge. I puzzled over it for a moment, and then realised that what I was looking at were the heaped sandbags lining the top of the Allied trench.

Which meant I was lying in the muddy hollow just beneath the trench itself! Perfect! It wasn't exactly home, but even so I could have wept with relief. I wondered whether Frank would hear me if I called out, but I decided not to risk it. Slipping the heart into my jacket pocket, and checking that my notebook was still in my breast pocket where I'd put it, I began to slither on my belly up the side of the hollow towards the raised hummock of sandbags.

Somewhere out in No Man's Land my past self would be crawling towards the German lines, which meant that gunfire from the enemy side would soon be blazing across the muddy wasteland between our two trenches. Did the fact that I was here mean that 'his' mission would be as successful as 'mine' was, that it would follow exactly the same pattern, or was there still the potential for things to go wrong? My uncertainty meant that the next few hours would be jittery ones for me. If I managed to make it through to dawn without winking out of existence, then I guess I could assume that things had worked out okay.

Reaching the sandbags, I took a deep breath, then crawled up and over them. Although there was no light for the Germans to see by, I still felt horribly exposed with nothing to hide behind.

I was groping for the top of the ladder on the inside of the trench when a black shape emerged from the gloom below and thrust upwards, jabbing me hard in the chest with the muzzle of a rifle.

'Who's there?' Nervousness turned the question into a wavery snarl.

Lying across the sandbags, my top half hanging over the trench, I raised my palms, hoping that even in the dark it would show my hands were empty.

'It's me, Frank,' I hissed. 'I said I'd be back, didn't I?'

The pressure on my chest eased as Frank lowered his rifle. 'Is that you, Alex?'

'No, it's the Archbishop of bloody Canterbury,' I said.

He grabbed my arms and directed them to the top rung of the ladder, then grabbed my muddy boots as I scrambled up and over to stop me from slipping all the way down the side of the trench and into the filthy water at the bottom. As I secured myself on the ladder and climbed down it, he danced around me like an excited puppy, clapping me hard on the back, his teeth white as he grinned.

'Bleedin' hell, it's good to see you! I was starting to think you were gone for good. Changed your mind, did you?'

'What makes you think that?'

'Well, you can't have been gone more than 'alf an hour – though it seemed a bloody age from down 'ere, I'll tell–'

Then his voice cut off as his eyes widened. I'd produced the heart from my pocket and was holding it up for him to see. In the meagre lamplight it seemed to sparkle as if inset with tiny crystals.

'Blow me!' he breathed. 'You ain't gone and found it?'

'It wasn't that far away,' I said. 'Told you I knew where it had landed.'

He continued to goggle first at the heart, then at me. He rubbed at his forehead, leaving a fresh smear of dirt. 'If I hadn't seen it I wouldn't've believed it,' he muttered. 'You're a bleedin' wonder, you are. Find a bedbug in a mattress, you would.'

I'd become very fond of Frank during the time we'd spent together. We'd been through a lot and he was genuinely like a little brother to me. But in the circumstances I couldn't honestly say it was good to see him again. And paradoxically, despite our closeness, there was always a sense of distance between us – on my part anyway. I didn't exactly hold him at arm's length, and I didn't shut off my feelings towards him (I could never be so cold), but at the same time, because I knew what was going to happen to him, I didn't feel I could allow myself to get *too* close. True friends have no secrets from one another, so in that regard foreknowledge is a terrible thing. Knowing Frank's fate made me feel terribly sad for him – not to mention terribly guilty. And although I maybe wouldn't have been able to save him even with the knowledge I had, what was infinitely worse was knowing that for the sake of others – most especially for Clover and myself, as well as for the integrity of the timeline in general – I couldn't *afford* to save him. When the time came I would *have* to let him die, and then, using the heart, drag him back into the half-life that he was living when I'd first encountered him.

But there was a lot of crap to get through before that happened – around twenty months' worth, in fact. I won't give you a blow-by-blow account of that period of my life, not only because I still find it hard to talk about, but also because much of it isn't relevant to this story. When I look back on the War, something I try to do as little as possible, I'm beset by a jumble of images and memories and impressions. Some are specific, and some are more general, and it's these that – if you'll allow me – I'll share with you.

We moved around a lot – that's one thing I remember. Before ending up in Ypres in August 1917, we were marched up and down the line of the Somme what felt like every few weeks. We fought in Arras and in French Flanders. We dug gun pits near Agnez-les-Duisans in the boiling July heat of 1916. In the late spring of 1917 we even had a little three-month sojourn to Italy to hold the line at the Piave River – a posting so quiet and uneventful compared to what we'd been used to that it almost felt like a holiday.

Mostly, it has to be said, the War was a battle not against the enemy, but against the weather and the awful conditions, and our own responses to the complex combination of boredom, misery and mortal terror that occupied our every waking moment. As I've said before, we were constantly filthy, wet, cold, hungry and exhausted – a state of mind and body that, in itself, has a grindingly accumulative effect. We were beset by rats and crawling with fleas, and most of us suffered terribly with dysentery, trench foot and a constant barrage of flu-like infections (though I fared better than most because of the nanites beavering away in my system). For all these reasons, those precious days – around three out of every nine – that we spent away from the front, recuperating in our billets, became blissful, almost heavenly interludes. During those all too brief times we'd relax by playing football in the afternoons and watching shows given by concert parties in the evenings. We'd eat huge amounts of egg and chips (proper food!) and occasionally we'd head into the local village to find an *estaminet* (a shabby pub or café), where we'd be sold cheap wine at inflated prices.

We knew we were being ripped off – and by the very countrymen whose land we were protecting! – but we didn't mind. We were just happy for the respite, happy to be able to do small, simple things, like walk upright, wear soft caps instead of uncomfortable steel helmets, and strike a match in the dark to light a cigarette without the fear of being picked off by a sniper.

The actual periods of direct conflict – not including the bombardments, which were both frequent and terrifying – were few and far between. We would shoot at the Germans from our trenches and they would shoot back at us, but unless you were stupid enough to stick your head above the parapet (which many were), or just incredibly unlucky, such tit-for-tat exchanges were generally not all that dangerous.

The bombardments, of course, *could* be dangerous, but only if the enemy managed to score a direct hit with a shell, which he didn't do all that often. Such a strike was akin, I guess, to hitting a bull's-eye in darts. Rare, but not impossible.

How rare? Well, it only happened twice during my two and a half years or so in the trenches, but on both occasions it was devastating. The first time Joe Lancing and Barty Trent were killed when a shell landed right next to them while they were on guard duty. The second time a much larger shell landed smack bang in the middle of our section of the trench, and although most of us were taking cover in our cubbyholes, five men were killed outright, including Reg Coxon and Geoff Ableman, and three died later from their injuries, including our good mate Stan Little, who had both of his legs blown off. I survived, of course, as did Frank and Jock McDaid – though Jock was hit in the face by a piece of shrapnel, which left him with a jagged scar on his temple and restricted the sight in his right eye for the rest of his life.

Emerging from our cubbyholes after the blast that day, covered in mud, flecked with cuts from flying shrapnel, and with our ears ringing so badly that we couldn't hear one another speak, was like stepping straight into Hell. The shell had hit the most populated part of the trench, and as a result the boggy, caved-in mud of the walls had turned red with blood, and there were bits of bodies everywhere. I saw arms, legs, rib cages, innards and plenty of things so badly mangled they were unidentifiable. A young officer called Potter who hadn't been with us long, found part of Geoff Ableman's crushed head under the twisted remains of the brazier, and screamed over and over, with the whooping shrillness of a child, until Jock silenced him by clamping a muddy hand over his mouth and dragging him away.

The closest I came to death during my time in the trenches was one winter's day early in 1917 when there was snow on the ground. We were fighting in French Flanders, and were going through a period where we were starting to make huge territorial advances, driving the Germans further and further back. Maybe we'd become complacent, but we were making another push across open, snowy ground, with the aim of taking what we thought was an unoccupied German trench, when we suddenly and unexpectedly came under fire. Immediately those of us who hadn't been hit threw themselves to the ground and began to crawl backwards, looking for whatever cover we could find. In the split second between being fired upon and hitting the deck, a bullet zipped across my chest, tearing the breast pocket of my tunic and leaving a scorch mark, before passing under my arm and killing an officer behind me. A few seconds later, as I was frantically crawling backwards, another bullet ripped through my water bottle and buried itself in the mud next to my leg.

I got away with that one, and so did Frank. Afterwards, safely back in our trench, he grinned and told me the two of us led charmed lives, and that we were one another's lucky mascots.

'We'll talk about this day when we're old geezers sitting in the pub,' he said. 'We'll bore our grandchildren with these stories.'

I grinned along with him, but my heart felt as if it was being squeezed in a vice.

One other memory, still vivid in my mind, is this one. On a late afternoon in, I think, the autumn of 1916, just as the sky was deepening to dusk, the rest of the men and I witnessed a distant aerial battle involving around thirty planes from both sides. As the fighters swooped and darted like insects, their machine guns emitting bursts of gunfire that from our vantage point sounded no more significant than a series of rapid, stuttering cracks – like the sound ice cubes make when you drop them into a drink – I remember thinking how like a film this was; a film or a dream. Even when one of the planes went down trailing black smoke, and hit the ground in a brief fiery flash, I found it hard to equate with reality. I looked around at the men watching with me, and saw a range of expressions on their faces – from mild interest and a dull kind of curiosity, to a kind of atavistic eagerness, and even, in one or two cases, a weird sort of elation. But there was no horror there, no pity, and although that might sound cold-hearted, I found it equally difficult to stir such emotions in my own heart, even though I regarded myself – and still do regard myself – as a compassionate man.

I was surprised by the depth of emotion I felt, however, when our company finally received orders to depart for Ypres in Belgium in July 1917. That night I wept, though only when I was alone, my muddy, rat-nibbled scarf (which had been Geoff Ableman's, and had been knitted by his mum) stuffed against my mouth to stifle my sobs. I felt such joy at the thought that my ordeal was finally coming to an end, and that in a few weeks I'd be reunited with the people I cared about most in the world. But tempering my joy was a profound and terrible guilt at the knowledge that my ordeal would end only at the expense of Frank's life. It seemed obscene to be looking forward to going home, knowing it would be facilitated by a young man's death. In those last few weeks it became more and more difficult to look at his grinning face, to engage with him, to laugh at his jokes – but I forced myself to do it. I didn't want him to spend his last days wondering why I was being so off with him, wondering what he'd done to make me suddenly so frosty. I felt torn apart inside. Often I felt as though I ought to prepare him somehow, or reassure him, or warn him. But I didn't. I stayed as 'normal' as I could. And I tried to convince myself that I was doing the right thing, that it was all for the best.

Passchendaele lay on the last ridge east of Ypres, five miles from a railway junction at Roulers, which was a vital supply line for the German army. The ultimate aim of the Battle of Passchendaele, a campaign launched by the Allies in July 1917, was to control the ridges south and east of Ypres, thus cutting the Germans off from their supplies. To do this we had to be forceful and aggressive; we had to go at them, all guns blazing, push them back. This inevitably meant we would sustain casualties – lots of them. But the entire campaign was predicated on the hope that the Boche would lose a lot more men than we would.

When we received orders on August 9th that our battalion was to embark on a 'bite and hold' operation further up the line, I had a feeling that this was it, that Frank's story, which he had related to me on the tube train after rescuing me from Queens Road Cemetery in Walthamstow, was about to play out. Our mission was to advance on a chateau close to the infamously desolate Menin Road. Held by the Germans, the chateau was surrounded by an interlocking series of pillbox defences, which, despite a prolonged shelling campaign, had so far stubbornly refused to yield. What we'd been ordered to do was launch an all-out attack – basically to charge into the enemy's line of fire and take the pillboxes, and hence the chateau, through sheer weight of numbers. We knew that many of us would die, that row after row of us would be torn apart by German bullets. But some of us would get through – enough, it was calculated, to do what needed to be done. It was a desperate, horrible gamble, but we had no choice but to obey the orders we'd been given.

On August 10th we marched fifteen miles through a landscape of mud and shattered tree stumps to our destination, acutely aware that a fair proportion of us wouldn't be coming back; wouldn't be seeing England, or our loved ones, ever again. It wasn't only because of our sombre mood that we marched mostly in silence, though. It was also because the going was tough, and we needed all our strength to keep putting one foot in front of the other. It had been a wet August and the mud was deep and clinging. Added to that we were each carrying not only our usual share of equipment, but also extra tools and ammunition, aeroplane flares, bombs, sandbags and various other bits and pieces. Plus we had to keep moving to the side of the road to let through droves of bedraggled-looking prisoners, or motor ambulances bringing the dead and wounded back from the Front.

Though distant, the noise of shell fire from up ahead was continuous and deafening. It went on all through the night, which we spent in the miserable remains of a wood, shivering and unable to sleep because of the relentless din. At sunrise we were off again, walking the last couple of miles to our rendezvous point – a bombed-out lodge adjoining a stable block. By the time we arrived we were pretty much the opposite of a crack fighting unit, but we had very little chance to rest and regain our strength. We were to launch our attack later that afternoon, and so, after a quick breakfast and a couple of hours of nervously sitting around, we were once more up and moving, all too aware that for some of us today would be our last on earth.

'Bit of a bugger, eh, Alex?' Frank said from behind me as we made our way in single file through a zigzagging maze of communication trenches. His voice was tight with apprehension and exhaustion. It was the first time either of us had spoken for a while.

I glanced over my shoulder, and the shock that went through me was like being doused with icy water. Frank looked *deathly*, his skin clammy and pallid, his eyes shadowed in hollow sockets. For a second I thought time was taunting me, thought I'd been given a glimpse into the future. Then I realised that Frank was just like the rest of us - scared, exhausted to the point of dropping, and so drenched in sweat that his hair was plastered darkly to his forehead. I tried to grin, but my lips were dry and peeled back from my teeth only slowly. The effect must have been both skull-like and sinister.

'That's an understatement,' I croaked

'*We'll* be okay, though, won't we?'

Maintaining my grin made my jaw ache. 'We can but hope.'

Doubt flickered across his face, and I realised how desperately he needed my reassurance. Almost bullishly he said, 'Course we will. There's no "hope" about it, old chum. We'll come through this lot with flying colours.'

We trudged on. Two hours slid by, then a third. At last a message began to filter back down the line: *Nearly there*. Even so, it was another twenty minutes or more of back-breaking plodding before we were finally able to halt. Regardless of the filthy conditions, we shrugged and wriggled free of our burdens, then pretty much collapsed where we stood into steaming, sweat-drenched heaps.

As soon as we were down the groans started. The pains we'd been holding at bay - from over-stretched limbs, aching backs, blistered feet -rushed in and overwhelmed us.

'My poor plates,' muttered Frank, who was slouched against a muddy wall, unconcerned by the fact that the wetness was seeping into his clothes.

A ginger-haired lad to my right, whose name was Jud Barclay, was in so much pain his freckled face resembled a clenched fist. 'No need to send me over the top,' he gasped. 'Just shoot me now and have done with it.'

It was an accepted fact among the men that the best cure for fear was tiredness. Get tired enough and you didn't care what happened to you. All you wanted was to let everything go, to slip into oblivion. There'd been a lot of unspoken fear in the ranks when we'd first received our orders. You could see it in every set of eyes you looked into. You could *feel* it too, like the low thrum of a generator. But as we'd neared our destination, some of that fear had drained away, along with our physical energy. Not all of it, but enough to enable us to carry out our orders without question, to do what was expected of us. That was why men were able to run into hails of bullets, why they were able to function in situations that seemed, to an outsider, so terrifying that it was impossible to contemplate anything other than curling into a ball.

Fatigue was the key. Fatigue combined with the adrenaline of battle. It was a fine balance. Fatigue made you fearless, whereas adrenaline restored the mental and physical sharpness you needed to carry out your mission without also restoring the more complicated bits, like emotions and self-awareness. Fatigue and adrenaline made you into a robot, a machine. And if you survived it was usually only later, when your body was resting, recharging itself, that your ability to think, to contemplate, to remember and to respond emotionally was restored to you. And it was often then when it hit you – what you'd been through, what you'd done. And *that* was when it became hard to deal with. When you stopped being a machine and became a human being again.

At that moment, sitting in the trench, we were *all* machines. Even me, who had the bigger picture to give him perspective, who was able to see round corners, was not entirely immune.

I was detached *enough*, though, as the officers in charge told us what our country and our loved ones back home *expected* of us, to feel like an outsider looking in. I noted the dull-eyed compliance on the faces of the men; I noted their sheep-like acceptance. They were boys, most of them. They'd had their innocence torn away in the most brutal manner possible, and yet their instinct was still to obey without question, to trust that their elders and superiors knew best.

It was obscene. Obscene and terrible, and yet at the same time unavoidable. And it was a story as old as time. Sacrifice yourself and the Gods will smile down on your people.

The rest of the day was a limbo. We sat around, waiting for the order to advance, machines waiting to be switched on. My hand kept creeping restlessly to my hip pocket, kept patting the heart as if to ensure it was still there.

Then suddenly it was time.

It felt like late afternoon, 5 or 6 p.m. maybe. We were ordered to stand, to get in line, to make ready. The men had the self-absorbed, slightly glazed look of footballers in a dressing room about to run out onto the pitch. A quick battle with Jerry and then home in time for tea.

The bombers went first, their mission to crawl forward and lob their bombs in and among the German pillboxes, try to create as much mayhem as possible. While they were doing that, those in the front line would provide them with covering fire from within the trench before going up and over the top themselves. Then the rest of us would follow, wave after wave, the idea being to pour forward more men than the Germans had bullets, or at least the ability to fire them.

'They're cowards at heart,' our officers assured us. 'Soon as the Boche realise what's happening they'll turn and flee. We'll do this with minimal casualties.'

Military spin doctoring bullshit, of course. Though some of the men might have believed it. We lined up like children in a school dinner queue, waiting our turn. Some way ahead of us – too far for us to see what was happening – a distant voice shouted an order. For long seconds there was silence... then the firing began, from both sides. Which meant the bombers were on their way.

We kept shuffling forward, until eventually we could see the men ahead of us, scaling the wooden ladders which had been set up against the long, muddy wall of the trench, plunging forward once they reached the top. Then starting to run – or rather wade – through the debris-strewn quagmire beyond, rifles at the ready.

'Don't start firing until you get a clear shot,' we'd been told – though how many would panic in the heat of battle and start blazing away with their friends and colleagues still in front of them? How many British soldiers would be killed not by a German bullet, but by a British bullet in the spine or the back of the head?

The noise was tremendous, the rain of explosions and bullets from both sides like a continuous, demonic screech of rage and fury. I felt a tingling like electricity inside me. *This is it*, a voice kept repeating inside my head. It was a voice full of disbelief, excitement and unalloyed terror. *This is it. This is it.*

But what if it wasn't it? What if something went wrong? What if Frank and I got separated? What if I got hit? What if, in this timeline, I died?

Or would that never happen? Would the heart rescue me? If a bullet was heading in my direction, would the heart snatch me away, to another place, another time?

The line of men ahead of us started climbing the ladders. The ginger boy, Barclay, was among them. I watched his mud-caked boots clumping up the wooden rungs. Smoke drifted over the parapet, like wraiths eager to snatch away those about to sacrifice their lives. The smoke smelled acrid, metallic. As it caught in my throat, I coughed; it tasted like blood. Barclay became swathed in smoke, and then he disappeared over the top. The last I saw of him was the heel of his left boot. I wondered what sights had filled his vision as he'd gone over, what horrors he was looking upon now. In a few moments I'd find out.

Climbing the ladder I was overwhelmed by the momentousness of the occasion. I couldn't get my head round the fact that the day I'd been grimly moving towards was finally here, and that in an hour or a few hours from now I could be a hundred years in the future, back with my loved ones, clean and warm, sipping the best cup of tea I'd ever tasted, sleeping in my comfortable bed.

But then another thought chased the fantasy down: What if today *wasn't* the day? Frank had told me he'd died at the Battle of Passchendaele in August 1917, but the Battle of Passchendaele wasn't a single skirmish; it was a campaign stretching over four months. So what if Frank *wasn't* destined to die today? What if he was destined to die next week, or the week after? I had to prepare myself for that eventuality, had to be mentally ready.

All these thoughts whizzed through my head as I climbed the ladder.

And then my head was above the parapet, and I was looking out over the battlefield.

Smoke. Mud. Hunched shapes running. The flash of explosions and gunfire.

And bodies. Strewn across the ground, twisted into such unnatural shapes that they didn't look human.

My gaze slid and jittered. Adrenaline revved my engine into overdrive, sped everything up, suppressed my emotions, erased my ability to think calmly and logically, while at the same time it boosted my instincts, my primal responses.

I went over the top and started to run, my hurtling thoughts carrying my cumbersome body along with them. My senses seemed to condense into a basic state – no frills, no subtleties. Tunnel vision; a roar of noise; the weight of the gun in my hand; the smell and taste of smoke and metal.

Did bullets whizz by me? Did they miss me by millimetres? If so, I wasn't aware of them. The situation narrowed further, became unreal, like a computer game. Dark, moving shapes ahead of me. One of them fell, then another. I couldn't see my destination, or what direction I was running in. All was haze, a shifting of light and dark.

Where was Frank? I should stay with him. I looked to my left, then my right, but couldn't make him out. All the running figures were nothing but black shapes wreathed in smoke.

Shit. I felt the beginnings of panic. Tried to tell myself to calm down. I looked to my left again, willing my mind and vision to clear. The future could depend on this. I couldn't afford to–

I ran into something. Or something smashed into me. I felt the impact in my right temple. My first crazy thought was that someone had hit me with a hammer. Whatever it was, it was powerful enough to spin me round. My body whirled like a top. Then I was falling. I hit the mud with a smack and seemed to keep on sinking, to slip right through the mushy outer skin of the earth. I put my hands out, but there was nothing there. I saw the sky beneath me. Was I dreaming? Had the heart snatched me away?

The barrage of gunfire, the roar of explosions so continuous they sounded like one unending burst, started to twist themselves into new shapes. I listened, convinced that something – the War itself, maybe – was trying to communicate with me. Was that a voice? What was it saying? After a moment I realised it was louder on my left side, and focused my concentration in that direction.

And all at once the blur of sounds became sharper. And I realised it *was* a voice. And the voice was yelling into my ear: 'Alex! Speak to me, mate! Speak to me!'

I didn't know my eyes had been closed until I opened them. I thought I'd been fully aware, thought I'd been falling upwards and trying to slow myself down by grabbing the edge of the sky. It was only when my eyes opened that I realised those thoughts made no sense, that they must have been part of a dream. But if I'd been dreaming that meant I'd been asleep, so where was I now? In bed? In which case, why was I so cold and wet? And why was my head hurting? And why were insects scurrying over my face, filling my eyes and stinging my eyeballs?

No, not insects. Mud. The voice was saying, 'Hold on, Alex. Hold on.'

Then something was brushing at me. Fingers. A hand. Brushing the mud off my face, picking flecks of dirt out of my eyes. My eyes still felt gritty, but now I could see Frank leaning over me, concern on his face.

'Wha,' I said, and felt mud in my mouth. I spat it out and tried again. 'What happened?'

Hearing those two words, Frank started to grin. 'You got shot, you daft old sod.'

'Shot?' I tried to shake my head, but it hurt like buggery. It felt as though my skull had been broken into several pieces and the sharp edges were rubbing against one another. The pain made my eyes water, which at least washed out more of the mud. 'No,' I said. 'It's not me who gets shot.'

'Well, you did,' Frank said. 'Right in the noggin.' He must have seen the expression on my face, or maybe it was his own relief that made him laugh. 'Don't worry. It was a glancing blow. Ricocheted off the edge of your helmet. Made a right dent, it did. I saw you spin and go down. Bang! Thought you was a goner.'

I was recovering now, starting to remember where and when I was, what I was supposed to be doing. The roar of battle was still going on. Men were running past us, their feet thumping through mud. I tried to rise, but the mud held me fast. Frank slid a supportive hand behind my back.

'Give yourself a minute,' he said. 'I don't reckon–'

Then he stopped talking, and suddenly, shockingly, the life went out of his face. I saw it go, like an invisible mask. He sagged, went limp, then toppled forward, right on top of me.

I caught him, wrapped my arms around him. 'Frank!' I shouted. 'Frank!' My right hand was on his back, and all at once I realised how wet and slippery it was. I held it up, raising it above his left shoulder to look at it. It was bright red, drenched in blood.

Using all my strength, I heaved myself on to my left side, Frank's limp body rolling off me. Now our positions were reversed. He was the one lying on his back in the mud and I was kneeling over him. And now I could see the hole in his chest, just left of centre. Blood had been pouring out of it like water from a punctured bag. The fronts of our uniforms were sodden with it. I realised the bullet must have entered his body through his back and exited through his chest, passing through his heart en route. What was it he had said to me about his own death? *'Bull's-eye, right in the heart. Snuffed out without so much as a by-your-leave.'* Something like that, if not those exact words.

Well now here we were, at that moment. When he'd related his story on the tube, it had been in his past and my future. Now it was in both our presents, and it was up to me to play my part.

Around us the battle raged on, but I felt as though we were enclosed in our own little bubble. My head throbbing from the bullet that had glanced off my helmet, I reached into my pocket with a hand covered in Frank's blood and withdrew the heart. I pressed it to his chest, as if plugging the hole, and held it there, closing my eyes and letting my mind go blank, trying to focus on nothing but siphoning my energy through the heart and into Frank. I didn't know if that was what I was *supposed* to do; I was operating purely by instinct.

I pictured the underside of the heart softening, changing. In my mind's eye I saw tendrils extending outwards, cautiously at first, probing at the ragged, wet edges of Frank's wound, and then sliding forward, into his body. I saw the tendrils working away busily inside him, like the nanites in my own body that were even now fixing whatever minor damage was causing the throbbing percussion in my head. I saw them repairing Frank's ruptured heart, sealing his wounds, patching him up. And then, once his body was whole again, I imagined life-energy pulsing from the heart and rippling along the tendrils, filling his body and bringing him back to life.

It was a simplistic image, perhaps even a crude one, but all at once I felt Frank's body twitch beneath me. I opened my eyes, and a second later Frank's eyes opened too, and stared into mine.

I saw no gratitude there, though, nor even confusion. What I saw was pain and regret and terrible knowledge. He said, 'What have you done?'

It wasn't an accusatory question – his voice was dull and emotionless – but even so, I felt a need to justify myself. 'I've brought you back, Frank,' I said. 'You were gone, but I brought you back. I've given you a second chance. Don't be afraid.'

I lifted the heart from his chest and put it in my pocket. There was no longer a wound underneath. After a moment Frank slowly raised a hand and put it on his chest where the heart had been. 'Where have I gone?' he asked.

'You're here, Frank,' I said, and I gripped his shoulders as if to assure him he still had a physical presence. 'You're alive. You're back with me.'

He moved his head from side to side, a measured but emphatic denial. Though his face was expressionless a tear trickled from his eye and forged a route through the mud on his bony cheek.

'No,' he said. 'There's nothing inside, Alex. The best part of me's not there any more. There's just darkness now.'

'I don't believe that,' I said, though what I really meant was that I didn't *want* to believe it. 'You're alive, Frank. You're whole. You've just... had a bad experience, that's all. But you'll be okay.'

Frank's hand, the one resting on his chest, suddenly reached up and grabbed my sleeve. 'I'm scared, Alex.'

'There's nothing to be scared of. I'm with you. We'll be okay.'

His eyes closed briefly, then opened again. Beneath the mud his flesh was so pale. 'I was always scared, Alex. Shit-scared. I joked around, but underneath...' He grimaced briefly. After a moment he said, 'It was you what kept me going. You looked after me. You didn't know you was, but you was. You were a mate to me. The best.'

'I'm still a mate. We'll always be mates.'

'Yeah, we will,' he said. 'Always. But what you did... I know you did it for the best, but... maybe you shouldn't have done it.'

I felt as though he'd reached into my chest and squeezed. A sick, fearful shame swept over me. What had I done? How thoughtless and selfish had I been? What right had I to make Frank part of my story, to use him like this? But at the same time, had I had any choice in the matter? Hadn't it been a *fait accompli* before I'd even been aware of Frank's existence?

'I'll take us away from here,' I said. 'We'll put all this fighting, all this death, behind us. I'll take us somewhere peaceful.'

'There ain't nowhere,' he muttered. 'Not for me.'

'There is,' I said. 'I promise there is.'

I took the heart from my pocket again. Put my left arm around him and held him close, so close that the rims of our steel helmets clunked together. I squeezed the heart and wished us away from there. The noise of battle receded...

The very air around us seemed to change, to settle; that's how I knew we had moved. I felt a warm breeze slide over me, brush across my face. I would have opened my eyes then if I hadn't felt the familiar bite of nausea in my belly, threatening to burst like a grenade and tear me apart. As the nanites rushed in to do their work, I instinctively curled up my body, locked down my senses.

When the nausea began to ebb, and I eventually stirred and opened my eyes, I was surprised to find it was dark. I looked up into a night sky unsullied by smoke, devoid of light pollution, and saw an array of stars glittering like diamonds scattered across black velvet, the sight so dazzling it took my breath away.

'It's over, Frank,' I whispered. 'The War's finally over. For both of us.'

I was still hunched awkwardly over him, my left arm wrapped around his back, my hand clutching his left shoulder. His eyes were wide open and he too was gazing into the night sky.

'How can it be?' he murmured. His eyes shifted and he looked at me fearfully. 'What are you, Alex? What you done to me?'

'I'm your friend,' I told him. 'And I saved you. With this.'

I showed him the heart. He looked at it, still with that fearful expression on his face, but he didn't touch it.

'What is it?' he said. 'That thing?'

'It's...' I began, and then realised I didn't know how to answer his question. Finally I said, 'It can do amazing things, Frank. Things you wouldn't believe.'

'Things I wouldn't want to believe,' he muttered.

I felt a flash of anger. 'How can you say that? If it wasn't for the heart you wouldn't be alive now.'

His gaze slid from the heart and locked on to mine again. 'Is that what I am, Alex? Alive? 'Cause I don't feel it. I feel cold.'

'Course you're alive,' I snapped. 'You're just in shock, that's all. Nice cup of tea, you'll be right as rain.'

He half-sat, taking note of his surroundings for the first time. He looked down and reached out, his hand hovering just above the ground. It was only then I realised we were no longer lying in mud, but on a soft, dry carpet of neatly trimmed grass.

'Are we both dead, Alex?' he asked. 'Are we both in Heaven or Hell?'

'We're in neither,' I said. 'We're safe.'

'And the War's over?'

'Yes.'

'So why do I still feel it?' He touched his chest. 'In here?'

I knew he carried the War inside him. The horror of it, the darkness of it.

'It's just an echo,' I said. 'Don't be scared of it. Soon you'll be able to control it. You'll learn to use it. For good.'

He didn't seem able to grasp that concept, or perhaps he was too distracted to take in what I was telling him. He was looking around again, clearly agitated.

'Where are we, Alex? Where is everybody?'

'Gone,' I said. 'Long gone.'

'But we'll get done. We'll get done as deserters. Getting shot I can take, but not as a deserter. I don't want my family to be ashamed of me.'

'No one'll be ashamed of you, Frank. The War's long over.' I paused. 'We've come forward. In time, I mean. That little black heart of mine, it can do that. It can take you forwards and backwards through time.'

I expected Frank to scoff, or at least give me a disbelieving look, but he didn't. He just touched his chest again, where the bullet hole had been. 'Regular box o' tricks, ain't it?' Then he half-turned, pointed. 'What's that?'

I looked in the direction he was indicating. The field we were sitting in rose behind us in soft, undulating waves, forming a gentle incline. Beyond the incline was the tip of a pale tower or obelisk, its edges limned in starlight.

I rose to my feet. The nausea and the throbbing in my head had gone. 'Let's see, shall we?'

I held out my hand and after a moment Frank took it. I pulled him to his feet and together we began to trudge up the gentle hill towards the white tower. Dressed in our mud and blood covered army uniforms, I hoped we wouldn't meet anyone. If we did, not only would we give them a hell of a shock, but we'd have a lot of explaining to do. I guess we'd have to say we were part of a First World War re-enactment group or something, though what explanation we'd give for being there in the middle of the night I had no idea.

Fortunately, though, we didn't meet anyone. We reached the top of the incline and began to trudge down the other side. And now we could see the white tower for what it really was.

Of course. It was a war memorial.

The obelisk was maybe twelve metres high and around three metres wide on each side. We only realised we were approaching it from the rear when we saw that on the far side was a long pale path, which led off from the wide square of gravel into which the memorial had been set. The path meandered through a beautifully tended park that I suppose, a century before, had been a churned-up battlefield strewn with mangled corpses. A trio of wide stone steps led up to the obelisk on each side. Dozens of wreaths had been laid at its base. In the moonlight they looked like dark wheels propped against the white stone.

'Did we... fight here?' Frank asked. There was a hushed kind of wonder in his voice.

I glanced at him. He looked colourless and insubstantial. I had the odd feeling that if I reached out to touch him, I'd connect with nothing, and he'd smear out of existence, the illusion broken.

'Yes,' I said. 'But it was a long time ago.'

'How long?'

'A hundred years, give or take.'

He was silent for a moment, then he said, 'And the land's been reborn.'

'Yes.'

'That's good.' He jerked an arm up, indicating the obelisk. 'And that's for us, is it? The men who fought here?'

'Yes.'

'So we ain't been forgotten?'

'No, Frank. You'll – *we'll* – never be forgotten.'

This time he was silent for so long that I almost asked him if he was all right. I was about to when he said, 'Can we have a look?'

'Course we can.'

We descended the incline towards the memorial, a couple of ghosts haunting the battlefield where thousands had died. The neat, gravelled square from the centre of which the obelisk reared, like a vast finger pointing at the sky, was bordered on all sides except the front by a black wrought iron fence, which was shin-high and comprised of a series of equidistant spikes linked by cross bars. We stepped over the fence and approached the memorial from the back, our feet crunching on gravel. When we got up close we saw that words had been carved into the stone on all four of the obelisk's sides. There was an elaborately bordered inscription on the front, in French, and lists of names – hundreds, probably thousands – occupying the other three sides. I wandered around to the left of the obelisk, and angled myself until the moonlight fell just so on the carved letters. Squinting a bit, I made out the heading at the top: CEUX QUI SONT TOMBÉS.

'Those who are...' I murmured, puzzling over the last word. Then it struck me. 'Fallen! Those who are fallen. Those who fell.'

It was a list of the dead.

I scanned it quickly, realising that this side of the obelisk was a record of all those whose surnames fell within the first half of the alphabet – A to M. This meant that my surname, Locke, and Frank's, Martin, should be towards the bottom of the fifth and final column.

But they weren't. I looked twice. The second time I even stepped right up to the obelisk and ran my finger over the letters carved into the stone.

We weren't there. Which meant that as far as history was concerned, it was as if we had *never* been there. I didn't particularly care for myself, because although I'd fought in the War, it had never really been *my* conflict. I'd known the outcome before going in; I'd been nothing but a temporal aberration, a man out of time.

But Frank... that was different. He'd been part of the generation of boys and men who had not only endured Hell but had made the ultimate sacrifice for his country in the pursuit of justice and liberty. It was Frank, and men like him, who *deserved* to be remembered. How could I tell him that he hadn't been?

I glanced at him. He was standing a few metres from me, peering up at the back of the obelisk, his lips moving slightly.

'Alex, what does dis-per-us mean?' he asked, saying the word slowly and pronouncing it with a hard 's' at the end.

I walked over to join him, tilting my head up to see what he was looking at.

'Disparus,' I said in the best French accent I could muster. 'It means... the lost, I think. No... the missing.'

He stepped forward, ascended the stone steps and jabbed at the obelisk with a long white finger. 'That's us then, is it? We ain't dead, we're just missing?'

I stepped up beside him. And there we were. There were our names on the list carved into the back of the obelisk. Alexander Locke. Frank Martin. It was a weird sensation, knowing that this memorial had been erected before I was born, and yet my part in a war that I'd learned about in history lessons at school had been immortalised on this stone monument in this Belgian field.

I ran my fingers over my own name, thinking that no matter how commonplace time travel might eventually become for me, I would surely never get used to moments like this; moments in which the rug was suddenly whipped from under me and I was struck with a sense of... I guess the word was 'wonder'. Maybe 'awe'.

'The missing,' Frank said again. He nodded. 'That's just right, that is. That's how I feel. In here.' He pointed at his own chest.

'I'm sorry, Frank.' His words brought me back down to earth. 'I was only doing... what I thought was right.'

'I know,' he said. 'I know you were.' He looked up at the obelisk once more, then he sighed and turned away.

'Can we go now, Alex?' he asked. 'I don't want to be here any more.'

TWENTY-ONE
THE GREAT BARNABY

A few weeks later I brought Kate home.

I *say* a few weeks, but that's only an estimation of how long it seemed in *my* terms. Because the fact is, between resurrecting Frank and seeing my little girl again, I did a hell of a lot of jumping about.

The jumping about constituted what I guess you could call housekeeping. Little – and sometimes not so little – jobs that needed doing in order to keep the machine oiled and running smoothly. With the War over, I was naturally desperate to see Kate again, desperate to bring her back to London and try to re-establish something like a normal life. But before I could do that I felt as though I ought to put certain things in place, simply because they were piling up and I didn't want my precious time with my daughter compromised by the knowledge that I had an accumulation of prior commitments hanging over me.

First and foremost, I needed to get Frank settled. And by settled, I mean I needed to stay with him while he acclimatised to his new... condition. Moreover, I needed to brief him. I needed to tell him where he had to be, and when. And what he had to do.

Compliant as he was, I found it tough. Tough because he trusted me and relied on me, and because in the twenty-first century he was a fish out of water, which meant I was responsible for him. And tough, to be perfectly honest, because I didn't truly know what he *was*, what I'd 'created', and so I was uncertain both how to handle him and how to feel about him.

Was he alive or dead? If the former, then why did he carry the darkness of war inside him, seemingly in place of a soul? And how was he able to access that darkness and use it like... well, like some kind of twisted super power?

More fundamentally, how come he never needed to sleep? I know he wanted to, but he found it impossible. Sometimes he'd lie on his back with his eyes closed and his hands by his sides, looking for all the world like a laid-out corpse, and he'd *rest* – that's what he called it anyway.

'Does your mind drift when you rest?' I asked him once. 'Do you feel drowsy?'

He shook his head. 'I don't feel nothing. I lie there and think about things – my family and the War and my old life – but I don't feel tired. Just like I don't feel hot or cold. Or hungry or thirsty.'

'But you eat,' I said. 'If I make you food, you eat it. And if we go to the pub, you drink. In fact, two nights ago we went to the pub because *you* wanted to. You said you could murder a pint.'

'Habit,' he said. 'It's all habit. If I have a pie and a pint I can feel normal. I can't taste it and it don't affect me – I could drink thirty pints and it wouldn't affect me – but at least by saying and doing normal things I can *pretend* I'm normal.' His voice dropped. 'But I'm not, am I? I don't know *what* I am, but I'm not normal.'

Did he bleed? Did he shit? Did his heart pump and his blood rush through his veins? We never got into that. I suppose I was partly in denial. I didn't want to think I'd done the wrong thing, a selfish thing, by bringing him back.

But I also didn't want to upset him by highlighting the differences between us. I'm sure he was aware of how he functioned, of his physical limitations and capabilities, but because he never brought the subject up, I didn't either. It helped to maintain that precious illusion of normality.

Another thing that helped was giving him a home, or at least a base, somewhere he could call his own. I could have booked him into a hotel, but I thought that would make him uncomfortable, so instead I installed him in my old flat, the one that the Wolves of London had trashed (unless, as I said before, I'd done it myself, perhaps as a warning not to go back there and become a sitting duck, and I simply wasn't aware of it yet).

Anyway, we cleaned the place up as best we could, and there we stayed while I filled Frank in on his role. Giving him a 'role' in the first place felt somewhat mercenary on my part, but that didn't get away from the fact that it was also something I needed to do in order to maintain the timeline as I knew it.

I didn't get heavy or lay a guilt trip on him. I didn't want to make him feel he *owed* me. On the other hand, I didn't want to make him feel resentful towards me either. So after wondering for a while how to approach it, I simply decided to tell him the whole story from the beginning, to give him all the facts.

Even now I'm not sure how he took it. He didn't give much away. He seemed to accept what I told him without question, in the same way he'd have accepted whatever orders a commanding officer might have given him during the War.

No, that's not strictly true, because during the War he'd at least had more verve about him. Before dying he'd been what is known in old-fashioned terms as a 'chirpy chap', one who was able to maintain his pluck and humour whatever the circumstances. But since coming back there'd been something missing. He'd lost his spirit, his essence, his *joie de vivre*. That wasn't to say he didn't occasionally smile, or make a joke, or show emotion, or talk with a certain amount of animation. He wasn't a robot. He wasn't a *zombie*, for God's sake!

And yet. And yet. There was a deep and abiding melancholy about him that hadn't been there before. I kept wanting to apologise for what I'd done to him; I kept feeling guilty about it. After I'd told him my story, and what (as far as I'd already experienced) his part in it was, I felt compelled to say, 'But look, mate, you don't *have* to do this. This is your choice, your life. You're not a puppet to be manipulated – not by me or anyone else.'

Having said that to him, though, I honestly don't know what I would have done if he'd said no. I like to think I'd have respected his decision, but in truth I would probably have reminded him once again of the visions I'd had – particularly the one in which his failure to show up at Benny's house had resulted in Clover's death.

Luckily, though, with no hesitation, and no apparent sense of resentment or obligation, he said, 'Course I'll help you out, Alex. We're mates, ain't we? It's what mates do.'

At last, when I'd briefed him as fully as I was able, and he was as ready as I felt he could be, I kitted him out with the overlarge demob suit, shirt, tie and brogues he'd been wearing when I'd first seen him (all bought from a vintage store down Camden Lock – so much for authenticity!). Then I used the heart to take us to Benny's house on the night he'd forced us to flee. I knew it had been around 5 a.m. on Thursday 4th October, so I got us there at 4:30. We arrived at the end of Benny's back garden, standing among the trees, swathed in shadow. There was nothing but blackness ahead of us, but after we'd been there about ten minutes or so, a light came on in the conservatory. It was the dim red glow of the lamp with the tasselled shade. From where we were standing the conservatory looked small and distant, though I could make out two figures – Clover and me – moving about in it through the glass.

'There I am, right on schedule,' I whispered to Frank. 'How are you feeling?'

'Fine,' he said, deadpan.

'So you know what you've got to do?'

'Yeah, you told me.'

'And you're happy with everything? You haven't forgotten that next time you meet me, after you've rescued me from Queens Road Cemetery, it'll be him, not me, and he won't know who you are, and you'll have to tell him what I told you? And remember, when he asks about Kate, you're to say that you know I'm looking for her, but you're not to tell him—'

He sighed, loud enough to cut in on my babble. I didn't know if his heart still beat in his chest or if the blood still pumped through his veins, but he was certainly still capable of sighing. 'I haven't forgotten,' he said. 'I won't let you down, Alex.'

'I know you won't,' I said. 'I know it'll happen exactly as I remember it, because... well, because that's how I remember it.'

'So stop worrying,' he said. 'I'll do exactly what you told me. Now bugger off so I can turn on the fireworks and give you all a lovely display.'

I grinned nervously, and although I itched to offer more advice, I decided it was time to go, and leave the rest of it up to Fate.

'Well, good luck,' I said, and I hovered a moment, not sure whether to say anything more, or whether to throw my arms around him.

We'd been through such a lot, Frank and me, and I owed him... well, potentially I owed him everything.

As if anticipating my half-intention to embrace him, and eager to deflect it (man-hugs just weren't the done thing in Frank's day), he thrust out his hand.

'Cheerio, guv'nor. See you soon.'

I took his hand. It was icy-cold, as always.

'See you, Frank. And thanks.'

He gave a single brief nod.

I went back. Not to the flat, which was Frank's to use whenever he needed it, but to my house in Ranskill Gardens. I wasn't quite ready yet for my post-war reunion with Clover, though, so I arrived on the afternoon of Thursday November 2nd 2017. This was one of the days I'd jumped to when I'd wanted to talk to my future self, and had found the house empty. I took advantage of that now, using my time alone to rest and recuperate. I had a long bath, went out for a meal, slept in my own bed. The next day I took out my little black book and knuckled down to a bit more 'housekeeping'.

I started small by jumping back to the day after Kate's abduction, finding an internet café and sending the email to Clover at Incognito, the one purporting to be from Kate's kidnapper. I felt bad having to type the threat to kill my own daughter, though I reasoned that it was better coming from me than from a real kidnapper, and that at least the only person I was truly hurting was my own past self.

Previously I'd have been worried that I might not remember the exact wording of the message, but I'd found that these things have a way of sorting themselves out. You find not that you're *remembering* the words as you type them, but that they're coming to you naturally, and that they *feel* right, as if they're being written for the first time – which, of course, in a way they are. It was exactly the same thing with Frank's suit. I'd been worried I might not be able to find a suit that matched the one I remembered him wearing the first time I'd seen him, but of course not only did I find a similar suit in Camden Lock, I found the *exact* one – which, again, is why he'd been wearing it when my past self had encountered him.

Time. It was neat in some ways, messy and convoluted in others. If you went with it, and tried simply to implement what in your experience had already taken place, all the pieces fell nicely into their allotted slots. But when you deliberately tried to change things... that was when the trouble started.

After I'd sent the email, wiped the account and offered a silent apology to my past self for the anguish I knew I was about to put him (me) through, I went back in time again. I went back to the summer of 1893, to a place in London I'd never been to before. It was a leap of faith, a leap into the dark, but I knew I'd arrived in the *right* place when I smelled the appalling stench of decay and unwashed flesh and human excrement, and when I felt things scuttling over my shoes that I knew were rats and cockroaches. I stood swaying for a moment, the nausea, both from the stench and from the effects of time travel coiling in my gut, threatening to overwhelm me. When I was finally able to focus I saw a tall, scraggly-bearded man in filthy rags staring at me in open-mouthed wonder, his eyes flickering from my face to the heart in my hand.

I swallowed and said, 'You must come with me, Abel. It's time.' Then I stepped forward and took his hand. And even as the nanites inside me were still doing their job, we were travelling again, though on this occasion we weren't moving through time, but simply slipping across London in the blink of an eye – from Newgate Prison to Ranskill Gardens.

That was where I stayed for the next twelve days. I stayed there with the man I'd called Abel, and who I renamed Hawkins to conceal his identity. He was broken when I found him. He was grieving for his murdered family, and he had resigned himself to the death he'd been facing for killing one of the men who had attacked the camp of travelling performers in which he, his wife Marta and their four children had lived.

But he was a proud, intelligent man with a strong spirit, and as the days passed, and he grew to trust me, we became friends. I told him my story – or as much of it as he needed to know – and by the time I left him, having given him his instructions and a letter to give to my past self in two years' time, not only was he on the road to recovery, but I knew I could trust him implicitly.

It was an honour spending time with him again. But it was heart-breaking too. It was the first time I'd gone back in time to see a dead friend, and although I'd been apprehensive about how it might make me feel, I'd had no real concept of what the true strength and depth of my feelings would be.

'Bittersweet' is the word that springs most readily to mind, but that doesn't even *begin* to cut it. Even though I'd seen Hawkins die, I'd always known that I had unfinished business with him. The reality, though, of actually *seeing* him and *talking* to him when I knew of his ultimate fate was both giddyingly glorious and gut-churningly harrowing.

I had to keep reminding myself that at this point in time he was *alive*, as alive as any of us were who were occupying the span of time between our beginning and our end. That wasn't the hardest thing, though. The hardest thing was dealing with my compulsion to keep trying to convince myself that what I had done for him – rescuing him the day before his execution, and giving him another couple of years' life he wouldn't otherwise have had – was a precious gift, and not simply a pragmatic, even callous, tactic on my part, designed simply to further my own cause.

Could I help it if I was bound by circumstance? Could I help it if there were certain things I *had* to do to maintain what I believed was a possibly fragile equilibrium? Whatever I did, I did with the best intentions. At no point did I set out to harm anyone or prolong anyone's pain. Sometimes stuff happened. Sometimes bad things happened to people because of my involvement with them – but was that my fault? Or just part of the randomness and complexity of life.

After leaving Hawkins, I jumped forward to the day after I'd received the letter from McCallum inviting me to his house. It was because of that letter that I'd been arrested and taken to the police station, and had ultimately ended up as Tallarian's prisoner in Victorian London, after trying to stop the shape-shifter, in the guise of DI Jensen, from stealing the heart.

My 'appointment' with McCallum (though I hadn't known it had been McCallum who'd contacted me until I arrived there) had been scheduled for noon that day, and that was the time I arrived back in town. Not at McCallum's house, though. My intention wasn't to warn myself, or to interfere in any way with what I knew had happened to me. No, I went back to see Clover.

Although I wasn't yet ready for a reunion with the Clover I'd left behind to continue my journey through the First World War, I was happy enough to meet up with Clover's past self in order to tick off another 'housekeeping' job in my little black book. I arrived as my past self was tentatively approaching McCallum's house at 56 Bellwater Drive. While he was occupied there, I turned up, once again, in the bedroom of my house in Ranskill Gardens. I arrived probably half an hour or so after my past self had left the house.

I went downstairs to find Clover in the kitchen making a sandwich.

'Hi,' I said.

She turned, bread knife in hand, eyebrows rising in surprise. 'Hi. What are you doing back so soon? Has something gone–' Then her eyes narrowed as she peered harder at me. 'Wait a minute. You're not "you" you, are you? You're not the you who left here. You're from a different time.'

I nodded. 'I'm from the future.'

'How far?' She wrinkled her nose. 'Three or four years? But you look thin.'

'I've been through the wars.'

'Literally?' Then she waved the bread knife vaguely in my direction. 'No, it's okay, you don't have to answer. And don't give me one of those enigmatic smiles of yours, because frankly you're not very good at them. You just look constipated.'

'What enigmatic smiles?' I asked.

She shrugged. 'That's probably the future you. You haven't perfected them yet – not that you ever will.'

I frowned. 'You're more *au fait* with the idea of time travel than you've been letting on, aren't you? This is just a few days after Frank rescued you from that basement in the Isle of Dogs, right?'

She nodded.

'And yet back then, when I mentioned time travel, after waking up having been unconscious for three days, you sounded surprised – like it was a whole new thing for you.'

She raised her hands in surrender, though the fact that she was still holding the bread knife kind of spoiled the effect. 'It's a fair cop. You've got me bang to rights.'

I frowned. 'So why did you lie?'

'Work it out, dumbo. Because you told me to.'

'Me?'

She pulled a face to let me know I was being *really* slow. 'You woke up here, didn't you? Who do you think brought you here?'

'You did?'

'Correct. And do you remember who I said the house belonged to?'

The penny dropped. 'A friend. Of course. That was the future me, wasn't it? So I appeared, told you who I was, and about this place, and you brought the unconscious me here?'

'Correct. That night in the Isle of Dogs I heard a commotion somewhere outside the room I'd been locked in, and started yelling, and next thing I knew the door was opening and there was Frank. He was surprised to see me at first, because he thought you and him had already rescued me, and that the two of us had legged it while he'd been holding off the shape-shifter. As soon as we realised what *had* happened – i.e. that you'd gone off with another bit of the shape-shifter disguised as me – we raced up top to try to warn you, but you were nowhere to be seen. I would have called you, but my mobile was back in the hotel room I'd been kidnapped from. Frank and I were just wondering what to do when a cab pulled up next to us and the bloke in the back told us to get in. Guess who that bloke was.'

'I'll take a stab in the dark and say me.'

'Correct. It was you as you look now, in fact – same clothes and everything. In the taxi you told us who you were and that you were from the future, and that we were on our way to pick up the past version of you – by which I mean *his* past, not my past.

'Anyway, the cab took us to some God-forsaken little street in the East End, and next second there you were. You just seemed to appear out of nowhere, lying in the street, clutching the heart and looking as though you'd had seven bells knocked out of you. We dragged you into the taxi and brought you here, and the future you told us to look after his past self, and said that this was his house, but not to let on to his past self yet – when asked, I was to say it belonged to a friend. And... well, that pretty much brings us up to date. Why are you looking so glum?'

I sighed. 'You said the future version of me that arrived in the cab was wearing what I'm wearing now?'

She nodded. 'So?' Then her face cleared. 'Oh! I suppose that means it was *you*! The "now" you, I mean?'

I nodded wearily and took out the heart. 'Why does one job always lead to another? Can you remember the name of the street the cab took us to?'

She frowned. 'Not off-hand.'

'Try. It's only if you tell me that I'll know where to go.'

She screwed up her face. 'It was something to do with birds. The name of a bird.' She closed her eyes and massaged her forehead with her thumb and forefinger, as if she could coax the memory out. It seemed to work, because her head suddenly jerked up, her eyes opening wide. 'Kingfisher something. Kingfisher Walk! That was it.'

'Great,' I said. 'Make me a sandwich. I'll be back in five minutes.'

I did what needed to be done. I went back a few days, hailed a cab, picked up Clover and Frank from the Isle of Dogs, and explained who I was and what was happening en route to Kingfisher Walk in the East End. Once there, we waited around until my past self appeared – this was the version of me that had been battered by Hulse and his cronies, and Jesus, was I in a bad way! – and then took the cab round to Ranskill Gardens. Once Frank and Clover had been briefed, I used the heart to take me forward, arriving back in the kitchen at Ranskill Gardens to find Clover sitting at the kitchen table, sandwich in hand, chewing.

'Turkey, salad and cranberry,' she said, her voice muffled by food. She nodded at the place she'd set for me at the opposite side of the table. 'Tuck in.'

I put a hand on my belly, lurched across and sank into the empty chair. 'Give me a minute.'

She regarded me steadily as I took deep breaths in and out, waiting for the nanites to kick in. 'Travel sickness?'

'Something like that.'

After a few minutes my guts settled enough for me to eat my sandwich. Once we were done and the plates had been cleared away, Clover said, 'So? You must be here for a reason. What can I do for you?'

'Have you ever fancied visiting the Victorian era?' I asked, and I watched her face light up.

You know the rest. Or, if not, I'm sure you can work it out. I took Clover back to August 1895, introduced her to Hawkins and the staff he'd employed during the two years since I'd rescued him from Newgate Prison, gave her some money to kit herself out in Victorian garb, told her as much as she needed to know and then left her to get acclimatised and to await the arrival both of Hope and my smoke-damaged past self – who Hawkins, having been briefed by me (I was getting pretty good at this by now), would rescue from Tallarian's lair in the early hours of September 3rd.

I still had things to do to establish myself in Victorian London – I needed to make some astute financial investments in order to accrue my fortune, set myself up with various business interests that would operate efficiently and profitably with minimal involvement from me, and buy the house in Ranskill Gardens – but by now I was reaching critical mass. I'd been desperate to see Kate since coming back from the War, but now I was so far beyond desperate that I'm not even sure there's a word to describe it. Added to which, the nuts and bolts of setting myself up as a Victorian gentlemen were so boring and long-winded, and seemed to require such a lot of thought and consideration that I simply didn't have the patience for, that I decided it could wait for another time.

I felt pretty much the same about the other big job that was currently nagging at me, which was the one concerning the Sherwoods. At some point I'd have to put three months aside, maybe more, to recruit them to my cause and then transform them, both practically and psychologically, from naive, strait-laced Victorians into a couple of tech-savvy whizz kids, capable of coping with the onslaught of the twenty-first century. But Rome wasn't built in a day, and the thought of undertaking that gargantuan task now, when I had already delayed my reunion with Kate beyond endurance, was too depressing for words. I'd tackle it at some point in the future. When Kate was ten maybe. Or fifteen.

Kate. She dominated my thoughts, and I felt sick with anticipation at the prospect of finally bringing her home. As I ascended the stairs to my bedroom on that day towards the end of August 1893, having just said goodbye to Clover and Hawkins, I felt as though electricity was fizzing through my veins. When I took the heart from my pocket, after changing from my Victorian clothes into my twenty-first-century ones, it was as if it too was aware of, and responding to, my almost feverish anticipation. It seemed to thrum with power, to vibrate with eagerness – or maybe that was just me. There was a part of me that wanted to use the heart to zap myself straight over to that little cottage in Wales where Kate was waiting for me, to finally have the lasting reunion I'd been working towards right there and then. But if I did that I wouldn't have a car, and would therefore have to use the heart to transport us both back to Ranskill Gardens - and I couldn't spring that on her, could I? Who knew what effect it would have?

So I forced myself to be patient. And instead of jumping the gun I moved forward in time, but remained at the same location - my familiar but ever-changing bedroom in Ranskill Gardens. I timed it so I'd arrive around five minutes after I'd left on the morning of November 2nd 2012.

The first thing I was truly aware of once the room had settled around me was the rushing sound of water. For a puzzled moment, as the familiar nausea swept over me, I wondered whether it was raining, whether the heart had brought me to the wrong time. Then I realised: it was the sound of the shower in Clover's en suite further along the corridor.

Once the nanites had done their work I moved along the landing to Clover's bedroom door. There was still a trail of dried mud on the carpet between my bedroom and hers. Not for the first time I wondered whether I'd ever get used to the vagaries of time travel. It was weird to think that while more than eighteen months had passed for me since I'd last seen her - at least in this timeline - it had been nothing but a matter of minutes for her since she'd hugged me and sent me on my way.

Although I could still hear the shower going, I knocked tentatively on her door, and then, when I failed to get an answer, opened it. Her duvet was in a rumpled heap on her bed and her clothes strewn untidily over the seat of a tall-backed wicker chair in the corner between the bedroom door and the door to the en suite. I crossed to the bathroom and knocked. The rush of water stopped abruptly.

'Hi, I'm back,' I called.

Her voice, from inside the shower, was echoey. 'You were eight minutes, not five. I was getting worried.'

'Sorry. I got held up in Ypres. Bloody Germans.'

Now her voice was sombre. 'How was it?'

I hesitated. How could I even begin to express what I'd been through? In the end I simply said, 'Not much fun.'

She was silent for a moment, then she asked, 'Are you okay?' More hesitantly, 'Nothing... missing?'

I briefly considered making a joke of it – *Only my sense of humour* – but it seemed neither funny nor appropriate. 'No,' I said, 'I'm fine. I'm going to make some breakfast. It's been ages since I had a proper full English. You want to join me?'

'Is the Pope Catholic?' she said. 'I'll be down in ten.'

She padded barefoot into the kitchen almost exactly ten minutes later, her maroon hair still damp. I had bacon under the grill, eggs and tomatoes frying in extra virgin olive oil (my only concession to healthy eating!), beans bubbling in a saucepan and four slices of bread browning in the toaster. I'd set the table and put ketchup, brown sauce, jam, butter, milk and a pot of tea on a mat in the middle. She nodded approvingly.

'You'll make someone a lovely wife one day.'

I shot her a grin. 'Talking of which, I'll hoover that mud up after breakfast. Don't want you traipsing it all over the house with your great clodhopping feet.'

The mood became more serious when we sat down to eat and I started to recount what I'd been up to since I'd last seen her. Despite it all, though, I couldn't help feeling both light-hearted and excited at the thought not only that I'd be seeing Kate later that day, but that I'd actually be bringing her home.

Clover's playfulness took a noticeable dip when I told her how I'd rescued Hawkins from Newgate Prison and installed him in Ranskill Gardens. She looked around the kitchen, as though mention of him might enable her to glimpse his ghost passing through.

'Poor Hawkins,' she said. 'He was a lovely man. A bit stuffy and... contained, but underneath it he was one of the kindest men I've ever met.' Her eyes suddenly grew dewy and raising both hands, she used the tips of her fingers to swipe her tears away.

'You okay?' I asked.

She gave a brisk nod. 'I'm fine. It was just you mentioning him like that. Caught me unawares.' She looked around again. 'You know, sometimes I find it hard to believe he was here in this house, that he walked through these rooms, that his voice echoed from these walls. It seems so unfair we can't just use the heart to go back and... save him.'

'I know. But we can't. Time wouldn't let us.'

'Stupid time,' she said with some vehemence. Then she smiled thinly, as though at her own childishness.

I took a bite of toast. There was silence between us for a moment. Then I said, 'Hey, guess what I did after rescuing Hawkins and getting him settled in?'

'Have tea with Queen Victoria? Punch Hitler in the face?'

I smiled. 'Remember the day I got that note and went to McCallum's house and ended up getting arrested?'

She looked blank for a moment, then her eyebrows shot up, stretching her eyes wide. 'That was the day you turned up and took me back to 1895! My God! Is that where you've just been?'

'About...' I looked at my watch '...forty minutes ago I was in Victorian London, saying goodbye to you and Hawkins.'

She raised her hands again and pressed her fingers to her forehead. 'Wow. Mind blown. For me... well, so much has happened since then. It seems like a lifetime ago.'

'The blink of an eye,' I said. 'All of it. Just the blink of an eye.'

She looked at me as though I'd said something profound. Or as though *she* was about to say something profound. Then to my surprise she reached across and took one of my hands between both of hers.

'What you've been given is an amazing gift,' she said. 'And I know it's caused a lot of grief, but it's also something you can use for great good. Something you *have* used for great good.'

I shrugged, embarrassed, and also a little uneasy. I couldn't help but think of people who'd suffered, even died, because of their association with me and the heart.

'I do my best,' I said inadequately.

'I know you do.' She squeezed my hand as though literally trying to press the conviction behind her words into my flesh. 'And that's all you *can* do. You're a good man, Alex. Don't ever lose sight of that.'

She broke the connection between us, turned her back and bustled away to make more tea. It was an odd moment, and one where I felt there was a hidden meaning behind her words, perhaps even something she wasn't telling me. But I didn't pursue it, because... well, because I felt afraid to, I suppose. Sometimes, instinctively, you don't *want* to lift the lid of the box to see what's inside. You just get a feeling that you shouldn't.

While she was making more tea, I took the opportunity to run up to the office and grab my laptop. I returned to the kitchen and cleared a space on the breakfast table, then opened the laptop up and started Googling car hire places.

After a couple of minutes Clover drifted across with a couple of steaming mugs. She put one down on my right, then moved behind me as she sipped hers, looking over my shoulder.

'How's it feel?' she asked after a second or two.

I glanced at her. 'How's what feel?'

'To know that today, after all you've been through, all your searching, you'll finally be getting your little girl back for good?'

'Wonderful,' I said automatically. Then, although I'd been thinking about it all day, the reality of her words hit me, and a warm glow of well-being rose up through my body. The grin that burst from me was a release of unadulterated joy.

'No, bollocks to that. It's better than wonderful. Better than anything. It's the best feeling in the world.'

'I'm glad,' she said. She squeezed my shoulder. 'So when are you heading to Wales?'

'We,' I said. 'You're coming with me.'

I thought she was being coy simply because she hadn't wanted to seem presumptuous, but she said, 'No, this is your day, Alex. Yours and Kate's. You're bringing her home, and that's a big deal. It's special. So it should just be the two of you driving back together. You need the time and space to get reacquainted. You deserve that. You've earned it.'

I swivelled to look at her. 'Don't be daft. We're in this together. We have been from the start. Whether you like it or not, you're part of this family now. And Kate will love you. I know she will.'

Clover crinkled her nose into an expression that indicated she'd been moved by my words, but didn't entirely agree with them.

'That does mean a lot to me,' she said, 'but honestly I'd feel awkward. And not because of how you'd *make* me feel, but just because... well, because I would.' Before I could respond, she rapped me on the shoulder and said quickly, 'Besides, if I don't come with you I'll be able to get Kate's room ready for her. It'll be weird for her to arrive at a strange new house, won't it? But if she's got a lovely room waiting for her, it'll make it much easier for her to settle in. She can have Hope's old room. I could go back to your old flat and fetch some of her stuff...'

She tailed off, breathless and bright-eyed. Again I couldn't help thinking there was something off about her manner, something she wasn't telling me, but I couldn't put my finger on it.

'Are you okay?' I asked her.

She laughed. 'Yeah, course I am. Why?'

'You're not in any trouble? You're not being threatened, or...' Then it struck me what it could *really* be. 'You're not feeling as though you're in the way? A spare part? Because Kate's coming home?'

She laughed again, though the way her eyelashes flickered made me feel I'd got pretty close to the truth.

'Course not. I just... I want to give you some space, that's all. Whether you want me to or not, *I* want to. It's important to me. You do understand, don't you?'

'Yes, sure,' I said. 'But don't ever feel you're not welcome here.'

'I won't.' She thrust her flat palm in front of my face like a teacher demanding a pupil spit out his chewing gum. 'So hand over the keys to the flat.'

'I haven't got them. Frank's living there now, remember.'

'No problem. I'll give him a call, tell him to put the kettle on and get some decent biscuits in.'

An hour later I was on my way to Wales in a hired Chevrolet Cobalt. It was a long time since I'd driven and it felt strange at first, the car responding more eagerly than I could initially cope with, which resulted in me stalling at a set of traffic lights in central London and spending an embarrassing twenty seconds re-starting the damn thing with horns blaring behind me. Once I'd been behind the wheel for ten minutes, though, I started to get the hang of it, and by the time I hit the A40 heading out of London I was cruising. It was a typical November day – cold and murky, the sky, streets, buildings and even people looking grey and drab, and somehow indistinct, like a charcoal drawing smeared by damp. But enclosed in my spotless, clean-smelling metal box, with the heater and the radio on, I was happy. I sang along to a bunch of songs from the '80s and '90s I only half-knew and didn't even like that much – Sting and Queen and Michael Jackson – and kept glancing at the sat nav as it counted down the miles. At around the halfway mark, on the M6 somewhere near Stafford, I stopped at a service station for a piss, a ham-and-cheese Panini and a cappuccino. I did it only because I didn't want to arrive at the cottage hungry and dying for the loo, though the entire time I was out of the car I found myself itching to get back into it again.

It was mid-afternoon when the sat nav finally informed me I'd arrived at my destination. I parked in the same lay-by I'd parked in the last time we'd been here and cut the engine. There was a part of me that wanted to leap straight out of the car and run up to the cottage, but I forced myself to sit tight for a few seconds so I could compose myself. I gripped the steering wheel to try to stop the trembling in my hands and took several deep breaths in a vain attempt to quell my churning guts. Now I'd finally arrived at this point, not just geographically but after a journey that had not only taken several years of my life but had also spanned centuries and turned my previously held notions of reality on its head, I was finding it hard to believe that it was over, that this was finally *it*.

And okay, so it wasn't *really* over. There were loose threads all over the place, and I still had the long shadow of the Dark Man stretching over me. But my search for Kate, and more specifically my desire for us to be reunited, and to resume our life together as a family, which had been my driving force for so long, was something I was now finally on the verge of turning into reality.

I turned my head and looked at the unassuming cottage perched halfway up the bleak rise of wind-swept fields that surrounded it. The white walls looked grey under the sloping slate roof; the windows were featureless black squares.

The lack of light and life gave me a sudden quivering pang of concern. What if they weren't there? What if they'd packed up and gone? What if they'd been *taken*?

Trying not to let my concern burgeon into panic, I fumbled open the car door, crossed the road in a staggering run and pushed open the gate in the black stone wall that surrounded the house. If I'd had any spare breath I would have shouted Kate's name, but my guts were so cramped, and my chest so tight, that it was an effort simply to breathe. By the time I reached the cottage sweat was pouring off me. I fought the urge to hammer on the door, and instead knocked with at least a semblance of composure.

I palmed sweat from my face and tried to stay calm as I waited. I was about to knock again when the handle first jiggled, and then turned...

Followed, moments later, by the door slowly beginning to open.

I resisted the urge to shove at it, and instead stepped back warily. The door opened like a sleepy yawn, seeming to take an age. And then a small figure leaped into the widening gap, shouted, 'Boo!' and started roaring with laughter.

The tension fell away and I laughed too.

'Were you scared, Daddy?' Kate yelled. 'Did I make you jump?'

'No, I wasn't scared,' I said – and she started to frown. 'I was *terrified*! I thought you were a ghost.'

She whooped and started laughing again. I grabbed her, scooped her up and blew a raspberry on her neck. She wriggled frantically, her laughter turning into gleeful shrieks.

The door opened wider, to reveal Paula/Maude Sherwood standing there, grinning. She snapped on the light switch beside the front door. 'She wanted to surprise you. I hope you were duly surprised.'

'I was,' I said. 'I was so surprised that I nearly ran away, jumped into my car and drove all the way back to London.'

'You can't do that, Daddy!' Kate cried.

'Can't I? Who'd have stopped me?'

'I would. I'd have chased you down the road and caught the car with my magic lasso and made you stop.'

'Really?' I looked at her, wide-eyed. 'Can you really do that?'

'Yep,' she said, nodding vigorously. 'And I can spin round, look. Put me down!'

This last command was delivered in a voice so imperious it warranted no refusal. I put her down and watched as she twirled around so vigorously she almost fell over.

'Wow!' I said.

'She and Hamish have been watching re-runs of a show called *Wonder Woman* this week,' said Paula drily.

I laughed again. Looking at Paula, it was astonishing how different she was from the young woman – Maude – I'd met in Victorian London, how quickly and completely she'd adapted to the twenty-first century.

I must have been a *very* good teacher.

I went into the cottage and Paula put the kettle on. Adam and Hamish came through from the front room, where they'd been watching TV. There was a lot of gooey, floury mess on the kitchen surfaces, and even on the floor, and pots piled in the sink and stacked up next to it. Paula saw me looking and said, 'The kids have spent the morning making buns in honour of your arrival.' She grabbed a big round cake tin from the kitchen counter and opened it, tilting it towards me to display the contents. I saw a pile of lavishly and messily decorated buns. Kate poked one topped by a dollop of dripping green icing that had the word 'Dady' shakily depicted in chocolate sprinkles.

'That's your one, Daddy,' she said proudly. 'I made it myself. Only you are allowed to eat that one.'

'Yummy,' I said. 'I'll have it with my cup of tea.'

When the tea was poured, Adam, Paula and myself sat around the kitchen table while Kate and Hamish, both of them carrying plates on which a couple of buns apiece were sliding about precariously, went through to the front room to watch TV.

'She's all packed up and raring to go,' Paula said.

I sipped my tea. 'Thanks for looking after her.'

'It's been a pleasure,' said Adam. 'Genuinely. As you can see, she and Hamish get on like a house on fire.' He hesitated. 'I hope the kids can stay friends. Once we're all back in London, I mean.'

'Of course.' I looked from him to Paula. 'You're staying in the twenty-first century then? You're not going back?'

'How can we,' said Paula, 'after seeing what this century has to offer? The advancements in technology and medicine and education, the opportunities for women, the cleaner air...'

I smiled. 'Many people think there's a lot wrong with the modern world, that we're on the verge of destroying it because of our technology.'

'Those people haven't lived in the 1800s,' said Paula fiercely.

More tentatively, Adam asked, 'It is okay for us to stay, isn't it?'

I spread my hands. 'I might have been your boss back in your old life, Adam, but I'm not your keeper. I'm not going to dictate how and where and when you live your lives.'

'I'm not so sure about the where,' said Paula.

'What do you mean?'

She took a piece of folded notepaper from the windowsill and handed it to me. I unfolded it and saw that an address in Crouch End had been written in block capitals, above a date: October 18th 2012.

'What's this?' I asked.

'When your older self came to see us before your last visit, he gave us this and said I was to give it to you the second time you came back to fetch Kate. He said to tell you it's the address of the house you've bought for us in London, and that the date is...'

'The date I bought it.'

She nodded. 'He said you were to write it in your book so you wouldn't forget. And he said to let you know there was no rush.'

'I'm such a manipulative so-and-so,' I said, smiling, and taking out my notebook, I slipped the sheet of paper inside. I put the book back into my pocket and patted it. 'I won't forget.'

'Thank you,' said Adam. 'We really appreciate all you've done for us.'

'I appreciate all you've done for me,' I replied. 'Without your help... well, who knows what might have happened?'

Ten minutes later, revived by tea and buns, I decided it was time to hit the road. With Adam's help I loaded the car with Kate's stuff – a suitcase of clothes and a couple of bags of toys and books, most of which she'd accrued since being 'abducted' – and then it was time to say our goodbyes. There were hugs and kisses all round, and even a couple of tears shed by Paula, and by 4:30 p.m. Kate and I were on the road.

Kate and I. Even now it feels wonderful to write those words, to remember how much they meant to me at the time. It was beyond amazing to be reunited with my daughter, for us to be together again, after all I'd been through. A few minutes into the drive, while I was still negotiating the rugged, hilly terrain leading away from the cottage, it struck me that this was the first time I'd been truly alone with Kate since the morning I'd got her ready for school and taken her across the landing to the Sherwoods' flat, prior to my reunion with Benny in The Hair of the Dog, and my first meeting with Clover. That was... forever ago. For me, at least. I looked across at Kate and grinned, overwhelmed, once again, by that glorious rush of well-being.

'Well, here we are, kiddo,' I said. 'It's just me and you again. The Gruesome Twosome.'

She wrinkled her nose. 'I'm not gruesome.'

'Yes you are. You're the most gruesome one of all.'

'You are,' she retorted. 'You're more gruesome than a hundred dog poos and fifty hundred smelly sausages.'

'Well,' I said, shaking my head gravely, 'there's no arguing with that, is there?'

What did we talk about on that long journey back to London? To be honest, I can't remember. It was nonsense mainly. The sort of nonsense that a father and his young daughter can talk about for hours on end, and find highly entertaining. The sort of nonsense that is accompanied by much name-calling, much laughter and much affection. The sort of nonsense that feels glorious, and happy, and *right*.

I told her about her new house (*our* new house) – *that* I remember. I broached the subject tentatively, knowing how much she loved being across the landing from Paula, Adam and Hamish. I feared she might be upset to find we wouldn't be living there any more, but I'd forgotten how adaptable and accepting kids are. She took the news on board with minimal fuss, and although I initially tried to over-egg the pudding by telling her about all the rooms and the garden, and the nearby park, and the new TV and computer she'd find when she got there, all she really wanted to know was whether she'd still have her own room, and whether she'd still see plenty of Hamish. As soon as I ticked all those boxes for her she was more than happy.

'Cool as a mule from Liverpool,' she said, which made me laugh.

'Where did you get that from?'

She shrugged. 'Dunno.'

I glanced at her for the hundredth time, marvelling at the sheer fact that she was *there*. She was too big for a car seat now, but sitting in the passenger seat, with an adult belt stretched across her and her little white-trainered feet dangling in mid-air, she looked so tiny, so vulnerable.

'Oh, there is one other thing,' I said casually. 'You remember Clover, that nice lady who came with me last time?'

She wrinkled her nose, as if trying to remember. 'Did she have purple hair?'

'She did.'

'Is she your girlfriend?'

'No, she's just a friend. A buddy. Like Hamish is your buddy.'

'Hmm?' she said.

'Well, Clover's got nowhere to live, because her home was burned up in a big fire. So, as we've now got a big new house with lots of rooms, she's probably going to be living with us for a while. Is that all right?'

'Will she have to sleep in my room?'

'No, she's got her own room.'

'That's all right then. Will she watch *Wonder Woman* with me when Hamish isn't there?'

'I'm sure she will.'

'Cool.'

But when we finally arrived back at Ranskill Gardens, at around ten that night, Clover was nowhere to be seen. Kate had fallen asleep in the car at around 8:30 p.m., and was still snoring gently when I turned in through the open gates and parked with a soft crunch of tyres on the gravelled drive. She didn't stir even when I unclipped her seatbelt, scooped her up and lifted her from her cosy seat into the chilly November air. She merely gave a little grunt and huddled further into me as I carried her up the path. Much as I wanted to show her our new house, I decided that now was not a good time. She'd be too confused and grumpy. Better leave it till the morning.

Supporting her weight awkwardly with one arm, I fumbled my key into the lock of the front door. The next ten minutes were spent putting Kate to bed and fetching her stuff from the car. I didn't call Clover's name, because I didn't want to wake Kate up, but I did think it odd she hadn't appeared to welcome us. I decided she must have had an early night or fallen asleep in front of the TV. No doubt I'd find out soon enough.

One thing Clover *had* done, which I discovered when I pushed open the door to Hope's old room with my foot, was fulfil her promise to make Kate's homecoming a pleasurable one. I was touched by how much care she'd taken to make the room look both beautiful and familiar. Not only had she fetched Kate's toys and books from our old flat, but she'd also transferred Kate's *Scooby Doo* bedding from her old bed (having, I noted from its fresh smell, washed and ironed it first) and had even taken the time and effort to bring – and hang – Kate's old curtains, which were pink with a big yellow and red flower print on them. And okay, so the curtains were a little short for the new window, and would have to be either replaced or lengthened, but it was a lovely gesture all the same.

That wasn't the *piece de resistance*, though. That particular accolade went to the objects sitting on the chair beside the bed. Beneath a jumbo set of felt-tip pens – *50 Colours!* – was a *Toy Story* colouring book. It was identical to the one Clover and I had found shredded the night the flat had been trashed.

As I gently laid Kate down and pulled her duvet over her, I'm not ashamed to admit that tears were not only pricking my eyes, but brimming over my bottom lids. What can I say? I'm a big softie and it had been a particularly emotional day. As I closed Kate's door behind me, I wiped the tears away with my sleeve, before heading along the landing to Clover's bedroom. I listened for a moment outside her door, then tapped lightly. No reply.

'Clover?' I said softly.

Silence.

I opened the door a crack and peeped in. Her bed was unoccupied and neatly made, the curtains open. I went downstairs, into the front room, which was empty. I was feeling not exactly uneasy, but a little disquieted, remembering how odd and guarded Clover had seemed that morning. At least everything seemed to be in order, and there was nothing to suggest that anything sinister had taken place. I checked in a couple of the other rooms, then walked along the corridor to the left of the staircase, which led to the kitchen at the back of the house. Although this place was my home, my sanctuary, and Kate was asleep upstairs, I couldn't help but think that it suddenly seemed hollow and empty. I pushed open the kitchen door and snapped on the light.

I saw the note immediately.

It had been written on a sheet of decent notepaper from the study. It had been folded in half and propped against the salt cellar, right in the middle of the table where I'd be bound to see it. My name was written on the front in swirly capitals, with an extra little x after the X of my name. I walked across, picked it up and opened it out. In Clover's scrawly handwriting, which gave the impression she was always in a hurry, it said:

Hey Alex
Please don't think I'm being weird, or that I feel put out by Kate coming home, because I'm not and I don't. I honestly, genuinely couldn't be happier that you've found your little girl and that the two

of you are back together. I know how much it means to you, and it's a lovely, lovely thing after all you've been through.
Whatever you may believe, though, I honestly do think that you guys need some time to get back into the routine of living a 'normal' life (ha! Whatever that is!) without a third person (i.e. me) around. I've therefore gone away for a bit (not for ever – don't think you can get rid of me that easily!) to give you some much-needed space.
Don't feel bad, it's not your fault. And don't get annoyed with me, because... well, because anger is a negative emotion and it's not good for the soul. And don't think for a moment this is forever, because it's not. I'll be there whenever you need me. In fact, I'll probably pop up like a bad penny when you least expect it.
For now, though, just enjoy having your girl home with you again, where she's supposed to be. Give her lots of love and hugs and try not to worry about the future (though knowing you as I do, it's almost certainly pointless me saying that!).
See you soon!
Your forever friend
Clover xxx
P.S. Hope Kate liked her pressie!

Despite what Clover had written, my first response was resentment, mixed with disappointment. I felt that by her actions she'd soured what had ended up being a pretty perfect day. I felt annoyed with her too for putting me in a position where I'd now have to explain to Kate why Clover *wasn't* here, when I'd told her earlier that she would be.

But no sooner had my bitterness started to bubble inside me than I started to see things from Clover's point of view. I guess if our positions had been reversed I'd have felt like a gooseberry too. Or maybe not a gooseberry, but certainly I'd have felt an urge to stay on the periphery, to give my friend and his daughter some space and time to get properly reacquainted. And with that I realised that Clover wasn't being selfish – that on the contrary, she was being *thoughtful*. Still, I felt bad for her. I felt as though I'd driven her out. I took out my mobile and called her, but got only her voicemail.

'Hey, it's me,' I said. 'We've just got back, and I've just got your note. I just wanted to say... um... that I understand where you're coming from, and... well, that you're welcome to come back any time – and I mean *any* time. Um... I also wanted to check that you were okay, so give me a call or send me a text to let me know where you're staying.' I hesitated. I wanted to tell her that if she was staying in a hotel, I'd happily pay for it, but it sounded mercenary; I didn't want her to feel she was dependent on me. So in the end I said lamely, 'So... yeah. Just let me know, okay. I'll see you soon.'

I was about to say goodbye when I remembered something. 'Oh, by the way, Jackie's coming by tomorrow with Hope. I arranged it before I left this morning. I wanted Hope to meet Kate. To be honest, I can't wait to see them together. It was something I used to wonder about back in 1895... whether they'd ever meet and become friends. Um... anyway, they're coming at 1 p.m., for lunch. It would be great if you could be here too. Anyway... I'll see you soon. Call me.'

She didn't call me. She didn't text me either. And she wasn't at the house at 1 p.m. when I answered a knock on the door to find a tentatively smiling Jackie and a grinning Hope on the doorstep.

It was okay, though. I was disappointed she hadn't been in touch, but I was focused mainly on Kate, and she'd been nothing but a delight. She'd woken early – earlier than me – and although I'd been worried she might come to in the morning disorientated and distressed to find herself in a strange bed, she'd instead woken up full of verve and energy. I'd been woken by a scream, which had caused me to leap out of bed and go haring down the corridor to her room, my heart thumping madly in my chest. When I threw the door open, though, I realised that the scream had been a squeal of delight. I found her sitting cross-legged on her bed, busily working away with her new felt tips at her *Toy Story* colouring book.

Even my dramatic entrance didn't faze her. As I burst into her room she looked up, still grinning, and raised the colouring book above her head, scattering pens everywhere.

'Look what I've got, Daddy!'

My heart was still hammering, but I tried to give the impression I hadn't just raced up the corridor in panic. 'Yeah, I know,' I said. 'Do you like it?'

'I love it!' she cried. 'I love it a million! It's new, Daddy! There's no colouring in it. It's all empty.'

'And what do you think of your new room?' I asked. 'Do you like that too?'

She glanced around, as if it had only just occurred to her to do so. 'Uh-huh,' she said, though she was clearly more interested in the book. 'It's awesome.'

And that was pretty much how the day continued to go. My concerns that Kate might be unsettled by her new surroundings turned out to be completely unfounded. She took everything in her stride. And like most five-year-olds it wasn't the bigger picture that impressed her, it was the smaller details. She laughed uproariously at the waste disposal in the kitchen and took great delight in putting tea bags down it; she loved the colours of the Tiffany lamp in the front room, and the piano in the corner, which she plonked away tunelessly on for several gleeful minutes; she marvelled at a squirrel sitting on the branch of a tree outside the window of Clover's room.

She didn't ask about Clover at all, and I guessed she'd forgotten until Hope asked where she was during lunch, whereupon Kate, who'd become uncharacteristically shy since Jackie and Hope's arrival, piped up, 'She's got purple hair, and she's very pretty, but she's not Daddy's girlfriend, because my mummy is.'

It wasn't only Kate who'd been shy since Jackie and Hope had entered the house. Both girls had been circling each other warily, occasionally casting one another bashful glances, as though *wanting* to make the first move, but uncertain how to do so. Now, though, Hope, who'd been nibbling a slice of pepperoni pizza (Kate and I had taken a trip to the local deli earlier that morning to buy provisions), slid a glance at Kate and asked, 'Does your mummy live here?'

'No,' Kate replied. 'She lives in hospital. She's sick.'

'But she's getting better,' I added.

Hope nodded, though barely acknowledged me. Her attention was now all on Kate. 'I don't have a mummy,' she confided. 'Not a real one. But Jackie's going to be my new mummy.'

'Do you have a daddy?' asked Kate.

Hope shook her head. 'Jackie's husband, whose name is Steve, will be my new daddy. He's nice. He's got an earring, and he does funny card tricks. And Ed will be my new brother.'

'I don't have a brother. But I've got a sister called Candice. Not a real one, though. She's a...' She squinted at me.

'Half-sister,' I said.

'Yeah, half-sister. That means she's half my sister and half somebody else's. But she lets me wear her lip gloss sometimes. It tastes like strawberries.'

And that was it. The beginning of what I hoped would become a long-lasting friendship. Not that I'd force it, of course. With Kate in London and Hope living in Hampshire with Jackie and her family, it was more likely the girls would remain only casual acquaintances; and it was perhaps even more likely that they'd lose touch completely in later years. But all the time I'd been in Victorian London, I'd harboured a desire that one day, in a happier future, the girls would meet and become friends. It was a hope that had comforted me, kept me going, through some of the darker days when Kate had been missing and Hope dangerously ill.

Seeing them together now, chatting away, becoming more relaxed in one another's company, was a wish fulfilled. And not only that, but a wish that had once seemed so far away as to be virtually unattainable. I caught Jackie's eye, and it was only when she gave me a big smile that I realised she must have been mirroring the joyful grin on my own face.

'Did you know, Kate,' I said, 'that Hope used to live in this house too?'

Kate blinked at me, then looked at Hope in surprise. 'Did you?'

Hope nodded. 'When my arm was making me poorly. Before I went to the hospital.'

'And did you know,' I continued, 'that Hope's old room is *your* room now?'

'Wowee,' said Kate. 'Wowee zowee.'

Hope giggled, which set Kate off too.

When the giggling had run its course, Kate asked, 'Can I show Hope my room, Daddy?'

'Course you can – when you've had your lunch. Now, who wants chocolate cake and ice cream?'

'Me!' both girls cried.

After lunch, when the kitchen had been cleared and the girls were playing upstairs, Jackie and I took our coffees into the front room and started talking about the mechanics of the adoption process. For me the conversation was something of a minefield. I'd already lied to Jackie about my profession, and about Hope's origins, and now I had to not only sustain the lie, but bullshit madly about a process of which I had only a vague understanding.

I think I just about carried it off. I managed to be – in my mind, at least – authoritative without actually saying anything specific. I told Jackie that she and Steve would have various forms to fill in, and that they'd have to be 'assessed', but that as Hope's origins were unknown that shouldn't be a difficult process, and that I'd do all in my power to make things as quick and painless as possible.

I was confident I could use the heart to ease proceedings along, to retroactively fix whatever paperwork might be required to give Hope an identity, and prevent her from being an enigma that the authorities might ask questions about in future years.

'Will we have to be interviewed?' Jackie asked. 'I've been reading up about it and it sounds as though prospective parents need to be interviewed and to attend various counselling sessions before–'

I held up my hand. 'Ordinarily, yes, that *would* be the case. But as I say, because of Hope's extraordinary circumstances I'm confident we can circumnavigate all that, especially if Clover and I deal with the paperwork from our end and provide you with references, which we're more than happy to do. Look, don't trouble yourself with it at all, Jackie. Just leave it up to us and we'll–'

At which point the welcoming chimes of the front-door buzzer rang through the house.

I excused myself and hurried into the hall, wondering if this was Clover, turning up late. If it was, there'd be no time to ask how she was feeling, or where she'd been. I'd simply have to fill her in quickly on what Jackie and I had been talking about so that she didn't contradict what I'd said. To be honest, I'd been on tenterhooks all through lunch, wondering whether Hope or Kate might say something that would tear apart the web of lies I'd spun for Jackie, and prompt her to raise some awkward questions. Both Clover and I had broached the subject with Hope in the past and impressed upon her how important it was that she not talk about her previous life. Although Hope seemed to understand the need for secrecy, I'd been afraid that in the heat of the moment she'd let something slip. Luckily, though, neither of the girls had said anything I couldn't have explained away.

I crossed the hallway and opened the front door. Standing on the step was a black guy wearing a blue cap and a blue jacket with a courier logo on the pocket. Propped against him, his hand resting lightly on its top edge, was a slim, rectangular parcel encased in strong brown cardboard; it looked like a giant credit card.

'Mr Locke?' he said, his voice so rich and deep he could have made a living doing voiceovers for TV ads.

'Yes.'

'This is for you. Sign here please.'

I signed for the parcel, carried it inside and propped it against the wall. I was curious, and slightly suspicious, but I didn't get chance to open it until much later that evening, after Jackie and Hope had left and Kate had been fed, bathed, read a Mrs Pepperpot story and tucked up in bed.

I carried the parcel into what I had used to call the drawing room, and now simply called the front room, where a fire was burning in the grate. I examined the parcel carefully before opening it, but there was no return address. Using a Stanley knife, I slit the parcel along the top edge and flipped it up like the flap of a letterbox. Now I could see what looked like the top of a picture frame made of some shiny dark wood. What was this? Had somebody sent me a painting?

Taking hold of the top corners of the frame, I lifted it from its cardboard packaging. I propped the picture against the side of one of the armchairs and stepped back to look at it.

Immediately I felt a little jolt of shock in my stomach. 'Fuck,' I said.

It wasn't a painting, it was a framed poster, and it was one that I had seen before. In yellow letters along the top were the words 'London Hippodrome, Friday 10th December 1948', and in larger yellow letters below that, forming an arch, 'THE GREAT BARNABY'. Beneath the lettering was a brightly coloured illustration of a grinning, bearded man in a red eye mask with a top hat on his head. He was wearing white kid gloves and was juggling a variety of objects, one of which was the obsidian heart.

The last time I had seen this poster it had been hanging on the wall in Barnaby McCallum's house. In the very room where I had killed him, in fact.

There was a cream envelope attached to the bottom of the picture, tucked between the edge of the frame and the glass. I plucked it out, opened it and read the carefully folded letter inside.

It was a solicitor's letter, and the message was short and to the point. It read:

Dear Mr Locke

Mr McCallum stipulated in his will that you should be sent this particular item on this particular date. He said that you would find it useful.

Yours sincerely
Jonathan Coulthard esq.

TWENTY-TWO

WONDER WOMAN

'Hey,' I said softly as Lyn slowly, and with obvious pain, turned her head to look at me. 'How are you doing?'

'Fantastic,' she replied, in a tone of such quiet and self-aware irony that I couldn't help grinning.

In truth, she looked dreadful, even worse than I'd been expecting. This, though, was only because the bruising had come out on her face, which meant that instead of looking her usual pale self her skin was now an interesting canvas of yellow, green and blue-black blotches. Her eyes were the worst, the pouchy black flesh beneath them making them seem even more sunken than usual.

'So how does it feel to be an action hero?'

'Painful.'

'You saved my life, you know. You were brilliant.'

She probably would have shrugged if, as she had told me on the phone, it didn't send shooting pains through her body every time she moved. Instead she merely grimaced. 'I didn't know what I was doing. I was overcome with rage. I'd never felt so angry before. All I really remember thinking was that I didn't want *him* to win.'

I nodded at the bandage, which still encircled her shaved skull like a turban. 'How's the head now?'

'Throbs all the time. It's just about bearable if I stay still and keep taking the tablets.' She gestured wearily at the chair beside her bed. 'Aren't you going to sit down?'

'There's a reason why I'm still hovering by the door. I've brought someone to see you. But I didn't want to spring it on you. I wanted to find out whether you were up to it first.'

She closed her eyes briefly, and I saw that her eyelids were purple-black too. 'I'm not sure I am, Alex. I'm not really up to visitors.'

'You might be up to this one. She's waited a long time to see her mummy.'

Lyn's eyes snapped back open. And now they didn't look sunken at all. They looked wide and full of disbelief. Then abruptly they went shiny and wet, and suddenly tears were running down her bruised cheeks.

'Are you okay?' I asked.

She blinked and made an attempt to wipe her tears away with a trembling hand – the one that wasn't encased in a pot that stretched from her fingers to above her elbow.

'Kate?' she whispered. 'She's really here?'

'She is. Shall I bring her in?'

Her eyes flickered towards the door. Her mouth moved, but at first no words came out.

Then: 'Yes.' It was little more than an expulsion of air. 'Yes, please.'

'Give me a minute,' I said.

I wanted to give Lyn a minute too. A minute to compose herself, to get used to the idea of seeing the daughter she'd never knowingly seen. I'd taken Kate along on my visits to Darby Hall in the early days, back when she was a baby. But Lyn had been too far gone to acknowledge her then – too far gone to acknowledge *me* more often than not. For the first eight or nine months of Kate's life I'd persevered, hoping that her presence might spark something in Lyn, might prompt a breakthrough in her condition. But it never did, and as soon as Kate began to become aware of her surroundings, and started showing signs of distress at her mother's erratic behaviour, I stopped taking her with me. Since then I'd taken along only photographs, and although Lyn had occasionally taken the photos from me and stared at them, I'd never been entirely sure whether she'd been fully aware they were pictures of our daughter.

'That's Kate,' I'd say. 'Kate, our daughter.' And sometimes she'd snap, 'Yes, I know it is. I'm not stupid!' At other times she'd repeat the name as though it was a word she'd never heard before. And sometimes she wouldn't even respond at all; she'd just stare blankly at the photo until I removed it from between her fingers.

One time she looked at me and frowned and said, 'I don't have a daughter.'

'Yes, you do,' I said. 'Her name's Kate. And that's a picture of her.'

Abruptly she'd become frightened, shrinking back into her chair. Then she'd become violent, screwing up the picture and throwing it at me.

'*I don't have a daughter!*' she screamed. '*I've never had a daughter! You're trying to trick me! Go away!* GO AWAY!'

With these old and troubling memories churning in the back of my mind, I went out into the corridor, where Kate was sitting on a chrome chair with grey leather upholstery, swinging her legs. Sitting next to her was the nurse who'd attended me when I'd first woken up here after four days of unconsciousness. She was tall with rust-coloured curly hair and her name was Patsy. The two of them were bent over a copy of Dr Seuss's *Green Eggs and Ham*, which Kate had brought from home. Kate was reading it and Patsy was chuckling at the illustrations and making encouraging noises.

They both looked up when I stepped into the corridor. Patsy raised her eyebrows and I smiled and nodded.

'Well, I'd better get back to making people better,' Patsy said as she stood up. 'Bye, Kate. See you again soon.'

'Bye,' Kate said.

As Patsy walked away, I knelt down in front of Kate's chair. 'Hey, pudding. I've talked to Mummy and she's very excited about seeing you.'

Kate nodded and put her thumb in her mouth. A sure sign she was nervous.

'There's nothing to worry about,' I said. 'Mummy's poorly, but she's getting better. But just to let you know, she's been in an accident, so she looks a bit... well, bashed about. You know when you fall and bang your knee and get a bruise?'

Kate nodded, her eyes big behind her pink-framed spectacles.

'Well, Mummy banged her head when she had her accident, which means she's got bruises on her face and bandages wrapped round her head.'

Kate removed her thumb from her mouth with a wet pop. 'Like Jack when he falls down and breaks his crown?'

'Yes, just like Jack.'

'Can she breathe?' Kate asked.

'Yes, the bandages are just round her head, not her face, so she can breathe and talk and everything. But when Mummy had her accident she also hurt her arm and her ribs here too' – I patted my side – 'so you mustn't jump on her, okay, because that'll really hurt her.'

'Okay.'

'And do you know *why* Mummy had an accident?'

'No.'

'It was because she was being very brave, and she was stopping a very bad man from doing a very bad thing.'

'Like Wonder Woman?'

'*Just* like Wonder Woman.'

'Wow,' Kate said.

'So you see, your mummy's very brave, and she loves you very much, and she hasn't seen you for a very long time, so she might get a bit...'

'Emotional?'

I blinked in surprise. 'Yes, emotional. Good word.'

Kate looked thoughtful. Then she asked, 'What does emotional mean?'

She looked so earnest that I suppressed the laugh that rose up in me; I didn't want her to think I was making fun of her. 'It means she might cry a little bit. But that won't mean she's sad. Sometimes people cry because they're happy.'

Kate thought about this, then nodded. 'Okay.'

I straightened up and took her hand, then led her over to the door to Lyn's room. I was about to push it open when Kate popped her thumb into her mouth again. I whispered, 'Don't suck your thumb, honey. You don't want Mummy to think you're a baby, do you?'

Kate shook her head solemnly and removed her thumb from her mouth.

We went in.

Lyn was sitting up in bed, her eyes fixed on us with such intensity that it was instantly unsettling. The expression on her face was a combination of hope, fearfulness and desperation, as if even now she couldn't quite believe I wasn't playing a trick on her. As soon as she saw Kate, though, her mask crumbled, her face becoming a mass of tics and twitches, her chin dimpling and trembling, her mouth writhing in an effort to form words.

'Oh, my,' she whispered finally, each word a warble of emotion, 'oh, my...'

I glanced down at Kate. She was clinging to my hand and half-hiding behind my leg, staring at Lyn warily.

I could hardly blame her, but I said softly, 'It's okay, honey. This is your mummy. Remember what we said about being emotional? Do you want to say hello?'

She didn't reply, but she didn't resist either. She allowed me to lead her to the bed.

Clearly aware of the unsettling effect she was having, I was relieved to see that Lyn was already making an effort to rein in her emotions. As we crossed the room, Kate moving slowly, hesitantly, Lyn swiped more tears from her face and took several deep breaths. By the time I sat on the chair beside the bed, Kate immediately clambering onto my knee for comfort, she'd regained most of her composure, though I could see her hands were still trembling.

'Hello, Kate,' Lyn said softly. 'Do you know who I am?'

Kate's head was pressed into my chest, but she gave a single nod.

'I'm your mummy,' Lyn said, a splintery, breathless laugh escaping her. 'I'm afraid I look a bit of a fright, don't I?'

Kate raised her head and murmured something I didn't catch.

'Sorry, sweetie.' Lyn's voice was soft. 'What did you say?'

Though still quiet, Kate's words were clearer this time. 'Daddy says you're like Wonder Woman.'

Lyn looked surprised. She glanced at me. 'Did he? Why did he say that?'

'Because you were brave. Because you got hurt fighting a very bad man.'

'Well,' Lyn said. 'I suppose that's true.'

Kate squinted at her. 'Are you *really* my mummy?'

'I am,' Lyn said.

'Are you going to live with us?'

Lyn hesitated. She glanced at me again, as if for guidance. I smiled and shrugged.

'Well,' Lyn said. 'Maybe. One day. When I'm properly better. Who knows?'

'I'd like you to live with us,' Kate said. 'If you lived with us, me and Daddy could look after you and make you better, couldn't we?'

Despite her gargantuan effort to keep her emotions in check, Lyn's eyes suddenly filled with tears again. They brimmed over her lower lids and began to run down her bruised cheeks.

In a husky whisper she said, 'I'd like that very much. I'd like it more than anything else in the world.'

TWENTY-THREE

MOVING ON

Could Lyn come and live with us? Would it work? Was it possible, after all we'd been through, to some day be the perfect, loving family I'd always hoped but never believed we'd be? Were there such things as happy endings?

I didn't know. And neither did I know how Clover, if she ever reappeared, would fit into this hypothetically idyllic scenario. There was nothing between us but friendship, but would Lyn see it that way? Perhaps more to the point, was there still the chance of a romantic relationship between Lyn and me? It had been so long since I'd contemplated such a thing that I'd all but abandoned hope that what we'd once had could ever be rekindled. I'd been madly in love with Lyn before the Dark Man had got to her, but however much her condition had improved recently, *that* Lyn was long gone; she was a completely different person now. And so was I.

I couldn't sleep. I'd been repressing my thoughts since leaving the hospital earlier that day, had devoted all my time and attention in the interim to Kate – we'd been to the zoo in Regents Park, and then for a meal at Zizzi's restaurant in Charlotte Street. But as soon as Kate had collapsed into bed, exhausted from her long day, the thoughts had resurfaced again, had begun to buzz and dart in my head like a nest of angry wasps.

It was now 2:30 in the morning, and I was in the 'parlour', cradling a glass of Southern Comfort and staring into the flames of the fire I'd built to keep out the autumn cold. It reminded me of the night in the cottage in Wales when I'd been too excited to sleep after first being reunited with Kate – except this time Clover wouldn't be turning up to keep me company.

Where was she? Why hadn't she answered any of the messages I'd left her? It occurred to me to wonder whether *I* was behind this latest disappearance – whether, for some reason, my older self had engineered it. Or *was* Clover simply giving Kate and me some space, as she claimed? Or was there something more to it? Could it be that, despite previous denials, she had stronger feelings for me than friendship and had gone away to think things through, consider her options?

I'd thought that getting Kate back would solve all my problems, that if only my daughter and I could be reunited, I'd be happy forever, and everything else would seem less than trivial. But happiness was a myth. None of us could ever be truly happy. There would always be some maggot somewhere, nibbling away at the apple.

I diverted my attention from the fire, and looked at the framed poster of The Great Barnaby, which I'd propped against the armchair on the opposite side of the hearth. There'd been no follow up to the gift, nothing to indicate why it had been sent to me or what I should do with it. I kept staring at the image of the masked, juggling man, at the yellow lettering above him. I held the heart in my hand and stared at the poster until it became meaningless, a melange of shapes and colours.

I had the feeling that something was beating insistently at a closed door in my brain, a thought or idea that I couldn't quite grasp. I felt as though I was underwater, and the door was somewhere above me, and I was rising from the depths towards it. I could see the handle through the murk. I stretched out a hand in an attempt to grab it, stretched and stretched, straining every sinew. As if sensing my proximity the knocking grew louder, more persistent.

...I woke up, or perhaps snapped from the fugue state I'd entered, to find that the knocking was real.

I struggled up from my chair, automatically slipping the heart into my pocket. I took a staggering step towards the door that led into the hallway. But I was confused. I had the feeling I was going the wrong way, that for some reason the front door was no longer out there.

Then I realised. The reason for my confusion was that the knocking wasn't coming from the hallway. It was closer by. It was here in this room.

It was behind me!

I whirled round, expecting... well, I don't know *what* I was expecting. Some ravening creature, its claws extended, its huge teeth clacking together? But there was nothing. Nothing but the windows behind me, concealed behind thick curtains. The knocking was coming from behind one of those. Immediately I was transported back to a snowy night over a hundred years earlier. Then my nocturnal visitor had been Lyn, or at least a vision of her that I'd come to think of as my spirit guide. Who or what would it be this time? Was I about to receive more guidance? Or could it be...

'Clover?'

Suddenly wide awake I crossed to the window in four strides and yanked back the curtain. I'd been so certain I'd see Clover out there, her hand perhaps raised in greeting, her lips compressed into an apologetic grimace, that when I didn't I was completely thrown. For a split second I failed to recognise the slight, pale figure standing on the other side of the glass. I thought I was seeing a ghost. Then my mind clicked into gear, and I berated myself for my stupidity.

It was Frank.

Of *course* it was Frank.

He was expressionless, but that wasn't unusual. A thread of pale grey smoke was coiling up from the roll-up held loosely between the index finger and second finger of his right hand. I indicated he should come round to the front door and he gave me a thumbs-up. I pulled the curtain back into place and moved across the room, into the hallway.

'I didn't want to disturb the little 'un,' said Frank when I opened the door.

'How did you know where I was?' I asked.

'Saw the glow through the curtains, didn't I?'

'But how did you know I'd be awake?' When his only answer was a shrug I said, 'It's getting on for 3 a.m.'

'Is it?' he said flatly. 'Sorry, guv. Time don't mean a lot to me these days. If I hadn't seen a light I'd've waited 'til morning.'

'So what you've got to tell me isn't urgent?' I said. 'You're not here because of Clover?'

'No. I ain't seen Clover since she popped round for Kate's stuff the other day.'

'How did she seem when she came round?'

'Fine.' He took a last drag on his roll-up, then flicked it into the darkness behind me. 'Mind if I come in? I want to talk to you about something.'

'Yes, course,' I said, pulling the door wider. 'Sorry.'

He stepped in, clasping his hands and rubbing them together in an old-fashioned 'right, let's get down to it' kind of way. I led him through to the parlour, where he barely gave the propped-up poster of The Great Barnaby a second look before standing in front of the fire, his back resting against the mantelpiece.

'You'll burn your arse if you're not careful,' I said.

Morosely he replied, 'Chance'd be a fine thing. Don't feel it these days, do I? Neither hot nor cold. When I was perishing me knackers off in the trenches, I'd have said such a thing was a blessing. But it ain't. I miss it, Alex. Even the things what used to make me miserable – the hunger, the cold, the fear that made you feel like you had a big black dog inside you, chewing on your guts.'

I didn't know what to say. Seeing my empty glass sitting on the hearth, I picked it up and, without thinking, offered him a drink.

'Makes no odds to me,' he said. 'I wouldn't waste it if I were you.'

I was already crossing the room to the table beside the sofa where I'd put the bottle of Southern Comfort. 'You don't mind if I have one?'

''Course not. You go ahead. You enjoy it for the both of us.'

I poured myself a drink and carried it back to the fireplace. Plonking myself in the armchair, I gestured at the other chair facing me across the hearth. 'Sit down, Frank. Just move that picture out of the way. I'm sick of looking at it, to be honest.'

Frank glanced at the chair, but shook his head. 'I'll stand, if that's all right with you.'

'That sounds ominous. What's on your mind?'

Frank was silent for a moment. I got the impression he was uncomfortable, though nothing showed on his face. Eventually he said, 'I don't want you to think I'm not grateful for what you did for me, Alex. Because I am. You gave me the best thing that anyone can give anyone. You gave me my life back.'

'I'm guessing there's a "but" coming,' I said.

His expression didn't change, but all at once I was overcome by a sense of deep melancholy. It was as if the emotion was pulsing off him in waves.

'The thing is... there's nothing for me here. And when I say "nothing", I mean, literally, nothing. I can't *feel*, Alex, that's the thing. I know what I *should* be feeling, and I know what's right and wrong, but although I'm moving about, and thinking, and talking, I'm just going through the motions, doing what I think I *should* be doing. But inside here' – he clenched a fist and gently thumped his chest – 'I feel dead. There's no love, no hate, no happiness, no sadness. Or maybe there's an... *idea* of sadness. But it's not really sadness, it's... emptiness. I'm empty, Alex.' He sighed and shook his head. 'I'm not explaining this very well. I've never been that good with words.'

'You're explaining it perfectly,' I said. 'And I'm sorry, Frank, I really am. I thought by bringing you back, I'd be restoring your life, making you just like you were before. Maybe even better.'

'I know that,' he said. 'I know you did what you did for the right reasons. And like I say, I ain't blaming you. You did what any real mate would've done in the circumstances.'

'So what do you want me to do now?' I asked. 'How can I put it right? Do you want me to take you back to your family? Because I could do that. I could fix it so that I took you back at the end of the War, so that you didn't have to fight again. I could–'

'No!' he said, cutting in. He'd raised a hand, but now he lowered it. 'No,' he repeated softly. 'I don't want that.'

'What then?'

'I want...' His eyes flickered from mine. He stared into the depths of the room behind me, as if seeing something that I couldn't. He was silent for ten, fifteen seconds. It seemed like an eternity. At last he said, 'I want peace. That's all. Just peace. I want to move on – if there's anything to move on to.'

I'd been expecting this, but I felt a tightness in my throat all the same, felt as if his sadness was infecting me, breaking down my defences, building up with a fever-like heat in my sinuses and behind my eyes.

'What are you asking me to do?' I said, forcing out the words.

'I thought... maybe that heart of yours could help. I mean, it brought me here... so maybe it can send me back.'

My throat was so clogged I couldn't speak. I swallowed, trying to clear the obstruction. When it didn't work I took a sip of Southern Comfort, wincing as it burned. I tried again, and in a hoarse voice I managed to say, 'You want me to reverse what I did? You're asking me to...' But I couldn't finish.

'Kill me?' Frank said. He shrugged, as if it was of no consequence. 'I don't really feel alive any more, so I don't think that's what you'd be doing.'

I swallowed more Southern Comfort – took such a big gulp, in fact, that my eyes watered. It did the trick, though. It unblocked my throat.

'I can't do it, Frank,' I said. 'You can't ask me to do it. I want to help you, but you're my friend. You can't ask me to...'

'Just give me the heart, Alex,' he said. He held out his hand. 'Just give me the heart and I'll do it myself.'

My instinct was to refuse. But if I did what would I be doing except condemning him to a living hell? Because he was right. There was nothing for him here. Nothing except me, and what could I offer him, aside from my occasional company? Refusing him access to the heart – which I wasn't even certain would do his bidding – would be nothing but a selfish act, even a cowardly one. And what would Frank do if I *did* refuse him? Try to top himself another way? But what if he couldn't? What if, whatever he tried, the heart kept him alive? The possible consequences of that were too horrific to contemplate.

A split second before handing the heart over to him, it struck me that this might be a trick. What if this wasn't really Frank? What if it was the shape-shifter? But I couldn't spend my life being suspicious of everyone. Although it terrified me to think of it, the shape-shifter could come in the night and replace Kate. Or it could imitate Clover again. Or Lyn. Or even a future version of me. I could become seriously paranoid if I started to think of *all* the ways the Dark Man might try to outwit me. All I could hope was that he was just as constrained by the 'laws' of time as I was.

I hesitated for maybe a second, then held out the heart and allowed Frank to take it from me. As soon as his fingers touched it, it reacted, myriad threads of darkness rising from its surface and not only writhing around his body but attaching themselves to it. The threads seemed to fuse seamlessly with his dark suit, as though they and the suit were made of the same substance.

As the threads crept upwards and outwards, twining themselves around Frank's body, he calmly opened his mouth. At first I thought it was to allow the darkness access to his body, but then I saw more threads of darkness, identical to those rising from the heart, curling from between his lips, just as they had when I'd first encountered him at Benny's house. The threads reminded me of black eels emerging from the parted lips of an underwater corpse. Once released from within him, they moved with purpose, slithering in all directions – downwards across his chin and throat, sideways across his cheeks, up across his face. Quickly they obscured his features – his nose, his eyes – and then continued to rise vertically across his forehead and eventually blend with his black hair.

It was a hideous process to watch, but Frank endured it without complaint. Indeed, he seemed to welcome it. Before his features were obscured completely I saw an expression of peace, perhaps of release, settle over them. Within a minute or less the man I had known was no longer recognisable; his form had become a writhing mass of darkness. Then the mass started to diminish, to break down, like a snowman exposed to strong sunlight. As it did so, it bled back into the heart, was absorbed by it, until soon all that was left of Frank was an inchoate haze of still-shrinking darkness. Within seconds that too was gone, the heart sucking up the last few strands of darkness like a sponge.

For a few moments the heart hovered in mid-air, as though held in invisible hands, and then it dropped to the carpet with a thud. Where Frank had stood there was now nothing. My gaze refocused, became fixed once again on the Great Barnaby poster, which Frank's body had been obscuring. The yellow lettering stood out bold in the dimly lit room. I stared at the date across the top: 10th December 1948.

And suddenly, as though Frank had somehow shown me the way, my mind was made up.

TWENTY-FOUR

FRIDAY 10 DECEMBER 1948

When I went back the house was empty, as I had thought it would be.

But preparations had been made. There was a full set of clothes laid out for me on my bed with a label pinned to them: WEAR ME.

I was getting used to such things by now. It was like having my very own Jeeves, except that that Jeeves was me – or rather, my future self. I took an inventory of the clothes – grey herringbone tweed suit, complete with waistcoat, white shirt, knitted green-and-red tie, trilby hat and a pair of highly polished brown brogues – and jotted everything down in my little black book, sighing despite myself at the fact that I was adding yet another job to the seemingly endless list.

I have to say, the suit bothered me a little; its presence niggled at my mind. Travelling through time changes the way you think. You no longer accept things at face value. You start to realise that everything has a consequence. In this instance, what bothered me was the question of where the suit had come from. Because let's say I simply wore it now, and then, when I'd finished with it, left it hanging in my wardrobe so that my future self could pop in, pick it up and bring it back to December 10th 1948...

You see where I'm coming from? Wouldn't such a chain of events suggest that the suit had been created out of nothing? That, stuck in this eternal loop of time, it had simply popped into being?

It was an anomaly, and one of several that I hoped wouldn't come back at some stage to bite me on the bum. I guess my main fear was that by using the heart I was becoming the temporal equivalent of a deathwatch beetle. I was worried that each of my trips might be creating a borehole through time that would eventually weaken the structure to such an extent that it would crumble and collapse.

But what could I do, except push my concerns to the back of my mind, and get on with the matter in hand? I transferred my notebook and the heart to the various pockets of the tweed jacket, and got changed. Dressing in my new outfit made me feel like an actor about to embark on a role in a period drama – which I guess, in a way, I was. As I pulled on the trousers I discovered something that necessitated me making another note: in the right-hand pocket was a leather wallet containing around £4 (the equivalent of an average week's wages) in date-appropriate currency, and a theatre ticket for that night's performance by the Great Barnaby at the London Hippodrome.

I left my own wallet in my jeans, which I laid on the bed in readiness for my return, telling myself that if anything went wrong I'd pick it up at a later date, and then I grabbed a dark-blue gabardine raincoat that was hanging on the outside of the wardrobe door. Before exiting the room I looked out of the window to check the weather. There was the suggestion of a hard winter sheen to the landscape, but I was thankful to see that it was neither windy nor snowing. As I descended the stairs I wondered how I'd get to the Hippodrome – did I have a car? Or if not, did I own a phone so I could call a cab? But no sooner had I stepped off the bottom stair and on to the tiled floor of the hallway than there came a knock on the door.

I opened it to find a short man standing on the doorstep. With his waxy-looking overcoat and his round, bulging-eyed face sprouting straight from the thick folds of his scarf, he reminded me of a toad. He touched a finger to the brim of his cap and said, 'Cab for you, sir. Ordered earlier today, I believe?'

Something else to add to the notebook. 'Oh, right. Yes, thank you.'

'I'm parked just outside the front gate, sir. Mind your step. It's a bit slippy.'

The cab was a black, gleaming Austin FX3, with an open luggage platform in place of a passenger seat. I've never been much of a one for cars, but this was a beauty. Yet despite its immaculate bodywork, the seats in the back were of cracked leather, and the interior smelled strongly of pipe and cigarette smoke.

'To the Hippodrome, isn't it, sir?' the driver said once he was settled in the front seat.

'That's right, yes.'

'Going to see anything nice, sir?'

'A magician. The Great Barnaby. Have you heard of him?'

'Can't say as I have, sir. I'm not much of a one for the theatre, I'm afraid.'

As he drove the driver chatted on – mostly about the London Olympics, which had finished a few months earlier ('Never seen so many foreigners in me life. Couldn't understand where half me fares wanted to go. Made a packet, I did, but I was glad to see the back of 'em.') and the new royal baby ('Charles they're calling him – that was me old dad's name, though everyone called him Charlie.'). I gave monosyllabic replies, most of my attention focused on the streets we were driving through. It was fascinating to see how much was familiar, and how much had changed. The structure of many of the buildings themselves, of course, was largely the same, though some were half-ruined and fenced off due to war damage. What was particularly striking was how few restaurants and cafés there were, and how the storefronts of the mid-twentieth century differed to those of the early twenty-first. There were no supermarkets or megastores – very few chain stores at all, in fact – and the shop signs were hand-painted, and therefore far more attractive than their modern counterparts; there was none of the ugly plastic signage that would proliferate in twenty or thirty years' time. Some of the buildings were emblazoned with big advertisements for the likes of BOVRIL and EXIDE BATTERIES, and some of the streets – again presumably due to war damage – were closed off. I saw one street being guarded by a couple of London bobbies, who were standing beside a pair of wooden signs propped open at its entrance. One of the signs read ROAD CLOSED and the other DANGER UNEXPLODED BOMB.

My driver dropped me off on the corner of Cranbourn Street, and I joined the throng of people streaming into the Hippodrome, whose impressive columned façade was lit up like a golden palace. Most of the men were dressed like me, in suits, overcoats, trilbies and brogues, whereas the women wore long pleated skirts beneath their winter coats, their hands encased in elegant leather gloves and their carefully curled or waved hair adorned with felt hats that sprouted bows or feathers.

I was pleased to discover that my seat was a fairly anonymous one, in the middle of a row about eight back from the stage. As I took it, noting with incredulity how many people were smoking, I wondered whether the Great Barnaby – or Barnaby McCallum as I better knew him – was aware of my presence here tonight. If I was to make contact with him after the show, then I guess he *would* know, if only because his older self, remembering our meeting, would surely have popped back to warn him I was here. The gift of the poster, and the message that had come with it, would seem to indicate I *had* made contact – though even now I still wasn't entirely sure what my plan was. I had come here ostensibly to play it by ear, to see what transpired. If it was possible to discover anything useful about McCallum without revealing my presence, then all well and good. On the other hand, there was every possibility I was being manipulated, moved into place like a pawn – though for what reason, only time would tell. But hey, in order to get answers I was going to have to take risks, wasn't I? Which meant following my nose and seeing where it led.

As I settled into my seat and ran my eye over the flimsy programme sheet – which I was hoping, in vain, might give some insight into the Great Barnaby's background – I wondered why I was pursuing this line of enquiry. I had Kate back (she was currently being looked after by the Sherwoods, who had returned from Wales and moved into their new London home – which I was still to buy), and my life, to all intents and purposes, was hunky dory, so why was I here?

Was it simple curiosity, or something more? Was it, in fact, a nagging sense of obligation, or even of destiny? Or perhaps it was a fear that if I didn't follow up this lead – dot all the i's and cross all the t's – I would come to regret it? Clearly McCallum had not bequeathed me the poster on a whim, which meant it must be significant. Perhaps it would lead me to an understanding of how to once and for all nullify the threat of the Dark Man. If so, I couldn't afford to ignore it.

The magic show itself was... well, I guess by 1940s standards it was impressive. Certainly the audience seemed to think so, oohing and aahing and gasping with wonder, bursting into applause at the culmination of every trick.

Watching it from a twenty-first-century viewpoint, it was evident that McCallum had used the heart to travel forward in time and borrow tricks from future magicians, so that here they seemed fresh and startling. There were card tricks, and tricks where handkerchiefs transformed into doves, and tricks where objects donated by audience members somehow ended up inside bottles whose necks were far too narrow to accommodate them. There were also a couple of sequences that seemed to be lifted straight from Derren Brown shows I'd seen on TV – one where McCallum correctly guessed the contents of audience members' pockets, and another based on what he called 'the artifice of spirituality', whereby an audience member, tied securely to a chair and concealed within a curtained box, would supposedly 'call on the spirits' to rattle a tambourine or shred a newspaper while he was restrained.

Although the audience lapped it up, what I found most interesting about the performance was McCallum himself, and particularly his use of the heart in his act. At one point he not only levitated it, but caused it to loop and dive above the heads of the audience like a bird. For the finale he set it on a glass stand in the centre of the stage, and then, to the accompaniment of a crash of sound from the musicians in the orchestra pit, he raised his arms dramatically to the heavens, whereupon the heart erupted into life, a mass of writhing tendrils shooting up from it and ascending almost to the ceiling of the theatre, accompanied by shrieks and gasps from the audience.

Both McCallum and his female assistant – who was small and slim, and whose age I was unable to discern from where I was sitting (she could have been anywhere between twelve and twenty-five years old) – wore red eye masks throughout the performance. McCallum also sported a waxed moustache with curled ends, and a luxuriant black beard, which made it impossible to tell whether he and the decrepit old man I'd accidentally killed while stealing the heart were one and the same.

As soon as the performance was over, I bustled outside with the rest of the crowd, then slipped down an alleyway at the side of the building, looking for the stage door. It had started to drizzle at some point during the evening, and within seconds of leaving the theatre the chill, biting rain had made my face feel like an ice mask.

The alleyway was adequately, though not brightly, lit, the semi-circles of yellow light spilling down the brickwork and across the ground from evenly spaced, wall-mounted lamps making no impression on the pools of black shadow that lay in between them. The rain made every surface gleam like plastic, and gave the scene a flickering, scratched quality like old film.

If I was to be ambushed – though God knew by who, and for what reason, unless in some crazily convoluted way the Dark Man was in league with McCallum – then I guess this would be the time and place it would happen. Experience at any rate had taught me to expect the unexpected, to take nothing for granted, and so I kept a tight grip on the heart in my pocket as I pressed yet deeper into the shadows.

About thirty seconds later, the bustle of the London street at the alley's entrance having receded to the point where it was no more than a glimmer of light and a rumble of distant activity, I was about to step into yet another pool of darkness when a scuffle of movement close to my right foot made me jump. I looked down to see a large black rat cross my path, then dart off into the even more profound blackness ahead of me. I shuddered, then grinned. I'd seen so many rats in the trenches you'd have thought I'd have been used to them by now. Even so my heart pumped a little faster as I moved deeper into the alleyway. Every patch of darkness ahead of me now seemed to teem with frantic life.

After another ten yards the alleyway came to an abrupt end. That's what I thought at first anyway, but then I took a couple of steps closer and realised that the wall I'd thought marked a dead end was actually set at an oblique angle, like a door pushed halfway open, and formed a right-hand curve that led around the back of the Hippodrome. I followed the curve, and almost immediately saw a shaded light illuminating a plain black door beneath it. Painted carefully onto the brickwork above the door were the words STAGE DOOR.

This was what I'd been looking for. This was McCallum's most likely exit point out of the theatre. All I had to do now was hide somewhere, and then, when he emerged, follow him and see where he went.

And then what? Confront him? Engage him in conversation? I guess I'd cross that bridge when I came to it.

I looked around for a hiding place, and spotted what appeared to be a dustbin set into a recess in the wall of the opposite building, about twenty yards further up the alleyway. I wasn't *entirely* sure what I was looking at, because the object was nestled in the darkness between one pool of light and the next, and only the vaguest outline of one side of it was visible. The far end of the alley was at least three hundred yards beyond that, and from where I was standing was little more than a slit of orange and the suggestion of faraway movement (would that be Charing Cross Road? I'd lost my bearings). Thinking how eerie it was that a lively city could have so many dead spots, I moved towards the dustbin-shaped thing, slipping from light into shadow, then back into light again.

When I got to the outer edge of the second pool of light, I saw it *was* indeed a dustbin. In fact it was one of four standing in a row in a recess the size and length of a bus shelter. I was pleased to find that if I crouched down behind the last bin in the row, it would not only provide a perfect hiding place and shelter from the rain, but would also give me an unobstructed view of the stage door.

It seemed like a win-win situation, though it wasn't *entirely* perfect, as I found out when I got close to the last bin in the row, and a couple of rats scampered out from behind it. Glancing back at the stage door, I kicked the bin lightly to frighten off any other rodents that might be lurking in the shadows, and then, wrinkling my nose against the ripe smell that rose up to greet me, I ducked into the recess and crouched down.

Despite the stench of rotting food, though, and the fact that the ground was too wet and filthy to sit on, which meant that my legs and feet soon began to prickle with pins and needles, my little hidey-hole could almost have been described as cosy. In my tweed suit, overcoat and trilby hat, I at least felt warm, and it was kind of nice, even comforting, to hear the patter of rain on the ground outside. After a while of staring at the stage door, I felt myself becoming drowsy despite my discomfort, and I shuffled around a bit to wake myself up and coax some life back into my numb limbs. But within a few minutes my eyelids were drooping again. *Just a quick power nap*, I thought, *to recharge the batteries. I don't need to stare at the door all the time. I'll hear it if it opens.*

What seemed like the next second I heard a clunk and a creak, and jerked awake. My head snapped up, and I saw a hooded figure emerge from the stage door. Was it McCallum? No, it was too short and slim, and although it was almost entirely swathed in a dark, hooded cloak, I got the distinct impression it was female.

McCallum's assistant then. Should I follow her, or wait for McCallum himself to emerge? She might be easier to speak to than her boss, who'd be more likely to be wary of me. Then again, I didn't want to frighten or intimidate her. And what if I did follow and question her, only to find that McCallum had simply employed her on a temporary basis, from an agency or something? On the other hand, what if McCallum had already left the theatre via some other exit, and following his assistant might be my one and only chance to get some answers?

All this raced through my mind (which was still edgy and brittle from having been snatched from its doze) in the time it took for the girl to half-turn and shut the door behind her. Still squatting on my haunches, I raised myself on my toes, ready to stand and follow her – and immediately felt a debilitating tingle of pins and needles rush through my feet and calves.

Shit. What if I couldn't walk? Or what if I tried to stand and ended up collapsing among the dustbins, causing her to bolt? In my still slightly befuddled state, I assumed she'd be walking away from me – if only because that was where I'd come from – and so was surprised when she turned and headed in my direction. Although I knew she couldn't see me in the dark, I instinctively shrank back – and promptly, because of the numbness in my legs, felt myself toppling backwards. I put a hand on the ground behind me to steady myself, and felt something cold and squishy ooze up between my fingers. I stifled a cry of disgust, hoping it was just mud, and willed myself to remain still as she approached my hiding place.

Would she see me? If she did, what would I say? That I'd been sheltering from the rain and had fallen asleep? No, that would sound weird and creepy. Better to just come clean.

To my relief, though, she kept her head down, her face obscured beneath her dark hood. She walked quickly and with purpose, looking neither left nor right. No doubt she wanted to get out of the alleyway as quickly as possible, and back among people again. As she came level with my hiding place I held my breath, but she hurried on without so much as a glance.

It wasn't until she was past me and striding towards the next pool of light that I decided to follow her. It could be a mistake, but if

McCallum had wanted me to come here tonight, he should have given me clearer instructions. I rose into a semi-standing position, gritting my teeth as my numbed muscles came alive with pins and needles. I shuffled from the recess, my legs feeling like lumps of dead meat animated by jittering jolts of electricity. Like Frankenstein's monster, I staggered after her, hoping my barely responsive feet weren't clumping too loudly on the ground. Apparently not, because she didn't turn round. Presumably her hood and the rain pattering on it – heavier now than before – were muffling the sounds of my pursuit.

She had a lead of about fifty yards on me, but that was okay. I didn't want to get too close and alert her. I watched her pass from light into shadow, light into shadow, light into...

Suddenly she stopped. Had she heard me? No, she wasn't turning round, and from her stance she seemed to be peering intently at the block of shadow directly in front of her. Even so, I slipped into the next pool of darkness ahead of me and pressed myself against the wall.

She edged towards the right-hand side of the alleyway, as though she'd seen or heard something in the darkness to her left. Suddenly she spoke, and although the rain was hissing and pattering, and the distance between us made her voice sound high and thin, I could just about make out her words.

'Who's there?' she said, though whether in defiance or fear was impossible to tell. Wiping rain from my face, I unpeeled myself from the wet wall and stared at where she was staring. Could I see something too? A swirling suggestion of movement in the darkness? I edged closer, thinking of myself not as a pursuer now, but a potential protector.

Then something detached itself from the darkness and lurched towards her, and she screamed.

It was a man, or a semblance of one.

He was little more than a silhouette, though not because of the darkness. Even when he stepped out of the shadows the light seemed to shun him, or to slide off him as if it couldn't get a hold. It was as if he wasn't quite there, wasn't quite part of this reality, though with each second he seemed to solidify, to become more real.

He reached a hand out towards the girl, who stumbled backwards, almost slipping on the wet paving slabs.

'Get away from me!' she yelled. 'Leave me alone!'

The man was becoming more solid now, the light falling on him as if there had never been any doubt as to his corporeality. I saw that he was wearing a black leather jacket with the collar turned up, a black baseball cap, black shades, and that his body was twisted and bent.

'Please,' he croaked, in a voice that sent ripples of disgust and fear through me, 'I only want to–'

'Get away from her!' I shouted, echoing the girl's words. My legs still shaky, I began to run towards the Dark Man and the girl, my hand – the one that had been covered in mud or something nastier – already delving into my pocket.

The Dark Man swivelled his crooked body towards me, and his damaged face – what I could see of it – scrunched into a sour expression. As I got closer I saw he was holding the heart, and like a gunfighter about to face a showdown I pulled my own heart from my pocket and held it up. The girl, meanwhile, taking advantage of the Dark Man's momentary distraction, slipped past him and began to run towards the end of the alleyway.

The Dark Man took one look at the heart in my hand and evidently decided to beat a hasty retreat. One second he was there, the next he was gone, leaving nothing behind but an almost subliminal impression of a patch of darkness folding in on itself.

There was no chance of surreptitiously following the girl now. I'd have to make myself known to her, see if she was willing to talk to me. Since darting past the Dark Man she'd widened the gap between us. If she had too much of a lead when she reached the end of the alleyway, there was every chance she could lose herself among the bustling Friday night crowd.

Starting to run, I shouted, 'Hey! Please stop! I just want to talk to you!'

But the girl didn't stop. If anything, she increased her speed. Swearing, I raced after her, trying to stamp the pins and needles out of my feet and legs.

By the time she reached the end of the alleyway, her dark cloak billowing like a sail, I'd halved the distance between us. The gap at the end of the alley had seemed to widen with each step I'd taken, the light from the street beyond streaming in. I could see now that the girl's hooded cloak was blue, not black as I'd originally thought. The flickering movement I'd glimpsed earlier resolved itself into people passing to and fro across the alley's mouth, many of them hunched under umbrellas. As the girl darted into the throng and turned right, I shouted, 'Please! I only want a quick chat! My name's Alex Locke!'

Whether it was recognising my name or simply a moment of indecision that caused the girl to pause I'm not sure. Regardless, she stopped directly in the path of a small, chubby man, who was bustling along the pavement, a black umbrella held in front of his face like a shield against the rain. Unable to stop, the man jabbed her with the point of his umbrella, and then barged into her, sending her sprawling. I reached the end of the alleyway just in time to see her fall forward on to her knees, her hands splatting on the wet ground. The impact caused the hood to fly from her head and droop down her back, giving me a glimpse of her chestnut-coloured hair. Then the little man tripped over and almost landed on top of her as he went sprawling too. His umbrella flew from his hand and skidded along the pavement, flipping over on its spiny claws.

'Good God, can't you watch where you're—' the little man blustered.

But the girl, perhaps mindful of the fact that I was close behind her, had already leaped to her feet, and was now darting into the road.

'*Stop!*' I bellowed, though this time it was not because I wanted to speak to her, but because of what I'd seen that she hadn't. A big green bus had turned the corner into the road and was now hurtling towards her. I took one glimpse of the driver's white-moustached face, his eyes and mouth open in shock, and then I threw myself into the road, arms outstretched. The horn of the bus blared, but instead of encouraging the girl to hurl herself out of the way, it had the opposite effect. Startled, she stopped and turned – and then froze in the middle of the road, unable to move.

I don't know whether I screamed something, or whether the girl suddenly became aware of my presence. It all happened so fast that all I knew for sure was that the girl turned and looked me in the eye a split second before my hands rammed into her back, shoving her to safety. She hurtled across the road, fell and rolled, but at least she was safely out of the path of the bus. Still reeling from what I'd seen, I fell too, then tried to clamber immediately to my feet.

But it felt as if I was moving in slow motion. I couldn't get my limbs to respond as quickly as my brain wanted them to. The blare of the horn filled my world. I glanced up and saw a huge wall of green metal with blazing white eyes glaring at me. I remembered the heart in my pocket. My hand darted for it. Too late!

The bus hit me. There was a horrible bang, a sensation of immense pain exploding through my body, and then I was flying through the air, helpless as a rag doll hurled from a car window.

I don't remember landing. All I remember is the notion of my broken body stranded on a tiny island with a vast black sea rushing in on all sides. As the black water engulfed the island and closed over my head, I clung to a single image, which burned like a flame in my mind.

The image was that of the girl's face in the split second when she'd turned to look at me. It was an image that was impossible, that made no sense. She'd been young, sixteen or seventeen, which meant she was a good ten years younger than when I'd first encountered her. Yet there was no doubt who she was. I was one hundred per cent sure.

The girl whose life I'd saved had been Clover.

TWENTY-FIVE

VISITING HOURS

I'm in the desert again, my hands delving into the sand. Only this time I'm standing to one side and watching myself doing it.

'Is this a dream?' I ask.

My other self squints up at me. 'That's what I've been wondering.'

'So if we've both been wondering the same thing, it can't be, can it? Because whenever you ask yourself that in a dream, you wake up.'

My other self shrugs. 'But if it's not a dream, how do you explain this?' He nods down at his hands. 'I don't know where I am, or when I am, but somehow I know what I'm doing. I'm digging for the heart... no, for its essence. I'm reaching into the core of the planet, so I can pull out the...'

'Primal stuff,' I say.

'Primal stuff, yeah. So that I can form it. Mould it.'

'Won't it mould itself?'

'I don't know. Will it?'

'Isn't that what we always wonder? Whether we came here to create the heart, or whether the heart brought us here to create itself? We wonder whether we started all this, or whether we're just...'

'Pawns.'

'I was going to say "being manipulated", but pawns will do just as well.'

The other me, his hands now buried up to their elbows, says, 'What do you last remember?'

I think about it. After a moment, surprised, I say, 'Nothing. My mind's a blank. What about you?'

'Same.'

'So what does that mean?'

'Fucked if I know.'

'Alex?'

The voice comes from just behind my left shoulder. I turn to see who has spoken, and am instantly blinded by the sun. I flinch and close my eyes. The voice, soft and feminine, speaks my name a second time.

Keeping my left eye tightly shut, I try to open just my right one, but even that is too much. The harsh light of the sun pierces my eye like the sting of a parasite, and then burrows deep, making my eyeball ache and throb. I must have groaned with pain, because the woman standing behind me says, 'Is it too bright? Hold on a minute.'

Next moment the sun is eclipsed by a soothing pall of greyness. As the ache recedes I try again, my eyes tentatively flickering open...

A face loomed in my vision. At first it was meaningless as a child's drawing – red mouth, two holes for a nose, almond-shaped eyes studded with blue pupils. Then my vision adjusted; the face became more defined. A few seconds later I recognised it.

'Paula! What are you doing here?'

What was wrong with my voice? I'd been speaking perfectly fine a moment ago, but now it had degenerated into a rusty whisper.

'I'm here to see you. You're in hospital. What do you remember?'

I stared at her. Hospital? No, that was before. I'd already done that.

'You had an accident, Alex,' she continued. 'Do you remember anything about it?'

'Green.' The colour flashed through my head, and emerged as a croaky whisper before I realised I was going to speak. Immediately more details seeped into my mind: not just green, but a wall of green metal studded with a pair of glaring white eyes. And there was a sound echoing in my memory: a blaring roar. And then the big green monster, it–

'Ate me,' I said.

Paula frowned. 'What?'

No, not ate me, it–

'Hit me,' I said. I struggled to concentrate, to make myself understood. 'The...' Not monster, but... 'Bus! It was a bus. It hit me.'

Paula Sherwood nodded encouragingly. 'That's right. You were hit by a bus. Your older self brought you here. That was three weeks ago.

It's the end of November, Alex. November 28th 2012.'

I gaped at her. Three weeks! No, I hadn't been gone for three weeks. It was impossible.

But she was still talking. I tried to concentrate.

'...in a coma. You had multiple fractures and ruptured organs. But you're making amazing progress. The doctors can't understand how quickly you're healing, but your older self told me it was because of the...' she floundered, searching for the word.

'Nanites,' I croaked.

'That's it. Nanites. Little machines that live inside you, and repair you when you're broken. Amazing!'

She grinned. I tried to smile back, but it hurt. *Three weeks. What about...*

'Kate,' I said.

'Don't worry, she's safe and well. I've been looking after her. I moved into your house, so that she wouldn't have to be uprooted again just as she was settling in. I hope that's okay. I told her you'd had a little accident, and that you were in hospital, but that you were fine and she'd be able to come and visit you soon. She sends her love. In fact, she made you this.'

She held up a slightly rumpled card, hand-made from a piece of folded white paper. In brightly coloured felt-tip pen at the top were the words GeT Well SOON Dady, the last three letters squashed together on the very edge of the card, because she had obviously misjudged how much room she'd need for her message. Below the lettering was a crude but very colourful drawing of a man and a girl – Kate and me presumably – holding hands in front of a big square house with lots of windows. On either side of the house was spiky green grass with flowers sprouting from it, and a few misshapen butterflies fluttering in the air.

This time I couldn't help but grin, even though it seemed to tug painfully on parts of my body I didn't know my mouth was connected to. 'Tell her I love her... and I'll see her soon,' I croaked.

'I will.'

With priority number one taken care of, I said, 'When my older self brought me back, did he bring the heart too? The one I used to bring you here – or will do.'

To my relief she nodded. 'He said to tell you he's taken it for safekeeping and will bring it back when you're capable of looking after it again. He said he didn't want anyone to steal it while you were unconscious.'

I felt a pang of anxiety. 'Are you sure it was me?' It wouldn't be the first time the shape-shifter had imitated me to fool my friends.

'Of course. Grey hair and a few wrinkles don't make you look *that* different.'

'How old was I?'

'Fifty-five, fifty-six? But he said to tell you he'd written all the details down in your notebook, which he's also got. He said he'd bring that back with the heart too.'

My gut told me it *had* really been me – why would the Dark Man's henchman take the trouble to imitate me, save my life by bringing me here, and contact the Sherwoods when he could just as easily have stolen the heart from my smashed and unconscious body? – but even so, after Paula had gone I couldn't help fretting. I was in hospital – Oak Hill naturally – for the best part of the next two weeks, during which time I received *lots* of visitors. God knows what the staff must have thought of me in there – presumably that I was either the most accident-prone man in the world, or that I had some hush-hush and highly dangerous job. To their credit, they never asked questions – probably because I was paying a lot of money, not only for their care and attention, but also (although it was an unspoken agreement) for their lack of curiosity, and their discretion.

My first visitors after Paula were, to my surprise, Lyn and Dr Bruce. To be fair, Dr Bruce – who I would now forever regard in a new light after witnessing how she'd repelled the shape-shifter, a matter I'd have to address at some point – was only there to accompany Lyn, and after a brief, awkward greeting she beat a hasty retreat.

'You look better,' I said to Lyn as she sat beside my bed and took my hands in hers. It was true. The bandage had been removed from her head, her bruising had faded and her hair had now started to grow back. She still had a pot on her arm, but it was smaller than her previous one. In fact, it wasn't dissimilar to the one I was wearing on my own right arm.

'You don't,' she said.

I laughed, and then immediately winced with pain. 'Ow, ow. Broken pelvis. Not good.'

Although some of my injuries echoed Lyn's – I'd broken an arm, several ribs, and had fractured my skull – they were only a few of many. I'd also bust my pelvis, shattered my left ankle, dislocated my jaw and dislodged several of my vertebrae. This latter injury meant that for the time being I had to wear a plastic neck brace, which was hot and uncomfortable, and which also made it hard for me to swallow – though that could have been more a psychological reaction than a physical one.

I had internal injuries too – punctured lung, ruptured spleen and various muscular tears – which had required emergency surgery. Quite how that had worked with the nanites bustling about in my system I had no idea, though it didn't appear to have disrupted either their presence or their work, judging by how quickly my organs and bones were now knitting themselves back together.

'So what happened?' she asked.

'I got hit by a bus. In 1948.' Quickly I gave her the details, though I didn't reveal that the girl I had chased, and subsequently saved, was Clover. I was still processing that one.

'The Dark Man,' she said sourly, hunching her shoulders as if bracing herself against a sudden chill.

'Don't worry about him,' I said glibly. 'He won't try anything now you've got Dr Bruce to protect you. How has she been, by the way, since...' I stalled, unsure for a moment how to put it into words. Then I said, '...since she did her thing?'

Lyn leaned forward, as if afraid of being overheard. 'I don't think she remembers. She hasn't mentioned it again.' She frowned, and I saw a little of the old confusion in her eyes, which caused my aching guts to flip over; it dismayed me whenever I saw even the tiniest hint of a possible relapse. 'What *is* she, Alex? How did she get like that?'

'I don't know,' I admitted. 'I think it was something to do with the heart. Something I'm going to have to learn.' I remembered how McCallum had manipulated the heart during his stage act. 'I think there's a lot it can do I don't know about yet.'

'Can I... hold the heart?' she asked shyly.

'You could if I had it.' When I explained where it was, her face fell like a patient denied vital medication.

'As soon as I get it back, though, I'll – shit!'

'What is it?' she asked.

'I've just remembered that my phone's in my jeans. In 1948. Which means I'm without the heart, my phone *and* my notebook. And I can't move. And this fucking neck brace itches like fuck.'

My grumpy mood lasted until the next day, when Paula returned with Kate. But lovely though it was to see my daughter, her visit was an all too brief blaze of sunshine between massing banks of storm clouds. As soon as she and Paula had gone the gloom set back in, and my thoughts turned inward again. I couldn't get that glimpse of Clover's teenage face out of my mind, couldn't think of a reason for her being there which didn't point to the fact that I'd been manipulated, deluded and betrayed by someone I'd grown to trust implicitly.

I asked for a phone, and was brought one. Luckily my whack on the head hadn't caused me to forget Clover's mobile number, and I tried calling her again – and again I got her voicemail. My first instinct was to put the phone down in frustration when her message cut in, but I didn't. After the beep I said, 'Call me at Oak Hill, Clover. We need to talk. If you're wondering why I'm in hospital, it's because I was hit by a bus. I'm sure you know why.' I hesitated, wondering whether I should say more, then I broke the connection.

I needed someone to talk to, though, if only to stop the ever-circling spiral of dark thoughts in my mind. Picking up the phone again I called Candice.

'Hey,' I said when she answered.

'Dad? Is that you? Oh God, where are you? I've left you, like, a million messages over the last couple of weeks. You still haven't told me anything about where Kate was found, or how. I've been worried sick about you. Where've you been?'

Though it was lovely to hear her voice, I felt pummelled both by the gush of words and the emotion behind them. Resisting the temptation to hold the phone away from my ear, I said, 'I'm really sorry not to have been in touch, love, but I've got a good reason. I'm in hospital again. I had a bit of an accident.'

'My God, you're kidding! What happened?'

'I got hit by a bus.'

'*Shit!* Are you serious?'

'I'm afraid so. I've been pretty much out of it these last few weeks.

Have got quite a few broken bones. But I *am* getting better. You don't need to worry.'

'Oh God, I feel awful that I didn't know. So where are you? Wherever it is, I'm coming to see you today.'

'I'm in the same hospital I was in last time. The one in Hampshire, near Farnborough.'

'The private one? Must be costing you a fortune, Dad.'

'I can afford it. I came into some money.'

'Well, I guessed you must have when you suddenly paid off Dean's debt.' After a beat of silence, she said, 'Do you mind me asking where it came from, Dad? It's not... dodgy money, is it?'

My bark of laughter sounded like someone scraping rust off an old bike. 'No, it's not dodgy money. It's... well, it's a long story.' All at once it struck me that in my search for Kate, and with everything else that had happened since I'd become involved with Benny and Clover and the obsidian heart, I'd seriously neglected my eldest daughter. Not that she needed me to look after her, but all the same I was suddenly overcome with an urge to see her, to hear her news, and to tell her some of mine. 'Look,' I said, 'if you've really got the time, jump on a train to Farnborough and get a cab from the station to Oak Hill Hospital. I'll pay.'

'I will do. I'll set off as soon as I put the phone down. But how's Kate? And where is she? Who's looking after her while you're in hospital?'

'She's fine,' I said. 'She's with friends. I'll tell you all about it when you get here.'

She arrived just after lunch, and we talked for almost three hours. When she walked into my room I almost lost it, partly because my injuries and the medication I was on were making me feel emotionally brittle, but also because, although I'd spoken to her on the phone a few times, the last time I'd actually seen her had been on the night of her eighteenth birthday at the Rusty Bucket in Covent Garden – which was only about eight weeks ago for her, but something like three years for me.

She looked surprised when I opened my arms to her – my right one still encased in its pot, which was no longer a pristine white since Kate had been at it with her felt tips – but stepped forward into my embrace willingly enough.

'You soft old sod,' she said, kissing my unshaven cheek. 'What the hell have you been up to this time?'

I told her a partial truth – that I'd been hit by a bus because I'd run into the road to push a young girl out of the way.

'Seriously?' she said, clearly unable to tell whether I was having her on or not.

I lifted my broken arm and clumsily drew an x on the left side of my chest with my swollen forefinger. 'Cross my heart and hope to die.'

'Bloody hell, Dad!' she exclaimed. 'That's amazing! You should get a medal or something!'

I shook my head. 'I don't want any fuss.'

Plus it happened over sixty years ago, I thought.

'What a hero.' She leaned forward and kissed me on the cheek. Then she sat back. 'So, tell me about Kate. I want to hear everything.'

I'd thought through what I was going to tell her between speaking to her this morning and her arriving this afternoon. I didn't like lying to my daughter, but neither did I want to drag her into the madhouse that my life had become. Plus, of course, if I'd told her the truth she'd have gone away seriously worried that my bump on the head had sent me completely nuts – particularly since I wasn't in possession of the heart, so had no way of backing up my claims.

'First of all, she's absolutely fine. The person who took her was a woman who'd had a child in Kate's class. A little girl called Jody. Her husband and Jody were killed in a car crash last year, and... well, I suppose the grief of it must just have got too much for her, and she snapped. So she went to the school the day Kate disappeared, and told Kate she was to take her home because I was busy with work and couldn't pick her up. Kate wouldn't normally go with strangers, but she must have thought it was okay because it was Jody's mum, and Jody had been her friend at school. So Jody's mum looked after Kate as if she was her own little girl. I think in a way she might even have convinced herself that Kate *was* Jody.'

Candice shuddered. 'Creepy.'

'Yeah, but sad too. In the end a neighbour got suspicious and called the police.'

'And Kate was all right?'

'Just a bit confused. She couldn't understand why I'd had to go away for such a long time, and why she wasn't going to school. I think Jody's mum told her it was the school holiday.'

'God, what a nutter,' Candice said. 'You must hate this woman for what she put you through.'

I paused. I'd plotted the story out so carefully in my head that I'd almost come to see Jody's tragic mum as a real person. 'At first maybe, but now I just feel sorry for her. She looked after Kate really well, doted on her, in fact, and Kate's absolutely fine. I just hope the poor woman gets the help she needs.'

'I hope they chuck her in prison and throw away the key,' Candice snapped, and then she instantly relented. 'No, I don't mean that. You're right, Dad. She sounds like a sad case.'

Before I could comment she continued, 'So tell me about this money. Where did it come from?'

I gave her a wry grin. 'I told you it wasn't dodgy. Don't you trust me?'

'Course I do, Dad,' she said innocently. 'I trust you implicitly. I'm just curious, that's all.'

Luckily I'd had time to concoct a story about this too, and spun her a tale about an old prison chum who'd gone straight thanks to my encouragement, and had started his own property renovation business after his release, which had made a pot of money. In my mind's eye my fictional prison chum, Reg Whiteley, had been an overweight workaholic with high blood pressure. He drank too much and smoked too much, and succumbed to a fatal heart attack at fifty-five.

'He always said he'd remember me in his will,' I said. 'I thought it was just talk, but it turns out he was as good as his word.'

'So how much did he leave you?'

'Enough to afford this place, pay off your boyfriend's debt and buy myself a new house.'

'A new house! Where?'

'Kensington. Near the park.'

'Wow! You *have* gone up in the world. Oh, and by the way, he's not my boyfriend any more.'

'What?'

'Dean. I've dumped him. Which *doesn't* mean it'll get him out of paying you back that money.'

'Oh,' I said. 'Well, I'm glad to hear it. I'm sure you can do a lot better.'

'I think so too. I'm like you, Dad.'

'Like me?'

'Yeah. I'm going places.'

Seeing Candice – who *was* probably more like me than anyone else in the world – cheered me up no end, but it still didn't rid me of the nagging desire to speak to Clover. I wish I knew where I stood with her, what was going on. Maybe I was wrong, but I couldn't help thinking that if only I could solve the riddle of why her teenage self was acting as McCallum's assistant in the 1940s, so much of what I still didn't understand would suddenly fall into place.

I still felt manipulated, but the more I looked back on our time together, the harder I found it to believe that Clover and I hadn't been genuine friends. Could it be that McCallum had initially *employed* her to manipulate me, but that during our time together she'd come to like me, and as time had gone on had therefore been struggling with a conflict of interests? Could that be why she'd now made herself scarce? Because she could no longer bear to pull the wool over my eyes? *Some* of that seemed feasible, but there was a lot that still didn't make sense. As I drifted off to sleep that night, I thought, *Maybe she'll call me tomorrow. Maybe she'll even visit me.* I couldn't believe that it was over between us, that I might never see her again.

Clover didn't call or visit the next day, or the one after, or even the one after that. I did get another visit from Kate, though, who this time was accompanied by all three Sherwoods. The following day Hope came to see me with her new 'mum' Jackie, and her new 'brother' Ed, and it was a real tonic to see her looking so well and happy. The most remarkable visitors I received, though, turned up the following day, by which time I'd been in the hospital for a month and the nurses were starting to put up Christmas decorations. I was dozing when my visitors arrived, and so didn't see them come in. Not that they used the door.

I was roused from sleep, as I'd been several times before, by the sound of someone speaking my name. I opened my eyes to see a long, grizzled face peering down at me. Then two hands rose into the gap between our faces, one holding the heart, the other my black notebook.

'Ta da!' said my older self. 'You can stop worrying. I've brought them back, as promised.'

I eased myself into a sitting position, grunting and wincing. My older self winced along with me.

'Take it easy,' he said. 'I remember how much that hurt. Still get a bit of an ache in my ribs when it's cold. Bloody nanites can't solve everything.'

I sensed movement behind him, the presence of others in the room, but I was too stiff and sore to peer around his body. 'Who've you brought with you?'

'Not even a thank you?' He pursed his lips in disapproval. 'I'd forgotten what a rude bugger I used to be.'

No matter how many times I'd seen my older self, it was eerie to see wrinkles I didn't yet have framing his mouth and grooving his cheeks.

'Thanks,' I said. 'I'm grateful – and relieved. You know I am.'

He half-turned to whoever was standing behind him, and took possession of a bright orange Sainsbury's bag, which appeared to be full to bursting.

'You'll be even more relieved to know I popped back to get these for you.'

He upended the bag on to the bed beside my left hip. Out tumbled the clothes I'd left in 1948, including my jeans, whose pockets contained my mobile and wallet.

'Thanks again.' I leaned back tentatively into my pillows, trying to get comfortable. I was improving day by day, but I still felt like I'd gone ten rounds with Mike Tyson every time I woke up.

'My pleasure. I'm doing it for my benefit as much as ours. Now, as you've already gathered, I've brought a couple of people to see you. You ready for this?'

'Just get on with it,' I said.

He tutted. 'You really need to develop a sense of occasion, son – and you will.' Then he stepped aside and raised his left hand in a gesture of introduction. 'Gentlemen.'

A couple of men stepped forward into the space that my older self had vacated, one grinning from ear to ear, the other peering at me shyly, almost sheepishly, from under a long fringe of hair. I looked at them, baffled. I had no idea who they were.

The older man, who must have been in his fifties, was mostly bald with a lumpy face partly hidden behind a thick, grey handlebar moustache, and a black eyepatch over his right eye. He was wearing a hairy brown suit over a checked waistcoat that stretched over his paunch, and he was holding a brown hat in his meaty hands.

The younger man, perhaps eighteen or nineteen, was slim, good-looking, and dressed in a black suit with waistcoat, white shirt and black tie.

The older man chuckled throatily. 'Has I really changed as much as all that, sir? I suppose I has. Though largely for the better, I 'ope you'll agree.'

I gawped in amazement as recognition set in. 'Mr Hulse?' I said.

'The one and only, sir, at your service.' He gestured with his hat towards his companion. 'And who might this young whippersnapper be, would you say?'

'It's not... surely it's not Tom?'

The young man blushed. 'Yes, sir,' he said, his voice soft and low.

Hulse chuckled delightedly. 'I can see you is mightily surprised, sir. 'Tis quite a transformation, is it not?'

'It's incredible,' I said. 'You both look... incredible!'

'All thanks to your generosity, sir. Your... er... generosity to come.'

I couldn't get over how much the two of them had changed. Despite being chubbier and balder and a good ten or fifteen years older than the last time I'd seen him, Hulse looked a damn sight cleaner, smarter, *healthier*.

But whereas Hulse's transformation was remarkable, Tom's was... *miraculous*. When I'd last set eyes on him he'd been a scrawny mute, almost feral, with a hideous metal lower jaw that had been created for him by Tallarian. Now his face was complete, flawless. There was not even the slightest evidence of scarring.

My older self said, 'Isn't it fantastic? Reconstructive facial surgery. *Future* reconstructive facial surgery. The details are all in the notebook.'

Despite myself, I laughed – and immediately set off a pinballing ricochet of pains in my bruised and battered body. Last time I'd seen Tom I'd been certain his life would be short, and that he would die an ugly and painful death.

'Fantastic's the word,' I said as the pain ebbed. 'So how are you doing, Tom?'

'I am doing very well, sir,' Tom said.

'And what are you up to these days? Both of you. Whatever it is you seem to have done well on it.'

Puffing his chest out proudly, Hulse said, 'Tom and I is respectable businessmen, Mr Locke. Partners we are. Ain't that right, my boy?'

Tom nodded.

'And what business are you in, if you don't mind me asking?'

Hulse closed his good eye in what it took me a moment to realise was a wink. 'We is in the business of death, sir.' Then, seeing my face, he guffawed. 'No, Mr Locke. Not in the way you is thinking. That was just my little joke. Tom and me run an undertaking business, sir. We ensure the final journey for them what has passed over is a satisfactory one. *More* than satisfactory! I would even go so far as to say: dignified, sir. Dignified and delicate. Tom and I is decorum personified. Ain't that right, Tom?'

'We do our best, sir,' Tom said to me, his face earnest.

'Our *very* best,' Hulse declared. 'Our utmost, you might say. And we are respected for it. Hulse and Son is renowned throughout London.'

'Hulse and *Son*?' I repeated.

Hulse nodded. 'I think of Tom as my son, Mr Locke – so that is what he is.'

I thought back to the first time I'd encountered Hulse, to how he and his cronies had chased me through the streets of the East End and given me a beating. They'd most likely have killed me if I hadn't used the heart to escape. And yet here my attacker was now, beaming, amiable and respectable.

And Tom! Tom who surely would have died if it hadn't been for the heart. So whatever trouble it had caused, here was proof – if any were needed – that it could be a force for good.

I held out my hand – my left one, as my right was mostly encased in plaster – and said, 'It's a genuine pleasure to see you both. It really is. I couldn't be happier to see you doing so well.'

Hulse stepped forward and enclosed my hand in his huge, scarred paw. 'The pleasure is ours, sir. I hope that we shall see you again very soon. Though as friends, o' course, and not in a professional capacity.' He guffawed.

Lying in my hospital bed that night, I had the feeling that things were coming full circle. If it doesn't sound too morbid, I felt not unlike a dying man who was slowly but surely being reacquainted with all the significant elements of his past, so that he might... well, if not make peace with them, then at least familiarise himself with them one last time.

In the previous week or so I'd been visited by Lyn and Dr Bruce, by Kate and the Sherwoods, by Candice, by Hope and Jackie, and by Hulse and Tom – not to mention my older self. The obvious omissions from that list were Clover and Benny. But I'd now come to a decision. I'd decided that if the mountain wouldn't come to Mohammed, then Mohammed would go to the mountain.

I'd pondered on various ways of seeing Clover again. I'd wondered about using the heart to jump back to the day she'd left, the day I'd driven to Wales to pick up Kate. But I'd already lived through that day. I'd come back to find her note on the kitchen table. So to go back and either prevent her from leaving, or find out her reasons for cutting herself off from me, would be to change a history I'd already experienced – and could I afford to do that? Or perhaps, more to the point, would the heart *allow* me to do that?

I also considered going back to 1948 and finding another opportunity to speak to teenage Clover. But what would that really achieve, besides perhaps giving me an insight into how she and McCallum had met, how they had started their association?

No, to find out the full truth without endangering the timeline I needed to speak to Clover as she was *now*, and the only person I could think of who might know where I could find her was Benny. Perhaps she was even staying with him? After all, with Incognito having been destroyed by fire, she had no home of her own to go to.

Ideally I could have done with another few days, if not another week or so, to recover and recuperate, but once the idea was in my head I knew I wouldn't be able to rest until I'd acted upon it. So at around 3 a.m. that night, with the hospital as quiet as it ever got, I pushed back my bedclothes and eased myself out of bed, wincing at the pain in my pelvis and ribs and neck, but relying on the fact that if I got into any sort of trouble, I could always use the heart to transport myself straight back to hospital again.

The clothes that my older self had brought for me had been folded up and placed on the shelves in the bottom of the bedside cabinet. I eased off the hospital gown I was wearing (I was issued with a fresh one every day) and got dressed slowly and painstakingly. It was an effort getting my T-shirt and hoodie over my neck brace and the pot on my arm, but luckily both items were pretty stretchy and I managed it eventually. By the time I'd tied my boots I was panting with exertion, and decided I needed a minute or two to recover. Impatience was gnawing at me, though, so only thirty seconds later I was sliding open the top drawer of the bedside cabinet and taking out the heart. Still sitting on the bed, I held it in my hand and closed my eyes.

When I opened them again, I was standing outside Benny's house. I leaned against the wall of the porch beside his front door for a moment, catching my breath and waiting for the nanites to dampen down the familiar waves of nausea that were sweeping through me.

By the time I knocked on his door I no longer felt sick, but I did feel sweaty and enervated, simply from being on my feet. I'd timed it so that I'd jump back in time a few hours and arrive not at 3 a.m. but at around 10 p.m. the previous evening. I took several deep breaths and closed my eyes as I waited for the door to be answered – which it was surprisingly quickly.

'Bloody hell, son,' Benny said, 'you look a fucking wreck. You'd better come in.'

I followed him into the house and down the corridor to the meringue-white sitting room that overlooked the front drive. Last time I'd been in here, I'd collapsed on top of the glass coffee table that had sat in the midst of a trio of white leather sofas and smashed it to bits. Its replacement was a highly polished wooden table (teak, possibly), on which sat two tumblers of whisky on metal coasters.

I pursed my lips. 'I'm guessing you're not surprised to see me. Who told you I was coming?'

'You did,' Benny said. He sighed.

'"Me" me?' I asked. 'Or...'

'You were older,' Benny said bluntly. 'I don't mind admitting, it gave me the fucking willies.' He looked suddenly weary. 'Look, I don't like any of this shit, Alex. People and business I can understand. Violence, and even death, I can accept as a consequence of what I do. But this... this fucks with my head. It unsettles me.'

'I know, Benny,' I said. 'I'm sorry.'

'Fuck your sorry. Just drink your drink, because you look as though you bloody well need one, and then we'll get going.'

TWENTY-SIX

ALL OUR YESTERDAYS

It was too uncomfortable to sit up straight in the passenger seat of Benny's Jag, so I stretched out in the back.

'Where are we going?' I asked him.

'I told you. To see Monroe.'

'Yes, but where's that?'

'You'll find out when we get there.'

By the time we started heading up the A3 it was obvious we were going back to London. But where in London? I kept a tight hold on the heart, ready to transport myself out of there if Benny did the dirty on me. I didn't think he would. I'd been paying him to use his contacts to look for Kate, and even though the deal I'd made with him had now paid dividends, I still hadn't cancelled the monthly payment, thinking I'd let it run for a while just to keep him sweet.

Even so, our alliance was an uneasy one. How long would it be before he decided that getting my 'voodoo shit', as he'd called it, out of his life was more important than any amount of financial renumeration? And what was the deal with Clover? She'd cut me off, and she'd been working with McCallum from an early age, and he was a rich man too, so could it be that my usefulness was now at an end, and despite the fact that financially McCallum had set me up for life, the three of them were now preparing to double-cross me in some way?

We didn't talk much in the car. Slumped in the back seat, I spent my time looking out of the window, trying to second-guess which part of London we were heading for. When we turned on to the A306 towards Barnes, I began to have my suspicions. These seemed to be confirmed when we then began to follow the A315 heading towards Kensington and Olympia.

Struggling into a sitting position, and wincing at the pain in my ribs and pelvis, I said, 'Are we going to my house? To Ranskill Gardens?'

Benny said nothing.

'Come on, Benny, speak to me,' I said. 'The silent treatment doesn't scare me or impress me. I can fuck off from here any time I want using the heart. If we're going to my house I want to know. Kate's in there. She'd better not be in any danger.'

Benny glanced at me in the rear-view mirror. 'We're not going to your house,' he said.

'Where then?'

'Another minute or two and you'll find out, won't you? Just be patient.'

It was when he turned off Kensington High Street on to Campden Hill Road that I guessed. A minute later we pulled up to the kerb.

'What are we doing here?' I asked.

As always Bellwater Drive was quiet and dimly lit, the light from the street lamps struggling to make an impression through the black, tangled branches of the trees that lined the road. Benny had pulled up right outside the metal gate to number 56, through which McCallum's house stood in darkness.

'Monroe's in there,' Benny said. 'She wants to speak to you.'

'Why here?' I asked.

'How the fuck should I know? I'm only the fucking chauffeur.'

'A highly paid one, no doubt.'

Benny's eyes flashed at me in the rear-view mirror. 'You want to watch your lip, son. I'll only be pushed so far, money or no money.'

I sighed. 'Who told you to bring me here? Was it the older me or Clover herself?'

'It was you. I haven't seen Monroe or spoken to her since our trip to Wales. And I don't give a shit whether you believe that or not. I've already been paid, so as soon as you get out of this car I'm fucking off. And if I ever see you again, it'll be too soon.'

I wouldn't trust Benny as far as I could throw him, but I believed him nonetheless. I looked up at the dark block of the house through the bars of the gate, and sighed again.

'Nothing good has ever happened to me in there,' I said. 'First time I accidentally killed a man. Second time I was arrested.'

'Third time lucky then,' said Benny bluntly.

'Here's hoping.'

I heaved and winced my way out of the car. As I hobbled across the pavement to the gate, the December cold throbbed in my bones, which were aching from exertion. Although I couldn't claim to have been on my feet a great deal in the past hour or so since leaving the hospital, it was still a more concerted period of exercise than I'd managed in the previous week, when the only time I'd been upright had been on the few occasions I'd hobbled to and from my en suite bathroom in the hospital. I hated being an invalid, but consoled myself with the thought that it would have been a lot worse without my little nanite buddies working away inside me. In fact, if it hadn't been for them I'd almost certainly be dead now.

Reaching the gate, I clung to it with my good left hand and half-turned. 'See you, Benny.'

His passenger window was down as if he intended to deliver a parting shot, but all he said was, 'I hope not.' Then the window slid up, the engine started and the car pulled away from the kerb.

I watched it until it was nothing but a pair of rear lights at the far end of the street, then I lifted my right arm with the cast on it and gave him the middle finger. 'It's been emotional,' I muttered, and turned back to the gate. I pushed it open and limped up the gravel path towards the house, not bothering to conceal my approach by walking on the grass.

I headed by habit not towards the front door, but around the side of the house towards the French windows at the back. I kept my left hand wrapped around the heart in my pocket the whole time. If there was anything about this situation that didn't smell good I was out of there.

The first time I'd come here, the house and grounds had been pitch black, which under the circumstances had been both reassuring and eerie, but as I neared the corner of the house that led around to the French windows, I saw a dim illumination seeping out from that area, flecking the trees and grass in front of me with brownish light. I paused a moment, licked my dry lips, then moved forward again, more cautiously. When I reached the corner I pressed myself against the wall, then slid around it. The glow of light was stronger now, yellowish-orange rather than brown. And it was flickering, not steady. Candlelight.

I sidled up to the edge of the French windows and peered through them. The drawing room beyond, where I'd first clapped eyes on the heart, and where I'd killed Barnaby McCallum, was illuminated by around a dozen candles. Around half that number had been set on top of the mantelpiece to my right. Sitting in an armchair to the left of the mantelpiece, with what looked like a big book on her lap, was Clover. When I moved into view she looked up, the candlelight falling over her face and making her skin glow like gold.

She raised her arm and mimed turning a handle, which I guessed was her way of letting me know the French windows were open. Her apparently relaxed demeanour was disarming, but I was still wary. I opened the French windows and stepped into the house, my eyes darting to check out the darker corners of the room.

'It's okay, I won't bite,' she said, sounding half amused, half sad. 'And neither will anything else.'

'What's going on, Clover?'

'It's explanation time. Time for you to be given some of the answers you've been looking for. You'd better brace yourself.'

At her words, my guts started crawling with excitement and apprehension. 'What answers?'

'Come and sit down.' She waved at the chair on the opposite side of the fireplace. 'I know you need to. How are you, by the way? That neck brace looks uncomfortable.'

'I'm fine,' I muttered. 'Well, no I'm not. But I will be.'

'I know you will,' she said. 'And thank you. For saving my life when I was sixteen.'

'What were you doing there? What's going on?'

'Please.' Her voice was soft and, so it seemed to me, genuinely pained. 'Please sit down. I'll tell you. But I need you to be calm.'

I hesitated a moment longer, then limped across the room and sat in the chair across from her. She looked nervous, which I wasn't used to. 'I'm sitting,' I said. 'Now what?'

'I want you to look at this.' She hefted the big book she was holding and offered it to me. It was an album of some sort, with a matt-black, spongy, leather-look cover. As she held it up, candlelight flashed on the word 'Photographs' printed on the front in a gold, calligraphic font.

I looked at the book, but made no move to take it, which she took as an indication that my injuries were preventing me from doing so.

'Sorry,' she said, a little flustered, getting up from her chair and crossing the divide between us. She offered me the heavy-looking book again, but because of my broken arm, taking it from her would have meant letting go of the heart in my pocket, and I wasn't prepared to do that.

When I didn't lift my arms, she apologised again, then turned the book the right way round before placing it carefully on my lap. Then, as though to reassure me she meant no harm, she went back to her chair and sat down.

I looked across at her and she looked at me. She looked more nervous than ever. She reminded me of one of my students, waiting apprehensively for my verdict on their end of term project.

Turning eventually to the photograph album, I opened it carefully, as though dealing with something volatile. There was a layer of flimsy protective paper between each page of photographs, and the top one crackled slightly as I opened the book. I peeled it back.

Baby pictures. I frowned. The book was unfamiliar, but the pictures weren't. I'd seen them before. I looked up at Clover.

'This is Kate.'

She nodded.

'What is this? Some sort of threat?'

'Just keep going,' she said.

I turned another page. Kate as a toddler. Wearing a sun hat. Eating an ice cream. Sitting on a picnic blanket. Perched at the top of a slide.

Another page. She was older here, three or four. Squinting at me through her first pair of spectacles. Opening presents on Christmas Day. Hugging her Jessie from *Toy Story* doll. Pointing out of a train window.

The next page. Wearing her uniform before her first day of 'proper' school. Playing in a ball pool. Competing in an egg and spoon race. Standing next to a tank full of sharks at the Sea Life aquarium, pretending to be terrified.

The next page made my heart leap. I felt suddenly dizzy, disorientated. Kate was only five, but in these photographs she was older. At least six or seven. She'd lost a little of her puppy fat. She looked taller, more willowy. There was more of a... it's hard to describe, but more of a *knowingness* about her. I tried to swallow, but my throat felt too thick and swollen. I looked at Clover and shook my head.

'Keep going,' she said softly.

I wanted to stop, but I couldn't. I had to see.

I turned another page. Kate was ten, eleven. These were all portraits now, all posed. They weren't shots captured on days out or when she was in the process of doing something. They looked to have been carefully manufactured to be neutral – neutral clothes, neutral backgrounds. As if whoever had taken them had known that one day I would look at them, and didn't want to give away too much information.

By the age of eleven she was wearing different spectacles – with thin silver frames instead of pink ones.

By the age of twelve she wasn't wearing spectacles at all.

By the age of thirteen her hair was longer and less unkempt, her face thinner and prettier; she was turning into a young woman.

By the age of fourteen the resemblance was undeniable.

I looked up at Clover. I was shaking. My head was swimming, and I thought I was going to faint.

Clover still looked nervous, but she was smiling now, and her eyes were full of nothing but love.

'You...' I said, my voice thick. And then my throat closed up and I couldn't say any more.

'I wanted to tell you,' she said softly. 'I wanted to tell you so much. But I couldn't. I had to keep it a secret.'

My head was not just swimming now, but spinning. I couldn't get a grasp on my thoughts. I felt as though I'd shattered into pieces, and the pieces were swirling slowly around me in a glittering parabola, caught within my orbit. I tried, through sheer effort of will, to rein myself back in, to make myself complete again. I squeezed the heart, but it made no difference. And the nanites inside me could not repair a blown mind. This was something I was going to have to accept and come to terms with on my own.

I forced myself to speak, if only to hear the words, to have them confirmed: 'You're Kate.'

Clover nodded. 'Yes. I'm all grown up.' She gave a nervous laugh and spread her hands, as though showing me a new outfit. 'What do you think?'

I didn't know *what* to think. Was I happy or upset? All I could really say with any certainty was that I was stunned.

'But how?' I said. And then all at once a splinter of denial mixed with anger slid into my thoughts, piercing my bubble of confusion. 'You can't be,' I said. 'You can't be Kate. It's not possible.'

Clover stayed calm – almost as if she'd been expecting my reaction. 'The evidence is there, Dad. Right in front of you.'

Dad. It felt *so* weird to hear her calling me that. A woman who was only a decade or so younger than I was.

And yet it felt right too. In my heart of hearts I knew she wasn't lying. I knew that this woman – Clover, who had become my great friend and confidante – was also my daughter, Kate.

Kate, who was currently only five years old.

'Why didn't you tell me?' I said, unable to keep the indignation out of my voice. 'You put me through all that heartache when all the time...'

My voice choked off. Though I couldn't help feeling it, I knew my anger was unjustified. Confirming what I already knew Clover said, 'I'm sorry, Dad, but I was under strict instructions. Instructions from *you*.'

I nodded jerkily, raising a hand to show that I knew, that I understood. My throat felt as though it had swollen to five times its normal size. As though to take up the slack, to fill the silence between us, Clover said gently, 'That was why it was so hard to be with you when you brought me – the younger me – back to the house a few weeks ago. It was too weird. I couldn't handle it. It was bad enough when we went to Wales that first time, but I knew I had to be with you then, because you were an emotional wreck, you needed my support. And there were other people around, so I didn't have to have much to do with my younger self. But if there'd been just the three of us in the house...' She shook her head. 'Too weird. And I was worried that with only the two of us to concentrate on, you might have started to see the similarities between us before the time was right. You might have guessed.'

My throat felt as though it was deflating now. I swallowed to enable myself to speak. 'I still can't believe it.' I looked at my hands. 'And I can't stop shaking.'

'It's the shock. Do you want a drink of water? Or something stronger?'

'No, I... I want to hear your story. I want to know how you got to this point. Sorry, but... I find it so hard to believe. So hard to get my head round.'

'I don't blame you.'

'But you look so different! You and Kate. How can you and she be the same?'

'I grew up, Dad. People do.'

'But your eyesight... and your learning difficulties.'

'I had eye surgery.' She made a 'going forward' gesture with her hand. 'In the future. You'll take me, using the heart. And as for the learning difficulties, I got over them. I was bright, I was determined, I worked hard.' She smiled. 'And you were a great teacher.'

'So how did you get to this point?' I asked. 'How did *we* get to this point? Tell me everything.'

Still smiling, she said, 'For you it started from this night. From the night you found out who I really was. You trained me, Dad – or you will. Because you knew from your own memories what my role would be in pointing you towards the heart in the first place, and helping you along the way. But you didn't tell me everything. You told me just as much as I needed to know, and then you threw me in at the deep end. That way my reactions and emotions stayed genuine. There was so much I had no foreknowledge of. I didn't know how Hawkins would end up, for example. Or poor Mary, who worked for me at Incognito. There were times when I hated you for not telling me. But I know it was right. I know you can't dare try to change what you know has already happened.'

'So those stories you spun me. About your background. About your dad, the vicar, and how you met Benny...'

'They weren't completely made up. Some of it was real – as far as Benny was concerned anyway. He was never in on what was going on, apart from you giving him a ton of money to look after your younger self in prison – don't forget to do that, by the way.'

I tapped the breast pocket of my jacket. 'It's all in the book.'

She nodded. 'You've got a load of setting up to do, Dad. I'll help you with it when the time comes. It's pretty complicated.'

'When is it not?' I said.

She laughed.

It was odd, but now that she had told me who she was, I could see Kate in her – the way she smiled and laughed, various little mannerisms. I was amazed now that I hadn't noticed them straight away – though of course I hadn't been looking for them, had I? Or maybe I *had* noticed, but only unconsciously. Maybe that was what had drawn me to Clover in the first place, had made me instinctively want to trust her even when I'd been wary and suspicious of who or what she might ultimately turn out to be.

Even now, though, I had burning questions that needed to be answered. The most pertinent of which was the one that had led to me being hospitalised again.

'What's the story between you and McCallum? How did you get involved with him? And from such a young age?'

She stood up. 'That's something it's better to show than tell.' She nodded towards my left-hand pocket. 'Power up the heart, Dad. I need you to take us on a journey.'

TWENTY-SEVEN
THE SAME RAIN

When we arrived it was raining again. No, scratch that. It was the same rain I'd been caught in when I'd last been here, about a month ago.

Anticipating my agreement to accompany her on the little jaunt she'd suggested, Clover (or should that be Kate? Even though I'd accepted she *was* Kate, it still seemed too large and crazy a thing to get my head round) had acquired a hat and coat for me to wear that would at least mostly cover my very modern plastic neck brace and enable me to blend in.

We arrived in a darkened doorway across the street from the Hippodrome just as the crowds leaving the theatre were thinning out.

'This time you'll be going in through the front with me,' she said.

'So where's my past self now?'

She pointed towards a dark slit between buildings on the opposite side of the wet and gleaming road. 'At a guess I'd say you've just settled down to hide behind the dustbins.'

'Happy days,' I muttered, which made her grin.

We waited a bit longer, until the last of the stragglers had dispersed, and then we crossed the road and ascended the steps to the theatre entrance. An old, saggy-jowled man in a light-grey doorman's uniform was closing and locking the various sets of doors.

'I'm afraid we're closed, miss,' he said, sounding genuinely apologetic.

'We're here to see the Great Barnaby. He's expecting us. Mr

Alexander Locke and Miss Clover Monroe.'

The doorman gave us the once-over, then touched a finger to the peak of his cap. 'If you'll just wait here a moment, miss, I'll inquire.'

He went inside, closing the door behind him. We stood at the top of the now wet and dirty steps, shielded by the theatre awning, and watched people hurrying by, coat collars turned up and umbrellas raised against the rain.

Now that we had a moment to reflect, I felt strangely tongue-tied. I glanced at Clover and she glanced back, smiling shyly.

'This is weird,' I said.

'I know,' she replied. 'Sorry.'

I shrugged. 'You did what you had to do.'

She was silent for a moment, then she said, 'It was weird for me too at first. Teaming up with my dad, who was only, like, eight or nine years older than me. It's a big relief the secret's out now, though, not least because I no longer have to worry about calling you dad by mistake.'

'Did you remember me looking like this?' I asked. 'From when you were little, I mean?'

She scrunched her face into a *very* Kate-like expression. 'Kind of. I remember my childhood pretty well. Going back to our old flat was weird, because before we got there I only sort of half-remembered it. But when I saw it again, even though it was smashed up, it all looked instantly familiar. But to answer your question – you didn't really look *all* that different to me. Just... well, as if you'd had some sort of extreme makeover or something. A few nips and tucks here and there. A bit of gravity-defying Botox.'

'You make it sound delightful.'

She laughed just as one of the theatre doors opened and the doorman poked his head out. 'Would you like to come through?'

We followed him through the lobby, along a corridor to the left of the main auditorium and down some carpeted stairs. Though the lighting was considerably better here, and the surroundings a lot grander, I was reminded of the time in Victorian London when Hawkins, Hulse and I had rescued Clover from the clutches of Willoughby Willoughby at the Maybury Theatre. At the bottom of the stairs was a fire door, leading into a narrower corridor with water pipes running along the ceiling. We passed various doors on our left as we were led down it, then turned left into another corridor. On our right was a long dark curtain (the side or back of the stage maybe), and on our left were yet more doors, framed posters for previous shows hanging on the patches of wall in between.

We stopped at a door about two-thirds of the way down the corridor. Like all the rest, it was painted a blue-grey colour, but this one had a yellow wooden star on it, above a sign that read 'Dressing Room'. As though checking for woodworm, the doorman put his ear to the door and rapped on it at head height with the middle knuckle of his right forefinger.

'Come in,' someone called, and the doorman pushed the door open just wide enough to thrust his head into the gap.

'Your guests are here, sir.'

'Thank you. Show them in.'

As if the voice had not been loud enough to carry, the doorman stepped back and turned to us. 'You can go in,' he said.

'Most kind,' said Clover in such an expressionless voice that the doorman looked unsure as to whether she was teasing him or not. She went in first, and I followed.

The dressing room was dimly lit, illuminated only by the light bulbs around and above the mirror on the left-hand wall. Beneath the mirror, stretching the length of the wall, was a long counter or table, cluttered with make-up, used hand towels, a glass vase stuffed with flowers, the remains of a meal and various other bits and pieces. There was a wooden chair set at an angle beneath the table and a threadbare rug on the floor over wooden boards. The back wall was of grey brick, to which various posters and notices were attached. To our right was a big chunky wardrobe, a rack of costumes, and, in the far right corner, an armchair upholstered in faded red velvet. The Great Barnaby – McCallum – was sitting in the armchair, smoking a cigarette, his right foot resting on his left knee. Despite the fact that he was still wearing his stage gear – spats, long fishtail jacket, red mask and all – he looked very relaxed.

'Come in,' he said. 'Have a drink.' He gestured towards the make-up area, where a bottle of whisky and a couple of crystal tumblers stood on a silver tray among the paraphernalia.

I would have refused – I felt too wired to drink – but before I could say anything, Clover crossed the room and poured us a couple of generous measures. She passed one of the tumblers to me, and despite myself I took a sip, which my nerves turned into a gulp, which made me cough, which ended up causing me to double over, clutching my ribs.

'Are you okay?' Clover asked, voice breathy with concern.

'Bust ribs,' I gasped. 'Hurts to cough and laugh.'

'You'll be fine once the nanites kick in,' said the Great Barnaby.

Still holding my ribs, I looked up at him. 'What do you know about nanites?'

Smoke was wreathing his face. When he smiled his teeth looked very white through his black beard.

'You'll enjoy this bit,' he said, 'when it gets to your turn.'

Maybe if my mind hadn't still been trying to process the revelation that Clover was my daughter, I might have understood what he meant. As it was, I frowned at him. 'What?'

He leaned forward in his chair, so that the light fell across his face. He peeled off his red eye mask. Then he peeled off his moustache and thick black beard.

I gaped. I could almost hear the cogs in my head, whirring madly, as I tried to make sense of this new revelation. I imagined the electronic voice of a computer from a 1970s TV show: *Does not compute, does not compute...*

My legs felt hollow. As if reading my mind, Clover grabbed the wooden chair from under the make-up table and swung it towards me.

'I think you need to sit down, Dad. You look a bit pale.'

I sat with a thump, my damaged pelvis groaning in protest.

I stared at the Great Barnaby, unmasked. 'This isn't right,' I said. 'You – I – can't be him. The Great Barnaby is McCallum.'

My older self grinned back at me. He looked a few years older than I am now. 'That's right,' he said.

'But that doesn't–'

And then it hit me. I looked at Clover. And then I looked back at my older self. He was nodding.

'We *are* McCallum,' he said softly. 'We've always been McCallum. It's an eternal circle, Alex. I found out ten years ago, because I was in your shoes, that I was destined to become McCallum, and that years from now I was destined to die by my own hand and be the guardian of the heart forever. You see, the heart has only had one guardian. *We* created it, and it, in turn, created...' he waved a hand '...well, who knows? But the path is a complex one, and even I don't know if it's always exactly the same. But I do know it's one we have to stick to, if only because we *remember* it. And also because, ultimately, this life of ours is a long one and a good one – so why would we *want* to change it?'

Glass chattering against my teeth, I took a gulp of whisky. It burned. My mind was a fairground ride, dipping and wheeling and spinning. I said, 'So you're saying that sometime in the future you'll force me to murder you?'

'Not *me*,' my older self said. '*Us*. *We'll* decide. And it's not murder, it was never murder. It's suicide. And it won't come from a bad place. It wasn't a mistake; it wasn't a robbery gone wrong. It'll only come when we've had enough, when we've lived a long life, and are too old and tired to carry on any longer.' He took another drag on his cigarette. 'You saw the old man you thought was McCallum about a week before he died. You remember? That day you were arrested?'

I nodded.

'You'll see him again. And he'll tell you what I'm about to tell you, what he told *me*. When you first met Kate as Clover, she told you McCallum was in his nineties.' (He nodded at Clover as he said this.) 'But that wasn't true. He was more like a hundred and forty, a hundred and fifty. He confessed to me he didn't know exactly, because he'd lived so many lives in so many times he'd lost count of his true age. Even now I'm living this life here and another life in "our" present day; I'm jumping between the two. We can be away for six months at a time and it doesn't matter. Because we don't age like normal people. The nanites keep us young and healthy. They slow the ageing process right down.'

I didn't know what to think. I didn't know whether to be happy at the prospect of a long – very long – and eventful life, or appalled at the thought that it was mapped out for me, that I had to stick to a pre-arranged plan.

I'd need time to think it through, to come to terms with everything. In the meantime, I focused on the fly in the ointment, the rogue element that could theoretically undermine everything.

'What about the Dark Man? Who's he? What's his role in all this?'

TWENTY-EIGHT

THE BELLY OF THE BEAST

It must have been weird for Clover, being in between two versions of her father, both of whom were holding her hand, but she seemed to take it in her stride. The time transition was infinitely easier for me than it normally was, travelling as a passenger of my older self and *his* heart. The only disadvantage was that I had no idea where we'd ended up, not even when we arrived. One moment we were in the Great Barnaby's dressing room, the next we were surrounded by chilling fog. I shivered and flapped at it, but it continued to press in, covering my face and hair with wet kisses.

Beside me Clover released my hand and gently rubbed my older self's back as he bent over double, hands on knees. He took a number of long, deep breaths, then slowly straightened up.

'So that feeling you're about to puke never goes away?' I said.

He gave me a thin smile. 'Hasn't done so far.'

To be honest, I also felt queasy, but it wasn't because of the journey. As I orientated myself, so my senses began to kick in, one after another, as if they'd taken a little time to catch up with the sudden shift from one location to another. What was making *me* feel sick was a stench, like rotting fish and raw sewage, which was wafting over us in waves. Accompanying the smell was a wet, surging slap, regular as breathing. As I put a hand up to cover my nose and mouth, I realised not only that it was foggy, but also that it was snowing – I might have thought it was a light rain if I hadn't seen it settling on the shoulders and hair of my companions. The fog, the snow, the stench, the slapping of water...

all these elements combined to spark a memory.

'Are we back at Blyth's Wharf?'

My older self nodded. 'We are. This is the night we went to the Thousand Sorrows. The night the Dark Man captured us and told us to get the heart for him.'

'Is this before that happened or after?' I asked.

'Let's get closer, shall we? See what's going on.'

I felt nervous, but I was guessing my older self had brought me here because he remembered *his* older self bringing him here when he was me. Which surely meant that everything would be okay? That whatever happened, we'd survive?

My older self led us along the edge of the harbour, the meaty slap of water to our left, the vague, dark blocks of buildings to our right. We sought cover where we could – behind packing crates, coils of rope, covered carriages on which goods were stacked, awaiting delivery or collection.

After a couple of minutes my older self halted and put a warning hand out behind him, encouraging Clover and me to stop too.

'What is it?' Clover hissed.

'Listen.'

I listened, but it took a few moments to adjust my hearing so that I could hear anything other than the movement of the Thames and the whispering of the snow. Eventually I managed to pick out a combination of gentle sounds – a nervous snort, the creak of wood, the tight clop of two hard surfaces scraping against one another.

'Sounds like a horse,' murmured Clover, working it out the same moment I did.

'Is it attached to a cart?' I asked.

'Let's get a bit nearer,' my older self said.

We sidled closer, trying to lift our feet fully clear of the snow, so they wouldn't make a *shhh* sound as they dragged through it. Little by little the area in front of us emerged through the murk, the objects in the foreground suddenly acquiring a solidity that seemed to make them loom, even lurch, towards us. I jumped when a huddle of headless, pot-bellied men turned out to be a dozen or so barrels clustered together. Clover, in front of me, turned to pluck at my sleeve to get me to duck down, which I did. Next moment, from much closer than I'd expected, came another equine snort and an uneasy whinny. I peered between the curved sides of two of the barrels and saw the dark shape of a horse attached not to a cart, as I'd expected, but to some sort of carriage, possibly a brougham.

I looked beyond Clover to my older self, intending to follow his lead, but just then he turned towards us, pressed a finger to his lips and flattened himself against the back of the barrel, trying to make himself as small as possible. Clover and I exchanged a glance, then followed suit.

Almost as soon as we'd done so, there came a huge leathery flapping sound from above us. My first thought was that it was a tarpaulin or something similar that had broken loose from a stack of goods and been plucked upwards by the wind. But when I tilted my head to look up (as best I could in my neck brace), squinting my eyes against the falling snow, I saw the dark, blurry shape of what appeared to be a vast bird descending towards us. I tucked my head in again, clutching the barrel so tightly that my fingers made dents in the wet wood.

The bird thing landed with a thump somewhere beyond the barrels, but close to the carriage. The horse whinnied in panic, but was quietened by what I imagined was the driver, perched on his seat behind it. Couldn't he see the bird thing? Hadn't he heard it? I half-expected the creature's landing to be followed by the crunch of wood, the screams of man and horse as it went on the attack. But instead all I heard was the sound of the carriage door being opened, and then the creak of wood or springs as someone or something clambered into it. Next moment, with a muffled clattering of wheels and the clop of horse's hooves on stony ground dusted with snow, the carriage was on the move. We listened until it had faded into the distance, though even then I might have remained where I was if I hadn't seen my older self rise up from his hiding place.

'One of the Dark Man's little gang?' Clover said.

My older self nodded. 'The shape-shifter, I'm guessing.' He looked at me. 'Escorting us home after our little tête-à-tête with the boss.'

I remembered how, after my meeting with the Dark Man in his most ancient state, his withered body reliant on a huge, metal spider-like conveyance to carry him around, I'd been drugged and had woken up back at home, my body having been dumped on the doorstep of my house in Ranskill Gardens. The carriage we'd just seen had presumably been my transport on that particular occasion. Which meant that, for a few moments, there had been not two but three of us – three of *me* – within feet of each other.

'I know what you're thinking,' my older self said, and a glint of mischief came into his eye. 'You know what we ought to do one day?'

'What?'

'We ought to have a party with just us as the guests. Not just me and you, but loads of us, from different time zones. Imagine what that would be like.'

'The ultimate ego trip,' said Clover.

'Just the thought of it gives me a headache,' I said.

My older self grinned and took his heart out of his pocket. Holding it up, he said, 'Arm yourself. We're going in.'

He led us around the barrels and into the fog beyond, bearing left, the river at our backs. In front of us loomed the dark blocks of buildings – storage warehouses, equipment sheds, the damp, mildewed premises of various shipping or export companies. Within thirty seconds we were standing next to a docking bay, from which a ramp rose to the open front of a huge warehouse. The sight made me think of the head of some vast creature, its mouth yawning open, its tongue unrolled. Of the interior of the warehouse itself, we could see only blackness.

'Ready to step into the belly of the beast?' my older self asked.

I frowned at him. 'Don't tell me you're enjoying this?'

'I've been here before. And as you can see, I came out of it okay.'

Now Clover looked at him disapprovingly too. 'That doesn't mean you always will, Dad. Don't be complacent.'

My older self looked suitably chastised. 'Sorry. I just remember how nervous I was the first time I did this.' He gestured towards me. 'I was only trying to keep everyone's spirits up.'

'Let's just get on with it,' I said.

We ascended the stone ramp, which was wet and slippery so we had to take it slowly. There was no sound from inside the warehouse, and I wondered briefly whether the Dark Man and his army of horrors had already cleared out. But if my older self had been here ten years ago, he had presumably found evidence to the contrary, otherwise why would he bother coming back? Surely it wasn't to preserve the timeline, because if I – and all the other mes caught in this loop – remembered this as being a dead end, then surely the timeline would never have been created in the first place?

We reached the top of the ramp and paused on the threshold of the warehouse, looking in. The square opening was comfortably wide enough to accommodate the three of us standing shoulder to shoulder, and tall enough to give us head clearance of at least thirty feet, but even now the foggy darkness ahead of us seemed impenetrable. Was it a natural darkness or something else? I shuddered as a chill swept through me, and I was glad of the overcoat that Clover had suggested I wear. My older self and I were like matching bookends, he with his heart held aloft in his right hand, me brandishing mine in my unbroken left. Clover stood between us, like a princess flanked by royal bodyguards.

Suddenly my older self shouted, 'Come out, Dark Man. We want to talk to you.'

Contained within the walls of the building, his voice boomed and echoed.

Was there a response? A stealthy shifting and rustling, as of many things that were currently motionless, readying themselves for action?

'We're coming in,' he shouted, and then he began walking forward, heading into the darkness. I felt apprehensive, and – because of my battered, broken, aching body – particularly vulnerable, but I followed his lead, anxious not to lose him. Clover walked close beside me, her fingers reaching for and then loosely intertwining with the fingers of my right hand, which were sticking out of my cast.

The shifting and rustling sounds were unmistakeable now. In moments they escalated into a plethora of other sounds as Tallarian's clockwork army and whoever or whatever else the Dark Man had rallied to his cause creaked and clicked and scuttled and slithered into life to defend their lord and master.

Clover gasped as *things* (it was inaccurate to refer to them as people, or even creatures) suddenly rolled and darted and scurried from the darkness around us. I caught glimpses of metal and flesh combined in hideous ways. I saw what appeared to be a flying crab trailing jellyfish-like fronds; something that looked like a jumble of human limbs sprouting from a metal box; a monstrosity that had goggling, fish-like eyes, a furry (possibly canine) body and long metal pincers.

They came at us, whether to kill or maim or simply drive us away I wasn't sure. Clover screamed and clung to me, and for a moment I braced myself, certain we were about to be overwhelmed.

Then the heart kicked in – *both* the hearts kicked in – and they created what I can only describe as a protective barrier around us. As when I had duelled with the Dark Man – me with the old and crumbling heart, he with the younger, more vibrant heart that he had stolen from me – I felt the heart sucking up the energy inside me and then spitting it out in a crackling blast of light and power. At the same time, in a display of perfect synchronisation, my older self's heart did exactly the same thing at exactly the same moment, the two eruptions of energy curving over and around the three of us until eventually meeting above our heads, where they formed a sort of arc or halo.

It wasn't this in itself that repelled the Dark Man's forces, though. His creatures kept coming at us, but now, whenever one or another of them got too close, thrashing, black, whip-like tendrils would shoot out from the arc of energy, like lightning bolts from a storm cloud, and drive them back. Several of them collapsed, or scuttled away, screeching in agony. One, a flying mechanical thing with a cat's face stretched over a metal frame and a row of spines along its undulating back, crashed and burst into flames, the organic parts of it bubbling and melting like cheese on a griddle.

'Come and speak to us, Dark Man,' my older self shouted into the foggy, smoke-filled blackness. 'Come to us or we'll come in there and drag you out, kicking and screaming.'

We waited as the Dark Man's creatures, having been given a taste of our resistance, now shrank back, cowed, into the darkness. We could still hear them, though, clicking and whirring and mewling, as though preparing to take advantage of any opening, any opportunity, that might arise. And we could smell them too – or at least those whose putrid flesh had been burned by heart energy. The smell was so abominable that all three of us couldn't help but put our free hands over our mouths and noses. Clover in particular looked as though she was having to draw on every ounce of willpower not to throw up.

The final echoes of my older self's challenge were on the point of fading when there came a shrill, metallic screech from the blackness in front of us. The screech culminated in the clank of something metal and heavy thumping down on the floor, which was then followed by another screech and another metallic thump, and then another, and another.

I knew what it was, of course. I had heard these sounds before. In fact, my younger self, whose unconscious form was now doubtless slumped in a carriage rattling through the fog-bound streets of London, had heard them minutes earlier.

It was the Dark Man's 'spider chair', the huge, clockwork conveyance on which his raddled body travelled from place to place. I had seen it on a couple of occasions, the last time in my own house on the night Hawkins died. Despite this, I couldn't help but feel a shiver pass through me as the first of its thin, jointed front legs emerged from the shadows, a gleam of brownish light from the murky sky outside slithering along the blade-like surface. The appearance of one leg was quickly followed by another, and seconds later, the mechanical conveyance, still mostly shrouded in shadow, was standing in front of us, poised as if about to spring. The Dark Man sat hunched and motionless on the dais in the centre of the conveyance, his emaciated form shrouded in an opaque, net-like substance.

There was silence for a moment, each side assessing the other. Then my older self said, 'Do you know who we are?'

The netting rustled as the Dark Man turned his head slightly. 'Of course,' he rasped.

'And do you know why we're here?'

The thin, brittle voice was just as flat, just as weary. 'As my executioners?'

My older self and I exchanged a glance. I wondered what he was about to say.

'Would you care if we were? Would you defend yourself?'

The Dark Man didn't respond immediately. I wasn't sure whether he was considering the question, or summoning up the energy to reply. Eventually he said, 'The heart would defend me.'

My older self snorted. 'That old thing? It wouldn't have the strength to defend you against a rat.' Then he shook his head. 'But we're not here to kill you. We're here to redress the balance. You know who we are. Now we want to know about you.'

This time there was a hint of surprise in the cracked voice. 'You want to talk?'

'Yes. And I know you do too.' My older self spread his hands. 'So. Tell us about yourself. We're here to listen.'

'Where should I begin?' There was an element almost of shyness in the Dark Man's voice. Wariness too.

'Tell us who you are,' I said before my older self could reply. 'Tell us where you came from.'

The netting rustled as the shrouded figure inclined his head towards me. It made me think of insect movement, of the frantic seething of a cockroach nest.

'You had an accident,' he rasped.

I assumed he was referring to my neck brace, to the cast on my arm. 'So?'

'I was... born from that accident.'

I frowned. I sensed Clover and my older self looking at me. 'What do you mean?'

The netting rustled again. 'I am... a splinter,' the Dark Man said. 'A shadow. You were almost... killed, Alex. You were... teetering on the brink. Your injuries were so... severe that the heart tried to... save you by opening up another timeline and... propelling an alternate version of you into eternity. I was... that alternate version. But you survived. You... clung to life. Which meant that I was... surplus to requirements.'

Was the Dark Man's breathy, tortured voice now tinged with bitterness? It was difficult to tell.

'I tumbled through eternity for millennia... clinging to the heart... to my heart... With your survival I should have been extinguished... wiped from existence... but I clung to life... I clung always to life...'

He made a thin, shrill sound that sounded like splintering glass, and that it took me a moment to realise was a laugh. It was a chilling sound, a mad sound.

And you went insane, didn't you? I thought, horrified at the notion of falling through time for what must have seemed like forever. Horrified too to think there was a part of me that was capable of becoming... this.

As if reading my mind, the Dark Man said, 'The process... scarred me... mentally and physically. It... fragmented my thoughts, my memories. I was... broken. But I survived.' His voice became an insectile hiss. '*I survived.*'

'How?' I asked.

The netting rustled. A shrug? 'By accident... by willpower... who knows? But I survived... and found my way back. By this time my heart... the one I had been lost with... that I had travelled with... was as broken and as old and as hollow as I was... And so I found you, Alex. My strength was... failing. But with the last of it, I created my army... my Wolves... and I used them to take your heart... the younger heart... from you.' His voice suddenly became a vicious hiss. '*It was my right! My right to live... to exist... I had just as much right to life as you...*'

'I'm not denying it,' I said.

He continued as if he hadn't heard me. 'In time, this heart too... became old... began to wither and waste away... My link to this world... to this reality... is tenuous... When I sleep I slip away... I travel... I tumble through decades... sometimes centuries... in a single night...'

'And so your plan was to steal the heart here,' my older self said. 'The heart that we created, that's been moving through the centuries towards this moment – towards a time when it and we are reunited.'

'Before it's used properly for the first time?' I said.

My older self nodded.

'The virgin heart...' the Dark Man rasped. 'Seized in its infancy... it would sustain me... for centuries...'

'What's the point?' my older self said brusquely. 'What's the point of carrying on, of surviving? Look at you. You're a wreck. You're clinging to life by your fingertips. So why bother? Why not just let go? Find peace?'

'*Peace!*' sneered the Dark Man. The netting shuddered, as though he was agitated, angry. 'Peace is for the dead... I want life... The life I'm owed... The life that was created for me and then taken away... before I could live it...'

'It's too late,' Clover said. She spoke softly, almost sadly. 'I'm sorry, but it is. You've missed it. It seems to me that you were never built to sustain it.'

'*No!*' This time the Dark Man's voice was almost a snarl. Then, as though he had expended too much energy in that one word, it became softer, weaker. 'No, it *will* work... it *must*... with the new heart... the unused heart...'

'It won't work,' my older self said. 'You're too weak to contain the heart's energy. It'll destroy you.'

'It will... *rejuvenate me*,' the Dark Man hissed.

I felt an urge to be spiteful, to tell him he was wrong, that I'd seen the heart destroy him, but I didn't want to tempt fate by giving him a glimpse into the future – besides which, I had another burning question on my mind, one from which I didn't want to get sidetracked.

'What about the innocent people you've destroyed? Hawkins, Mary, countless others? What about Lyn? You took away her sanity, and for what reason? Because you were jealous? Because you were resentful of the life she and I had together? Is that it? You wanted to get at me, and so you did it through her?'

I felt almost choked with anger and horror – to think that *I*, a version of *me*, was capable of this. The Dark Man's response, though, surprised me.

'*No!*' Though little more than a croak, his denial was vehement. 'I wanted only... acceptance... love... I wanted to regain what was rightfully mine... You and I are the same, Alex...'

'We're *not* the same,' I retorted.

'We're the same,' he said adamantly. 'I never hurt you, Alex... I never hurt your loved ones... though I could have done... I could have killed your daughter... this one... when you knew her as Clover... but I didn't. I captured her and imprisoned her... but I didn't harm her... because she's part of us... she's part of all of us... I love her... as I love you... as I love all of us...'

'Love?' I sneered at him. 'What do you understand about love? You *killed* people. You tortured people – you tortured *children* – to create your Wolves. What about *their* lives?'

'Their lives... don't matter,' the Dark Man rasped.

'Of *course* they matter!' I was almost screaming now. Not only because I was furious, but because of the Dark Man's association with me, the awful knowledge that deep inside me was... what was it he had said? A *splinter*. A splinter that, given the right circumstances, was capable of such atrocities, and such a lack of compassion, of morality.

Clover squeezed my hand, as if to calm me, to reassure me. It helped. I reined in my anger, shook my head. I didn't want to believe what the Dark Man was saying. I thought back, trying to find a chink in his armour, desperate to prove he was lying.

'If you're telling the truth, then what about the visions I had?' I said defiantly. 'In those I saw Clover – Kate – die. I saw Candice die...'

The netting was rustling and twitching; he was shaking his head. 'I know nothing about those... it must have been a construct... a false future... created by the heart...'

To keep me on my toes, I thought. To instil in me the imperative to manipulate my present and future so as to fit in with my past as I remembered it. In truth, it was something I'd already half-suspected.

'But you still drove Lyn mad,' I persisted. 'Why would you do that to someone you claim to love?'

'It was a mistake,' he rasped, and there was such sorrow in his voice that, despite myself, I found it hard to disbelieve him. 'I never intended... for it to happen... I loved her... I wanted to prove to her... who I was... what I'd been through... how my love for her had sustained me... helped bring me back... I thought if I gave her a glimpse... of the eternity I'd endured... it would prove... I was telling the truth... but it was too much for her... the effect was...' His voice tailed off.

'You drove her mad,' I said.

His reply was barely a whisper. 'Yes...'

I glared at the shrouded figure, but although I still couldn't shake off my anger, my revulsion at what he had done, there was also a part of me that felt utterly horrified – that perhaps even pitied him – because of what he had had to endure, and what it had driven him to.

'You see,' my older self said gently.

I turned to him. 'See what?'

He smiled. 'I know what you've been thinking about, Alex. I know what's been keeping you awake at night. You've been thinking that your life would be perfect if it wasn't for the threat of the Dark Man. You've been worrying that he'll sneak into your house at night and take away everything you've fought to protect.'

'He means me,' said Clover.

'But he won't,' my older self continued. 'Because he's part of us. He's part of *this*. And although he's desperate he'd never intentionally harm us, our family – not physically anyway.'

'So it's over?' I said, feeling a growing sense of... of release maybe. Even wonder.

'Oh, it'll never be over,' my older self said. 'But this bit is. From here on in, it's a fresh start. For both of us.'

Clover linked her left arm gently with my broken one, then leaned in to give me a kiss on the cheek. 'Go back home, Dad,' she said. 'And bring me up properly. And just remember to give me everything I ever want.'

Despite our surroundings I laughed. 'I'll do my utmost to ensure that you turn out like my good friend Clover.'

'That'll do,' she said. 'Clover's cool. I'm sure you'll make a brilliant job of it.'

EPILOGUE

TUESDAY 2 OCTOBER 2012

So here I am, and here we are.

Tonight's the night I die. But that's okay.

I'm old now. Older than old. Not exactly ancient, but something like a hundred and fifty, a hundred and sixty. Jumping between time zones, living here and there for days or weeks or months at a time, it's hard to keep track. But I reckon the nanites have at least doubled my natural life span, kept my bones and organs strong, kept me cancer and infection free.

But everything has its time, and everything dies. Even nanites give up the ghost eventually. Even the obsidian heart will one day crumble to dust.

That night all those years ago, when I discovered the true nature of the Dark Man, did not mark an end to the story, because real stories never end, they just go on and on. But it did mark the end of my battle with him. It allowed me to draw a line in the sand, to live my life without being haunted by the fear of what he might do.

The Dark Man was so obsessed with prolonging his life that his ultimate plan, after only partially succeeding in stealing the heart from my younger self before I could find out its true worth, was to go further back and steal the heart in its infancy – or at least at the point when it emerged from its centuries-long journey to be reunited with its 'creator'. But the power of the heart was too strong for him, and it destroyed him – an action undertaken by the heart that I still see as a mercy killing. The Dark Man was the embodiment of the very worst that I could have become. And as well as being insane, I believe he was in terrible torment. I know that at this particular moment he's out there, ready to make his bid to steal the heart from my younger and far more innocent – or at least unknowing – self. But in the great scheme of things I hope the Dark Man managed to find peace. I truly do.

As for his Wolves, I have no idea what became of them. Perhaps they died when he did. Perhaps the shape-shifter lost its abilities. Perhaps Tallarian went into hiding. Perhaps, perhaps, perhaps.

They too are still out there right now, though, of course. My younger self is destined to encounter them in this time period, and others. To me they're long gone, but to him, who is also me, they're about to become a real and terrifying threat. Such is the elasticity of time. Such is its nature.

As I say, real stories never end.

If you've journeyed with me this far in the hope that everything will be tied up in a neat bow, then I'm afraid you're going to be disappointed. Even now I don't have all the answers. I don't know, really, how and why the heart came into being, what its ultimate purpose is – or even if it *has* an ultimate purpose.

As human beings we like answers, don't we? And we like patterns. We're frightened of randomness, of chaos, and therefore we like to believe that everything has a purpose, a meaning; that somewhere, just out of sight, is an ultimate truth, a Grand Design.

But we're flailing in the dark. We'll never find what we're looking for. If we *did* one day discover all the answers, what would we do with them? I doubt we'd be satisfied. We'd only set out to discover the answers behind the answers. Or we'd slump into despair. We'd think: *Is that it?* And then we'd wonder what to do next.

But time is short, and I'm beginning to ramble. I make no apologies for it – I'm old, I'm *allowed* to ramble – but if I'm going to say what I want to say before the Reaper comes to claim me, then I'd better get a move on.

As I've already said, my story didn't end on the night I discovered the true nature of the Dark Man. There was still plenty to do, plenty to learn. I had my little black book to work through, things to set in motion.

I had to learn stagecraft, so that I could become the Great Barnaby. That took a while. And I had to train the Sherwoods, so that they could comfortably cope in the twenty-first century and play their part in my story. That took even longer.

As Barnaby McCallum, I lived through the '40s, the '50s, the '60s and the '70s, and it was glorious and exciting and unexpected and surreal. I learned that a man with foreknowledge can make huge amounts of money – and I did. I made pots and pots of the stuff.

Sometimes I used the heart for fun – to meet people, to be present at historical events (and sometimes to be *absent* from historical events). I saw the Beatles' first gig at Litherland Town Hall on 5th January 1961, with Pete Best on drums. I saw the Sex Pistols' last gig at Winterland in San Francisco on January 14th 1978, at the end of which Johnny Rotten slumped on the stage and uttered the now immortal line, 'Ever get the feeling you've been cheated?'

Just under a year earlier, in February 1977, I toasted my own birth. I wasn't present, of course, though Kate was with me on the night I was born. We stood outside the hospital and I told her what was happening inside, and then we popped over to a nearby boozer to wet the baby's head.

Kate, needless to say, had a nomadic childhood, and although she didn't accompany me on all my little jaunts (it would have become too disorientating and disruptive for her), she did adapt quickly to the various time periods we found ourselves in. She learned so much too. With the extra mental stimulation that was part and parcel of her upbringing, she not only quickly shrugged off the learning difficulties she'd been born with, but soon superseded her classmates in terms of intelligence and maturity. When I finally installed her in 2010s London, so that she could aid my younger self during his difficult early days after procuring the heart, she was more than ready. Through my careful manipulation – a process far too complex and, frankly, boring to go into here – she had already inveigled her way into Benny's affections. As far as he was concerned her name was Clover Monroe, and she was a vicar's daughter from Kent.

Like I say, it was complicated. If I had time I'd draw you a flow chart – but thankfully I don't.

As for Lyn, she became what I'd always hoped she'd become before the Dark Man got to her: the love of my life, and a fantastic mother to Kate. With the help of the heart, she was able to finally and irrevocably cast out her demons, and regain her mental and physical health.

She left hospital and came home to live with Kate and me in Ranskill Gardens in June 2013, just before her thirty-third birthday. When I became Barnaby McCallum she and Kate both travelled back in time with me, and then Lyn decided she liked it so much that she subsequently hardly ever accompanied me on my trips back to the future. Instead she stayed (most of the time with Kate, apart from on those occasions when I had to take Kate with me in order to play the vicar's daughter and inveigle her way into Benny's affections) in the house – and the time period – in which we'd made our home. We lived out our lives together through the '40s, '50s, '60s, '70s and '80s and we were as happy as I think three, and then two people can be (though even when Clover flew the nest in order to establish her life in the 2010s, I made sure she popped back frequently to visit Lyn). Although I was away quite a bit – sometimes for months at a time – as far as Lyn was concerned we were barely apart, as wherever I went I always made sure that I timed my return to only a few minutes after I'd left. She died in 1992 at the age of eighty-two, and although it broke my heart, it comforted me to think that somewhere in London was a twelve-year-old Lyn, with seventy years of mostly happy life in front of her.

As for Candice and Hope, I've used the heart to stay in their lives beyond this point, to be as good a dad as I can manage to one and a surrogate uncle to the other. They're both great girls, and although they've suffered the usual bumps and bruises that most of us endure on this rocky road through life, they were both doing okay the last time I saw them.

And that's about it, I think. That pretty much brings us full circle.

Life is a funny old thing, especially when you live it outside the restrictions of linear time. You achieve a kind of immortality – or, looking at it another way, you die over and over.

It's getting late now, edging towards 11 p.m. It's quiet outside on Bellwater Drive, and the house – aside from this lamp I'm using to write by – is dark. My younger self, who I know is sick with worry after what he thinks is the abduction of his (our) youngest daughter, will be leaving Incognito in a few minutes. In less than an hour he'll be here to steal the obsidian heart, in the hope that he can use it to procure Kate's release.

Soon I'll go downstairs, place the heart under the glass dome on the sideboard, and then sit quietly in my chair in the shadows and wait for him to arrive.

Thinking of how distraught he'll be after he kills me makes me feel bad, but at the same time, despite knowing what he has to go through, I can't help feeling envious of him. In the years to come he'll encounter horror, and heartbreak, and terrible hardship, and more than his share of crippling physical pain, but he'll also experience wonder beyond his imagining, and excitement, and unbounded happiness, and deep, abiding love.

Life is an adventure. It is there to be lived and relished. And although mine is almost over now, at the same time, through him, I know it will go on.

Because time is forever.

And stories never end.

ACKNOWLEDGEMENTS

Writing this trilogy (and in particular working out all the time travel shenanigans) has been a long, complex and mind-warping endeavour, and thanks must go to my wife Nel Whatmore and my two gorgeous children David and Polly for their incredible love, support and sympathy, to my agent John Jarrold and my editor Cath Trechman for their suggestions and enthusiasm (Cath is, without doubt, the best and most insightful editor I have ever had the pleasure to work with), and to my father-in-law Trevor Whatmore and his friends at Toc H in Walsall for their information, suggestions and advice regarding the First World War. Thanks again too to Johnny Mains for lending me his book-lined study to write in for a few days, to Christopher Golden (and family) and Jim Moore for looking after me during my recent trip to the USA, and to everyone at NECon for making me feel so welcome. There are literally dozens and dozens of other people who have helped in so many different ways during the writing of this trilogy, who are far too numerous to name – thank you all. And finally, thank you to those readers who have contacted me via Facebook and Twitter to express their enthusiasm and excitement for the ongoing adventures (now ended) of Alex Locke and Clover Monroe.